"Have you come upon any of the Red Emperor's declared enemies at this time?" she asked.

Her mouth said this, but what her eyes really said was *Are you the Red Emperor's enemy?* to which Danso's eyes were, unwillingly, answering *Yes.*

"Not any that I have recognised, officer," he said, forcing his lips to ignore his brain. This question was another trap, and the next was likely to be the one with the trip rope, the one that snapped and held the weak animal tight in place, helpless.

The mouthpiece took a moment before she posed her last question.

"Have you, at any point, aided any enemies of the empire, or those who have strayed from the Red Emperor's guidance?"

Yes, yes, yes, Danso's brain said. Thankfully, his mouth did nothing but gulp. And perhaps that moment of pause was too long, because the peace officers responded. Their arms, which once hung by their sides or were folded across their chests, dropped to rest on their cutlasses, spears, axes.

Praise for
Son of the Storm

"A mesmerizing coming-of-age tale set against a thrilling, fantastical adventure that introduces a beguiling new world...and then rips apart everything you think you know."
—S. A. Chakraborty, author of *The City of Brass*

"Ambition and intrigue cause surprises on nearly every page as characters reach for power in unpredictable and nuanced ways....The effect is rich, wild, and occasionally dizzying." —*NPR Books*

"Okungbowa weaves an intricate and irresistible plot around the tensions and contradictions of a corrupt, decadent society. The result is a vibrant tale of betrayal, intrigue, and revolution, which benefits greatly from an original setting, a fresh take on magic, and deftly executed characterization." —Anthony Ryan, author of *The Pariah*

"Fantastical beasts and forgotten magic propel a story about ambition, conspiracy, and the elusiveness of belonging. This is epic fantasy that will make you think and leave you unsettled."
—Fonda Lee, World Fantasy Award–winning author of *Jade City*

"An epic fantasy set apart by how deftly Okungbowa unfurls his intricate, richly imagined world. It's not often you get to read a fantasy novel that spans not only ancient magic, sinister machinations, and monstrous forests but courthouses, college classes, and hairdressers too, evoking the terrible and fascinating city-state of Bassa in living, breathing detail."
—A. K. Larkwood, author of *The Unspoken Name*

"Highly recommended for fans of epic fantasy based on non-European mythologies...readers who enjoy protagonists on troubled journeys...or anyone who likes to chew on stories with complex shenanigans."
—*Library Journal* (starred review)

By Suyi Davies Okungbowa

THE NAMELESS REPUBLIC
Son of the Storm
Warrior of the Wind

David Mogo, Godhunter

Warrior
OF THE
Wind

The Nameless Republic: Book Two

Suyi Davies
Okungbowa

orbitbooks.net

Copyright © 2023 by Suyi Davies Okungbowa
Excerpt from *The Nameless Republic: Book Three* copyright © 2023 by Suyi Davies Okungbowa
Excerpt from *The Jasad Heir* copyright © 2023 by Sara Hashem

Cover design by Lauren Panepinto
Cover illustration by Dan dos Santos
Cover copyright © 2023 by Hachette Book Group, Inc.
Map by Tim Paul
Author photograph by Manuel Ruiz

Orbit
Hachette Book Group
1290 Avenue of the Americas
New York, NY 10104
orbitbooks.net

First Edition: November 2023
Simultaneously published in Great Britain by Orbit.

Orbit is an imprint of Hachette Book Group.
The Orbit name and logo are trademarks of Little, Brown Book Group Limited.

The publisher is not responsible for websites (or their content) that are not owned by the publisher.

The Hachette Speakers Bureau provides a wide range of authors for speaking events. To find out more, go to hachettespeakersbureau.com or email HachetteSpeakers@hbgusa.com.

Orbit books may be purchased in bulk for business, educational, or promotional use. For information, please contact your local bookseller or the Hachette Book Group Special Markets Department at special.markets@hbgusa.com.

Library of Congress Cataloging-in-Publication Data
Names: Okungbowa, Suyi Davies, author.
Title: Warrior of the wind / Suyi Davies Okungbowa.
Description: First edition. | New York, NY : Orbit, 2023. | Series: The Nameless Republic ; book two
Identifiers: LCCN 2023013528 | ISBN 9780316428972 (trade paperback) |
    ISBN 9780316428958 (ebook)
Subjects: LCGFT: Fantasy fiction. | Novels.
Classification: LCC PR9387.9.O394327 W37 2023 | DDC 823/.92—dc23/eng/20230330
LC record available at https://lccn.loc.gov/2023013528

ISBNs: 9780316428972 (trade paperback), 9780316428958 (ebook)

Printed in the United States of America

LSC-C

Printing 1, 2023

For those buckled and bent, but never broken.

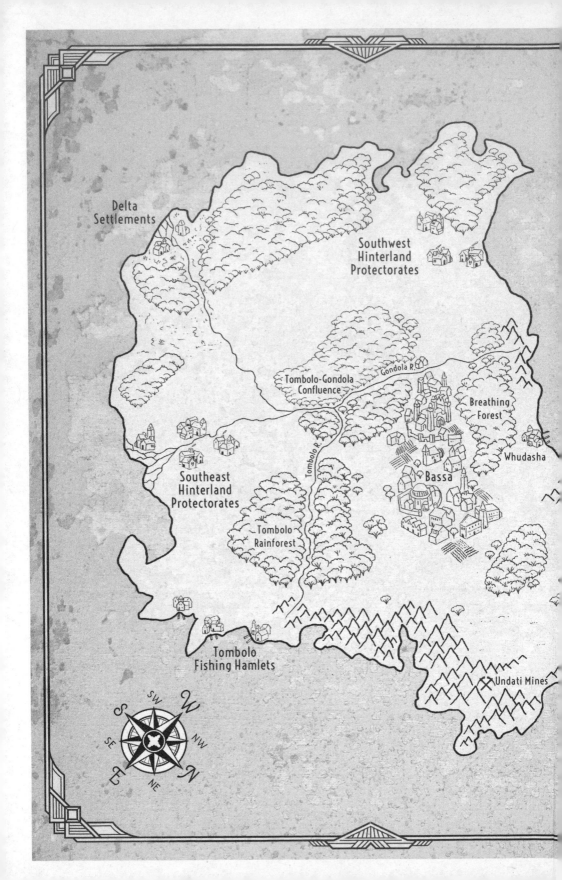

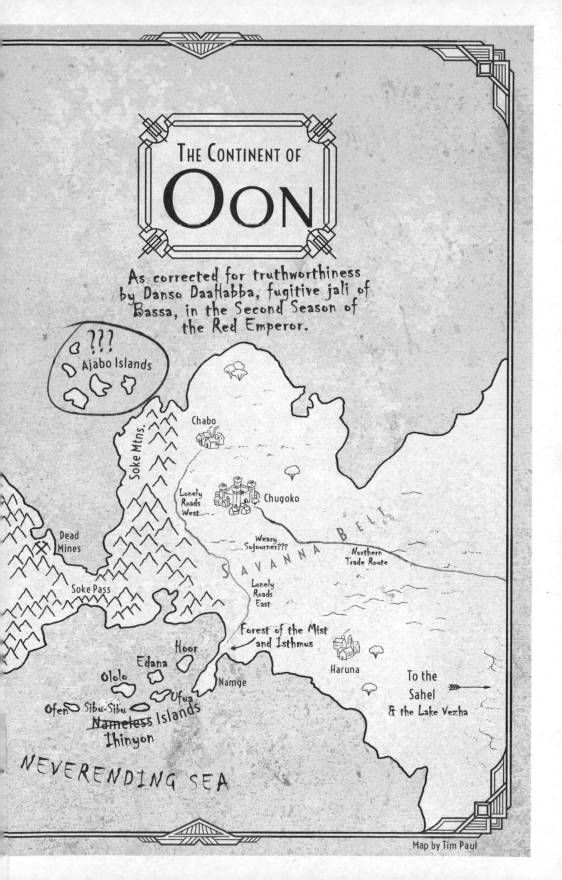

THE CONTINENT OF OON

As corrected for truthworthiness by Danso DaaHabba, fugitive jali of Bassa, in the Second Season of the Red Emperor.

Ajabo Islands ???

Chabo

Soke Mtns.

Lonely Roads West

Chugoko

Dead Mines

Weary Sojourner???

SAVANNA BELT

Northern Trade Route

Soke Pass

Lonely Roads East

Forest of the Mist and Isthmus

Hoor

Haruna

Edana

Ololo

Namge

To the Sahel & the Lake Vezha

Ofen   Sibu-Sibu

Ufua

Nameless Islands
Ihinyon

NEVERENDING SEA

Map by Tim Paul

Content Note

This book is intended for an adult readership, and contains themes, depictions, and/or instances of: albinism, animal death, artificial insemination, blood/gore, caste and class segregation, colourism and discrimination, death, pregnancy loss and miscarriages, murder, PTSD and anxiety, violence, and xenophobia.

Reader discretion is advised.

The Story So Far

IN THE UNICONTINENT OF Oon, surrounded by the Neverending Sea, the prosperous city of Bassa sits at the geographical and political centre of the mainland. Being the most fertile of all three regions (mainland, desertland, and islands), the empire of Bassa has long ruled by might and by tale. But everything is changing—the land, the winds, the seas. As resources dwindle, so does Bassa's might. And unknown to the city, its story is about to be rewritten.

BOOK 1: *SON OF THE STORM*

DANSO, a disillusioned scholar at the University of Bassa, stumbles upon an ancient manuscript while skimming a restricted section. The written codex of the Manic Emperor contains stories about Bassa's past that challenge everything Danso knows about his nation, raising even more questions about his past: his mixed heritage of an islander mother and mainlander father, which has earned him the lowest caste position of Shashi (though he is let into the scholar guild reserved for the elite Idu nobles, the highest caste position, due to his excellent memory). The codex also discusses a mythical mineral called IBOR, with which a gifted user, called an IBORWORKER, can perform supernatural feats. His quest for further answers puts him in trouble with his family, the university (which suspends him), and most importantly, ESHEME, his intended.

Things come to a head when an intruder breaches Bassa's border. LILONG, from the Nameless Islands (believed by most Bassai and mainlanders to be extinct, alongside its peoples), is chasing the Diwi, a family heirloom of inert red ibor that has been stolen by NEM, a fixer (and Esheme's mother). By a twist of fate, Lilong ends up in Danso's family barn, where she is spotted by him. Her presence confirms Danso's beliefs that the codex's words were true: Islanders aren't extinct, and ibor is real, proven by Lilong's use of amber ibor (to change her skin shade and control her blade, among other feats). When Lilong leaves, Danso opts not to report her presence.

In the course of retrieving the Diwi, Lilong discovers that Nem has learned iborworking, and ends up attacking her. Both get wounded, Nem more so than Lilong. Lilong returns to Danso's barn, and Danso helps her, but encounters Esheme in the process. In a bid to protect herself, Lilong attacks Esheme, and Danso's Second, ZAQ, is dutifully required to attack Esheme's Second, who intends to harm Danso. With a search for the intruder on, the three—Danso, Zaq, and Lilong—are forced to flee to Whudasha, a coastal protectorate where other Shashi are permitted to live outside of Bassa. To do this, they must head through the Breathing Forest.

Their journey through the forest is filled with challenges, including constant quakes and an attack by a lightning bat called a SKOPI. Here, Danso learns that such beasts are attracted to ibor and feats of iborworking. But after killing the beast, the Diwi—which has been inert in Lilong's family for generations—is awakened by Danso's touch, and the dead bat is brought back to life under his command.

Back in Bassa, Esheme has taken over Nem's affairs while she recovers from a coma. She comes into possession of a broken-off piece of the Diwi, held by Nem. She also inherits a debt Nem owes to the powerful First Elder DOTA. Dota, who knew about Nem's dalliances with ibor, wants his hands on the mineral, and tasks Esheme with retrieving the full Diwi from the fugitives, threatening consequences if she doesn't. This sends Esheme down two paths. The first: sending her Second, OBODA, to Whudasha in pursuit of the fugitives. The second: a meeting with the Coalition for New Bassa, in which the coalition's leader, BASUAYE, and one of his generals, IGAN, sign up to protect her and her house until Dota's threats wane. But Basuaye wants something else in return:

to use the funeral of the Bassai Speaker—who died in a strange attack (later revealed to have been facilitated by Nem for his knowledge of her actions)—to push his goals for the coalition, which are to disrupt the Bassai elite and galvanize the people to his cause. Esheme, chosen to give an address (on behalf of the absent Nem) about the recent attacks (which have been pinned on the intruder), is asked to speak in favour of the coalition.

On the day of the funeral, Esheme delivers her speech, which she infuses with her own rallying cries, revealing truths about the Bassai elite's secrets. Her speech ignites a fracas, during which Esheme is rescued by Igan. Afterward, Dọta sends his people after her, but due to the protection of the Coalition for New Bassa (and her newfound respect by the Bassai), is unable to reach her.

Back on the road, the fugitives (Danso, Lilong, Zaq) arrive in Whudasha on the back of a tragedy: an attack by a crop of bounty hunters on their tail, which Danso deals with by setting the Skopi's lighting on them. They are discovered by BIEMWENSÉ, a Whudan outcast who nurses them back to health. Zaq, harbouring doubts throughout the trip, finally abandons Danso, but is picked up by the Whudasha Youth, led by the Supreme Magnanimous, KAKUTAN, who pressures the truth out of him. Kakutan sets upon Biemwensé's home, hoping to avoid Bassa's wrath by rounding up the fugitives and returning them to the city. But Biemwensé holds her ground, defending Danso and Lilong—before Danso quells the attack using the Skopi. Kakutan allows the fugitives to go if they leave immediately, which they agree to. They head for the headquarters to retrieve Zaq, but more surprises await.

Oboda, who has traced the fugitives to Whudasha, has commandeered the Whudasha Youth and set Zaq to a pyre in order to draw out the fugitives. This leads to a battle wherein Oboda is killed by Lilong, and Zaq is burned at the stake. Zaq's death weighs greatly on Danso. Kakutan, realising what Oboda's death means for her people, decides to lead all of Whudasha across the border—*underneath* the Soke mountains, through the Dead Mines—to the desertlands beyond, where they may be safe with a secret group who runs these passages. Danso, Lilong, and Biemwensé follow on this journey.

In Bassa, Esheme learns she is pregnant with the child of her desertland immigrant lover. While processing this, she receives Oboda's deceased body, which, upon her touch with the small piece of red ibor, is brought back to zombie-like life (like Danso's bat) and is compliant to her commands. When Dọta shows up in person with his personal army to retrieve the red ibor, she decimates him and his group in a bloody attack by her newfound weapon, Oboda. Afterward, Nem awakes from her coma, and Esheme fills her in on everything. Nem pieces together that Esheme's carriage of a mixed-heritage child must be the reason she can wield red ibor (giving us an insight as to why Danso also can). Nem believes that protecting this secret is important, and therefore all mixed-heritage peoples must be prevented from learning it—especially Whudans.

This leads Esheme into capitalizing on her newfound power (and support from the people) to take over the Coalition for New Bassa (which she does by murdering its generals and imprisoning its leader, Basuaye). With a rousing speech, she commandeers the coalition into an attack on the Great Dome, which she leads herself, using Oboda and Igan. In view of the public, she gives the Bassai elite over to the people to be maimed, after which she is rewarded with their support and loyalty, and is proclaimed by them as saviour and the new emperor.

With her newfound position, Esheme gathers Bassa's best forces and sets upon the Soke border, catching the escape of the Whudans in the nick of time. On the last bridge across the moats, where Danso, Lilong, Biemwensé, and Kakutan are escaping, she tries to barter the Diwi for Danso's father, whom she has brought along. This ends in a battle where Danso's father dies at Esheme's hands (by burning), Oboda and the Skopi are lost in the moat, and the four fugitives escape. They are picked up by the secret group, who they learn are called the Gaddo Company.

Back in Bassa, Esheme is crowned the new emperor.

WARRIOR
OF THE
WIND

The Written Codex of Danso DaaHabba, First Jali of Bassa to Journey over the Soke Borders: Hereafter lie his personal accounts of travels and travails through the desertlands, from the western vagabond colony of Chabo, to the fabled eastern Forest of the Mist.

The Third Account: The salt-taste of triumph.

Triumph is salt. It is blood rushing back from throat onto tongue, warm and stale and sick. It is the ache of bones after victory, the agony of wounds treated.

—The Manic Emperor, Nogowu,
Twenty-Third Emperor of Great Bassa

I FIND SOLACE IN a madman's words once we have crossed underneath the border's mountains and make our way to a future beyond Bassa. Our journey across the lower Savanna Belt lasts many days and ends in a colony obscured from the naked eye, whose roads only familiar feet know. Here, we dismount and venture into the shadows.

In the quiet, I discover madness. What else is left to lose but sanity when one has lost everything they love, has left behind all whose freedoms may well depend on their actions? So, while around us people sing happy songs, seek friendship, eat good food, and make home, I find no respite, and neither do my companions; there is only dust and sweat and hearts jumping into our mouths.

Silence is safety, but also anticipation.

As an old jali's saying goes: *There is no rest under the throne.* But a child who says their parent will not rest, will not rest either. All of us, eyes open, will stand through the dark of night.

ochela

Second Season of the Red Emperor

1

Five Hunthands

The Lonely Roads West
Fifth Mooncycle, 19–21

CHABO WAS A COLONY of vagabonds.

Every soul in Chabo was running from something. People of disrepute who, if their feet were to touch the dust of any city or settlement in the Savanna Belt, would be pounced upon and sent into a forever darkness. Those who lacked ambition, aspiration, or resourcefulness, making Chabo the only place on the continent that would not eat them alive for it. Those who moved between worlds, who needed a place of dishonour that operated by its own rules to pause and rethink their strategies.

Chabo asked nothing of those who came. There were no councils, no civic guards, no warrant chiefs, no vigilantes, no peace officers. Nothing but a haphazard collection of rogue communes in the western armpit of the Savanna Belt. It was generally agreed that any soul without a wish to be absorbed into this colony was to remain on the northward trade routes that sprouted from Chugoko, a *real* city. It was advised not to turn even one's neck westward, let alone one's kwaga.

Except, of course, if one *wanted* to turn their sights on Chabo in search of something that did not wish to be found.

Five mooncycles into the second season of the Red Emperor, a wagon carrying five men turned westward like so, sidling the Soke mountains and border moats, and set themselves upon the Lonely Roads West to

Chabo. Each man was dressed in armoured hunthand garb—skirts, chest plates, iron headwear—and bore a short spear and long blade. Faces half shielded by veils, eyes alone betraying grim temperament. In their wagon: shackles, blindfolds, an iron crossbolt.

They rode in the open wagon and spat in the browning grass by the wayside, not an eye taken off the roads, minds focused on the colony ahead of them. They camped without event on the first day. By the next day, they came upon the first person they had seen in a long time: a wrinkled old desertlander who sat in the dust and batted flies from his lips.

They kicked aside his alms bowl and shoved a worn leaflet into his nose.

"In the name of the Red Emperor, tell us what you know of this," the leader of the hunthands—a dark man with tribal marks etched into his cheeks, remnants of his hinterland origins—said in halting Savanna Common.

The almsman cocked his head and licked his dry, cracked lips. He squinted at the sheet of paper, struggling to make out the faint markings in the glare of the sun. It was unclear what language the words were written in. Besides, the man couldn't read. He shrugged after trying, pointed at his ear, then at his head, to say he understood neither their words nor the markings.

"We seek the jali who made this," said the leader, switching to a smoother border pidgin, more easily understood. "We are led to believe it came from Chabo."

The almsman shrugged again. The leader smacked him on the cheek.

"Listen, you millipede," he said. "This jali and his accomplices are fugitives of the Red Emperor. If you have seen a Shashi in Chabo, you better tell us now." When the almsman struggled to process the word *Shashi*, the leader added: "He rides a dead bat that is not dead, and can call on lightning. He may be travelling with a yellowskin."

The almsman blinked at that, then stifled a chuckle, and that was all it took.

One of the men punched him in the face and broke his nose. They left him bleeding into the dry grass, red reflecting in the hard heat of noon.

Next, they came upon a nomadic group of cattle and goat rearers. They stopped and asked the same questions. The rearers, a ragtag group of poorly armed men, said they sounded ridiculous. A bat-riding Shashi and a yellowskin? They had walked the length and breadth of this Savanna Belt and had never seen such things. They waved the hunthands aside and asked to be left alone.

One of the hunthands took off his veil to reveal his mouth: lips sewn shut, copper wires criss-crossing top to bottom, leaving dark, reddish patterns where they pierced.

Immediately the nomads saw this, they fell to their knees, heads bowed in the sand. "We did not know you were the Red Emperor's peace officers," they pleaded. "We thought you were bandits or swindlers trying to take our goats."

The lead hunthand, in response, mounted the crossbolt and shot it between three goats. The rearers swallowed their hurt and rage and sorrow as the hunthands made them chop up the meat, dry it over a fire, and salt it for the rest of their trip.

On the third day, a few hours outside of Chabo, the hunthands met another vagabond.

This man happened to be headed away from Chabo, toward Chugoko, and luckily for them, knew about the tract. He had seen others like it being read back in Chabo, passed from hand to hand. All nonsense stories, he said, lies about the Red Emperor and Bassa. But it was popular in the colony, often read around night-fires among the companies that plied their trade there.

They thanked him, but for good measure, stripped him of his belongings.

They had barely gone another hour when they met another vagabond, this one cloaked in every sense of the word. Their wrappers went up to their wrists and ankles, and a veil shielded their face, leaving only their eyes visible. Even their hands and feet were wrapped in strips of cloth, as if they'd once been buried beneath the sand.

Upon sighting the hunthands from afar, the vagabond stopped in the middle of the road.

The men, unsure of what they were dealing with, disembarked from their wagon. The leader shouted his questions—in Savanna Common, in Mainland Common, in two border pidgins. None evoked any response. Then the man with the sewn lips revealed his face, and the vagabond snickered.

"If you were truly peace officers," the vagabond said in High Bassai, "I would already be dead."

The leader's eyes narrowed. The man with the sewn lips removed the false wiring, tossed it in the sand, and wiped the fake blood from his lips.

"Who are you?" asked the leader.

"Come and find out," said the vagabond, then ducked into the bush.

The men moved before they thought, drawing, unsheathing, a synergy born of seasons of hunts together. They piled into the bush, but one ran to the wagon, mounted the crossbolt, aimed it in the general vicinity of the vagabond, and fired. The iron bolt whizzed through tall grass, parting vegetation, headed for the retreating figure's spine.

Out of nowhere, a flash of colour, as a gem-hilted blade appeared and struck the crossbolt clean in the head, altering its trajectory. The bolt missed the vagabond narrowly, tearing through their wrappers, splintering one tree, embedding itself into another.

"Ambush!" cried the leader, but it was too late. The vagabond had stopped running and had now turned to face them.

A second figure materialized in the grass: a man in a boubou kaftan, head in a turban, the curved sword in his hand pointed at the hunthand leader. Various people dressed and armed in a similar manner began to appear, their curved swords pointed likewise. In a moment, the hunthands were outnumbered, outarmed, outfoxed.

"If you know what is good for you," the man in the boubou said, "drop your weapons."

The lead hunthand, though not fully understanding the Savanna Common spoken, recognised the language of a well-executed trap. Especially once he spotted the vagabond from much earlier—the one who'd told them about the tract—among the group.

He surrendered his weapons and signaled for his men to do the same.

The cloaked vagabond stepped forward. Up close, he could see it was a woman: young, low-brown, desertlander. Raised scars peeked out near her collarbone, stretched and leathery, as if belonging to some other skin.

"You will be returning those," she said, of the belongings they stole.

The lead hunthand nodded solemnly, then asked again, softer this time: "Who are you?"

"We," she said, "are the Gaddo Company."

2

Lilong

Chabo
Fifth Mooncycle, 21, same day

LILONG RODE BACK TO the colony beside Kubra, in the lead and on the kwaga gifted to her by the company. This was how crucial she had become to company affairs over the few mooncycles since her arrival. So integrated, in fact, that she barely spared a thought for their targets anymore, especially when they deserved it like the hunthands they had just stripped of everything and abandoned in the savanna.

It'd started with Kubra asking her to join their raids. Not a request per se: It was customary for Bassa escapees to work off the cost of their escape. Between the four in her group, Lilong was the best choice, being the most skilled, most easily adaptable, and least recognised.

Initially, she'd accompanied them only on food raids, robbing Bassai merchant caravans along the trade routes. But the caravans soon became harder to defeat as the routes saw increased patrols by the Red Emperor's bounty force of peace officers. So Lilong opted instead to provide first points of attack closer to home, fitting so seamlessly into the role that, within the season, she had become Kubra's second-in-command.

They rode into the colony through the widest of the four mainways, that which contained both the depository and the public house. At this time of day—early evening—a motley selection of people milled about at the height of their business. There were no stables, so most tended to their mounts—camels and kwagas both—in back corridors. Most also trained their wild beasts in the street, like the feral camel that spat in Lilong's direction as they went by, the owner trying to rein it in.

Chabo welcomed them as it often did: by paying no attention at all. The colony had a character of its own, a spirit of organised chaos that possessed all who arrived here. It had to be a possession, Lilong surmised, since no matter how deadly a vagrant one was before joining the colony, it was only a matter of time before they turned out differently (*though worse in other ways*, she thought with an eye on their tattered clothing, rotten teeth, and general lack of hygiene).

There was an odd sense of belonging one developed to the place, something Lilong had sorely missed in all her time traipsing the mainland. The full-bellied laughter of colourful strangers who did not wish her death, and whom she did not want to strangle in turn. Singing by the night-fire. Combat training with fighters she barely knew yet shared a common goal with.

But that feeling, she reminded herself often, was dangerous. No one here had anything in common with her. No one here had to return home—a home that awaited with jaws open—to reclaim their family's honour. No one here held the future of the continent in their hands.

"It's time," said Kubra, pulling Lilong out of her thoughts.

She blinked. "For what?"

"The meeting. The audience with Gaddo you asked for?"

Lilong's eyes narrowed. "You said after fifty successful raids. I have not done fifty."

"And yet they would like to see you anyway," said Kubra. "Something urgent. Come by our quarters tonight and I'll take you."

Lilong wanted to allow herself a moment to exhale, to scream with joy and say, *Finally, Lilong, you're going home!* She wanted to envision her daa's face, pretend he was still alive (until she knew otherwise for sure). She wanted to imagine her siblings' excitement when she returned with the Diwi in hand. She wanted to envision the Elder Warriors of the Abenai League patting her on the back for doing the right thing.

None of those things were going to happen. But that was not the reason for holding her breath.

She didn't detest the Gaddo Company. She could even say she enjoyed working here. There was recreation, camaraderie, gifts like the kwaga. Two mooncycles in, Kubra bestowed upon her a "colony name," which the company used in the field in lieu of one's true name. (He named her Snakeblade—*snake* for her ability to, in his words, "shed skin," and *blade* for her skillful ability with her short sword). It was a nice gesture, even though it was in keeping with the Code of Vagabonds—the loose list of rules of conduct by which every resident of the colony lived—which stated: *Never inquire about a person's past or their true name—a colony name and all the past they offer is sufficient.* (Other rules: *Stay within assigned territories; keep weaponry unconcealed at all times; company leadership must remain secret.*)

Regardless, her impending journey east was an open secret. Traversing the Savanna Belt to the eastern coast where the Forest of the Mist lay would be a perilous task. There was a bounty on her head. Peace officers prowled the region. Bandits and wild beasts littered the open savanna. Even if she could somehow overcome these, there was the little matter of food, water, and reliable transport for the length of the trip, costly things she could not afford. She'd learned the hard way on her initial trip to Bassa that lacking these could kill you just as quickly as a sword.

So she'd requested a meeting with Gaddo to ask for help.

The Gaddo Company was one of the largest companies headquartered in Chabo, bigger than the Savanna Swine, Ravaging Mongrels, Tremor of the Sands, and other fledgling companies roaming the savanna but keeping base here. The Code of Vagabonds ensured that every company adhered to Chabo's rules, but also served to strengthen the standing agreements between the companies and the law, which once consisted solely of vigilantes employed by Bassa-ordained warrant chiefs. But with peace officers now in the region, the warrant chiefs' vigilantes no longer held as much sway—not even in Chugoko. The identities of company leadership were now at a premium. *A headless group is a multi-headed one,* Kubra had said, *not as prone to decapitation.*

So Lilong ended up never meeting Gaddo, despite working for them for a season and a half. But suddenly, out of the dust, an invitation?

"Tonight is not good," said Lilong. "That is no time to prepare."

"There's nothing to prepare," said Kubra. "They know all there is to know about you."

Lilong eyed Kubra. "What have you gossiped?"

"Me, gossip?" Kubra chuckled. "Your suspicion knows no bounds, Snakeblade. You four need to keep an open mind until the meeting."

Lilong lifted an eyebrow. *"Us four?"*

"Yes: you, the Whudans, the jali. Gaddo wants to meet you all."

Lilong did not like the sound of that.

"And speaking of the jali," Kubra continued, "can you tell him to stop distributing those tracts? We have better things to do than intercept hunthands."

Lilong pursed her lips. "He is . . . going through some things."

"Then he better go through them fast," said Kubra. "Or one day, it will land in the hands of a peace officer who can read, and then we'll all be doomed."

·—◦—·············—◦—·

Back at her quarters before the sky turned sunset orange, Lilong took the secret entrance—the rear one built of wood, made to look like an abandoned shack. She made straight for the washroom, wiped her sweaty parts, and switched back to her regular complexion before heading for the common area, praying that the evening dish would already be laid out. Sure enough, as she emerged from the darkness into the only room with windows not boarded shut, Biemwensé and Kakutan sat on short stools at the dwarf roundtable, surrounded by pounded yam, dika nut soup, and ram.

"Ooh, ram," Lilong said, reaching for the bowl of meat. Biemwensé, without looking, stretched out her stick and smacked her hand before it reached the dish.

"Wait until your brother joins us," she said.

Lilong massaged her smarting hand. She wasn't sure if it was just a language thing, the way Biemwensé used *brother* to refer to Danso and *auntie* to herself and Kakutan. Other things she insisted upon: all four of them living in the same quarters; requiring everyone to be home before dusk; having the evening meal together. It was play-acting family, a fantasy, and Lilong hated it. Each had their own family, and this little gang of four was not it. Biemwensé herself never wasted an opportunity to speak about how much she missed her children, how much she wished she was back in Whudasha with her boys. Even Kakutan spoke often of returning to do right by the Whudans, gather them from every corner of the mainland and lead them back to safety.

Each had their own way of coping with the limbo they were stuck in, but Lilong's patience for indulging them was wearing thin.

"Maybe you should tell *brother*," Lilong said, "to stop leading bounty hunters here."

Biemwensé pretended not to hear, instead resetting each dish in scalding water to keep the food warm. Lilong took the opportunity to snag one of the diced chunks of papaya lying in a side dish and stuffed it into her mouth.

Kakutan, transformed from Supreme Magnanimous to Chabo commoner by losing her warrior garb and cutting her hair short—*part camouflage, part comfort*, she'd say when asked—leaned in. "What happened?"

"I have good news and bad news," said Lilong. "Pick."

"Bad," said Kakutan, at the same time Biemwensé said, "Good."

"More hunthands who can read," Lilong said, pulling out the yellowed tract seized from the men and slapping it on the table. "Mainlanders, these ones. I don't know how this travelled all the way there."

The women stared at the tract. Not that they needed to. As much as Danso denied it, everyone in this house knew it was him writing and distributing them.

Kakutan shook her head, saying, "Several times I've warned him. And yet."

"Please don't bring outside on my table," said Biemwensé. With her stick, she shoved the tract onto the floor.

"He has to stop *now*," said Lilong, "or all this hiding is for nothing."

"Then tell him," said Biemwensé. "He listens to you."

Lilong shook her head. "Not anymore."

Silence bit at them, interrupted only by Biemwensé's impatient tapping of her stick.

"What's the good news?" asked Kakutan.

"Meeting with Gaddo. Finally."

The former Supreme Magnanimous sat up, flush across the face. "Say again?"

"Tonight. Kubra will take us."

"Us?" Biemwensé said, at the same time Kakutan said, incredulously, "*Tonight?*"

Lilong nodded. "They want to meet with all of us."

"Why?" asked Biemwensé. "You're the one who needs help."

"You are the ones going back to the mainland," Lilong retorted.

"Right," said Kakutan, rising. "Well, we can't eat now! I hear meeting company leaders is like meeting royalty. I suspect there will be a hearty meal, and we cannot disrespect them by suggesting we're full."

"So what happens to all this?" Biemwensé gestured at the meal. "After I spent seasons preparing it?"

Kakutan shrugged. "We are sorry?"

"I can eat," said Lilong, reaching for a bowl. Biemwensé's stick came back up, but this time, Lilong was ready and caught it.

"What is wrong with you?" said Lilong. "You are not anybody's maa here. Stop this."

"*Lilong*," said Kakutan, cocking her head. "Be gentle." To Biemwensé, she said: "You know she's right." Then the former Supreme Magnanimous left it at that and went to prepare.

Biemwensé remained unfazed. "We all eat," she said, strengthening her grip on the stick, "or no one does."

Lilong slapped the stick away and left the room.

· ○ ···————··· ○ ·

Danso was holed up in the dark, writing in his codex, when Lilong knocked and entered. He did not acknowledge her.

"You missed evening meal," she said. "Biemwensé is upset."

"Not hungry," he said without looking up.

A beat, then she said: "We caught hunthands today. They had your tract."

"Not my tract."

Lilong collected herself. *Be gentle.*

"I know you are bursting with stories, and that you want to"—she put on his voice—"*liberate people's minds.* But this actually hurts us."

Danso said nothing. Lilong changed tack.

"Listen," she said, stepping closer. "As a jali, I know this is the one power you have." She did not mention the *other* power, the one he had forever abandoned and forbade her to speak of. "Your codex—its purpose is storytelling, yes? Tell all the stories you want in there. I promise you these tracts will not be missed. Nobody wants to hear the truth about Esheme—"

"Don't say her name."

Lilong held up her hands. "Fine. *The Red Emperor.*"

"Don't say that either."

Lilong scoffed. This was fruitless. "Look at us, arguing about names and tracts. We could be putting this time to better use. Like practicing with the Diwi."

Danso stiffened. She hurried forward, giving him no time to respond.

"I have thought it through, Danso. We wrap ourselves up like I do on raids. No one recognises me out there, even when I do not skinchange—no one will be able to tell! We ride off to the outskirts, start out with the small critters—lizards, scorpions. Try bigger after." She waved a hand over the scattered papers of his codex. "*This* isn't the power that will save us if we come upon the emperor's forces. *Ibor* is."

Danso's writing hand stopped moving. A shadow of a smile tugged at his lips.

"You have been practicing that argument."

Lilong wrinkled her nose. "And what if so?"

"It's a good argument." He went back to writing. "But I told you. I'm not touching it again."

Lilong exhaled, defeated. "Danso…"

He turned, anticipating the rest of her sentence. His hair, now moon-sized and unbraided, had not seen grooming in many mooncycles. His beard was the same, encroaching down his neck, moustache threatening to block his nostrils. His eyes were bloodshot from peering in the dark, refusing to light anything more than one candle.

What exactly are you going to say, Lilong? she thought. That she understood what it meant for one's family, friends, home, livelihood—everything they loved, knew, and believed in—to be snatched away forever? Had she seen her daa murdered by her own intended's hand? Had her closest associate been burned to a crisp right before her eyes? Had her sole actions broken the world and cost *everything* in the process?

She, too, had lost things, but not like this. It had to be hard, living every day knowing he escaped Bassa's grip, but everyone else he cared about was still trapped there: friends, uncles, mentors. Had to be hard knowing he could do little or nothing to help them—not even with stories, the one thing he was good at. And how could he save them if *he* wasn't safe, if he couldn't even go outside without a disguise?

At least everyone under this roof had something to look forward to, a people to return to, no matter how fractured the situation. Danso had nothing.

So what did she really know about what he was going through?

"Never mind you," she said. "I just came to give the news."

This made him perk up. He put down his charcoal stylus and gave her his undivided attention.

"We have the meeting. Tonight."

His eyes lit up. "Gaddo?" She nodded. *"All of us?"* She nodded again.

"The *aunties* want you to . . . make yourself proper."

"Ah," he said, then chuckled. She hadn't heard that sound in a while.

"So, this is real?" A small vigor had crept back into his once-defeated manner. "We're going home?"

He said *home* like the Ihinyon islands were theirs to share. Maybe they were. Agreeing to come east with her was the right choice, seeing as he had nowhere left of his own. Perhaps it wasn't a bad idea to start thinking of Namge as home. And who knew? Maybe the seven islands might be more welcoming than she envisaged.

3

Lilong

MEETING GADDO WAS INDEED like meeting royalty. Now that company leaders were only learned of by word of mouth, tales about them abounded, each trying to outdo the others through exaggeration. Lilong doubted the commander of the Tremor of the Sands had ever slain a lion with his bare hands, or the matriarch of the Savanna Swine truly descended from a desertland goddess of war. Such tales were primarily to instil fear into merchants who were unlucky enough to encounter their companies.

Of Gaddo, the songs were more realist. No one had seen enough to tell if they were man or woman or neither or both. While every other company leader was a fugitive of some sort, Gaddo was best at disguises, hiding in plain sight, and therefore had never been caught or imprisoned. Lilong knew it was a huge feat to orbit the savanna in this way yet remain anonymous, so she was equal parts curious and anxious about this meeting.

Kubra took the party of four on a trek through an extensive thicket, one of the last few of such still standing in the desertlands. Chabo boasted a couple only due to its closeness to the coast.

"You'd think that weeks in the Breathing Forest would make me less uneasy about walking into forests at night," Danso, beard and hair now trimmed, whispered to Lilong as they went deeper and deeper into the thicket. "But look." He stretched out trembling hands.

"Kubra cannot harm us," Lilong whispered back.

Danso appraised the man, who was walking in front of the Whudan women.

"I wouldn't know," he said. "He and his employers are still blank slates to me."

Lilong shrugged. "Do we have a choice?"

Kubra meandered some more, holding a lantern up, until they finally arrived at a dense wall of vines. He handed the lantern to Kakutan and pulled the vines apart. Behind them was a sturdy wall built with slender trunks, disguised as trees by greenery tied to the top of them. Kubra led them in, squeezing through some space, and they finally arrived at a tunnel-like opening. They trudged forward, toward light streaming in from the opposite opening.

A scent wafted over to greet them.

"Is that—" Danso started.

"Bean pudding?" Lilong said.

"We call it moi-moi here," Kubra said. "Come, let me show you."

They emerged from the opposite end into a clearing, and it was all Lilong could do to keep from gasping.

Before them was a garden, set into the mist of night. Lanterns hung from branches and cast soft glows on flowers arranged in various patterns. At the centre of it all was a large hut—couldn't call it a hut, really, because it was too large, but it was built to look like one anyway. The grass was soft and inviting, meticulously tended to. Off to a side was a tiny patch of farm with various plants growing. In that farm were two figures: a woman, holding up an open-flame lamp, and a man, bent over and picking some fruit from a shrub.

"They are here," Kubra announced.

Both figures rose as one, and the woman lifted the lamp to show their faces. They were both elderly—Lilong surmised them to be about the same age as Biemwensé. The woman—mainlander, high-black as humus—had a permanent warm smile affixed to her face in a way that uneased Lilong. The man—low-brown, desertlander—presented as aloof, as if only just remembering people existed outside of the woman next to him, and Lilong couldn't decide if this was a front or not. He rubbed the fruits he had been picking up—yellow lantern peppers—in his palm.

"Welcome, dear ones," the woman said in crisp High Bassai. "Please, have a seat." She waved them toward open space outside the hut, mats spread over the soft grass. To Kubra, she said, in Savanna Common: "You may guard the entrance."

Kubra went over to do just that. The party remained standing, confused. When no one else seemed willing to ask the obvious question, Lilong blurted out: "Is it you we are supposed to meet?"

"Ah," the woman said, dusting her palms together and interlinking her arm with the man—Lilong assumed they were some sort of partners. They made their way over to the group.

"You must be Lilong," the woman said, the smile still plastered on her face. "The Snakeblade."

"And skinchanger, don't forget." The man had a shrill voice, as if he was perpetually excited. "Also: extraordinary Ihinyon warrior."

Lilong frowned. Kubra had been right. They knew a lot.

"We take it upon ourselves to know everyone who works for us," the woman said. She pointed at Danso. "You're the scholar—my apologies, *jali*, yes? And you"—she pointed to Kakutan—"must be the Supreme Magnanimous of Whudasha. Well, *former* Supreme Magnanimous." She looked Biemwensé over. "And you're the one we're still trying to piece together."

The Whudan women glanced at each other. Danso, the only person who seemed pleased to be recognised, offered a wry smile.

"Jali *novitiate*," he corrected. "But I was close to graduating."

Lilong offered nothing, turning things over in her mind. She had expected to be recognised, sure, but these people did not even refer to the seven islands as *Nameless* like everyone else. They had used their *real* name.

"So you are . . . Gaddo?" asked Kakutan.

"As we live and breathe," the man said. "You may call me Pa Gaddo. This here is Ma Gaddo."

"And those are your real names?"

The two looked at one another and smiled.

"Real enough for our purposes," said Ma Gaddo.

"So there are *two* of you," Danso added. "And, you are..."

"Old? Not warriors? Warm and welcoming?" Pa Gaddo said.

"From opposite sides of the border?" Ma Gaddo said.

Lilong was wary of people who answered questions before you asked them.

"There is nothing to be said about us that we haven't heard. Come, sit." Pa Gaddo placed the lantern peppers in Ma Gaddo's hand. "Let us spice up that moi-moi and then we will tell you everything you need to know over a meal."

Lilong watched the couple through the door of what she assumed was their kitchen as they fussed over steaming pots. She noticed that Kakutan, seated next to her in the grass, watched with the same intensity. Biemwensé and Danso had wandered off to a corner of the garden, whispering over flowers and fruits.

"You really believe it?" she whispered to Kakutan. "Chabo's biggest company led by two old lovers living jolly in the bush?"

"They sure have much explaining to do," Kakutan whispered back. Lilong, who once found the former Supreme Magnanimous a risky ally, considered this moment one of the reasons Kakutan was a good fit for their group. She often held a healthy amount of scepticism, a trait useful for continued survival.

The moi-moi, when it came, was indeed spicy—those peppers were no joke. When the leaf wraps were opened, steam rose from the pudding-with-meat, stinging the eyes. With it came the wave of a memory for Lilong: Ma Guosa doing the exact same back home, though her daa's wife made her pudding with a different kind of beans, steamed with a different kind of leaf and often containing fish and shrimp rather than meat. She remembered her older brother, Issouf, and her younger brother, Kyauta, scrambling to open every wrap to find the one with the biggest fish and take it for themselves. They would dig in, just like Biemwensé and Danso did now, sucking in their breaths to calm the pepper's heat, eyes watering. Lilong would fight them for the biggest piece of fish or crayfish they had found, and hand it to their baby sister, Lumusi.

Lilong shut her eyes, letting the memory wash over her and remind her why she was here. *Ground yourself, Lilong.* She opened her eyes, but did not touch the food. Kakutan, next to her, did not either.

"The doubters of the bunch, I see?" Pa Gaddo said.

"We just want to know why we are here," said Lilong. "And present our ask."

"We know your ask," Ma Gaddo said. "You want to journey east, so you'll need a mooncycle's worth of food and water, maybe a few weapons, all stocked in a sturdy travelwagon drawn by kwagas trained for the wilderness." She angled her head. "Well, at least *you* need that. These two"—she pointed at the Whudan women—"want to return to the mainland."

The four glanced at one another.

"I reckon you must've heard," Ma Gaddo said, "what the Red Emperor is doing to your people?"

Biemwensé and Kakutan tensed. The news had indeed filtered into Chabo little by little—a companyperson here or there, returning with tales gleaned from those who had managed to escape the mainland. They had learned that every Whudan left on the mainland who wasn't old, frail, or a child too young to possess agency had been given two choices. One: leave Whudasha and be integrated into Fifteenth Ward, where the civic guard could keep an eye on their activities, but they'd still be far enough from the centre to bother anyone of note. Or, two: be taken into First Ward's prisons and left to rot for the rest of their days. Seeing that both were the same imprisonment by different names, many Whudans opted for Fifteenth Ward. Only a few had ended up in prison.

"How do you know so much?" Kakutan asked.

"Our job is to know things," Ma Gaddo said, then tapped a bowl. "Now eat. It would be disrespectful for us to put forward our proposition before you have eaten."

"What is the proposition?" Lilong pressed.

"Eat," Ma Gaddo said. "Talk after."

So Lilong ate, reluctantly at first, but soon a bit more eagerly than she'd expected. The food was surprisingly tasty, the black-eyed beans well ground and the chewy bits of meat—camel or goat or kwaga, she still couldn't differentiate—soft.

"If I may ask," Danso said, mid-meal. "What is the tale here?" He pointed to each half of the Gaddo couple.

"Is this going to be in one of your tracts?" asked Pa Gaddo.

Danso swallowed and looked away.

"If we tell you," said Ma Gaddo, "perhaps it will make you trust us a bit more?" She said this with an eye on Lilong, who didn't respond. Ma Gaddo continued anyway.

"I was given over for joining at a young age. Too young. The man I was joined to was . . . well, *bastard* is the kindest word I can use to describe him. Pa Gaddo was a soldier—too young, just like me—conscripted under the Manic Emperor to fight for the Bassai side. He helped me cross the border. Back then, the Soke Pass was more porous than it is now."

Danso's eyes widened. "You two were alive for the Second Great War?"

"The tail end of them, mostly," Ma Gaddo said. "I was much too young to remember anything of note. Pa here might have some stories for you."

Pa Gaddo shrugged. "Eh. I never fought, was never close to the coast, which is where the real battles with the first landers happened. For me, it was mostly orders, orders, orders. I was in supplies transport, see. Scrawny little travelhand driving teams of kwagas. Boring, depressing. Most exciting thing was meeting Ma when she stowed away in one of my wagons."

Lilong noted how much of their story—stowaways, intendeds, sneaking past borders—mimicked hers and Danso's. Was this why the Gaddos took an interest in them, among all the people they had liberated from the clutches of the mainland?

Danso, on the other hand, seemed ready to burst with curiosity. "I have *so many* questions."

"I have only one," Lilong said, cutting in. "We have yet to pay the debt for our crossing, and you have said nothing about erasing the rest of it. If we are not yet free to leave, then why do you speak of our journeys?"

"As I said," said Ma Gaddo. "We have a proposition."

Lilong rose. "Then say it now, or we are done here."

"Sit," Ma Gaddo said, so sharply Lilong had no choice but to obey.

She started to speak, but the woman held up a silencing finger. The couple, done with eating, washed their hands together, a small, silent ritual they seemed to take seriously. As the group watched, the couple muttered prayers under their breaths, whispering into the air, turning their faces up, down, side to side.

"To the Four Winds," Pa Gaddo said, after they were done. "One must give thanks after a meal and ask for favour." He waved his hands in the air to dry them.

"You are indeed correct," said Ma Gaddo, finally. "We do not speak of your debt, because we are willing to erase all that's left of it. Transport, supplies, maps with the safest routes—name it, and you'll have it for your journey east. For those of you who wish to return to the mainland, we will sneak you back in and connect you with our network, who will hide you until you can make your move."

Lilong nodded. "But you want something from us first."

"Yes," said Pa Gaddo. "We want you to break into a prison."

4

Lilong

Chabo
Fifth Mooncycle, same day

"You want us to do *what*?" Lilong spat.

Ma Gaddo shushed her violently. "You will wake the baby!"

A gurgle started up somewhere within the hut, then broke into a cry that pierced the stillness of the thicket's night.

"Ah, now you have done it." Pa Gaddo kissed his teeth and went into the hut.

"You have *a baby* in there?" Kakutan asked. "Who are you people?"

The crying soon stopped. Pa Gaddo emerged, a wrapper tied about his midriff. Nestled in the cocoon of wrapper folds at his back was the child—less than three seasons old, by Lilong's guess. Pa Gaddo danced foot to foot, bouncing and humming a song to lull the child back to sleep.

"This one has peed," Pa Gaddo whispered. "I've wiped her, so she will be back asleep soon, if you can manage to keep your voices down."

Lilong watched Pa Gaddo with the child, images flashing through her mind: her daa, the day Lumusi was born, strapping her to his chest. Dancing in the house to keep her quiet. Chiding the boys for playing noisily while she was asleep. It was a long time ago and the details were fuzzy, but Lilong remembered how she'd felt back then: jealous, upset that her daa had chosen someone else over her. She shook off the memory.

"What is in this prison?" she asked.

"Not what, *who*," Ma Gaddo said. "And perhaps that answer will interest you more than you think. But first, I will tell you the story of this baby."

Ma Gaddo rose, went over to Pa Gaddo, and patted the child strapped to his back.

"This is Thema, daughter of our one and only son, Alaba." Ma Gaddo kissed the baby. "Now, Alaba should be here to take care of his child, should he not? But our son, winds bless his soul, is a coconut head with a heart of gold, a burdensome combination. He is off in Chugoko, seeking to release Thema's maa—whom he has decided is the love of his life—from the Chugoko Central Prison." She patted the baby once more, then turned to face the group. "Now, I understand young love. I have felt it once, and look, Pa Gaddo and I are still here because of it. But this foolish quest Alaba is on, he cannot succeed. Reasoning has never been his strength, though, and Thema's birth has made him all the more determined to free her maa. So, because we are loving parents and do not want our son to needlessly perish, we've decided to get help—*proper* help—to see it through. That is where you come in."

"We are to help him...break his lover out of prison," Kakutan said. "Are you being serious?"

"Am I smiling?" Ma Gaddo shot back. "Do you see my teeth?"

"Let me understand," said Lilong. "You want us to risk our lives for your son because he is foolish."

"Or," Pa Gaddo inserted, "maybe wait until you hear the person you're rescuing."

Ma Gaddo turned to Kakutan. "The high-ranking Bassai you once helped secure passage through our route in the Dead Mines, you know who she was, yes?"

"Oke," Kakutan said, nodding. "The former speaker's daughter."

"Surely you must know her story?"

"I hear she got lost over the border."

"Not lost, no," Ma Gaddo said, turning to Danso. "But did you know that she *also* read the Manic Emperor's codex? And left the mainland right after too? Luckily, her leaving didn't raise as much dust as yours.

But unluckily, before she could do anything with that information, she was caught by vigilantes, arrested, and placed in prison. The Chugoko Central Prison." She angled her head further. "You see what I'm getting at?"

Danso's and Kakutan's eyes bulged.

"So *that* is who you want us to risk everything for?" Biemwensé, since quiet, suddenly found her voice. "A spoiled Bassai Idu and her wayward desertland lover?"

"Wayward desertland lover, yes," said Ma Gaddo. "Spoiled Bassai Idu, no."

Ma Gaddo turned to Lilong.

"You are here because someone from your side of the continent was at the Weary Sojourner Caravansary when it burned down. Meeting with someone from this side of the continent. A Bassai." Ma Gaddo held Lilong's gaze. "A Bassai who knew about *ibor*."

The mention of ibor stiffened the group's countenance. Humidity sucked away, leaving behind air that was bone-dry, prickly, prone to catching.

"No," said Lilong. "It can't be. Everyone who didn't die in that fire was a merchant or worker. The housekeep told me so."

"That's because Oke wasn't there when it burned down," said Ma Gaddo. "She left long before, sensing something amiss. She was captured in the wilderness nearly a season later, dehydrated and pregnant. She'd been trying to make her way east." She held Lilong's gaze again. "*East.*"

Lilong looked at the baby on Pa Gaddo's back, now fast asleep. She tried to imagine the parents' faces—the stubborn daa, the dogged maa. She tried to imagine Oke and her own daa, Elder Warrior Jaoudou of the Abenai League, seated together at the Weary Sojourner, ibor on the table between them, him divulging the secrets of the seven islands, inviting her to the Forest of the Mist. She tried to imagine Oke in the middle of the savanna, wading through grass, evading bandits and wildlife, regretting leaving the comforts of her daa's wealth.

The web was simply too tangled, even a spider couldn't weave it. A tale so convoluted could be only one thing.

"Let us assume what you say is not a lie," Lilong said, slowly. "Why me?"

"There's not a skilled companyperson I can hire who will not immediately be recognised in Chugoko and rightly pounced upon. Now someone who can alter their appearance..." She left that trailing.

"A throwaway Bassai escapee is not worth the risk," said Lilong. "And your son does not deserve my sacrifice."

Ma Gaddo smiled, then ushered Pa Gaddo to return the baby to bed. Once gone, she sat back down.

"You know what it means to traverse this Savanna Belt. You've done it once before, Lilong—have you told your friends what it's like? If I remember correctly, you got wounded by bandits on your way west— and that's you, a trained warrior with... *abilities*. Now imagine all that, tripled by the dry harmattan, plus a bounty on your heads." Ma Gaddo sat up straight. "Stop being so stoic. You need help, and we are willing to give it. You need answers, too, or you'd never have come west in the first place. If this goes well, you get both those things."

Lilong hadn't really thought of rescuing Oke as a pathway to finding answers. Mostly, it was anger that filled her belly. Like: How dare it be a Bassai that may have led her daa to his demise? Like: How dare her daa spill the secrets of the seven islands to some stranger, when his own daughter was *right there*? If anything, she was happy to rescue this Oke person from prison if it meant she'd get to put a blade through the woman herself.

But then there was also the promise of return: of traipsing the Forest of the Mist, crossing the isthmus, Diwi in hand. Receiving a hero's welcome. Reclaiming her family's honour. Saving the continent. Saving her daa—if he was still alive.

Ma Gaddo was right: The next best thing to killing Oke was finding out all she knew about the islands, ibor, her daa's plans—then using that to her advantage.

Lilong turned to her comrades. "Thoughts?"

The Whudans looked conflicted and Lilong could guess why. They now understood why the Gaddos had wanted to meet with all four of them—to make it difficult for Lilong to refuse their offer, since they'd all benefit from her success. If Biemwensé and Kakutan told her to accept the proposition now, it would seem selfish. But telling her not to would sound like they didn't care about her own desire to return home. It was a perfectly laid trap, and Lilong decided that the Gaddos were much more calculating than their warm disposition let on.

"Maybe," said Kakutan, canny as ever, "it doesn't have to be just you? Partaking in the heist, I mean." She turned to the Gaddos, Pa Gaddo now returned from laying the baby down. "We can all play a part, can we not?"

"Depends," said Ma Gaddo. "What can you bring to the table?"

"Assume we possess a variety of useful skills."

The Gaddos glanced at one another, shrugged. "I guess we can use more hands with no ties to the company," said Pa Gaddo. "Four of you plus Kubra could mean no one else need be involved."

"Four plus Kubra *and* Alaba," said Ma Gaddo. "He'll be there to represent our interests."

Kakutan turned to Lilong. "You stand to lose the most if something goes wrong, so I say it's your decision." She nudged Biemwensé. "Right?"

Biemwensé, who had something else at the tip of her tongue but decided against it, acceded: "Your decision."

Lilong turned to Danso. "What about you?"

Danso looked distant. "I don't know. If we get caught, you—*we*—will never go home. Everything we've struggled through, everyone who's died, everything we've lost..." He trailed off, a faraway look in his eye. "I just want a chance to fix things, and I need to be alive to do that, you know?"

"We understand it's not an easy decision," said Ma Gaddo. "Go home, sleep, speak among yourselves. But be hasty about it."

"Why?" asked Lilong.

"Because the Ochela, Chugoko's Festival of Nomads, is about a fortnight away. And that is when we move."

5

Lilong

Chabo
Fifth Mooncycle, 23

Two days after the meeting, Lilong ventured into the outskirts of Chabo at twilight, soon finding herself in a less crowded locality. Here, all the roads disappeared, and the real belly of the colony showed itself. Unlike the abodes near the centre where company powers held sway, constituents living closer to its edges had less of an affinity for order.

Lilong's path took her into the only thoroughfare available—the space between ramshackle abodes and lean-to constructions, stacked precariously upon each other like chickens in an acrobatic pyramid. All navigation was done via such alley-like connections, zigzag mazes no person in their right mind could memorise. Lilong herself had learned to navigate by using the clotheslines criss-crossing overhead from one abode to the other. Most residents labelled their clothing and wares tied to the lines using personal symbols, and Lilong had learned to read these and use them as her cardinals.

Soon, she found the door she sought and rapped on it in quick, coded knocks.

"What's the word?" a low voice inquired from inside. Lilong whispered it and the door opened. A hand stretched out, gripped her tunic, and pulled her inside.

The clandestine public house was soaked in darkness and near empty.

Lilong did what she did each time she came here: She went to the counter, ordered a spirit, hunched over the drink when it was offered, but did not touch it. As usual, she was approached by at least one drunk who wanted to know why she was so tense, if they could give her a massage and remedy that. She offered her usual response: *Touch me, lose your hand.*

After she was sure she hadn't been followed, she poured the drink in the dirt and took the back exit. Behind the building was the shed she sought, and within the shed was the trapdoor to which only she had a key—because she had paid for that privilege. She opened it quickly, and within it was a strongbox, demanding another key, which she also had. Soon, that one opened as well.

Inside, an object was bunched up in rags tied with strips of cloth. Usually, all Lilong would do was to open it and inspect, ensuring the Diwi was still in one piece. But tonight, she simply laid down the strongbox, trapdoor, and key, and walked away with the wrapped stone-bone tucked into her wrappers.

She left the public house as quickly as she'd arrived and plunged back into the outskirts. Night had fallen proper, making navigation more difficult. A deep chill had set into the air. Lilong draped an extra wrapper over her head, holding it tight and close.

Perhaps it was that which prevented her from seeing the movement around the corner. It was right next to her before she sensed it—the warmth of a person—reaching out.

She swivelled, primed to Draw and Command. Her blade rattled in its sheath, ready to swing into the face of the figure before her.

"It's me, it's me," Danso said, hands up. He pulled his wrapper over his head.

Lilong swore under her breath and recalled her power. The blade stopped agitating and settled back into the sheath with a snap.

"What are you—" She stole a quick glance back at the corner she had just turned. "Are you *following* me?" Lilong swore again. "I could have wounded you! That is a risky joke you are playing."

"And that was a very long evening stroll you were taking," he said.

"What are you doing here?" She eyed the lump in his own wrappers, the shape of rolled-up papers. "Let me guess—new invitations to our enemies?"

Danso scoffed. "Whatever." He walked away. Lilong sighed, caught up, and fell in stride.

"I did not mean it like that," she said. "But you know me, I will not stop saying this—what you are doing is dangerous for us."

"I know."

"And yet you continue."

"Because I have no choice."

What does that even mean? Lilong wanted to press, but decided against it. She had learned the hard way that Danso was like a lever with no balance on the other end. If you pushed too hard, the return swing could knock you out.

For their first few days in Chabo, Danso had been close to delirious, muttering half sentences in which Lilong only managed to catch a name here or there—often *Zaq* or *daa* or the names of his triplet uncles and friends. Then a fortnight or two in, he stopped talking altogether. All he did was write, throwing himself into the codex (and as they would soon discover, the tracts). Lilong tried everything she could to get him to open up to her, offering everything from promises of Red Iborworker training to stories of Namge to cheer him up. Danso was a stone wall. Only after she stopped trying did the wall start to come down. But even then, he only let himself show in trickles.

"I know what you have tucked under there," Danso said, motioning to her own wrappers. "You went to get it because you're ready to leave." He glanced at her. "I guess you've made up your mind, then."

She had, and it hadn't taken long. The stakes of getting caught and imprisoned or killed were high, yes, but the costs of saying no, of never going home, were even higher. What life awaited her out here, where she could never be who she truly was, who she really wanted to become? What kind of life would it be to never find her voice, her truth, her heart?

The tipping point, therefore, had been the promise of answers. The opportunity to learn what her daa had been up to. Whether she liked it or not, her fate here or in the islands was tied to those events, and she needed to understand them through and through. Better, even, if she could do so before taking a step toward the journey home.

"I want us to have a safe trip," she said. "If that means we break into a prison, then we break into a prison."

They had come upon an overlook, one among many present in the only ridge in Chabo. The colony wasn't mountainous, but being so close to the Soke mountains, one rogue ridge had slipped off and run its way past the colony's southwest edge. This gave passers-by a scenic view in four directions: the Soke mountains to the south and southeast, the coast to the southwest, and the expansive Savanna Belt everywhere else. They stopped and sat in the sand, gazing out to the horizon, as the two moons overhead prepared to cross.

Danso pulled the tracts from beneath his wrappers and laid them out. They were not freshly written, from the look of them, but old and worn, already read.

"Oh, that's what you were doing—*gathering* them."

He arranged them in a stack, pulled out a fire striker, and struck. Sparks flew.

"You're not the only one who's ready to leave," he said, setting the papers on fire. They watched the tracts burn, Danso's loopy markings becoming even loopier as orange flames encroached on them.

"I want to defeat the empire," Danso said.

So *driven*, so *raw*, the way he said it. Lilong had always known, from the moment Esheme had set his daa ablaze in the Dead Mines, that Danso would want some kind of revenge or retribution. But this was bigger than that. This was about defeating the *empire*—not just one woman, but the entire infrastructure that held her up.

"I can't just escape Bassa, then run away forever," he continued. "What happens to everyone I've left behind?" He shook his head. "No. If these tracts have proven anything, it's that I can't truly help them if I cower in hiding, and stories alone cannot do the job. I need something else. Or *someone* else."

Lilong could see where this was going.

"You want to meet Oke," she said.

Danso nodded. "Someone who also read the Manic Emperor's codex, who was also moved by its revelations to leave Bassa, seek truth, find ibor. Someone who was driven to bring change and was willing to brave a journey east to do it."

He was right. Their journeys were truly similar.

"But she didn't even get halfway."

"And maybe that was fate!" A feverish quality had crept into his voice. "Now, we get to rescue her, maybe join forces, maybe finish whatever it is she started with your daa."

That last part stunned Lilong. There was *no chance* that Lilong was going to help Oke with anything, especially not revealing even more secrets of her islands to strangers and outsiders. But she reminded herself that this was not the best time to have that debate.

"So you think we should do it," was all she said.

Danso nodded. "I think we should do it."

A handful of onlookers arrived to watch the mooncrossing happen, causing Danso to stamp out the fire. They tightened their cloaks around themselves to retain their disguises. Chabo wasn't under Bassai rule, so there was no mooncrossing festival to speak of, but watching the sister moons cross was still an event of note for some. Sitting here together, Lilong felt this was of note for them, too, in a way. It was the closest she'd felt to Danso in many mooncycles.

"I've been thinking about it," he said, motioning toward the Diwi tucked in her wrappers.

"Yes?"

"Should we destroy it?"

"*Destroy?*" Lilong scoffed. "What is doing you today?"

"I just thought, on the journey, we don't want it to attract . . . *them*."

She assumed he was referring to the wild beasts like the Skopi that could sense ibor's presence. They hadn't encountered any so far since the Breathing Forest, but if she had to guess, the probability of encountering one on their journey east may not be low.

She had once considered destroying it too, for this same reason, but quickly reminded herself that if she returned without it, her chances of being arrested and imprisoned by the Abenai League would rise. Worse, she would be putting Danso at risk. Though the Elder Warriors weren't known for summarily executing people, she was sure they could make an exception for a Bassai who knew all there was to know about the islands.

But the real reason she had decided against destroying the Diwi, the one reason she didn't want to admit, was that no matter how troubled she was by her daa's choices, by the league's choices, she was still an Abenai warrior through and through. She still had her duty and honour. Without those, who was she, even?

"We will need it to gain entrance," she said. "Remember that I left without asking permission. We will not be welcomed with open arms."

"What if we shatter it into many pieces, then, like the ones in your arm? Won't attract them in that size."

"We would have had to shatter it *before* you bonded with it. Shatter it now, and it will simply become dust." She paused. "Besides, we would not have to worry about beasts if someone among us would just, you know, *Possess* the stone."

He stared into space, impassive. The moons above them came together and shone brighter as one. The onlookers, having had their fill, began to wander away. Lilong reached out to pat him on the back, then decided against it.

"Something leaves them, you know?" he said out of nowhere.

"What leaves who?"

"When they die. You can see it fade, the *life* or whatever it is. And then I touch them, and you can see it return, but not really. Like it pauses midway and just never makes it back. Like I've stolen it from them, then prevented its return so they can come under my Command. When they open those red eyes..." He gulped.

"I'm sorry," she said, suddenly feeling horrible for asking him all this time. *Is that what red iborworking feels like?* Now she understood why he struggled to accept that the Skopi was gone, why he would forever be haunted by the image of Esheme Commanding undead humans.

"I know I'm tethered to the Diwi, so I can't run away from it," he said. "But it deals in death, and I don't know how much more death I can take, Lilong. I don't know."

He took a stone and tossed it so that it bounced down the overlook, skidding before embedding itself into a mound, spraying a cloud of sand below.

"You don't have to touch it ever again if you don't want to," said Lilong.

"I know." He paused. "You think Zaq would've—" He gulped again. "You think this—all of this—is what they would've wanted us to do?"

They, she understood this time, were all the names that hurt.

"I think they would be glad we tried," she said. *And I think*, she didn't say, *they would wish they had done better by us, and that we do better for them.*

6

Kangala

Sahel: Lake Vezha
Fourth Mooncycle, 17

MOY KANGALA WAS KNOWN as the Man Beyond the Lake because he did not need to be known by anything else. The Sahel had only one lake—the whole of the desertlands did, to be precise—and he was the only person that mattered where it was concerned. The *beyond* part was a misnomer because Kangala did not actually live on the Idjama side of the Lake Vezha, but existed in various places at once, culminating in him existing nowhere in fact, other than on lips whispering into ears and tongues held back in silence.

Still, when desertlanders spoke of Kangala, the image that came to mind was uniform: He was the man who ensured that whatever crossed the Savanna Belt into the Sahel with the aim of heading into the Idjama desert—or had any interest in moving in the opposite direction—went through his multitude of ventures. The few who thought themselves clever and attempted to bypass this did not, as many believed, come to violent ends by Kangala's hand. Kangala prided himself in not being a violent man, but a man of the greater weapons of words, tact, and innovation. But if said people thought they would not come to other sorts of ends—violent or otherwise—by hands not his, they were sorely mistaken.

Kangala himself was an unassuming fellow. He was sugarcane-thin, lanky, and often picked at his teeth. Sometimes, they bled while he did business, and he would swirl with spit and swallow, then flash a bloody grin at his guests to discompose them. He performed the same ritual at home with the youngest of his twenty-seven children, who was only nine seasons old. His young daughter would giggle with a childish mix of disgust and pleasure. He could not say the same of his guests.

Few knew what Kangala looked like, because he only met with guests of the highest calibre, and delegated everything else to his eldest children, his seconds-in-command: Oroe was head enforcer, and Ngipa ensured all the moving parts of his enterprises kept running. Together, the three ensured that the communities of travellers, vagrants, and mainstays that sprouted from the lake and made home in trading settlements littering the routes down south, or scattered across the grasslands to the east and west, knew who they must pay fealty to whenever they wished to cross the Lake Vezha.

So, it was with great reluctance that he decided to meet with a woman who was from neither of these places. His seconds-in-command informed him she was a former member of the now overthrown Bassai government on the mainland, and had arrived from exile in Chugoko to seek his audience.

When Kangala's canoe pulled into shore on the waterfront, gentle water slapping against the wooden hull, he stepped onto the jetty less than eager. It was high afternoon, and though he walked beneath a canopy held by attendants, he sweated beneath his headdress, wrapped so intricately as to disguise his features. The heat did not stop the lakeside from buzzing, dockworkers sweating as they moved crate upon crate. Most paid little attention to the entourage; it was a recognisable though infrequent sight. Kangala prided himself in being a master of performance, establishing the element of mystery: Show the people just enough to keep them guessing, but never enough to give them understanding. Understanding, Kangala believed, bred comfort, comfort bred contempt, and contempt in the hearts of a significant populace was a considerable threat. Look at what happened to Bassa, for instance.

They crossed the jetty quickly, Oroe's party clearing a path. The air stank of raw fish brought here from all around the lake for export. Smoke from the large smoking houses employed in drying them hung low in the air. But it was not the only thing that hung low. Kangala could see the uncertainty in the eyes of his workers, the sag in their shoulders, the conversation in hushed tones. They worried about their futures here, as did he. The coup down south and its infamous new emperor had shaken up the rest of the continent. Trade along the northbound routes had significantly dwindled, stores were getting empty, and no new stock was coming in. Everyone was waiting for the emperor's long hand to reach north before deciding their next steps.

Kangala was less worried about the emperor and her antics and was more concerned with the things he could not control. His wells, for instance, which were drying up at an alarming rate. Salt yields from the Idjama side were dwindling. But worst of all, the lake itself was *dying*. He had canoed here on tide that was so low he could see the bottom of the lake even though the water was not clear. Soon, it would be impossible to canoe at all. There would be no lake, and with that, no enterprise.

He pushed the worries aside and focused on the business before him.

The woman who sat in his workroom rose when he arrived and greeted him with the Bassai bow and hand on the bridge of her nose. He'd heard enough about hair arches to tell that the number on this woman's head meant she was high-ranking. Or *once* was, if she was now here seeking his audience. Her clothes were more sensible, the dust of a trip through the savanna evidenced in corners where her wrappers folded. Her travelling party, a bunch of attendants and armed private hands, carried the same signs of travel.

"DaaKangala," the woman said in High Bassai, and Ngipa translated to Kangala's native Sahelian. "It is an utmost honour to make your acquaintance."

Kangala sat before the woman and waited. Another thing he understood about performance was that it wasn't always about the things said and done, but things left unsaid and undone. Empty space was not *empty* just because one couldn't see air. But people who didn't understand this always tried to fill that perceived emptiness. And when they did, they divulged more than they'd initially planned to.

"My name is MaaButue," she said. "I have come from Bassa to seek your audience."

Ngipa continued to translate. Kangala nodded but remained silent. The woman took that to mean she could continue.

"I would like to propose an agreement, if you are willing to hear it."

Kangala nodded.

"I have come this long a way because Bassa is in turmoil. The nation I once knew is no more, now in the hands of a brutal yet inexperienced emperor. As a former Second Elder and member of the Lower Council, I cannot in good faith continue to work with and for a government that does not serve my interests. To that end, I have put Bassa behind me and decided to move my interests here. I would like to settle along the Vezha, but I would also like to retain sovereignty for me and my family. Perhaps we can come to an agreement beyond fealty. I bring much that can be beneficial to you."

Kangala cocked his head.

"I am a trained member of the craftworking guild with a specialization in textiles, and I bring with me that expertise. I can offer consultation for best practices in handling of raw textile sources, including cotton and leather. I am well aware you are a savvy man of commerce and innovation—your well pumps are acclaimed all over, and no one has yet to replicate their secret technology. But I presume you do not currently possess the kind of expertise I just put forward. Perhaps we can help each other."

Kangala asked for a toothpick, and when it was brought to him, he began to pick and suck at his teeth noisily, mulling over his next step. She was not wrong—that was indeed useful expertise. But it did not solve his current problems with the drying lake. Worse, what she was offering was not on the same level as what she was asking for, and she knew this. She was attempting to be crafty. Kangala didn't like people who started out crafty. They were future problems disguised as current opportunities.

"What say you?" Butue asked. "A deal? I have brought a few of my most precious textiles with me. I am willing to offer some as a gift. A sign of goodwill, if you say." She waved her people forward, and they presented bales of various textiles to Ngipa: wrappers, headcloths, leather wraps, wool overcloths, velvet spotted with coral, bronze, gold.

Kangala eyed the bales without acknowledging them, then leaned forward, looking Butue in the eye, before saying to Ngipa: "I want her to tell us what this new emperor is like."

Ngipa related the question. Butue frowned.

"That is not in my place to say," the woman replied. "I would rather refrain from speaking about Bassa's emperor, if you will."

"Then tell her we are done here," Kangala said. "She either offers me this information, or we do not even discuss a deal."

After Ngipa relayed Kangala's words, Butue was pensive, then began to speak. She spoke about the Red Emperor's powers, about how she could command the dead. She spoke about how her eyes would turn red, and how anyone who spoke against her often ended up dead, and then resurrected again, a reanimated corpse. She commanded the corpses of her enemies like so, building a personal undead protection unit known as the Soldiers of Red.

She spoke of the emperor's preoccupation with demanding respect and enforcing loyalty from all corners of the continent; how she was currently touring the mainland to ensure this in person. The desertlands were next, that was sure. The emperor's continued search for her former intended, believed to be travelling with a yellowskin warrior from—Kangala couldn't believe his ears—the extinct Nameless Islands, was sure to bring her here, if the peace officers were not already a sign. Both fugitives were said to possess a mineral called ibor, which helped the bearer perform supernatural feats—the same mineral the emperor employed in reanimating corpses.

Kangala had heard snippets of all of these before, gossip curated from traders who came up here from the settlements along the trading route. He considered it typical gossip from the mouths of merchants, traders, and dockworkers, sources that could not be trusted. But hearing it in such detail, coming out of the mouth of a Second Elder who used to walk in the very halls of the Great Dome of Bassa—now *that* was privileged information. In fact, more privileged than whatever else she thought she was bringing to the table.

Moy Kangala rose and walked out without offering Butue a response. His group converged to shield him, but he waved them aside, taking off his headdress and walking into the light of day. The sun beat down on his face, caused his cheeks to shine and his face to look radiant. Most workers gasped upon seeing him. Some shielded their eyes, unsure if they should be looking.

"What are you doing?" Oroe said, he and Ngipa coming to stand beside their daa. "They can see you!"

Kangala shut his eyes and inhaled the salty, smelly air.

"You see all of this, my children?" he said. "This is ours. It was not given freely to us. We have earned it through sweat and innovation, without lifting a blade in conquest. Perhaps it is time people see the face of their leader. A leader with a face means a striking hand, and a striking hand may be feared and respected. But a faceless leader is a conquerable one and encourages dissent, a lesson Bassa has learned the hard way and that perhaps we need to learn sooner." He glanced at his employees on the dock, then turned to his children. "This new emperor the woman speaks of, ehm—"

"The Red Emperor," Ngipa offered.

"The Red Emperor, yes. She sounds a bit foolhardy, heavy-handed, but she understands this lesson. One suspects she can be reasoned with. And this Butue woman has just given me an idea."

He stepped forward, walking along the pier. His children followed. Workers scampered out of the way, one man falling off the jetty and into the water. At the end of the pier, he turned to look out to the lake, watching the water lap softly against the abutment. Far in the distance, on the opposite docks of the Idjama side, canoes dotted the horizon. Soon, they would be stuck there forever, unable to cross a dry lake.

"We will go to Bassa," he said.

His children's eyes widened.

"No," said Oroe. "No, no, no."

"We cannot grovel to the emperor," Ngipa said. "We mustn't."

"We will do a great many things, but grovelling is not one of them," Kangala said, patting his children's shoulders. "We will offer gifts, loyalty, a proposition. A *good* proposition, one with heft, not the diluted kind Butue has brought to us."

"Like what?" asked Ngipa.

"The secrets of our pumps."

Ngipa was aghast. "That is your life's work! You cannot barter with that."

"Look around, daughter." He waved his hand over the lake. "Those pumps will be useless soon either way, if this lake turns to nothing but sand. We must diversify, and if we don't, we will perish anyway."

"What do we get in return, then?" Oroe asked. "Just ask her not to kill us? Yes, I'm sure that madwoman will listen."

"Mad, yes; stupid, no," said Kangala. "She single-handedly took the Great Dome. She will recognise a good opportunity and won't be as eager to put a spear through it. All we need is to gain an audience." He counted on his fingers. "Gifts. Our pumping secrets. The services of our champions, if she needs them. In return, we ask for the same thing Butue has asked for: land to install new ventures, and the self-governance of it."

His children regarded one another. They were used to Kangala by now, the way his mind ticked, sometimes too quickly for them to catch up. But they knew he was right. Each day saw more migrants crossing from the Idjama side, moving southward due to a complete lack of water up north. That complete lack of water was bound to catch up with the Lake Vezha at some point. Catering to their extensive dynasty would be impossible without a venture on its banks. Bassa or no Bassa, they were going to have to make the decision to leave sooner or later. Better sooner than later, if they were to have a chance at negotiation.

"Gather your champion siblings," Kangala said to Oroe. "Prepare your parties, all of you. We head into the savanna in a matter of days."

"All eighteen of us?" Oroe frowned. "That's a company of hundreds. Will the emperor not think us an invasion?"

"We will camp outside Chugoko. I alone will meet her in Bassa."

His children did not like the sound of that, but they trusted his judgment.

"What about this Butue woman?" Oroe asked. "What do we do with her?"

"Same as the others."

"Are you sure?" Ngipa queried. "This is a Second Councilhand."

"*Was* a Second Councilhand," Kangala corrected. "Now, a mere fugitive of Bassa. And as we have always said, Bassa's rejects will have no place with us." He looked to Oroe. "Try to be quieter about it this time."

Oroe nodded and left, calling his party along. Soon, there were faraway sounds of struggle, iron clanging iron, tumbles, crashes, thuds. Cries of pain, whimpers of persons succumbing to death. The dockworkers continued to work, unperturbed. Kangala and his daughter remained at the end of the pier, unmoved, their wrappers swaying in the light afternoon breeze.

7

Esheme

Southwest Hinterlands
Fourth Mooncycle, 32

THE HINTERLAND SUNRISE WAS a loud, ever-present orange. Back in Bassa, Esheme barely saw the sun manifest this way. Even high up on the Great Dome's portico, the Soke mountains to the east prevented such a sight until it was too late, when the skies had already left their beauty behind. This was her life in a nutshell: something delicious and exciting within purview, yet fleeting, still out of reach.

Esheme shut her eyes and focused on the moment, drinking in the sounds and smells of nearby forested areas as the royal caravan trudged into the hinterlands. The constant shrill of cicadas. The babble of streams branching from the confluence. The prevalent stink of rotting bark. Nothing particularly exciting, but at least different from the drudgery of the Great Dome.

The trip wasn't without its inconveniences. This far south, the terrain was denser, the clayey roads soaked and sticky. The royal travelwagon had gotten stuck once already, so that Igan's posse had to come down and push. It rained hard and often despite the fact that it was harmattan season everywhere else on the continent. Satti, who hailed from the hinterlands, had warned the royal planners of these ghost rains, explaining that even hinterlanders themselves didn't know what caused them. The royal planners had, in turn, advised Esheme against a trip south, citing these challenges.

But Esheme had persisted. When she overthrew the empire's leaders, it was so she could be free, not become shackled by duty and performance. She couldn't stand another season of mundane appearances in the city. Emperorship, it turned out, was its own prison. Any reason to escape the overwhelm of the Great Dome was a good one.

This trip south, however, was for more than just that.

"Who would have thought," Esheme said to Ikobi, "that all those times you tried to get me to venture outside Bassa, see more of the world—that I would be doing it eventually, and with you in tow?"

Her mentor-turned-advisor chuckled. Igan, the only other person in the travelwagon, said nothing.

"Perhaps it was your destiny all along," Ikobi said.

"Destinies are never written in stone, unless one does the writing themselves."

"Let me guess," said Ikobi. "Your lips, but Nem's words."

Esheme smiled wryly. She had chosen Ikobi to be her second advisor not because of her scholarly accomplishments, but because the woman knew her well. She'd also needed someone to rely on during this trip. As First Consul, Nem had to remain and handle the Great Dome's affairs while the emperor was away. And Igan... well, Igan had been unrelenting in their disapproval of many things, current trip included.

Her Second-turned-lover-turned-Second glared out the window, refusing to meet her eyes. Esheme chuckled quietly. Any other person, and she would have them put to the dust. But Igan was special in many ways— and worse, they knew it. Perhaps that, too, was why Esheme found herself drawn to them anyway. Someone who did not simply bow to her every whim. Nem and Igan were the only two people on this continent who complemented her desire for resistance, who gave her something to push against.

Voices brought her to the present. The two lookouts who regularly rode ahead of the caravan galloped back to detail their sightings to Igan.

"A welcome party," Igan reported in a businesslike tone, avoiding Esheme's gaze. "Clan leaders have heard of our arrival."

They said *heard* with a blade in the back of the tongue, like: *I told you so.*

"If you have something to say, say it," said Esheme. "I may tolerate your petulance, but I will not have dissent on this trip."

Igan, never one to back down from a challenge, dug in. "I told you," they said. "We should not have abducted the Tombolo leaders."

"*Abducted*—" Esheme kissed her teeth, long and hard. "You know what, I take that back. Maybe it's better you stay quiet." To the lookouts, she said: "Tell the party they may present their best face."

When the royal caravan met the welcome party, it was quickly established that they were there only to offer gifts. Oxen, ass, and buffalo drew wagons that bore the southwest's most precious prizes: maize, beans, cassava, kolanuts, craftwork, ornaments in various metals.

"Announcing!" said the royal jali. "The Twenty-Fourth Emperor of Great Bassa, Sovereign Scion of Moons, the Red Emperor of Oon and all that light touches, Emperor Esheme and the Royal Court of the Great Dome."

The welcome party already had their heads bowed, eyes lowered to the ground. The jali looked to Esheme for instruction. She gave a slight nod.

"You may speak," said the jali.

A small person of a third gender—an envoy, perhaps—stepped forward. They were dressed the same way as every member of the party: headwrap, short wrapper beneath the arms, and another from the waist down, leaving the midriff bare. Esheme marvelled at how beautiful and fascinating it was, but her excited questions rested at the tip of her tongue. This was what being emperor had reduced her to: someone who could not smile, lest it be mistaken for approval. How different was that from the average Bassai woman?

"Sovereign Scion of Moons," the envoy announced, "I am Gevah, leader of the clan of Enuka. On behalf of the clan leaders of the protectorate lands west of the confluence, I welcome you. We are here to guide the royal caravan to our home. We have prepared festivities in your honour, and it will be our pleasure to celebrate your name, if you let us."

Esheme glanced at Igan, who eyed her back. They had both expected a different response, something akin to the one they'd received at the Tombolo hamlets. The Elders there had been mostly demure, but two of them—the eldest and the youngest of the lot—bore dispositions that were not as welcoming. The youthful Elder in particular had worn a steely gaze, all but frying the sand between his feet. So Esheme had had Igan rest the sharp edge of their axe on his shoulders and drop him to his knees.

She nodded to the jali before her, who turned to the welcome party.

"Do you know why the emperor is here?"

Gevah looked at their fellow party members. "I'm . . . not sure?"

"But you are aware of the royal tour west and south?"

"We only heard about the . . . events at Tombolo," said Gevah. "That is all we know."

"What did you hear?" the jali pressed.

Gevah swallowed. "That a number of Tombolo leaders now ride with the emperor? And a new civic guard battalion was installed there? Among other events."

Smart, thought Esheme. Managed to avoid the snake pit that was that question. She decided she liked this Gevah person.

"Let's see what these festivities look like," said Esheme.

Igan waved them forward. The party turned about and led the royal caravan off the muddy roads and onto a wide earthen way, clean and polished.

"Looks like an Emperor's Road, does it not?" Esheme asked.

Ikobi nodded. "Satti says they've preserved it all this time. My belief is that they hoped for a return."

"Of emperors."

"Yes."

"And you think that means something."

Ikobi shrugged. "Perhaps not everyone is as opposed to your rule as you believe?"

Esheme chuckled. Ikobi often thought good things, offered people and circumstances the benefit of the doubt. It was the reason she agreed to be Esheme's mentor at the university in the first place. Where other scholars had eschewed the task of moulding a fixer's daughter into a model of the Bassai Ideal, Ikobi had relished the challenge. And though she never quite succeeded, she still believed, to an extent, that her role as advisor offered her the opportunity to continue where she had left off.

"Only those doing the ruling remain unopposed to it," Esheme said. "It is in the very nature of ruling to be resisted."

"Another one of your maa's adages," said Ikobi. "Tell me—if you believe that, then why are you so worried about what the citizens think?"

Because thoughts are dangerous, she wanted to say. Most Bassai were no different from those two Tombolo Elders. They worshipped her only because they had no choice; duty out of fear, not respect. They were happy for her to be their redeemer, but emperor was a role too far. *For someone so young!* they said, words spoken in the wards filtering back to her court at the Great Dome. *When has an emperor so youthful ever done anything but destroy us?*

And she did want to destroy them, when these words reached her ears. Gather all her disparate pieces of red ibor and ravage the city. *That* would teach them to respect her.

But then Nem would speak, and they would be back to useless politicking and administration, and her fantasy would be squashed there and then. It didn't help, of course, that Igan thought Nem was right to, in their words, *find non-violent ways to solve this problem.*

"I believe," Esheme said to Ikobi, "that you get what you demand. So I will demand what I want, including how and what they think about me."

The caravan snaked deeper into the heart of the hinterlands. Soon, the silty and rockier terrain began to give way to flatter, muddier undulations and even thicker vegetation. For a moment, Esheme forgot she was the Sovereign Emperor of Bassa and Scion of Moons. She pushed open the window and poked her head out of the travelwagon.

Nothing she had seen in Bassa prepared her for what the hinterlands would look like. She had heard little in all her time of counsel study, and therefore believed their ways to be unsophisticated, uncivilised. But as she neared Enuka, the seat of the southwest hinterlands, clan abodes began to come into view. Multi-storeyed houses of mud sculpted in the shape of bananas, with exterior design patterns of okras. The architecture stood sturdy on opposite sides of streets as smooth as those in Bassa, in just as orderly a fashion, and lined with all the accoutrements she was used to seeing in the capital city: street lamps, sculptures, trimmed bushes, canals. She also noted the advanced trading and commerce infra-structure, including various warehouses.

As they neared the city—because she had started to think of it as one now—she noticed every activity seemed to be halted in favour of a welcome for the emperor's caravan. Clan members stepped out to each side of the road, waving broad leaves and palm fronds. Many had the red mud of the hinterlands smoothed over their faces and bodies in decoration.

"Well, there you go," Ikobi said to Esheme, who peered through the obscured blinds. "Now you have what you want."

But *this* was not what Esheme wanted—subjects compelled to do things in her name. She already had that back in the city, and as long as she had iborworking, she could eke it out of anyone. No, she wanted people to come out and welcome her because they *believed* in her, because they *respected* her, *loved* her from the bottom of their hearts.

She just needed to show that she was mighty, powerful, that she could protect them. This was why she had come here: to dissolve the doubt in their hearts, make space for love and adulation. Moons willing, she would find a way.

After another hour of hinterlanders lined up in welcome, the royal caravan finally arrived in the centre of town in Enuka, where the emperor's meeting with the clan leaders was to take place. The buildings were of the same okra-banana style as the houses she had seen before, but much larger and sculpted by obviously more experienced hands. Seven of such abodes interconnected into one, which told her that this was their Great Dome of sorts. The leaders of all the clans in the southwest hinterlands were gathered there, and before them were spread out even more gifts to be presented: plantains, yams, textiles, livestock.

Igan got down first, and their posse followed. Then Ikobi and the jali, followed by the civic guard squadron travelling with the caravan. And just like they had done back at the Tombolo hamlets, the emperor would emerge last. But first, she would send the Soldiers of Red ahead to set the stage.

Esheme closed her eyes and Drew.

The pit of her belly stirred, and painful anguish tightened in her stomach. She gritted her teeth, the effects of losing her last conception to iborworking now commingling with the demands of employing this new conception in its service.

Breathe, Esheme, breathe. She Drew further, biting her tongue to keep from screaming, stretching her consciousness until it gripped every Soldier of Red, locked itself around them. Then she breathed and gave the Command.

The last wagon in the caravan, where the Soldiers of Red lay in stasis, rocked. The Soldiers jumped down one by one and marched in loose formation, limbs in the staccato movements of something caught between living and dead. Heads shaved, feet unsandaled, skin grey and devoid of shine. Eyes brimming red, lifeless and demoniac.

The crowd stepped back as one.

Esheme had not quite meant to start an army of undeads. After losing Oboda to the moats, she had only wanted a replacement. But it turned out that a usurper emperor had no shortage of people who needed booting out of her path. Both goals simply coincided: Why waste a good corpse when she could collect them and Possess and Command at will? What better assurance of safety than an army she could trust to carry out her commands to the letter?

What better way to become invincible?

The Soldiers of Red encircled the royal travelwagon in a ring of protection and stood still in wait for the emperor.

"The Royal Scion of Ashu and Menai," the jali announced. "The Sovereign Emperor of Bassa and of all the world, she who slays her enemies with nothing but a look—the Red Emperor of Oon."

Every person in sight bowed, eyes to the ground, as Esheme stepped from the travelwagon onto the stool-cum-dais placed on the wrappers the people of Enuka had spread out for the emperor to walk upon. This part of being emperor—revealing herself to those who did not know her prior—she enjoyed. It reminded her that three-quarters of retaining power was all about performance, and only one-quarter actually expending it.

"People of Enuka," the jali continued. "You may announce your address."

Another person dressed just like Gevah stepped forward gingerly.

"I turn to the right, I turn to the left," they said. "May the crown last on your head, the shoes on your feet, the command in your mouth. Hail the Red Emperor, Sovereign Scion of Moons."

"Hail the Red Emperor, Sovereign Scion of Moons," the people chorused.

"Permit me to speak in Mainland Common?" the speaker said. "High Bassai is as far from our tongues as the Great Dome is from us."

Esheme glanced at Ikobi, who nodded and gave the go-ahead.

"Thank you, oh most gracious Sovereign," the clan leader said. "Permit me to introduce myself: I am Manemena, leader of the clan of Wanneba. Along with Gevah, clan leader of Enuka, whose sands your esteemed feet now bless, we welcome you on behalf of all of the clans of the western protectorates."

The jali told them their welcome was accepted.

"We have waited for this day, Most Sovereign, for true leadership to return to our land, true leadership to which we can fully demonstrate our fealty." Manemena dared to glance up for a moment. "And we have spared no thought or expense in showing you, today, that we wholly succumb to your leadership. We have prepared a feast for your welcome, and if you do wish to bless us with your presence for longer, we have an abode fit for the gods themselves. We have prepared gifts from our land—*your* land—to go with you on your journey."

With that, the clan leader fell back in with the rest.

Esheme stepped out of the encircled protection of the Soldiers of Red so she could stand in full view of the people.

"Look up," she commanded. Tentatively, they lifted their heads.

"I do not come here for festivities," she said. "I come here as a reminder to you of whom this land belongs to. The waters you fish from, the crops you grow, the timber you fell, the forests you fell them from—all that the wind touches on this continent belongs to the nation of Great Bassa."

She searched the line of leaders. Not a squeak. Nothing like the Tombolo Elders.

That was power. Now *love*.

"But I will abide your festivities," she said. "You have demonstrated faith in me, and I will therefore return the favour. I will remain with you for the night and will partake of the gifts you offer. And while I am here, you may consider my blessing and protection, and that of the moon sisters, granted upon you."

A cheer rose from the crowd of clan onlookers. Esheme let it last its course, then quieted them down.

Now, *respect*.

"From this day forward, consider your arrangements with the old Upper Council gone. You may now conduct your business and pay taxes according to the new Great Dome's laws." She motioned to her caravan. "And to help you do it, I will leave a battalion of civic guards with you like I have done everywhere else I have visited. In the coming moons, I will send even more."

Murmurs. Some movement. She held up a finger.

"I have promised to protect you," she said, "and protect you I will. Whatever enemies may rise against you, you shall not fear, for the Great Dome will be with you, even when you are far from it."

A small lift of their heads, a tiny puff of their chests. This was that hinterlander pride everyone spoke of. But this one wasn't pride in themselves, but in *her*.

Best to press home the advantage.

"Lastly," said Esheme, holding up a finger, "if you wish for your voices to be heard all the way up in the Great Dome, then your voices must get there and be loud on your behalf." She pointed to the clan leaders. "So, decide among yourselves which two of you will return with me to the Great Dome."

This raised eyebrows, but not from the clan leaders. It was Igan, perhaps not quite thinking, who stepped forward.

"*Esheme*," they said, before correcting themself. "Emperor—"

"Back," Esheme hissed. Igan bowed their head and stepped back. Esheme gave the clan leaders the go-ahead to respond.

"We are your subjects," said the clan leaders, speaking through Gevah and Manemena. "We will do as you wish."

◇·----------·◇·

After, while the caravan offloaded and Esheme had been shown to her quarters—the interconnected abodes, as she had guessed—Igan came in.

"I want to apologise, Emperor," they said. "It was reckless of me to behave like that in public."

Esheme regarded her Second with amusement. Even though their relations were not quite a secret to those closest to them, Igan had always maintained a determined effort to keep public interactions respectful and professional. In fact, they often did it with such precision that it sometimes unnerved Esheme—if they could keep this appearance up with such ease, what else could they hide from her? Igan didn't know it, but today's outburst was a breath of fresh air to Esheme, a reminder that they were just as fallible a human as anyone else. That didn't make it any less egregious, though.

"*Now* you call me *Emperor*," said Esheme.

"It was a slip of tongue."

Esheme scoffed. "It's not about the mode of address, and you know it."

Igan nodded solemnly.

"Why do you do that?" Esheme asked. "Why do you try to be my Second *all* the time?"

"I *am* your Second."

"Yes. But I don't always need a general watching over me like a hawk, tracking every step and relaying back to me how wrong I am. We have Nem and the rest of the Great Dome for that." She gazed into their eyes. "Sometimes, all I need is a lover."

Igan bit their lip and nodded. Esheme tapped the beddings where she sat. Igan unlatched their long axe and laid it down, then their boots, then their armour, then their underclothes, until they were standing there with nothing on.

"Latch the door," Esheme ordered.

Once it was dark, and they were alone, Esheme let them undress her with the small, patient motions that Igan never exposed to anyone else. Then she lay in the beddings, and Igan came and lay behind her, encircling her in firm, muscled arms.

Warmth, small and intimate, gathered between their bodies. Skins— one battle-hardened but moist, the other suppled by fine essential oils— melded into each other in a way that felt both familiar and new. Into a private universe of their own they sank, an eternity held in silence, the world disappearing around them.

This was yet another reason Esheme was always wanting for the road, though not one she could admit to anyone else. Out here, Igan was always within reach, never far away. Esheme wanted to feel safe, and in Igan's embrace, she always did.

"I say these things because I care for you," Igan whispered into her back, breath hot on her neck. "I do not want to see you come to harm."

Esheme reached back a hand and clasped her Second's thigh, wrapped their leg tighter around herself.

"I am the emperor of the world," she said. "I think I will be fine."

Nem

Undati
Fifth Mooncycle, 28

NEM DID NOT APPRECIATE the Undati prison holdings. They were below ground, dug into the eastern half of the Soke mountain range, only sharing a name with the nearby new mines but not a part of them. They had once been located in First Ward, but were moved out here when the old mine was emptied out and relocated. The move had been triggered by a spate of successful escapes from the Chugoko Central Prison and beneath the border, where escapees disappeared into the desertland populace. This new location meant civic guards had the higher ground, preventing escapees from crossing the Pass or going westward and disappearing into Bassa. Such escapees would be forced to wander east instead, and surely get lost in the mountains and wilderness, where they would eventually die of starvation.

There had been no successful escapes in many seasons.

Had Nem not been First Consul of the Royal Court of the Great Dome, her foot would never have touched these grounds. It was much too far from the Great Dome, and having spent two days on the road, seated, only moved from rolling chair to travelwagon and back, her bottom had begun to ache. And now, being carried down the steps that led deep into the heart of the holding facilities, she wasn't looking forward to the time she was going to spend here.

"We can leave if you want, MaaNem," Satti said. The woman, now transformed in title from Nem's regular Second to Royal Second to the First Consul, walked behind the two civic guards tasked with carrying Nem down the stairs. She still used Nem's old title out of habit, and Nem didn't mind. She liked that there was always a close-by reminder of who she once was, who she would always be.

"We'll be gone as quickly as I can help it," Nem said. "But this bit of business must be done first."

Once at the bottom, Satti rolled her the rest of the way. The warden assigned to guide them to their destination ushered them past packed holdings that might as well have been pit latrines. The people in them stank just as badly. Most were dressed in rags, a few completely naked. Coughs aside, each had at least one skin disease, fluids oozing out of some orifice. Nem tried to keep from retching. Since her accident, her body had become more unforgiving, and offered fewer ways to resist such discomfort.

This level seemed to contain a lot of mainlanders, judging by their complexions. But Nem knew that this prison held more desertlanders than any other people, as they were the most susceptible to landing here. Illegal border crossers were often sent back over the Pass and handed over to the warrant chiefs of Chugoko and their vigilantes to handle. The same was done to those who crossed legally but ended up convicted on the mainland for small crimes. But the ones held here were those whose crimes were far more egregious, to the point that they had been deemed a danger to both mainland and desertland. Bandits, armed robbers, murderers. Victims of political warring. Nem had sent a few people here herself, in her heyday. She wished not to run into any of them.

Her daughter, the Red Emperor, had also sent a number here since her rule began. A significant number, in fact, especially if one included the recaptured escapees from Whudasha. Those, Nem also hoped not to see.

"Here," said the warden, putting a key into a keylock and turning it. The pins within snapped, and he pushed the gate open. "Would you like a guard inside with you?"

"That won't be necessary," said Nem. "He's not dangerous."

The warder bowed and left them alone with the person in the holding area. The prisoner was the only one in here, isolated upon Nem's request.

"Dehje, Cockroach," Nem said.

The man before her was a shadow of the fearless one that once ruled the Coalition for New Bassa with a shrewd sure-handedness. Basuaye had always looked undernourished, sure, but now each bony joint jutted out at an impossible angle. When he rose to greet her, he stood tall, gaunt, emaciated. His neck had holes deep enough to hold water, his eyes buried deep within their sockets.

"Dehje, MaaNem," he responded.

"That's First Consul Nem to you now."

"Ah." He nodded. "Permit me to sit, First Consul? My body is not equipped to hold itself up as long as it used to."

"Permitted," said Nem. Basuaye slowly lowered himself to the dirty ground. Nem took the time to request some privacy. Satti stepped out, the gate clanging behind her, and the two were soon alone.

"How are you doing, old friend?" asked Nem.

Basuaye chuckled. "*Old friend*, is it? I bet the new emperor doesn't think of me that way."

"You will have to forgive her," Nem said. "She is doing what she believes is right in the circumstances she has found herself."

"*Forgive.*" He chuckled again. "I don't know what that word means anymore. Captivity does something to your head, you know?" He tapped his temple and laughed. Nem thought he looked a little bit unstable.

"It does, does it?"

"Yes. Helps you appreciate life, the little things once taken for granted. Insects: ants, houseflies, mosquitoes, cockroaches. Water and thirst. The sweet, welcome taste of bland, unsalted bread. Sanity—particularly in isolation such as this. You learn that memory is more of a thing you create and shape rather than one you are burdened with." He smiled. "Perhaps this is why the concept of forgiveness is like a raindrop on my already wet tongue. It relies on memory, doesn't it? Yet memory is only what you make it. And if you think that raindrop nothing but the spittle already in your mouth, it doesn't exist now, does it?"

Nem wasn't sure what to think of his rambling, but understood he meant to say he could forget whatever he needed to if he wished. So perhaps, all he needed was the right motivation.

"I need your help," she said, plain and simple. "And if you agree to give it to me, I will get you out of this dungeon."

Basuaye sat quiet for a long beat. Nem let him take his time. She had known this man for almost all of her fixer career. Back when she was a young girl far away from the Great Dome and closer to the hinterlands than she'd liked, Basuaye had only just been a jali hopeful at the university. He never made it to graduation, which was why he took his oratory gifts to the streets, where his more direct methods were most useful. There, he could speak in words that the Emuru welcomed, refraining from dipping his tongue in haughty High Bassai like most scholars did.

He'd been written off as a madman, back then. But Nem had seen his power early enough. Once she had begun to make her way into Bassa's upper echelons, she had been wise to find him and add him to her list of allies. It did not matter that, soon, he guided the Coalition for New Bassa from being a fringe group into becoming the central opposition to the Idu nobles. They had continued to help each other whenever needed, and their goals never came into opposition because Nem served no master— her only master was herself.

Then ibor happened. And the yellowskin. And Esheme.

So Nem gave him time to think, because she knew he understood that the circumstances that had caused their parallel roads to split apart were just that—circumstances. And though he may have harboured resentment against the current emperor, it was nothing throwing him a few bones wouldn't fix. A place at the university, perhaps. But only after he'd done what she needed of him.

"Tell me," was all he said when he finally spoke.

"Your coalition," she said. "You will need to corral and put an end to them, once and for all."

He scoffed, then coughed. His ribs showed with every flex of his chest muscles.

"Me?" he said, wiping his mouth. "Corral—*corral*, is it?—a nonexistent coalition? All the way from my holding cell a whole day's ride from Bassa."

"No," said Nem. "I will get you out. *Then* you will corral them."

"Who are this *them* you speak of? Am I going insane, or was it not your same daughter who usurped me, murdered my generals, co-opted brave ordinary citizens, and took the Great Dome? What *them* is left to corral?"

"There are still loyalists," said Nem. "In Fifteenth Ward and in the outskirts of the city, some spreading as far as the forests of the confluence. Too far for us to reach from the Great Dome. I hear whispers, stories. They dream of a return—of *your* return. You have fed them a diet of messiahs for so long that they do not know how to live without one. And so they have made one up in their heads. I want you to go there and tell them to stop whatever it is they're thinking or, worse, planning."

Now Basuaye frowned, and Nem could see the cockroach in him rise to the surface.

"Interesting," he said.

"What is?"

"This." He gestured between them both. "You coming to me, asking for my help."

"We have always helped one another, Basuaye. We have always been friends."

"Indeed we have. But you have not always had the kind of power that you now have at your side. You have not always had, for a daughter, an emperor that can command an undead horde to wipe out whomever she pleases." He leaned forward. "So it begets the question: Why would you, despite that power and access to it, take a day's ride from the Great Dome to meet me down here and ask for help toward a peaceful solution?"

Cockroach indeed, thought Nem. Skittery and sly. In only a few moments, he had deduced the reason she was here: because she did not trust her own daughter to make the right choice.

"The time for violent solutions is over," she said instead. "Bassa needs the peace—"

Basuaye's laughter cut her short. "Over?" he asked, once done. "I lie here, in this dungeon—do you not consider that a violence? Is it not violence that I'm forced to knock my knuckles bloody simply to converse through walls with my fellow man? Is it not violence that we now treasure the smell of paper because it's the only thing that reminds us there's a life outside these walls? Nothing is *over*, my dear friend. Not while I and others like me whom your emperor considers enemies are kept imprisoned."

Nem hated that he was right. She *did* want and cherish this power. She had to protect herself and her family in a world designed to keep them under, so she was willing to do what it took to hold on to her new-found status. But this, right here, was a reminder that she was not the true holder of this power, that it was all in the hands of someone else, who could do with it as she pleased, including making all the wrong decisions. So here Nem was, yet again, trying to hold on.

"I could have done things differently in the past," said Nem. "But the past is gone. I strive to do things better going forward."

Basuaye leaned forward. "Tell me—does the emperor approve of this?"

Nem shifted uncomfortably. "I did not come here for a dance, Cock-roach. Tell me now: Will you, or will you not?"

"What if I say no?"

"Don't be daft," Nem snapped. "I am well aware of your physical ail-ings, worsening every moment more you spend in this place. I am willing to put an end to that and, at the same time, apply a salve to our singed relationship. Neither of these will come without exchange. If you are as wise as you claim, then you will accept my proposition. I will get you out of here, you will travel to the fringes of Fifteenth and down to the con-fluence, and you will rein in those who have strayed from the emperor's guidance."

Basuaye let another moment of silence pass, then said, "Fine. But only on one condition."

"Which is?"

"It must be genuine."

"What does that mean?"

"It has to be real, otherwise they will not believe me. And if that hap-pens, they will simply slit my throat and continue on their business. As you and your emperor know from experience, you can hold back the tide of a misled people for only so long. If I am gone, someone larger than life will simply appear to mislead them into even greater things."

Nem considered his words. "What do you have in mind?"

"A place at court."

"Excuse me?"

"Hear me out," he said. "Once, they believed in my name, but only because my name demonstrated a power they could look up to: that of revolution. I don't know about you, but losing a revolution to someone else tends to strip one's name of said power. If I must approach them and hope to get them to listen, I must approach from a position of power—a *new* power. And the only power worthy of any ear right now is that of the Court of the Great Dome."

"Then that defeats the whole purpose," said Nem. "They will simply know you came from us."

"Perhaps you're not quite keeping your eye on the goal, here, First Consul Nem. The goal is to prevent agitation. Whether they know on whose behalf I come is irrelevant."

Nem turned to look at the walls of the holding cell. "This will require me to convince the emperor. And the current members of court."

"Then I believe you have more convincing to do, don't you? Judging by how you have convinced me, I believe this will make for small work."

Small work indeed, thought Nem, clapping her hands loudly. The gate reopened, and Satti and the warden came to her attention. To Satti, Nem said: "We're leaving." To the warden, she said: "Get him some clean clothes."

The warden looked flabbergasted. "May I ask what for, maa?"

"No, you may not," she snapped. "Get him the clothes and bring him up to my caravan."

She signaled for Satti to roll her away. Down the corridor, the civic guards carried her back up the stairs and out front. Outside, as dome-hands put Nem's chair back into its place in the travelwagon, Satti asked, or more like said: "The Cockroach is coming back to the Great Dome with us."

"Yes," said Nem, twisting her fingers, nervous in a way she hadn't been in a while. "No matter how big you are, some wars are just too big to fight all on your own."

9

Lilong

The Lonely Roads West
Sixth Mooncycle, 4–6

A DAY BEFORE DEPARTURE, Lilong and her group returned to the thicket with Kubra for a final meeting with the Gaddos. After pleasantries, Ma Gaddo spread a map of the Savanna Belt over a table in the garden.

"We've decided each one of you is going to play a crucial role," said Pa Gaddo, who was still on child duty, Thema strapped to his back.

"Is that—" Danso leaned over. "This map is wrong. It's too—"

"Large?" Ma Gaddo leaned away to pull another, smaller, worn map and spread it over the table.

Lilong could immediately spot the difference. The bigger map covered a large swath of the Savanna Belt, with many cities, settlements, hamlets, and nomadic group hotspots noted, and major trading routes labelled and named. The smaller map was much sparser. The mainland and desertlands were both represented, with the Soke mountains and its Pass separating them. But the desertlands were depicted as half their true size, with only Chugoko and one throwaway settlement named. The rest of the desertlands were presented as bare and unpopulated.

"This was made by your Emperor of Enlightenment—Tumwenke, fifteenth or sixteenth, I can't remember now," Ma Gaddo was saying to Danso about the smaller map. "Jalis drew this falsity right there in your university library."

Danso looked crestfallen.

"Don't take it personally," said Pa Gaddo. "Tumwenke knew that if desertlanders believed their land—the biggest arbiter of property and influence—was smaller and less populated than it really was, they'd be smaller in mind too." He tapped his temple. "Power is only where they make you think it is, son."

"Okay, that's that." Ma Gaddo placed a hand on the big map. "Now, the desertland's annual Festival of Nomads—the Ochela—brings travellers from across the Savanna Belt, even up from the lower Sahel. Lasts three days, so it's a good enough reason to have strangers like you there. But most importantly, the show-off parade for the pageant contestants happens here on the third day." She jabbed at a spot in Chugoko marked with an emaciated skull, then traced a finger along the zigzaggy roads that led to it. "Starts in the outskirts but moves through the city square, right past the central prison, where large crowds will gather." She straightened. "It is the most chaotic event of all three days of the festival. Everyone, even the warrant chiefs and chief warden of the prison, goes to those parades. This is why we have chosen this day to get you in."

Lilong realised Ma Gaddo was pointing at her. "Oh, *me*."

"Yes, you. In your...whatever shade you decide is least conspicuous, of course. You will be dressed as a vagrant, blending in with the prison population so you can find Oke and then use your—I don't know, what is it that you do? Anyway, you get her out. Also, your blade will be within calling distance, in case you need it, though it is our hope you won't."

Then Ma Gaddo turned to Danso. "You—you will be the spectacle, provide our distraction. And you will do so by enrolling in the pageant."

"Excuse me?"

"It is a pageant for young men, and you're the only young man here, so there's no argument. We need a spectacle to draw as many people as possible toward that parade. And if there is anything you can provide, it is spectacle."

"Why can't your son do it?"

Ma and Pa Gaddo glanced at each other.

"Alaba will do his part," Pa Gaddo said. "Which will mostly involve staying far, far out of your way. He may offer useful information, perhaps a better description of Oke than we can give you. Maybe a map of the prison, even. But on that day, he cannot be seen within spitting distance of that place."

"Preparing you will take some work, seeing as you have not worn face-paint in a while," said Ma Gaddo to Danso. "Alaba's other lover, Ugo, will help you see to it. Nothing some dye and shea butter cannot fix."

Lilong could see everyone had a question about this second lover on their lips, but no one asked it.

Ma Gaddo pointed to Kakutan and Biemwensé. "Biemwensé will keep a lookout and be ready with a wagon. Kakutan, you will be dressed as a prison guard and will get Lilong in, then wait to offer support in getting Oke out. Then, we will—"

"I'm sorry, I'm sorry," Danso interjected. "This plan has *way* too many possibilities for failure. One thing goes wrong, everything comes falling apart. And guess who will be in the public eye if that happens—me! I do not see myself escaping peace officers while dressed in colourful regalia."

"Nothing will go wrong," Pa Gaddo said. "Kubra has networks in Chugoko he can call on for emergencies. Alaba can provide other forms of assistance too. Plus, don't discount the Chugoki. Majority of them are not content with Bassa's fingers everywhere in their business. They might just be happier than you think to see their prison wardens bested."

"And peace officers?" asked Lilong. "If we come up against them?"

Silence settled among them. This was the one part no one had an answer for.

"What if Oke doesn't want to come?" Kakutan asked, breaking the silence. "Or what if she is weak and we have to carry her?"

"Oke can take care of herself once freed," Ma Gaddo said, then paused. "If she still has her powers, that is. Which would cause one to wonder why she has not yet used them to escape…" She trailed off when she saw Lilong's quizzical expression.

"Oh, you don't know?" She glanced around, and after seeing no understanding, turned to Lilong and said: "The Speaker's daughter—she can *do things* too."

Lilong rode to Chugoko in a travelwagon with Danso, Kakutan, and Biemwensé, with Kubra outside driving the team of kwagas. Beyond stowing away on the one that took her into the mainland, Lilong had never travelled inside one of these things. Abenai warrior life demanded nothing more than riding on kwagaback and in open wagons. In here, she felt cut off from the outside world, like a stowaway all over again.

She tried not to think about what she'd learned from the Gaddos about Oke being an iborworker. A Grey Iborworker, from the descriptions they'd received from their son. Lilong tried to envision the situations that would explain how she'd come to know about this power as well as come into possession of the stone-bones required to wield it. No matter how much she skirted the matter, the same bitter truth always reared its head: Her daa, an Elder Warrior of the Abenai League, had sold all their islands' secrets out to a mainlander.

A deep and ugly anger welled up inside her, one that she could only avoid lest it burst open and spread through her chest. She spent the trip in solitary quiet, watching the bare roads.

The Lonely Roads West, which connected back to the northern trade route, took them through parts of the desertlands unfamiliar to all four of them. Danso, who had grabbed the errant map from the Gaddos and sworn to rectify it, had his nose in the large sheet, scribbling in any new locations they managed to identify. Most of these they gleaned from the conversations Kubra had whenever they came upon one of the several checkpoints patrolled by vigilantes of warrant chiefs. Each time, the process was the same: pleasantries exchanged, the company's travelwagon identified, the distance to the next settlement or checkpoint discussed, and then a few copper or bronze pieces changing hands.

"No wonder the Gaddos were so confident," said Kakutan. "All these people are tucked into their wrappers."

Soon, however, the checkpoints thinned, and it didn't take long to see why. Charred remains of small settlements and hamlets soon came into view whenever such a checkpoint was missing. The ash mounds of once-standing abodes tussled with dust in the restless desert air. Silhouettes of burnt trees and tentpoles posed at high noon, shadows like black webs in the sand. Scorched skeletons mimicked their poses, legs still lifted mid-flail, arms still held up mid-shield, mouths still opened mid-scream.

The weight of those images pressed them into silence for the rest of the trip. No one said it, but Lilong knew what they were all thinking. This—all of it—was *their* fault. They had let Esheme get away with that tiny piece of the Diwi, and with it she had conquered the mainland and empowered these murderous peace officers. Now they roamed the desert-lands in search of the emperor's enemies, real or imagined, catching innocents in their web of brutality.

·◇·⋯—————⋯·◇·

Chugoko was a shining city overcast by a perpetual cloud.

At least that was the impression Lilong had when they finally arrived after a day of travel. They did not enter through the city's main entrance, but through one of its side gates, sparsely guarded and poorly coordinated, especially now that the festival had almost begun. They changed into dust-laden wrapper-cloaks more suited to visitors attending the Ochela and merged into the crowds before them. As Lilong would come to realise, every district in Chugoko was a market. Chugoko was really just a large trading settlement in itself.

But that was where its major differences from Bassa ended. Lilong soon began to see similarities between both cities that ran far deeper. Many buildings here were mudbrick and thatch, despite the heat of the savanna. Then there was the streetside art. Imagery of the sister moons—the mother hen Ashu and the fiery leopard Menai—splashed over pillars and walls. Even the trading stalls that bore titles had them written in High Bassai.

Then, of course, there was the melting pot of peoples, rhythms, and languages, a chorus and dissonance all at once.

"They don't call this place Little Bassa for nothing," Kubra said, reading their quizzical expressions.

"High Bassai for the signs is a little extreme, I think," said Danso.

Kubra snorted. "If you were a shopkeeper seeking to attract customers—half of whom are the mainland elite travelling for trade, and the other half of whom are desertlanders seeking to curry the mainland's favour—tell me, in what language would you title your business?"

The districts ballooned in size and bodies as they moved closer to the city centre, where there was more activity pertaining to the Ochela. Vendors cooking fast food at the roadsides, offering tasting portions to willing passers-by. Hawkers hassling people with their trinkets. Shopkeepers calling out to whoever could hear for trading contracts, storage services, hair and makeup ahead of the next day's pageant. One hairdresser pulled down Danso's cloak and ran her hands through his hair, explaining how he would surely win the pageant once she was done.

Lilong was still struggling to adapt to this frenetic pace when Kubra suddenly put out an arm and held all four of them back.

"There," he said, jutting his chin forward to avoid pointing with his finger.

Lilong had never seen a prison before. Namge had no prison, and as far as she knew, Hoor, the island next to them, did not either. She could not speak for the islands farther down the archipelago, but the Ihinyon people simply did not favour imprisonment as a pathway to restitution. Punishment that placed offenders in the eye and service of the people was preferred, with said penance producing benefits to the community. In many ways, shame was the real punishment there, and she suspected the other islands in the archipelago thought so as well.

The building stuck out like a sooty pot among washed ones: gargantuan, monstrous, devoid of life. Its stone walls seemed to go on forever, lengthward and upward, uninterrupted by windows or airways.

"Ugly," said Biemwensé.

Kubra began to pick fruit from a nearby stand to blend in with the crowd. Lilong and crew followed his cue. The fruit seller suddenly materialized and asked them to leave if they were not going to buy anything. Kubra apologised and asked for a handful of dried dates. The seller wrapped it in leaves, he paid, and they were back on their way.

They ate the small, sweet fruit as a group, each pinching a couple at a time and munching. They went past the front of the prison, pretending to be seeing the sights, even stopping for a moment and pretending to marvel at it. Lilong and Kakutan used this time to glean information for their walk in and disguise: guard numbers and shifts, entryways, windows or the lack thereof. Afterward they split into two groups to circle the prison and meet at a distance from its rear. Danso and Lilong made sure to split themselves between each group, being easier to recognise together.

Lilong went with Biemwensé. A distance away from the building, the older woman stopped to stare back at it, not taking in any detail in particular. Lilong knew she was thinking again about her children, stuck in the prison that was the mainland.

Lilong, too, took this moment to remind herself of why she was doing this in the first place. This was but one step in her path toward return, a journey that was more than just going east. This was her way back to the league's blessing, to an honourable reward for herself and her family. This was the way back to answers, to the truth, to fulfilment. This was the *right* thing to do.

Biemwensé resumed, but there was a pronounced droop in her shoulders, a resignation. Lilong put her hand around the woman's shoulders in comfort, but pretended it was an act for the onlookers—just a young desertlander helping an elderly one catch the sights. Biemwensé did not respond with her customary rebuff. Instead, she put her own arm around Lilong, as if to say that she, too, understood this sacrifice.

· —◦— ··· ———————— ··· —◦— ·

Once done with scouting the prison, Kubra led the group to meet Alaba, who would show them to their hideout. The travelwagon took them through a convoluted route down darker, dirtier streets and corridors. Here, the city's cultural potpourri resided neck to neck, bald Chugoki beside those who imitated the Bassai with outrageously plaited arches, beside those who simply let their hair hang loose. The Savanna Common spoken here was so intertwined with border pidgins that Lilong could not understand it.

After some meandering, the travelwagon finally drew to a halt in front of a public house of lax build, zero decor, and lowlife clientele. Inside was darker than Lilong had expected—she had never been in one of these either. She'd heard stories of the kind of debauchery that happened in such places, but there seemed to be none of that excitement here. It was boisterous, yes, but that was quickly overshadowed by the smell of sweat and stale spirits, and the inability to hear herself.

"Stand tall, don't look guilty, and we should be fine," said Kubra to them all, before going over to the housekeep.

"What are you doing?" the housekeep, a lanky man, whispered fiercely, leaning over the counter. "You're not supposed to be in *here*."

"We're looking for somebody," Kubra said.

"Go look for them outside," the man snapped.

It took Lilong a moment to process the reason for the man's insistence. It became clear when she looked outside, into the backyard where he was pointing. Everyone seated inside was Bassai, and everyone outside was not.

"Never mind," Kubra said. "There's who we're looking for."

The outdoor drinking area Kubra was looking out to had dwarf stools spread out in the dust before low tables, a range of desert palms providing canopy from the harsh sun. There, among a row of bickering and laughing drinkers, sat a man who was immediately set apart. The moroseness of his posture, how distinctly hunched over his drink he was. No sandals, hair that hadn't seen oiling or grooming in a while, and as Lilong could see when they moved closer, skin that was flaky in places, not oiled well enough for the desert's climate.

But most importantly, this man was not a desertlander like those seated around him. He was a proper high-black Bassai like those inside the house, yet for some reason, refused to be seated in the place of privilege reserved for those like him.

"*That* is who is supposed to help us?" Danso asked, perplexed.

"No," Kubra said. "That is Ugo. He will tell us where to find Alaba."

Perhaps they had been standing and talking for longer than was natural, because eyes began to wander in their direction, and eventually one of them was Ugo's. As soon as he sighted Kubra, he shot to his feet, too quickly for someone who had been feeding his body with a lot of wine and spirits. He lost balance just as quickly, and righted himself, only to upturn his calabash in the process, as well as that of the person next to him, and the person after that. His fellow drinkers rained expletives in his direction, but Ugo seemed unfazed, holding Kubra's gaze. On second thought, Lilong realised he was looking at someone behind them. Lilong turned.

The man was tall, with a similar complexion to Biemwensé and Kakutan, but with hair more akin to Danso's, difficult to stay in a plait—so he held it up with twine, like a kwaga's tail. His wrappers were starched, knots and lines holding firmly. His feet were oiled and toenails manicured, a worthy feat in the desertland's dust. There was pride in the way he stood, his squared shoulders, his angled chin, his charming smile.

"Kubra," he said warmly, then looked at the rest of them. "Friends."

"Dehje, Alaba," Kubra said, putting his hand to the bridge of his nose.

"Ha, stop it." Alaba wrinkled his nose. "We don't have to pretend to be Bassai out here." He held up a hand. "Excuse me a moment?" He went up to Ugo and embraced the other man, and they kissed. Alaba leaned back, observed the spilled drink on his lover's wrappers, made a click at the back of his throat, then pulled Ugo along, beckoning to everyone else to follow him.

The group went around the building this time, rather than through. But just as they came out front, a band of peace officers pulled up at the public house.

Danso

Chugoko
Sixth Mooncycle, 6

THERE WERE FIVE OF them, given a wide berth as they descended from their kwagas. People re-congregated a distance away, murmuring with dread. Not many could say they had met a peace officer and lived to tell the tale. Rumours had it that peace officers spoke only the language of violence; that all their words were spoken by a separate mouthpiece—often a local assigned to speak for them in exchange for protection. The mouthpiece asked the same three questions each time, to which the wrong answers would invite anything from a bruising to instant death. The first step toward staying alive was never to get in a conversation in the first place.

The dust of their entrance cleared, and Danso could see the mouthpiece of this group—a young desertlander woman with a bald head—descend from one of the kwagas. She moved with swagger and intent, a person who knew the power they possessed and was unafraid to use it.

The five peace officers came into full view.

The stories had not been wrong. They were indeed a motley collection of former hunthands, ranging in gender, complexion, hairstyles, clothing, and even weaponry of choice, but bound together by tall and muscular builds, a grim demeanour, and a general air of otherworldliness. They wore no uniforms, emblems, or any such identifying items. Save for the fact that their weapons were all visibly Bassai-made, they could otherwise have been bandits.

The stories had also been incomplete. No one had mentioned that silence was not a choice the peace officers made, but that speaking was something they simply could not do.

All five peace officers had their mouths sewn shut. Copper wires dug into the flesh surrounding their lips, binding them tight in puffy ridges, like stray dogs muffled by a barbarous hand. Dark red patches surrounded their mouths, perforated wounds never healing. This explained their perpetual scowls, the intense, carnivorous gaze that made Danso's blood curdle.

"Scatter." The voice was Kubra's. "*Now.*"

The command was delivered with a whisper, but that did not dull its acuity. The group separated like sand particles in the desert wind. Kubra and Lilong went one way, Alaba with Ugo, Kakutan with Biemwensé. Danso suddenly found himself standing alone, frozen with fear.

The public house emptied just as quickly. The peace officers themselves did not seem harried, simply standing around and waiting for their mouthpiece. The woman prepared a sheaf of papers, approaching the public house. But then she stopped mid-stride, turned her eyes, and settled them on Danso.

Later, Danso would come to attribute this action to the innate feeling of being watched, the weight of a gaze resting on the nape of one's neck. But in that moment, he did not waste time pondering. The look, though brief and fleeting, was enough to get his feet moving.

He did not turn around and run, fearful of being too conspicuous, but instead began to move sideways along with the crowd, allowing the wave of exits from the public house to carry him. But he was too late, or too slow, because the mouthpiece's eyes did not leave him. They shifted when he did, staying locked on his face. There wasn't quite recognition yet in her gaze, only a wondering, quizzical.

Then she turned, as if resigned, and went up to the nearby wall at the front of the house, where public notices were hung. She took out one of the papers from her sheaf, planted it on the wall, fished a nail from somewhere inside her mouth, and nailed it into the mudbrick with a nearby stone.

Danso was still within reading distance, so he stopped to squint at the public notice. It was written in High Bassai, but also translated to Savanna Common and supplemented with plain symbols for those who couldn't read either language.

His chest went cold at the words.

A BOUNTY OF TWO HUNDRED GOLD PIECES, it read, FOR THE INVADER AND HER ACCOMPLICE, ALIVE. ALL COMPANIONS TO BE EXECUTED ON THE SPOT.

Beneath the description were two hasty sketches of him and Lilong. His portrait was a stripped-down version of his official portrait at the university, the one all graduates were required to get done. Which was why it still had the former Bassai plait, the novitiate wrappers, the Idu jewellery and facepaint, the intense gaze the painter had insisted upon. Thankfully, he looked absolutely nothing like that now, with his new hair and beard, no earrings, no facepaint, and a sea of desertlanders with complexions not too far off from his. It would be near impossible to match that portrait to him.

Lilong, on the other hand, looked exactly as she did now. Her short clumps of hair had grown somewhat fuller, but that was all that had changed about her. The drawing was pretty close to accurate, complete with the scars on her clavicle. It wouldn't take a smart person to recognise her from this sketch.

Beneath his own portrait, just one word was written: JALI.

Beneath Lilong's, there were more warnings: ARMED AND EXTREMELY DANGEROUS. SKILLED WITH A SWORD. A PRACTITIONER OF SORCERY WHO MAY CHANGE APPEARANCE AT WILL. COULD BE ANYONE. BEWARE.

The onlookers who had once given the peace officers a wide berth began to inch closer, whispering among themselves, discussing the bounty, the scandal, the assassinations. Danso decided this was the time to go. But when he lifted his head, the mouthpiece's eyes were back on him.

Her gaze was surer this time, less hesitant. She flung her sheaf of public notices in the air, letting them scatter into the crowd and be plucked by interested hands. Then she beckoned to the peace officers to follow her and strolled forward—toward Danso.

Moons.

For a second time, he found it impossible to move his feet. The shadow of the advancing gang drew closer and closer, until suddenly, all six were upon him. The mouthpiece was smaller than he'd thought, so that even though he tried to keep his eyes down, he ended up looking right into hers anyway. They were accusatory, almost like they could see past the beard and hair and lack of adornment, and match him with the public notice by his eyes alone.

"Citizen," she said, "have you strayed from the Red Emperor's guidance at this time?"

Danso's brain, the only part of him that did not seem to be frozen with fear, recognised this as the first of the three standard questions the mouthpiece of the peace officers always asked. It was a trap, this question, to lure one into a lie, to make a dishonest person out of them. Because, as far as Danso was concerned, most people this side of the border strayed from the Red Emperor's guidance just by existing.

"No, officer," Danso lied. He spoke in broken and accented Savanna Common, in the way Kubra had taught him to make him sound Sahelian, as if he had migrated southward from one of the settlements farther north along the trading route. "I have not break any of the Sovereign's laws."

The peace officers shifted on their feet, impatient. The mouthpiece tilted her head and squinted. He could tell she had a different kind of question on her lips, one that tied him to that public notice. But he assumed she couldn't ask it yet until she had completed the three standard ones.

"Have you come upon any of the Red Emperor's declared enemies at this time?" she asked.

Her mouth said this, but what her eyes really said was *Are you the Red Emperor's enemy?* to which Danso's eyes were, unwillingly, answering *Yes.*

"Not any that I have recognised, officer," he said, forcing his lips to ignore his brain. This question was another trap, and the next was likely to be the one with the trip rope, the one that snapped and held the weak animal tight in place, helpless.

The mouthpiece took a moment before she posed her last question.

"Have you, at any point, aided any enemies of the empire, or those who have strayed from the Red Emperor's guidance?"

Yes, yes, yes, Danso's brain said. Thankfully, his mouth did nothing but gulp. And perhaps that moment of pause was too long, because the peace officers responded. Their arms, which once hung by their sides or were folded across their chests, dropped to rest on their cutlasses, spears, axes.

"There you are!" a voice said.

The mouthpiece and all five peace officers shifted their gazes to the speaker behind Danso. Danso did the same, turning around to see Ugo walking up to him.

"I've been looking everywhere for you, brother," Ugo said, shaking his head like an exasperated parent. He was speaking in the same exaggerated Sahelian accent that Danso was. "You run off without finishing our game, eh?"

The mouthpiece's death stare was enough to slow Ugo's pace, though he kept advancing anyway, throwing the whole gang a formal salutation.

"Dehje, officers," he said, hand on the bridge of his nose. "I hope my little brother have not disturb your activity in any way?"

The mouthpiece's eyes roved over Ugo, then over Danso.

"Little brother," the woman repeated, with enough snarl to signal that she did not believe it one bit.

"Oh, yes," said Ugo, inching closer. "Different daa, of course, as you can see. You know them Bassai merchants love everything between desertlander thighs, yes?" He chuckled good-naturedly, and therefore alone. The peace officers had faces of stone.

"You are Shashi, then?" the mouthpiece asked.

"In a way," said Ugo, beating his chest. "Born and raised up and down the northern trade route, me. Lucky to take the bones of my desertland maa, but sadly little else." Then he reached forward and patted Danso's head. "Jhobon is not like me, though. There is no mainlander blood in him. This one is through and through desertlander." He cleared his throat. "Again, I hope he is not causing any trouble? He only just come down to enjoy the Ochela with his big brother, you know? Still struggle with the language, the customs. Maybe he will stay back and learn a little, eh, won't you, Jhobon?" He slapped Danso on the back.

Danso looked hopefully at the mouthpiece. She wasn't buying it, but she looked tired. It was days to the Ochela's main events and she probably had many public houses to visit and put up notices. She also seemed rankled by Ugo's drunkenness.

The peace officers themselves remained expressionless, waiting for nothing but the word *Go*. Danso reminded himself that these were not civic guards, Seconds, or hunthands. They were not even bandits. These were people given the licence to be worse than all those put together, to deal out nothing but pain. One wrong word from this mouthpiece and it was all over for him.

Which was why he almost wept with relief when the mouthpiece shook her head, irritated, and said: "Be good citizens, both of you." Then she turned away, and the peace officers went with her.

Ugo grabbed Danso by the arm and yanked him in the opposite direction.

"Don't run," he whispered, his Savanna Common suddenly correct and unaccented. "Walk, slowly, casually."

They had barely taken two steps when a voice called out: "Wait."

They turned. The mouthpiece was facing them again. Danso's heart pounded.

"You never answered my third question," she said.

Indeed, Danso hadn't. As he opened his mouth to say the words, he realised this was a life-saving lie indeed.

"I have not, at any point, aided any enemies of the empire," he said, repeating her words haltingly, "or those who have strayed from the Red Emperor's guidance."

The woman's eyes rested on both men for a beat more, then she said with finality: "Go in peace."

11

Lilong

Chugoko
Sixth Mooncycle, 6–8

THE HIDEOUT WAS A small hut in a run-down part of the city outskirts. It was built in a clearing obfuscated by tall grass and crafted in the crudest way possible—mud-clay mixed with straw—to better blend in with its surroundings. The structure was fragile, its largest pillars a pair of wooden poles to which sinister winds could do real damage, but it was sufficient for the singular purpose of lying low. Alaba had also stocked it with more than sufficient resources needed for their stay and the mission—food, water, clothing, weapons, and other items for disguises.

"That was close," said Alaba, to everyone and no one. "*Very close.*"

They were all gathered inside the hut, halfway between recovering from Danso's near miss and acclimatizing to their new surroundings. Kubra, Danso, and Kakutan offloaded the remaining supplies from the travelwagon, which was parked some distance away. Ugo helped Biemwensé find a comfortable corner in the cramped quarters. Having now been seen with Danso, he could not return to the city, so he had come along with the group. He would be staying at the hideout for the remaining days until the heist.

Lilong thought the location was pea-sized for the original party of five, not to talk about a sixth person.

"Make that seven," Alaba said when she raised this concern. "I've arranged for Thema to join us with the next company travelwagon that comes this way."

Lilong frowned. "These are no conditions for an infant."

"True," he said. "But you must understand: Oke has not set eyes on her child since Thema's birth in the prison. We were even lucky I made arrangements to receive the baby, or Thema could have been sold to any interested party out there." He shivered at the thought. "I just want Thema's face to be the first Oke sees when she regains her freedom."

Lilong regarded the man. He had the presence and carriage of a Bassai Idu, but a warmth and earnestness that felt antithetical to that. The resulting dissonance had a disarming effect that made Lilong uneasy. Being capable of getting people to let down their guard was a weapon in itself, just as useful for good as it was for evil. She realised, now, that this was why she'd felt just as uneasy about the Gaddos. Though she was yet to see the foolishness they had spoken about in this man, she considered him to be unlike them anyway. His eyes simply did not possess the same sharpness of a predator.

It was late evening once the unloading was done and everyone was rested. Kubra pulled out the map, and they went over the finer details of the plan.

The group was to be split into three teams. The first, the duo of Lilong and Kakutan, would make it into the prison itself, release Oke, and find a way to get her back out. Kakutan would dress up as a prison warden. In the heat of the pageant and parade, when half the wardens were out to watch the procession, she would slip into the prison by pretending to arrest and bring in Lilong, who'd be dressed in rags, playing the role of a drunkard caught causing havoc. Such arrests were reserved for the lowliest of wardens, making it less out of place if Kakutan were not to be recognised.

Ugo—who it turned out was skilled in costumes and makeup and had acquired the right clothing for everyone's roles—presented his procurements. Lilong looked perfectly ragged in her wrappers. Kakutan tried on the warden uniform—thicker wrappers stitched into a robe—and it suited her just as well. The warden baton she tested, swinging with practiced ease, as if she had once been a warden herself. Lilong thought that per-haps, in a way, that was what a Supreme Magnanimous was.

"We still haven't answered the question of how we get her out," Kaku-tan said.

Alaba turned to Lilong. "Can you"—he wriggled his fingers—"Possess the lock?"

Lilong frowned at his use of the correct term. How much had Oke divulged?

"If you can, then Ugo will give you another warden uniform. You change into that, Oke changes into your rags, and it can be like she is your prisoner and you are transferring her somewhere."

"Sounds risky to me," said Danso.

"*And* demanding," said Lilong. "The Possession you describe is not as easy as you think. It has... effects. I may become a handicap."

"Make that *two* problems," said Ugo. "Because I could only manage one uniform." He made an embarrassed face.

Alaba sighed, then said to Lilong and Kakutan: "I can't say I have an answer, but what I do have is trust, and I trust that you two can find a way that works for us all. Because if we can't get her out, then no part of this plan is useful."

The second team was made up of Danso and Ugo. Ugo would be Danso's handler for the pageant, which he had already signed him up for. Now came the hard part of preparation. Ugo detailed the differ-ent aspects of the pageant—makeup, clothing, headpieces, song and dance—required to create the kind of spectacle that would pull enough eyes toward him, prison wardens included. As he laid out the specifics, Lilong saw Danso's initial excitement slowly wane, and could not help but feel that his job might just be the toughest of them all.

The last team was to be made up of Biemwensé and Kubra. Being the least mobile of the crew, Biemwensé would drive the travelwagon that would whisk the escapees back to the hideout. She was to be sta-tioned nearby in wait, away from the parade's route and ready to go at a moment's notice. Kubra was to be the middleman between the prison exit and the travelwagon's location, ready to adapt to any changing situa-tions at a moment's notice.

It was a good plan, but not great. So much room for failure, no one fully convinced of its success. But, Lilong decided, if she was ever going to return home, this was her best—if not only—chance.

⋄ ⋯ ⋯ ⋄

The next two days at the hideout were filled with preparation. Alaba, the only one who could leave the hideout, went into the city to procure further supplies, and returned with news of the festival, which had already begun. On the last of such trips, he also returned with something—or someone—unexpected: Thema. Everyone crowded around the child and cooed, the persistent dour mood lifted. Lilong peeked through the sea of heads to catch a look. Her toes were so tiny. She was so small, so vulnerable.

After Alaba left, Ugo took her into his care—it took Lilong a while to realise that he, too, was *also* her daa of sorts. Whenever he needed to train with Danso, Biemwensé helped care for the baby.

Theirs was the most intense of the preparations, Danso and Ugo. Lilong observed them on the last afternoon as they took a break from the dances. Ugo was teaching Danso the meanings of the words the judges, who were mostly women, would be using. He also explained the role of the leader of ceremonies, who would do the work of connecting the crowd with Danso. Lilong failed to catch much of it—too much information all at once—but Danso drank every word with practiced ease. It was her first time seeing his famed memory in action. Ugo even put him to the test, stopping periodically to offer a question. Danso's answers were languid, bored even, but all exactly correct. Not one sentence or word gone awry.

He did not fool her, though, Danso. She could see the folds beneath his eyes, grief scribing lines at their edges. She saw the way he threw himself into every dance move, every lesson. He was trying to escape something that could never be escaped, only faced. Lilong crossed her fingers and hoped he could hold out for much longer. Such torments often came to roost at the worst of times.

Later that evening, she sat with Kakutan on small stools outside the hut and unfurled the crude prison map Alaba had drawn on a piece of cloth. They were still trying to figure out a clean exit. So far, they had nothing satisfying.

Kakutan lit a pipe and smoked, offering Lilong a puff, which she declined. The woman chuckled.

"You may die tomorrow, or anytime on your trip after," Kakutan said. "Don't you want a taste of everything life has to offer before then?"

"I have tasted what I need to, thank you."

"Well, there are *some* things I have not seen you taste," said Kakutan with a raised eyebrow. "At least tell me all your secret sojourns into Chabo's outskirts were not just to check on your heirloom. Surely you must have…" She lifted her eyebrow higher. "Found someone desirable?"

This was not the first time Kakutan had attempted to inquire about her sexual life. Back in Chabo, she'd insisted that there was no shortage of charming young vagabonds eager to take off Lilong's wrappers— and she had not been wrong. Opportunity was never the issue. Lilong was on a mission, and casual matters like sex were distractions that only increased the chance of being discovered.

But there was something else, something she had never told them— not even Danso: that family and the Diwi weren't her only reasons for returning to Namge.

Lilong did indeed know what desire tasted like. She had loved and been loved, once. A fellow warrior in the Abenai League called Turay— a wisecrack, sturdy like a dwarf palm. Son of the oldest warrior in the league, and an Abenai warrior himself. Unfortunately, that had been the same reason it never worked out—romantic relationships within the league were absolutely forbidden.

Turay had been ready to elope if need be. Take a dhow, find a Grey Iborworker of dodgy means, and sail south in search of a new coast, *any* coast. Start a new hamlet together away from prying eyes.

But Lilong had believed in the league's purpose, considered loyalty to them to be loyalty to the islands, and therefore ranked these above her personal desires. Much of her still did, though recent events had caused her to wonder: If, upon her return, Turay asked again, would her answer really be the same?

"I know desire," she said to Kakutan, and left it at that.

"Ahh. An old flame. Those die slowly, don't they?" Kakutan tapped her pipe on her stool to get rid of ash. "Did I ever tell you that I never wanted to be Supreme Magnanimous?"

"No."

"True story. I loved a woman, once. She wanted to go to Bassa, make a life there. She was going to be a weaver and wanted me to come with her. Said I could become a civic guard." She chuckled. "Imagine that."

Lilong wanted to tell her that a Supreme Magnanimous and civic guard were the same thing.

"I'm happy I stayed. I believe in making one's way in the world, but there is no *way* to be made if fences lie in every path. We only get the destinies we're dealt. You don't go out to the world and waste it. You go to the place where you can make a difference. You go home."

This was Kakutan's way of saying why she was doing this heist, Lilong surmised. Why she wanted to return to the mainland and do right by her people. And though she didn't know it, she was reminding Lilong of why she was doing this too.

They got to work seeking a solution to their exit problem. Alaba's map showed that the prison had three floors, none of them below ground. The route to Oke's holding unit went up to the middle floor. At the time of the map, it held just her as a solitary occupant, a precaution once due to her pregnancy, but which could have since changed—Alaba wasn't sure. Yet another hole in the plan.

"Which of these do you think is best?" Kakutan asked, pointing to the three possible exit points Lilong had identified and marked.

"By *best*, do you mean least physical or least risky? Because those are not the same."

"Start with least risky."

"That is here." Lilong pointed to a marked spot on the second floor. "A window, but large enough. The trouble will be sending her down without injury, especially if she is too weak to climb down on her own."

Kakutan clicked her tongue at the low odds. "And the risky one?"

"Through the front, as Alaba said. Walk out like we walk in."

"But you don't have a uniform."

"So we get one before leaving."

"How?"

"Take from a warden, maybe."

Kakutan lifted an eyebrow. "Without causing a ruckus? I doubt that's possible."

"We can if we are quick. Few blows, no bloodstains. Hide them so they are not found until we are safe."

Kakutan gave Lilong a look she hadn't been given in a long time. The one where the person was suddenly reminded of how deadly she could be, and with how much ease. It used to give her pride, this expression on others' faces. Now, though, she did not enjoy being thought of as this islander warrior who did nothing but kill. She wasn't even planning to kill said warden, just render them unconscious. Kakutan had been Supreme Magnanimous once. She understood these things were sometimes necessary.

Kakutan cleared her throat and pointed to the third exit. "And this one?"

"Final option if the plan spoils: the roof."

"Roof will be suicide."

"Not for me."

Kakutan gave her the look again, then said: "I guess I need some light training before tomorrow. In case I have to climb with a whole person on my back."

After Kakutan left, Lilong studied the map some more, trying to fashion a better escape route that didn't involve running into stray wardens. Her eyes began to hurt after a while, even with the reading stones Kakutan lent her, so she abandoned the attempt and went off to the edge of the clearing to stare at the tall grass. Once there and out of sight, she pulled aside her wrapper and looked at the stones embedded in her arm.

Of the twelve embedded when she'd started at the Abenai League, she had used up a couple making the journey to Bassa alone, and then a bunch more between Bassa and Chabo. In Chabo, she'd used one up just to keep her complexion a steady desertlander at all times. Now there were only four left. She had to conserve these for the long journey back east and use more of her physical abilities for everything else, this heist included.

No more iborworking. Or violence. Not unless it was absolutely warranted.

12

Esheme

Deltalands
Fifth Mooncycle, 16

DAYS AFTER THEIR STOP at Enuka, the royal caravan was deep in the hinterlands, headed for the swamplands. Word of their exploits had reached the clans farther south, so that every new clan they passed, they found empty, with only the youngest and most elderly remaining. Everyone else had fled into the bushes, trying to escape—as one elderly hinterlander put it—"being included in the emperor's collection."

Esheme, frustrated, had trudged through the mud and ordered a nearby travelwagon be opened. Inside were four people: the two clan leaders from Enuka...and the young and old Elders from the Tombolo hamlets.

"Elders," she said in Mainland Common. "Do you have any reason to fear for your lives?"

The four looked at one another, dread and perplexity commingling in their expressions. "No, Sovereign."

"Do you believe my invitation to the Great Dome to be a mistreatment?"

"No, Sovereign."

She turned to Ikobi, to Igan, to everyone in the caravan. "Then tell me why everyone thinks us here to capture and enslave them."

Her advisors shuffled on their feet, answers on the tip of their tongues, but decided that the emperor was being rhetorical, that she didn't really want an answer because she already knew it.

Now, the royal caravan was charting its way through the bush paths of the wetlands. With the mainland's waters thinning each passing day, the swamplands had shifted farther inland than expected, leaving behind pitchy ground that had seen no human feet. Though the swamp peoples of the delta settlements lived in the core of the wetlands, the region was still considered uncharted, mostly because no emperor had ever come this far south. This was evident in the lack of a royal road, and the only bush paths had been overtaken by forest. The caravan had to be brought to a halt for hands to clear a way through.

Esheme took the time to muse with her advisors about solutions to the misinterpretation of her attempts at reconnection.

"Hinterlanders have a deep connection to their land," Ikobi was saying. "They consider removal from it akin to the removal of their souls."

"And yet all they complain of is distance from the Great Dome," said Esheme, beckoning to a nearby hand to hold closer a dish of mixed sliced fruits, which he did. She plucked a slice of mango and ate. Iborworking always made her ravenous, a situation doubly exacerbated by her current pregnancy.

"How can they not see I'm giving them an opportunity for representation?"

"Because it is not on their own terms," said Igan. "And they know that."

Esheme took off her substitute crown, the smaller one she wore often in lieu of the larger, official one. She set it aside, extending a finger through her hairdo to scratch her scalp.

"I hear your calls for integration, but this empire cannot be ruled by assembly. We have learned that much from the Upper Council." She leaned back in her chair, shut her eyes. "They will like it. They have no choice."

The way had been cleared, and the hands and guards outside shouted commands to get moving. But the caravan soon stopped again.

The wetlands were not a kind place. Floodwaters covered every area as far as the eye could see, and there was more mist in the morning than could be travelled in. The size and ferocity of plant and beast multiplied exponentially, with many prone to stealth and attacking without provocation.

"Emperor," said Igan, while their posse and the civic guards tried to spear a stray crocodile outside. "I have been thinking—maybe this is a good time to turn back?"

Esheme frowned. "Where is this coming from?"

Igan tilted their head. "There is a reason no emperor has ever tried to contact the swamplanders, and why they do not want to be contacted. Who can blame them? This place…" Igan looked out at the crocodile, whose hide was so thick the spears weren't going through. "There is something *wrong* with this land."

The crocodile was eventually driven off, but Esheme insisted the caravan press on. Igan did not understand, did they? This trip was not really about the things that would be done while here. It was about what they brought back: the trophies, the pride, the tales of the emperor's exploits. Bassa's power and might were built on such things.

It was also about the reverence the Bassai would be forced to have for her. The emperor they thought was too young to rule over them would now be the first emperor to traverse the swamplands and make contact with the delta settlements. Such an accomplishment could not be denied, not even by the most disillusioned Bassai.

Igan might disagree, but for Esheme, at the end of this road lay nothing but success.

⋅◦⋯————⋯◦⋅

By evening, after moving with more care and deliberation, the caravan came upon a massive wall built of bamboo and mud. This was the first wall Esheme had seen that rivalled that of the Soke Pass. It stood tall—so tall that looking up at it made her dizzy. She wondered if it was the product of iborworking, as it also ran as far in either direction as the eye could see. Despite the material, it looked sturdy and fortified.

Behind the wall, a number of lights flashed.

"Arrows!" Igan ordered. "Positions!"

Archers from their posse and the civic guard squadrons popped out in formation and stretched their bows, strings taut in wait. But the attack they were waiting for did not come. Esheme nodded to Ikobi, who nodded to the jali, who stepped forward.

"In the name of the Red Emperor of Bassa," the jali announced, his voice ringing throughout the swamp, "the Scion of Moons and Sovereign Ruler of the world—"

A lone arrow flew from behind the bamboo wall and struck the man in the neck. He fell, gushing blood into the swampwater.

And it was in watching him fall that Esheme noticed what the others around her also did: that the swamp was not quite filled with rotten foliage as they thought it was, but bones and rotting flesh, human and beast alike.

Every person with a shield stepped back and surrounded the royal travelwagon. Though fortified to withstand even the most ardent of attacks, the wagon would need to be held until the emperor could make a clean escape.

From behind the wall came an ululation, which started in one location, but was soon picked up at various points along its length, escalating down the line until it became a chorus, an alarm. Behind the bamboo, there was significant movement. All spaces between the sticks began to close up, quick fortifications set up behind the barrier. Large shields appeared from nowhere and covered the top row of the walls.

The ululation came to an abrupt end, but no attack followed it. The emperor's guard stood, waiting.

Then came a long and perilous trill, a rumble buried under breath that shook the very trees of the swamp to their roots and caused the still water to tremor. A ripple began around the swamp. In the distance, a submerged creature peeked above the water. Even in the small light of the setting sun still filtering through the canopy, its two eyes, parted by a snout and crested by a rugged ridge, were clearly visible.

It swam toward the caravan with a fierceness, begetting waves that knocked bone against bone and swayed reed against reed.

"More crocodiles!" Igan screamed. "Guard the emperor!"

In a great wave, the advancing head rose, and a great long neck emerged and continued to rise and rise until it was almost as tall as the canopy of the swamp forest itself. Every head in the caravan tilted to follow its rise, and every eye blinked as it opened its mouth and let out another bellow that blew a gust over the swamp.

Four legs, separated by a thin yellow belly, and a great tail so long it snaked out of sight. Mirror-like scales, reflecting a rainbow of the sun's stray beams across the swamp. Eyes as orange as a bushfire. A great many pointed teeth. It was beautiful.

"Oh Menai," Ikobi whispered breathlessly next to Esheme. "A Ninki Nanka!"

Out of the beast's mouth came a large rain of yellow saliva. It bespattered the man foremost to the creature, whose face immediately melted into a puddle, followed by wherever else on his body had been smeared.

"Shield!" Igan screamed, and everyone with a shield held it above their heads. "Back away! *Back away!*"

But Esheme, stretching to catch a glimpse of all this from the royal travelwagon, was struck with awe. She felt the tug of red ibor on her consciousness, and instantly knew why the beast was heading her way, what it had smelled. Fear and fascination gathered in her chest, just like back in the Dead Mines, when she had first witnessed Danso give life to the large undead bat.

And just like that, she looked up and saw opportunity. An image clouded her mind: riding into Bassa on the back of the Ninki Nanka, the jali singing the tale of the Red Emperor who killed and commanded the fabled dragon-serpent of the swamps, so elusive no one on the continent had ever seen it. The jali's voice filled her head, songs about an emperor so mighty she reduced her enemies into a puddle with one drop of her beast's spittle.

And in response to the songs, every citizen of Oon, every person who resided wherever the light touched, looked up at her with the same feeling: fear, fascination, *respect.*

Esheme stepped forward, beyond her line of protectors, and despite the shouts of warning from Igan, she shut her eyes and Drew.

The Ninki Nanka sensed it, turned to Esheme, and snarled.

"What are you *doing*?" This was Igan.

But Esheme was already neck-deep in the costs of ibor. A wrenching in her belly. The stone-bone attached to her upper arm—the very last one, she remembered now—began to falter, nearing its end. One more Draw, and it would disintegrate completely. The pain stung deeper than she'd felt in a while. There was sure to be blood after this.

But for control of this mountainous beast? Any price was worth it.

The Ninki Nanka let out another ear-rending bellow, then dove into the swamp and shot toward Esheme.

"Protect the emperor!" Igan rallied their posse and the guard.

Esheme hurled the first Soldier of Red at the dragon-serpent.

The undead woman, a former Second Elder, had been one of Esheme's first converts, and was the strongest and longest-served Soldier of Red. She flew with the alacrity of something fearless, eyes gleaming red. In the air, she drew her cutlass, landed on the dragon-serpent's head, lifted, and struck downward.

The cutlass broke in two, succumbing to the superior strength of the beast's skull. The Soldier of Red, unfazed, pushed down the remainder of the broken blade, breaking skin and bone both.

The Ninki Nanka hollered, black blood running down its crest, into its face. The Soldier pushed harder, muscles straining to keep balanced on the beast's head. The beast, angered, swayed vigorously, until the woman lost her balance and fell.

The beast didn't wait for her to reach the swamp floor. With a great swoosh, it brought its tail around. Ridged as its crest and back, twice the length of its body, with a sharp end like a blade.

The tail sliced the Soldier of Red clean in two. There were multiple splashes, syncopated, blood and body and organs separated from their host.

Esheme sent three Soldiers of Red a more refined Command:

Aim for the neck.

The Command, once delivered, drained so much energy that it brought her to her knees. Her aides and Second, still circled around her, attempted to hold her up, but she put up a hand.

"Focus," she said. "If they don't succeed, you will need to finish the job."

The three Soldiers were already in motion. The Ninki Nanka, now back to its full height, was impossible to reach by normal means. The Soldiers found the nearest trees and scurried up them with bare hands and feet, pulling themselves up with superhuman strength, lacerating limbs but bleeding nothing.

The closest Soldier of Red flew spear-first, plunging a weapon into the beast's neck before falling the too-high distance into the swamp and promptly breaking both legs. The two Soldiers left descended upon the beast and did the same. Dark blood filled the swampwater.

But the dragon-serpent, stunned from the attacks, was not done yet. It located the Soldiers crawling in the swamp—now that their legs were useless—and promptly stamped on their heads, iron-like claws finishing what its thick feet didn't. Then, the beast turned its sight back on Esheme, baring bloodstained dentition.

Esheme pushed her final Command with everything she had left—to *all thirteen* Soldiers of Red remaining.

Finish it.

Thirteen undead Soldiers moved as one.

The Ninki Nanka dug its head and pitched forward. Esheme couldn't see much now, her vision dwindling, body straining past its limits, the power taking a toll. Her belly tightened like a washcloth, twisting harder, past the cloth's ripping point. She felt a rip of such manner now, somewhere in the depths of her insides, a snap, crackle, click.

The Soldiers of Red, as if sensing her waning consciousness, fought faster, faster. Bodies flew from trees at the dragon-serpent, slashing, slashing. Alas, one by one, they were caught between ferocious teeth, torn to parts, unceremoniously discarded. Esheme saw them only in blurs now, dissolving in the beast's corrosive spittle. Those that remained upright went at it again and again. On her knees, Esheme watched the chaos unfold through cloudy vision and muffled sound.

Then, a large shadow, and many shouts, as the beast finally came down in slow motion. A strong arm—Igan, she recognised from their armpit musk—picked her up as if she was a weightless sack, and pulled her out of the way of the falling giant.

The Ninki Nanka hit the swamp with a deafening crash, raising a great wave and drenching every last person in swampwater stink. A loud silence befell the swamp after, a silence that spread through the delta settlements so that even the frogs and crickets withheld their songs, and only the sloshing of water and the swaying of reeds stood between them.

A fine misty spray settled on Esheme's cheek. She could see that not a single Soldier of Red had survived. She could also see the outline of the Ninki Nanka where it had fallen, where its head lay.

"Take me to the head," she said to Igan.

Igan stood still. *"Emperor—"*

"Take me to the head," Esheme repeated, and Igan obeyed. They laid Esheme down in the swamp, next to the bloodied head of the great beast.

Esheme put her hands to its head, ran them across its bloodied face. Dead for sure. The images and jali songs from before flooded her mind. She leaned in close, hands on the beast's head, and Drew.

This was the last of the red stone-bones she had brought along, on its last dregs. She felt it disintegrate from where it was attached to her arm, scatter into sand and seep into the swampwater. Power surged through her body, shaking her in small convulsions. Her stomach roiled, her insides knotting, fighting back. But she kept her hands on the beast, kept her focus steady as she Possessed it with every last strain of ibor in her body.

Rise, she Commanded the Ninki Nanka. *Rise and be mine.*

Beneath her came a huff, a puff, a snort. The beast's eyes fluttered, and opened into a deep pool of red.

Then, the world stopped. Everything was suddenly too far away from Esheme. There was shouting, or maybe singing, or maybe both, too distant to decipher. Hands, elongated, reached for her. But she had already fallen too far into the darkness.

13

Nem

Bassa: The Great Dome
Fifth Mooncycle, 29

NEM WILLED THE TRAVELWAGON to go faster. The royal stablehands drove as hard as they could, the kwagas' necks straining to their last sinews, but Nem needed to be in Bassa as soon as possible.

The Red Emperor was coming home.

She did not often think of Esheme as her daughter these days. Save for quiet moments when it was just them two in a room—which happened less as the seasons wore on—Nem did not so easily step past *emperor* into the zone of *daughter* with her. Since the coronation, the most time she had spent with Esheme was at court.

Not that Esheme didn't want her by her side. She had made her First Consul after all, the most senior position in the Court of the Great Dome, second in command only to the emperor. Nem was proud of the woman Esheme had become—Scion of Moons, Sovereign Emperor of Great Bassa and the world! But all it would take to come crumbling down would be one wrong move, one hasty decision. And Esheme was full of nothing but wrong moves and hasty decisions.

They reached the Great Dome before noon. Word of the emperor's approach had reached Nem on her slow trip back from the prison via a sole rider from the Great Dome. The Consul's travelwagon had cut away from the caravan, and she and Satti covered the remaining distance, leaving the rest to catch up, including the travelwagon bringing Basuaye back to the city.

Satti pushed Nem's chair from the royal courtyard up to a nearby hoist. Esheme had these hoist cages constructed at various points around the compound to make it easier for Nem to access wherever in the Dome she pleased. Nem's chair could be pulled up or down by the cages, which were connected to a system of pulleys and ropes, drawn by a team of oxen guided by a domehand. One of such cages took her and Satti up now, swinging them in the air as the oxen drew the ropes taut.

"You think her tour was a success?" Satti asked.

"Depends on our definition of success," said Nem. "Or worse, *her* definition."

"I think it may be good, eventually," said Satti. "My family are among those who believe that hinterlanders will have a better chance of making it to Bassa and thriving here if they have a stronger relationship with the Great Dome."

"True," said Nem. But she did not tell her Second that were she not in service of the royal court, her family would never have been brought from the hinterlands into Bassa. Nem didn't think Esheme was trying to open the city up to hinterlanders. She simply needed them to *believe* that was what she was doing.

"You think her journey unwise, regardless," said Satti.

"Very much so." Nem had been staunchly against travelling into the farthest reaches of the mainland with such paltry resources. The civic guard squadrons and Igan's posse were trained, but not in the hinterlands or coasts. They had no advantage there. And with ibor's effects on the body, the Soldiers of Red were more liability than asset. Any dogged and industrious people unwavering in their traditions—the kinds of communities the hinterlands was rife with—would be a hard nut to crack.

"Maybe she will find a way," said Satti, a confidence in her voice that Nem didn't have in Esheme. "On the night of the invader—remember she had taken a beating too? But she stood up because someone had to. She dusted herself and faced Dọta even when the circumstances did not favour her. She led a whole city to revolution. I don't see how the hinterlands may offer a challenge bigger than that."

The cage came to a halt at the highest level of the Great Dome. Satti pushed Nem along the promenade that led to the portico, where emperors of old often stood and spoke to citizens assembled in the streets. One could see all of First Ward from here—the mainway, the nooks, the crannies.

As Nem expected, the streets were already lined with Bassai citizens, most of them supporters of the Red Emperor, patiently waiting for her caravan to come riding through mainway one. Her first trip—west, to Whudasha, to assess the remnants of the protectorate—had not received as fevered a reaction as this. It was the idea of an Idu noble—an *emperor*—going south to the swamplands, that captured the minds of citizens.

The people were dressed in bright colours as if on a mooncrossing night. Some entertained with singing and dancing as they waited. Others came with baskets and passed food and drinks—akara balls, rice beverages, roasted corn—to those waiting in the sun. There was the same energy in the air as that of a festival.

The members of the Court of the Great Dome were already gathered on the portico, all present for the emperor's welcome. They were dressed in their courtly wrappers, starched and ready, hair freshly plaited and oiled. Compared to them, Nem's travel clothes made her look like one of the emperor's undead soldiers.

"Dehje, First Consul," said Elder Yao, the scholar, as Satti pushed Nem into view. "Glad you could make it in time!" He sounded genuinely excited about her arrival, but then Yao, like most jalis, sounded excited about everything.

The other court members, all four of them, had more balanced dispositions. Elder Oluodah, the moon temple's representative, was wordless as usual, even in his greeting. Elder Mawuli, the merchantry guild's proxy, offered a warm smile alongside her slight bow. Elder Ebrima was the farming and hunting guild's voice, and Elder Inyene was the craftworkers' mouthpiece. Their greetings were ungarnished but deeply respectful.

Nem responded non-committally and pointed to a spot with a good view where she wanted Satti to place her chair. Domehands planted shade in the form of woven raffia on a stick next to each court member. Others brought forward cool drinks, which Nem's parched tongue gladly welcomed. She considered testing the waters about Basuaye joining them, get the court on her side early on, but decided against it. There was truly only one person she needed to sway.

After an hour of wait, the front riders of the royal caravan came into view. The cheers from the citizens started from those farthest down the road, cascading down the lines. The plain travelwagons came into view. Then, ambling slowly behind them was the decorated royal travelwagon, surrounded by civic guards.

Nem peered closer to see if her daughter was already in her usual place: the top half of her body out of an aperture at the roof of the wagon, substitute crown perched on head held high, drinking in the veneration of her supporters. But there was no Esheme there. Just the gloomy faces of the front riders.

Nem sat up. Something was wrong.

The Bassai nearest to the royal travelwagon fell silent, as if acceding to Nem's thoughts. The hush travelled down the line as quickly as the cheer had. Then, cries, erupting faster than the silence, as the citizens farthest down the road scattered and ran, screaming at the top of their lungs.

"What in Menai's name—" started Elder Ebrima, and then he was cut short, as a lengthy shadow began to appear at the rear of the caravan.

"By moons!" exclaimed Oluodah, who never swore, being a priest. "Is that—?"

Even this high up, Nem had to tilt her head to look at the Ninki Nanka, so long was the beast. Its head and face dripped blood down its neck, tall as a giant giraffe's. The smell of death and blood and what she believed to be swamp rot hit her with the full force of the wind that brought it, and she choked. From this angle, she couldn't see the rest of its body, which was being carted in a hasty collection of stripped-down travelwagons. But its tail, just as long as its neck if not longer, dragged behind the caravan.

Nem, watchful, noted that the emperor was still nowhere to be found.

By now, all the gathered citizens had done their share of fleeing, the once-filled road now emptied, save for a basket or two still circling in the dust after being pushed aside. But then someone—a child—walked out from behind the street walls the people were hiding behind, back into the road, and stood there, gazing at the undead beast as it rolled by. The child's parent or caregiver ran out and yanked them back, but somewhere within the struggle, even said parent became mesmerized by the beast, captivated by its soulless presence.

Someone else stepped out and joined them, and another, and another. Soon, once they had judged that the beast was doing nothing but lying there, dead but awake, all who had run away began to emerge, one by one.

"By Ashu's grace!" Oluodah said. "The Sovereign Emperor has conquered the unconquerable!"

The Bassai citizens were coming to the same conclusion. From their hushed silence came murmurs, then cheers—small, tentative, at first. Then louder and louder as the beast neared the gates to the Great Dome. Soon, they transformed into raucous exaltation, a full and exuberant glee, a true saviour's welcome.

But Esheme was still nowhere to be found, and Nem knew something was indeed very wrong.

"Satti." She clapped at the woman, who was still transfixed by the presence of the undead dragon-serpent. "The emperor's quarters. Now."

·⋄· ⋯ ⋯ ·⋄·

When Nem rolled into the emperor's private quarters, her daughter lay in bed, broken.

Not her body—her body seemed fine. Nem had been broken before, just like her daughter here: joints swollen, limbs dangling of their own accord, hair matted to her sweating face, eyes set deep into their sockets as ibor sucked all the nutrition and consciousness from her body. But the body could be repaired. One look, and Nem knew it would be her daughter's spirit that would need the most stitching.

The Ninki Nanka display had been a distraction. Nem had deduced that the moment she couldn't spot the emperor's inner circle—Ikobi, Igan, the Soldiers of Red. It was clear now that, hours before, this group had peeled away from the royal caravan and snuck the emperor's limp body through a separate route, arriving at the Great Dome unnoticed and unannounced. Ikobi had secretly assembled the royal healers and brought them to the emperor's private quarters, which Igan and their posse guarded while the rest of the court waited on the portico, unaware that the emperor had already arrived.

Now, Nem stood with Ikobi and Igan and watched as the healers and their attendants, supported by a bevy of domehands, flitted around Esheme, trying everything to resuscitate her, to no avail.

"Days upon days of riding and...nothing," Ikobi muttered. "We tried everything."

"Leave us," Nem announced, when her patience had worn thin. The healers bowed low to her and cleared the room. Nem nodded to Satti to shut the door after herself, leaving Nem alone with Ikobi and Igan.

"What happened?" Nem asked.

She already had an idea, but she let them fill in the missing parts. The story was the same: Esheme had seen an opportunity, one too big to ignore, and had chosen to ignore the *too big* part of it. Now it had sapped all the life out of her and rendered her bedridden.

Ikobi narrated while Igan filled in the gaps with a veneer of annoyance. Nem felt seen by their mix of anger and frustration. But there was something they still held, buried beneath the exasperation: a quiet pride. That, Nem recognised too. Being the emperor's lover wasn't much different from being her maa, was it?

"She will be fine," Nem said, once they were done.

"How so?" Ikobi had still not lost the stricken look she'd worn since arriving. "Her breathing is shallow. The healers said—"

"The healers don't know what's wrong with her," Nem said. "I do." She clicked her fingers. "The stone-bones—where are they?"

"Crumbled," Igan said. "Nothing but dust in the armlet after."

Igan produced said armlet, which Esheme used to hold small pieces of ibor in contact with her skin at all times. It was indeed empty. Dust from the disintegrated stone-bone sifted into Nem's palm. She tucked the armlet into her wrappers.

"Are the Soldiers of Red still standing?" Nem asked.

Both advisors shook their heads.

"And the beast?"

"Put away from sight," said Igan.

"Then the emperor remains fine. If her power did not still hold the beast in command, it would not have remained in stasis. Fret not. She is simply resting." Nem paused. "Make sure that is exactly what you tell the rest of the court."

Nem beckoned to Igan to help push her chair toward Esheme's bed. Then she asked both advisors to join the rest of the court and wait for an address from her. She wanted a moment alone with her daughter.

"Call in my Second, will you?" she said as they left the room. Satti came in soon after.

"A message for the kitchen," said Nem. "I want food, water, drink. Every form of nourishment available in this dome and in this land—I want it in this room, today, and for as many days as we'll need it. There will be no healers, no medicines. Just me and the emperor for as long as she takes to regain her strength. There will be no visitors unless the emperor wills it or I do. Go."

Once Nem was alone, she stared at the ashen face of the woman in the bed, weak and ailing and nothing like the daughter she knew. Or maybe exactly like that, because what was Esheme if not ready to put herself in the way of the greatest harms in order to gain more power? Nem felt pity for her daughter, for the prices she had to pay for this power, and a little guilty for benefiting from these sacrifices herself.

So this is how our roles reverse, she thought. Once, ibor had brought her down and Esheme was forced to fill her shoes. Now was the time for Nem to repay that debt.

⋅◇⋯━━━━━━⋯◇⋅

The grand room of the Great Dome, where the Red Emperor herself had prised control from the corrupt and irresponsible former leaders of Bassa, was being redecorated. Everything in the image of the last emperor—the Manic Nogowu—had been stripped away, save for a few: the crimson draperies, the gold and bronze melted into the walls, the carved stools with leopard and tortoise feet for bottoms. Even the throne, a thick, dense affair constructed with the finest ebony and adorned with gold—known colloquially as the *elephant throne* for its size—had been retained.

Esheme rarely sat on it herself, and as First Consul, Nem was the only other person authorised to sit there in the emperor's absence, though Nem had no such interests.

The court was already seated when Satti pushed Nem to her place at the grand table. All seven advisors were present.

"What has happened to the emperor is a great inconvenience," she began. "But the emperor will be back soon, ready to take up her role again. Until then, the only thing that holds this empire together is all of us in this grand room."

The advisors solemnly nodded their heads.

"The first thing I will ask for is your ultimate discretion. It is our royal mandate to ensure the citizens of this great empire are kept from speculating, because speculation eventually breeds truth, and we do not need said truth in the wrong hands. We must have a word ready for the people."

"We can tell them the emperor is ill," offered Inyene, the Elder craftworker. "Everyone understands road sickness. And with such a long journey..."

"Wrong," said Nem. "The people must never believe their Most Sovereign Emperor, the Scion of Moons, is given to illness. Illness means weakness, and any inkling of weakness means people get funny ideas. Funny ideas beget coalitions, rebellions, usurpers. And what better time for such thinking to take even greater hold than when an emperor is ill and unable to command her people?"

"On another trip, then," Mawuli offered. "Perhaps we could say she went north immediately after arriving?"

"Without the royal caravan and her Soldiers of Red?" Ikobi said. "Not very believable."

"Perhaps a story—true or false—is not what we need," said Igan.

Everyone turned to look at them.

"Go on," said Nem.

"Back in the coalition," Igan started, then paused for the table to register its discomfort. Few were allowed to speak about the Coalition for New Bassa anymore, especially with Basuaye imprisoned and his most ardent followers scattered to the wind. But it was understood they hadn't heard the last of the coalition, or coalitions in general.

"Back in the coalition," Igan continued, once the table had recovered, "we learned that sometimes, where a story cannot be used to explain, it must be used to distract. If the tale we want to tell will not suffice, we tell a new one, one so tall and fearsome that it strikes terror in the hearts of those who hear it. Enough terror that they forget to question its veracity, or even question the previous story, the one we don't want to be questioned at all."

Nem nodded. "You're talking about the Ninki Nanka."

"If we can find a way to tell the tale of how the emperor conquered the Ninki Nanka," Igan said, "one so tall and fearsome that it strikes terror into the hearts of those who hear it, that terror may soon become reverence. Said reverence may stand in stead of the emperor's physical presence, so much so that many will forget to ask where the emperor herself is."

Nem regarded the emperor's Second. Igan barely spoke at court, but when they did, it was to offer insights that were as useful as gems. Nem was reminded, once again, that though she did not choose Igan and Ikobi herself, they might just be the most useful voices in this court.

"The forthcoming mooncrossing festival," Ikobi pitched in. "We can use that. Show off the emperor's latest and biggest conquest for all to see. Make a spectacle out of it, even. The best jalis can put together an epic tale, the best of the performance guild can make an engrossing presentation. It'll be the talk of the city for a long time."

Nem liked what she was hearing. She set forward her orders: No one was to leave the walls of the Great Dome unless by her command. Then she gave the advisors instructions to prepare for this performance. After sending everyone off to their duties, Ikobi came up to her.

"First Consul," said the woman. "There is yet another matter from the expedition—perhaps even more important than our planned performance."

Nem lifted an eyebrow. "What has she done this time?"

Ikobi explained the situation with the leaders from Tombolo and Enuka, who had arrived with the royal caravan. Nem shook her head the whole time.

"Where are they now?"

"Here," said Ikobi. "Confined until we're sure what to do with them. Or until she wakes up and offers instructions. Her plan was to have them in this court, but I couldn't think of a worse time for that to happen."

Nem took a moment to ponder. She agreed with Ikobi that Esheme's plan was noble, yet ill-timed and risky. But she wasn't thinking about that. Rather, she was weighing the opportunity that this situation offered to her own planned addition to court.

"Let me think on it," she said.

Satti wheeled her away, and Nem, forever a fixer at heart, decided that this tragedy may not be a tragedy at all, but many blessings in disguise.

14

Nem

Bassa: The Great Dome
Sixth Mooncycle, 1–8

ESHEME FIRST AWOKE AFTER three days of intense nutrition. Her eyes opened, but she couldn't speak until the next day, when she managed to utter the word *water*. Nem, spending all her time by her daughter's bed, gave her a jarful, and after gulping it down, the emperor promptly went to sleep.

More nutrition followed. Domehands brought in platters of food and fruit, everything from roasted cocoyam to boiled maize to pawpaws and guavas. Nem mashed and spooned each down her daughter's throat. Though Esheme was unconscious, her body still worked, which meant that the food went down only half the time, and the other half, she threw up all over her own face. Nem would set down the food, wipe her daughter with a wet cloth, change the stained sheets, and resume the ritual.

Esheme did not awake again until the fifth day. Nem was sitting in the room, resting, when Esheme came to and sat up. Their eyes met, silence pressing between them.

"Thank you," Esheme said hoarsely.

Nem nodded.

Esheme looked around, blinked. "I'm sorry."

Nem wasn't sure what Esheme was apologising for: for being a bad daughter and refusing to visit her maa's bedside when she had been down, or for being a bad emperor and putting herself in peril.

"I understand," Nem said anyway, unsure which she herself was referring to. "I know your actions at the time did not mean you don't care."

Esheme blinked in response.

"You and I, my daughter—we are of a kind," Nem said. "We do not fare well with charades. We understand our desires, and we pursue them accordingly. I have understood mine and done the same. So have you."

Esheme nodded slowly. "Okay." Then she lay back down to sleep.

Nem thought she looked so young all of a sudden. No longer the Red Emperor of Bassa, but the little girl she once was over twenty seasons ago. The one who used to enjoy sports in the courtyards, mingling with the street rats in Fourth Ward against her maa's warnings. And she was good at them too, the sports, beating most at kwaga racing in the fields and stickfighting duels in the back corridors.

Nem remembered the day that phase ended, when Esheme had returned home with a bloodied nose. She had lost in stickfighting for the first time and, new to the feeling, demanded a best of three, the majority of which she went on to win. The street children did not take kindly to a little girl from Fourth beating them at their own game, and during the fights, had made sure their sticks found her nose in "error." Yet Esheme had come home triumphant, grinning through bloodstained teeth, narrating the ordeal as her Second wiped her nose. Her eyes had lit up at the need for her maa to share in her pride.

Nem was indeed proud of her daughter, for understanding how to bend the rules in her favour and take the pains that came with winning. For understanding that no one else needed to be proud of her deeds before they could be deemed worthy. And though she had left to go ensure the street children were carted off to Fifteenth, she remembered Esheme's eyes then, filled to the brim with *need*.

There was still some of that little girl in the woman lying in the emperor's bed, the exuberance of *want* having never left. There was still some of that proud maa in Nem, too, watching her recover and conquer this burden of power over and over again. And oh, how she wanted to tell Esheme that she was indeed proud of her, that she indeed cared for her, even if she disapproved of the harm it brought to her body, her reputation, her self. Just like back then, when she had wanted to leave the street children alone and simply embrace her daughter, bloodstained teeth and all.

But this woman was not her little girl anymore. She was the Twenty-Fourth Sovereign Emperor of Great Bassa, the Scion of Moons. She belonged to the world now. And the world did not just offer bloodstained teeth in return—it ravaged until there was nothing left. If Nem did not remind Esheme of that, both as maa and First Consul, then she had failed at her job.

She clapped her hands for Satti to come roll her away. The emperor might be asleep, but her enemies were wide awake. It was Nem's job to put them to sleep once and for all.

·—◦·⋯————⋯·◦—·

Between the Great Dome physician's brews and potions, and Nem's nutrition regimen, Esheme began to walk within a day of awakening. Mostly with aid, resting the weight of her body on the back of Nem's chair as she rolled forward, maa guiding daughter. Often, they would go up to the window and look out at the city. The city they had conquered, together, even if at separate times. The city for which they had both given up their bodies, their selves, their lives, in exchange for the opportunity to stand here and look upon it.

This routine was broken by some bad news from the Great Dome's chief physician, who had been monitoring the emperor's health for changes. The woman, whose name was Anuli, waited for them to be alone in the emperor's quarters before divulging it.

"These are not words the emperor may welcome," she said, shuffling on her feet.

Nem waved her forward. "Speak them all the same."

"Fire of Menai," Anuli began, addressing Esheme. "Your body has possessed so many fires since the day you were blessed to lead us. The light of the sister moons shine in you. Perhaps this is the reason that whatever life is created in you has so far not been able to withstand for long." She swallowed. "But your future scions may not be the only ones now at risk of surviving this fire. You, Emperor, now also share this risk."

"What do you mean?" queried Nem.

"I cannot say what illnesses have intermittently taken over the emperor's body these past seasons," Anuli said. "But what I can say is that putting even the strongest of bodies through the rigor of conception, loss, and recovery, over and over, wears away at it."

"You are calling me weak?" Esheme asked.

"No, Sovereign!" said Anuli. "I am saying all worldly flesh—even that propped up by the sister moons like yours, Emperor—has a limit. Yours has been stretched repeatedly in recent times. So stretched that its limit has become much closer than you know."

"How close?"

The woman swallowed again. "Very close, Emperor. So close that, if you were to conceive again, it may be your last. And if your scion does not survive it, neither will you."

Nem glanced at her daughter and found her pensive. They were probably thinking the same thing. Anuli did not know about the way ibor worked, and therefore did not understand the gravity of what she was saying. If the emperor could no longer use ibor, she was nothing without the power and control that iborworking afforded her. She would not be emperor for much longer.

"So how do we avoid that?" Nem asked. "Better diets for improved nutrition? More water? Less travel?"

"All of that and more, First Consul," the chief physician replied. "Most of all, I cannot advise that the emperor carry a new scion until further notice. Bodily demands only escalate with such a situation, and the life expectancy of any such scion is unknown. Also, it will be impossible to gauge the emperor's health from too far a distance. My humble suggestion is that the emperor remain in the Great Dome until we can chart a way forward."

Esheme, who was lying down, swung her legs over the bed and tried to stand without the help of Nem's chair. She had been getting more walking practice periodically, having almost forgotten how to use her legs in all the days of being bedridden.

"You are saying this place should become my prison," Esheme said, still trying to stand, to no avail. "I should trade the prison of the wards for the prison of the Great Dome."

"I suggest only what I believe is best to keep you alive to continue to guide us, Sovereign," said Anuli. "That is all."

Esheme made a few more attempts, then gave up and simply sat.

"Thank you," she said. "Leave us."

After the woman had gone, Nem said: "She is right. You broke a lot bringing that beast here, and not just in your body."

"My body is fine."

"You cannot walk. Only two days ago, you coughed up blood. You are not a cat, Esheme. You do not have multiple lives."

Esheme shrugged. "So long as I occupy this Great Dome and rule over this land, I will bleed one way or another." She turned to Nem. "Those are your words."

Both women sat in silence after, until Esheme put an end to the conversation by saying: "Let me think about this for a while."

⋄⸺⸺⸺⸺⸺⋄

The day after, Esheme, back at the window of her private quarters—without leaning on Nem's chair this time—made a request.

"I want another one," she said.

Another one, in Esheme parlance, meant another conception.

Nem, seated alone at the beverage table and sipping weybo, decided it was pointless to argue.

"Okay," she said. "But perhaps when your body is stronger." For this past conception—Esheme's third since she took over the Great Dome—they had waited a significant amount of time before taking her in. A new conception would require an even longer wait, possibly several mooncycles.

"I am strong enough," Esheme said, her gaze remaining fixed on the city outside. "We only need a fortnight to take in again. Enough time has passed since..." She let it hang, but Nem knew what the missing words were.

"Your body has seen multiple misfortunes at once," said Nem. "It bears a physical and mental weight. You must exercise caution, or risk death."

"I risk death every day I sit in this room and refuse to show my face out there," said Esheme. "Do you know that those two Tombolo Elders were emboldened enough to show displeasure at my presence? They do not respect my name, even with the Soldiers of Red at my back." She stood arms akimbo, defiant. "I captured the Ninki Nanka and brought it here because I want them to see what I am capable of. I will not step back onto that portico until I am able to Command my new conquest before them."

They will never respect you, Nem wanted to say, because she knew this exact feeling. She had wanted it so badly too, in those first seasons of being a fixer. She had learned to play all the right politics, made others do the dirty work for her, gained power without striking a blow with her own hands. She had devoted her time and energy to keeping power rather than chasing more to her detriment.

And it worked—really well. But she had still never gotten the respect she craved, so she'd learned to stop expecting it. The one time she had lost focus and tried to gain access to more power, to eke more respect— look where that landed her.

"Trust me when I say I understand all you're saying," said Nem. "But the court and I are working on solutions to occupy the minds of the people until your return. For now, all you need to do is rest while we—"

"I don't need you to *occupy* anything, thank you very much," Esheme said. "Either you can help me, or I will find someone who will."

Esheme clapped in the quick, sharp manner that Nem often did. The door opened, and Satti walked in.

"It's time," was all Esheme said, and Satti, who was often privy to these conception procedures, understood.

·⸰·⸳⸳⸳⸳————⸳⸳⸳·⸰·

Nem never asked how the seed they used was collected. Satti and a few of her trusted hands often did the deed, selecting inconspicuous Shashi men who would never care what their collected seed was used for, or even had the option of caring. So, when Satti brought in the freshly collected seed—Nem knew it was fresh from how warm it was—she did not ask. Satti had been a midwife in a former life back in the hinterlands. Part of her work had been to assist joined couples who found it difficult to conceive to do so. If there was ever a person best equipped to do this work, it was her.

Nem also did not ask about the person chosen for this particular seed. Satti knew the routine well already. The last two times, Nem had explained the criteria for each choice, which was always the same three: They had to have a penis; they had to be of visibly mixed heritage, whether socially marked as Shashi or not; and they had to be so disenfranchised that this service could easily be bought from them, and they could be persuaded to forget it ever happened. Or, if they turned out to prove difficult after the fact, they could be made to forget, or be forgotten.

The first two criteria were often easy. Most of the Shashi in Fifteenth Ward, now that the western protectorate was nothing but a ghost settlement, were not faring particularly well. Amid their economic hardship, it was easy to find willing sellers of their seed if paid handsomely. But, as Nem and Esheme had learned the hard way the first few times, Fifteenth was far away, and the potency of seed waned quickly. So Nem had opted for another approach: whisk a number of able Shashi into the inner wards and place them in conditions much better than Fifteenth's. The catch was that they were forever in the crown's debt, to be collected at any time and in any manner. Things had become much easier since then, often as easy as Satti showing up at such a door and requesting a penis.

As for the latter part of the criteria, they were yet to run into any problems of indiscretion. Nem didn't anticipate any troubles. If the Second to the First Consul of the Red Emperor showed up at one's doorstep and asked for one's seed, it went without saying that the punishment for speaking about it without express permission was instant death.

"Thank you," said Nem to Satti, who pushed Nem's chair over to the bed where Esheme lay asleep, then shut the door and locked them in. Once alone, Nem turned to her daughter and tapped her awake.

"It's time," she said.

Esheme, her strength now regained, made the remaining arrangements as she always did, albeit slower than usual. She pulled the special bench from the wardrobe and laid it down. It was a special piece of woodworking Nem had had made—half a flat surface, the other half separable and branching away. The separable parts could be levered up and held at an incline. This way, Esheme could lie with her back on the flat portion of the bench, then hook her legs over the inclined parts, with her genitals in the middle: high up, parted, and welcome for insertion.

Once the bench was set up, Esheme rolled Nem into the appointed space, then began to undress. It was not really required, but again, Nem let her have her way of coping. Perhaps there was something about her being completely naked, bare and vulnerable, that made this process bearable; this opening up of herself to something that would first come into her and make life, then proceed to be destroyed in order for her to gain power she could wield in the world.

Once Esheme was in position, Nem removed the stopper atop the small gourd and brought it between her daughter's thighs. When she tilted it, her hands shook. Her fingers grazed the inside of Esheme's thigh, and her daughter shivered too. Even though they were performing this ritual for the third time, they were yet to become used to it.

"Are you sure you want to do this?" Nem asked, fingers paused right at the opening.

"You know I have to," was Esheme's reply.

Nem tilted the little gourd between Esheme's thighs until it was empty. Esheme shook her legs as Nem poured, mostly because it tickled, but also to ensure more than enough seed made its way into her. Some of the slimy contents spilled over onto her legs, too much to go in at once. Nem found herself chuckling as she reached for a rag to wipe the spillover.

"Want to share the joke?" asked Esheme, who couldn't see Nem due to her elevated legs blocking her view.

"I was just thinking that this must be a big man to produce this much seed," said Nem. "But you know the joke about small men, yes?"

"I don't," said Esheme, and Nem was reminded, for a moment, that the emperor was just, in truth, a young girl.

"It's an old women's joke," said Nem. "We say that the smaller the man, the bigger his coconuts and the water held in them. Some say it's a joke the moons have played on us, giving the best gifts to the ones we think least desirable."

Esheme chuckled. "That I cannot dispute."

Afterward came the waiting, giving a little time for the seed to crawl deep inside her and plant itself. Or at least, so they thought. Neither woman really knew anything of the sort—they were operating on Satti's advice. Nem did what she often did during these periods to avoid sitting in silence and staring at her naked adult daughter: She asked Esheme to tell her about her journey.

Throughout the narration, Esheme stared at the ceiling, not meeting Nem's eyes. Her account of the events differed markedly from that of Igan and Ikobi, in that she seemed to spend more time speaking about what Nem surmised were the enjoyable aspects of the journey. When she got to the events at the swamp, she slowed, as if still traumatized by the events. Then she stopped altogether once she spoke about the moment when she had lost everything: herself, her power, her unborn child.

Silence drowned the two women after. Then Esheme began to shake, first her body racked by small sobs, then a sudden burst of tears. She crossed her arms around herself, letting—pain? fear? sorrow? regret?—take over her body.

Nem rolled herself over to her daughter and put out a tentative hand, then leaned forward and lay her body over Esheme's in an embrace. Esheme wrapped her hands tightly about Nem, and they held each other close, in a way they hadn't in a long, long time, right until late into the evening, when the seed between Esheme's thighs became dry and flaky.

15

Lilong

Chugoko
Sixth Mooncycle, 11, heist day

ON THE THIRD DAY of the Ochela, a crowd prepared for the parade at high noon.

Biemwensé parked the travelwagon at a distance from the prison, with Lilong, Kakutan, and Kubra seated within, blinds drawn, doors locked. The desert sun cooked them slowly inside. Lilong wiped her dripping forehead with the back of her hand and counted numbers, reminding herself to breathe.

Kubra, eyes like a hawk, opened the window every now and then to see if he could spot the eager child he had paid as a lookout to inform him of the procession's arrival. Kakutan offered Lilong some water from her waterskin.

"You must remain calm." The older woman wiped dripping sweat off her own face with a rag. Earlier, Lilong had asked for a rag to do the same, but Kakutan declined, stating that she needed to look like a true vagrant for her role, so it was in their best interest if she sweated as much as possible.

"Calm indeed," Lilong replied. "I did not have good sleep, I am being baked, and the procession is late. I feel like piss."

"The procession is always late, from what I hear," said Kubra to no one in particular. He had opened the window again. The vagrant boy was

back, whispering softly. Kubra nodded, pressed something—a coin—
into his palm, and the boy ran off.

"It's time," said Kubra, and opened the travelwagon door.

Noise and heat rushed up to meet Lilong as they descended onto
the roadside, the smells and colours of the Ochela washing over them.
Every corner was packed full, lined with children, women of all ages,
elderly men. Most of the younger men had gone off to watch the contestants prepare, Lilong had learned, a private performance that was its
own spectacle—the dressers and makeup artists flaunted their own skills
there, often drawing accolades. Lilong hoped Danso had prepared adequately for so many eyes on him. If there was a time to unlock his jali
skills of crowd management and put them to use, it was now.

The three of them clung to the walls as they inched closer to the
prison, sidestepping trinket vendors with wares spread out, or those who
cooked or fried or brewed in carts. Kakutan's warden uniform helped
chart an easier path. Lilong kept an eye out for local vigilantes, the easiest to overlook of their many adversaries. She spotted a few who did not
seem particularly attentive, instead anticipating the parade like the rest of
the crowd.

When they arrived at the point that was equidistant between prison
gate and parked travelwagon, Kubra stopped.

"This is my spot," he said, then looked Lilong and Kakutan in the eye.
"Be careful. Those wardens are faster than they look. Make sure you wait
for the signal. Don't move until you—"

"Hear the drumbeats," Lilong and Kakutan finished.

Kubra held up his hands. "Okay, then. Moons go with you."

He disappeared into the crowd.

They found a shaded corner out of common sight and waited. Children ran around them in long tunics, headgear, and facepaint that Lilong
understood to be a mimicry of the contestants' regalia. The tunics were
homemade, different materials woven together, beautified with any shiny
object they could find. They sang in a bevy of languages, not all of which
made sense to Lilong, but from which she gathered that they wished
blessings on all the contestants, that they may be spoken for and receive
an offer of intendedship.

Lilong was beginning to wonder if Danso had been informed of this part of the contest, when the drumbeats began. Big, quick, and booming rhythms from down the mainway. The crowd responded with cheers and ululations.

Around the bend came the first of the contestants, riding in wagons refitted as small stages hitched to kwagas, each decorated according to the personality of the contestant. The contestants themselves—at least the first three or four Lilong could see coming down the mainway— were all young desertlanders of different physiques, complexions, predicaments. Tall, thin, short, portly, muscled—all stood in the wagons and presented themselves in a myriad of intricate poses, dances, and interactions with the crowd. One contestant leaned over to get patted— blessed—by prominent Elders on the roadsides. Another with a headgear built of sticks twirled in his carriage, so that the assorted textiles dangling from his headgear formed a carousel whenever he did so. The crowd cheered encouragingly.

"Do you know what he's wearing?" Kakutan asked.

Lilong shook her head. They wouldn't recognise Danso easily anyway. Not after the heavy makeup and elaborateness of the outfits.

"Well, then, moons be with him," muttered Kakutan. "Here we go."

* * *

"Move there, you *fowl shit*."

Lilong braced for the shove on her back. When it did come, it was as hard as she'd anticipated, Kakutan really putting energy into her role. She staggered just the right amount to sell the role of a drunk.

A few more shoves, and they found themselves at the gaping maw of the prison. Tall, gated with steel pegs, and guarded by four people who did not seem interested in doing any sort of guarding, their eyes fixed on the parade. Other than a short glance at Kakutan's uniform and Lilong's rags, they paid little notice, which made sense. No one worried about those going into a prison. It was those who wished to leave that raised eyebrows.

Kakutan gave Lilong one last shove into the darkness, and they were in.

A registering station welcomed them. Wardens milled about the entry-way, half their eyes and ears on the parade outside. Only one warden, standing behind a demarcated platform, beckoned them over. Kakutan shoved Lilong in that direction.

"Temporary or permanent?" the warden asked in Savanna Common, without looking up.

"Temporary," Kakutan said. "Need to teach this one a lesson that fighting in the street is—"

"Clothes," the warden interrupted.

"Excuse?" asked Kakutan.

"Take off your clothes," the warden said in Lilong's direction, then to Kakutan: "Next time, make sure they take off their clothes before they come in here."

Lilong tried for a glance at Kakutan. *This wasn't part of the plan!* But Kakutan refused to meet her eyes, staying in character. Lilong had little to lose other than her dignity—her blade was stuffed in Kakutan's own warden uniform. Perhaps this was even good for the last stage of the heist—no one would recognise her if they obtained new robes and walked out.

Lilong took off her wrappers and placed them on the counter. The warden picked up a stick, and with it, shifted them into a heap of other clothes.

"Find a free spot in general holdings," the warden said, and waved them away. No question about a name or any sort of identity. It didn't matter, apparently. Each new prisoner was simply one more of the face-less mass.

The two women followed the directions and found themselves in a poorly lit corridor, lacking any openings, and therefore filled with smoke from the oil lamps. They hustled down its length, thankful to run into no one. A number of doorways appeared, and Kakutan produced her cloth map and peered at it before selecting one of them. They went in, bumping into a warden patrol of three.

Kakutan pulled her uniform's hood over the front of her face, nodded a greeting the way of the group, and shoved Lilong for effect. The wardens paid little heed.

The two women ascended the stairs, running into patrolling duos every two or so entryways. Each also paid little heed. The combination of Lilong's lack of clothing and Kakutan's demeanour seemed to do most of the trick.

Soon, they were on the middle floor, and after a few manoeuvres, losing their way once, they ended up in the main corridor where the prisoners were held.

The smell hit them first. Filth of unimaginable proportions, hanging so heavily in the air. Both women covered their noses.

"Down the corridor, to the left," Kakutan directed, muffled by her sleeve over her mouth.

When the prisoners spotted the women, they rose and began to holler. Lilong did not look—the smell had already told her all she needed to know. It was no ordinary stink, but that of decay, of rotting meat left in water too long, of something once alive that was no longer quite so. The hoarse voices followed as they ran past, each *please* and *help* in whatever language they could muster a sting to Lilong's chest.

Lilong willed her gaze to remain straight, to remember the mission, what she was doing this for. Her family, her people, her league. She could not afford to break.

They turned the corner, toward the solitary holding cell—

—and stumbled into two wardens.

The wardens weren't particularly alert, busy squatting in the dust, playing a board game with squares and round discs. They looked up and spotted Kakutan. But unlike the wardens on patrol from earlier, it took them only a short moment to put things together and draw their batons.

16

Danso

Chugoko
Sixth Mooncycle, heist day

UNDER THE RISING TIDE of drumbeats, Danso's wagon tumbled over pebbled ground and rolled into the parade route. He counted the number of oxen-driven wagons ahead of his—twelve, so far. Subtracting the first two contestants who had been presented—he could tell because the drums stopped each time a contestant was presented—that was fifteen, him included. Behind him, three, totalling eighteen. They were still a way off from the prison.

"I'm going to pass out before we get there," he said to Ugo, who drove the wagon. He swatted at a fly that had opted to settle on his matted eyelash.

"Don't," Ugo said sharply, and with practiced ease, turned and swiped the fly from Danso's eye, flicking it away. "What is our first rule?"

"Don't spoil my makeup?"

"Not even to wipe sweat or tears—I'm not playing! We may be covering for a prison break, but believe me when I say we must make an impression anyway." He eyed Danso up and down. "Try to stay on your feet. Remember your performance is not only during the presentation. It is for the duration of the parade."

"So I can start dancing?" Danso twirled on a toe, and every part of his ensemble jangled: the beaded headdress accessorized with feather and cowrie; the flared velvet tunic criss-crossed with beads and goldstones at the neck and sleeves; the earrings, necklaces, armlets, wristlets, and anklets of copper and coral and wildcat bone.

"Conserve your energy for the real thing," said Ugo. "The others depend on us making the right moves."

The drums started up and stopped multiple times—Danso counted six contestants. He could see the crowd ahead, eager, lapping up the performances. He bit the inside of his cheek.

"Can we . . . go over it again?" he asked. "One last time?"

"Now?" Ugo was distracted by familiar faces who recognised and greeted him. He returned their greetings with a practiced smile and grace, then returned to Danso. "We don't need any more practice. Just dance from your heart, okay?"

"You know music and dance are the exact parts of my jali education I failed at, right?"

"Yes, but you don't *have* to be good at it to do it well. It's all an act, yes? Dancing is the easiest thing to fake because it's *really* fake, isn't it? Dancing is *acting*! You hear the music, you let your body do the talking, and then you put some energy behind that bodytalk. Forget about doing it correctly—there is no *correctly* with dancing. Only energy." He turned to move the cart one more contestant step forward. "Besides, it's the best for our spectacle. Who doesn't want to watch a young, energetic man dance his cares away?"

Soon, they had crawled up by four more contestants, rolling into the thick of the parade. The crowd swarmed Danso's wagon as they came in. Child, adult, old, young—it didn't matter. They all reached out to touch him, their fingers caressing his skin, their lips chattering in his ear, crooning about how good his makeup looked, how wondrous his tunic, how sublime his headdress. One man offered to give Danso a house if he agreed to be joined to his child. Another wanted to know if Danso was looking for a Second.

Danso neither loved nor hated it, being the object of such desire. It was a strange and new experience, being adored in this way. He had spent so much of his life trying to prove that he was worthy of admiration such as this, but he had always done so by wielding intellect because it was the only part of him that seemed worthy of notice. To be admired just for existing—as is—was unnerving, but gladly received.

Now they were two contestants away from being presented. Danso reviewed the judges, who sat in a row where the crowd was thickest. They were a motley group, all eight of them, bested in dress and intensity of expression only by the contestants themselves. He'd heard they were usually selected from the heads of all working groups in the city, since they didn't quite have guilds in the same way Bassa did. Among them, Danso guessed, would be warrant chiefs or their representatives, heads of vigilante groups and unions like trading, craftworking, and the likes. At least one of them was the Chief Warden of the prison, though Danso couldn't tell which.

When he was only one contestant away from being presented, Danso regarded the eyes on him, searched within them for hostility, confusion, dismissal. But all he saw was expectation. They wanted him to not just stand there, but do something.

That was all he'd wanted, all this time—to *do something*. Now he could.

The drums began, the wagon rolled forward, and over the sound of the welcome song, the herald spoke Danso's name and announced his arrival.

Moons go with you, Lilong, Danso thought. Then he began to dance.

When Danso was a child, long before he joined the jali guild, Habba had taken him to his first mooncrossing festival.

Not really his *first* festival, but his earliest memory of the event. Danso most remembered it being so loud, and there being so many bodies. The mainway had been packed as they went up to the arena. They'd had to push through the crowds because they did not have a kwaga or a Second yet. Habba had to carry him high on his shoulders to prevent them from getting separated.

They had sat among the lowliest tiers of society, although Danso didn't know it back then. Habba had been freshly stripped of his scholar status and was yet to make any headway with his private healing practice.

But to Danso, they might as well have sat in the highest of all tiers. The loud cheers, booming drums, and piercing flutes; the crowds singing the Bassai Pledge in one voice; the smells—roasted corn, roasted meat, armpit sweat, the burning wood of the bonfire, the dust raised by acrobats and wrestlers.

But it was the dancers and their disguises that most enthralled him. Many wore fearsome masks made of wood or bone or thatch, and attires of woven grass and cloth, from which dangled all manner of trinkets and accessories. Much like the Ochela parade, in fact.

And they danced. Oh, they danced.

Danso remembered watching them, gyrating with purpose and agility, twisting and turning and swaying and flailing, telling stories with their bodies. This was the *bodytalk* Ugo spoke of.

Only once he'd used that expression did Danso get a flash of this memory, an image that truly represented what he was being asked to do.

So when the drums began, and the herald spoke Danso's name and announced his arrival, Danso threw himself into the memory, and began to bodytalk.

· ◇ ··· ———— ··· ◇ ·

The bodytalk was a spectacular failure.

The spectacular happened first. Danso began with the opening act as Ugo had suggested: jumping out of the wagon. The expectation was that all contestants remained in their wagons, so jumping out was operating outside the lines, enough reason for a spectacle all by itself.

The crowd gasped as a collective when Danso landed in the dust. He began the first pattern, an arm and leg dance based on Ugo's lessons about joints, how understanding them as the real tools for dancing was the secret to looking assured. Neck, shoulders, elbows, wrists, hip, knees, ankles—knowing what joint to twist and in what specific pattern was the important thing. Head, buttocks, and torso movements were only to add flair.

Danso moved to the second pattern, a predominantly waist dance, to the third, a foot and hip dance, and then promptly forgot what the fourth sequence was supposed to be, so circled back to the first.

The crowd's appreciation rose, then waned when they recognised the repetition. The light in their eyes tapered, and he could see the judges' eyes lower, the slant of the sun over their faces as they angled their heads and whispered to one another.

I can't fail, he thought. *Not again.*

He was thinking of Lilong and the heist, but drowning in the memory of being at the bonfire with his daa. The Ochela drums and cheers blended with the snap and crackle of the mooncrossing bonfire, smells and sounds and people becoming one.

Habba turned to Danso from where he was seated atop the wagon, smiled, big and warm. Danso stared back at his daa, but also at Zaq, also his friends Abu and Uria and Nowssu, also his triplet uncles and Elder Jali Oduvie at the university, also the face of his maa, how he had always imagined she would look.

All the faces, together, said: *Then do something.*

Danso's knees gave way, and his body began to tremble, his chest heaving, his breath coming only in short gasps. He dropped to the dust. His limbs were too heavy, his joints too stiff. His shoulders shook as his body ejected a stifled, ravenous sadness, a too-full wineskin finally burst open.

He did not notice the tears at first, confusing them for sweat. But when he tried to rise, a weight came over him, so heavy that he relented and stayed down, tears dribbling down his cheek. In his periphery, he caught a glimpse of various faces: perplexed, concerned, displeased. He touched his cheek with a dusty hand, facepaint staining his fingers, before realising he had broken Ugo's first rule.

"Danso!" Ugo's voice, up in the wagon's seat behind him. He looked. Habba and the other faces were gone.

"Get in!" Ugo was motioning him back into the wagon.

Danso crawled back in, to tepid applause from the disappointed crowd as the drums rose again to welcome the next contestant. He glanced at the judges and saw them watch his wagon ride away, irritated. He turned and hid his face.

"You did well, my friend," said Ugo. "You did what was needed."

They had barely ridden a few feet when a shout broke their stride.

"Stop! Stop that wagon!"

A small man came barreling through the crowd, gasping but focused, and only pausing when he had brought Ugo's ox to a halt. He stood in the way of the wagon and pointed at Danso.

"You," he said. "The Chief Warden would like to have a word."

17

Danso

Chugoko
Sixth Mooncycle, heist day

Danso and Ugo stood in the sun with the Second, waiting to be summoned by the Chief Warden, who was still engrossed in watching the last few contestants of the parade.

"Can you at least tell us why he wants to meet us?" Ugo asked the Second. There was a little tremor in his voice.

"The Chief Warden wants to meet with only the contestant," the Second said, referencing Danso. "And no—I do not know why."

Danso leaned toward Ugo. "You think he knows?"

"That we may be connected to a prison break that we don't even know has happened yet?" Ugo whispered back. "I doubt it."

"Then why are you afraid?"

"That he might recognise you?" Ugo tilted his head. "From the notice?"

Danso grew cold. He had completely forgotten about that. Before he could gather his wits about him, the Chief Warden turned toward them and beckoned. The Second led them forward to the hastily constructed platform under whose shade he sat.

The man himself was not quite impressionable. Danso had thought he'd look like a hunthand, being the most senior of prison wardens, but no—he was languid, genial, affable, wearing his wrappers with stature, like a councilhand. Even his makeup was similar to that which Danso used to wear as a jali novitiate.

"Ah, welcome," he said, looking to Danso. "Wonderful dancer, you. I never quite caught your name when the leader of ceremonies mentioned it—you are?"

"Dehje, Elder," said Danso, slipping into a Sahelian inflection. "You may call me Jhobon."

"Jhobon of . . . ?"

"Gwagwamsi." They had not planned this part, he and Ugo, so he picked a random settlement from the northern trade route, building on the lie that Ugo had begun with the peace officers and their mouthpiece.

"Gwagwamsi?" The Chief Warden's expression was quizzical. "Interesting. So you made it all the way down just to participate in the Ochela?"

"Yes, Elder."

"Hmm, yes, I did wonder about your origins." The man waved noncommittally, in what Danso assumed to be a reference to his complexion. "But I think I see it now—makes sense. You have that Sahelian agility. And those tears—oh, that was really good! To weep on demand like that—what a performance!" He paused. "Though, I must say, you look familiar? I feel like I've seen you somewhere."

Danso's heartbeat sped up.

"I sincerely doubt it, Elder," he replied. "I only recently arrive Chugoko for the contest."

"I fail to remember where exactly," said the Chief Warden, ignoring Danso, a finger on his lip. "But I feel sure of it." He studied Danso's face some more. "You only recently arrived, you say?"

"Yes, Elder," Danso said, pointing to Ugo. "My brother live here, and he is housing me. Perhaps it is his face you remember? Though he is not one for trouble, so perhaps not. But he is known inside beautification circles."

The man looked to Ugo, uninterested. Ugo made the requisite bow and hand-nose gesture, but the Chief Warden's eyes were back to Danso, giving him another once-over.

"Eh," he said finally. "I guess it doesn't matter anyway." He wrinkled his nose, considering it for another moment, then acceded. "I guess you'll do. More northerner than I'd have wanted, but whatever makes her happy, I guess."

Danso cocked his head. "I will do for . . . what, if I may ask, Elder?"

"Consider yourself spoken for." He snapped a finger at his Second, who hustled away. "My daughter finds you desirable and would like a walk of intendedship with you."

"We need to find a way out," Ugo was whispering. "You *cannot* follow this man's daughter."

But Danso wasn't hearing him. He was far, far away again, swallowed in memories.

He and Esheme, walking down mainway one, saluted by fellow Bassai. The firm grip of her hand in his, insistent on the right performance. The kindless gaze she cast at him when he slipped up. The disquiet he would carry in his heart for days after. The apprehension that rose to his throat, that threatened to choke him whenever a forthcoming walk neared.

He shut his eyes, trying to breathe away the weight sitting in his chest. What he would give to never feel that way again! But here he was, helpless, on the verge of being roped into another long-term commitment, living in someone else's shadow, unable to do or be anything other than be a tail.

These were the days he missed the Skopi the most. Now that he had nothing to call on to get him out of trouble, he'd become acutely aware of his vulnerability. Without Lilong or the Diwi nearby, he was exposed. Anyone with the slightest veneer of power, this man included, could simply smother him if they wished.

Lilong was right: Stories were powerful, but they were worthless in the wrong circumstances. Only true might could prevail here. And oh, what he would give to feel such power again!

A pull on his arm yanked him back to the present.

"Danso! Are you hearing me?"

Danso blinked.

"*Do not* perform that walk," Ugo pressed, hiding his lips behind a hand so they couldn't be read. "You will *never* leave this place."

Danso blinked again. The Second had returned with the young woman.

"Ah, yes, my treasure," the Chief Warden said, rising to present his daughter. "Meet Jhobon of Gwagwamsi—exciting contestant, interesting young man. Jhobon, meet my daughter, Abunni DaaAwa." He patted his chest. "And forgive my rudeness—I may not have introduced myself. I am Elder Awa, Chief Warden of Chugoko Central Prison." He waved his hand above his head and behind him, at the prison, like it was a beautiful thing to behold.

The young woman, standing next to him, lifted her head and smiled. She was of pleasant demeanour, hair done in a mix of dangling desert-lander styles in the front and upheld in Bassai rings to the back. Her makeup was a derivative of her daa's, but with smidgens of gold dust to make her cheeks stand out. She smiled shyly and cast furtive glances at Danso.

Her kind disposition softened the moment for Danso, but he could not find it in him to smile back. Which was just as well, because behind her, a bustle had broken out near the prison entrance.

Danso angled his body to get a better view, alerting both Chief Warden and daughter to the ruckus. The whole group turned, watching the scene unfold with interest.

Then came a loud clang that caused the ground to shudder, the dust to rise.

Two wardens spilled out of the prison's entrance and into the street, one supporting the other, preventing them from keeling over. After looking both ways, both wardens limped off in the direction opposite to where Danso's group stood.

"What—" the Chief Warden started, but a third warden came running out of the same entrance, also looking in both directions. The warden's eyes found Danso's.

Lilong.

She held his eyes only long enough to register recognition, but also confusion. Then she turned and sped off in the same direction as the last two wardens.

A large, heavy gong began to sound, and commotion took over the mainway.

Danso felt an arm grab him—Ugo again—and then together they were cutting through the crowd, slipping between people. Danso, still in regalia, struggled to keep pace.

"The wagon!" he was saying to Ugo. "We need to go back."

"*Forget* the wagon!" Ugo said, and yanked at a dangling piece of Danso's clothing. Danso followed his cue, ripping extraneous elements from his clothing. He tossed his headdress aside, wiped his facepaint.

Vigilantes began to appear from every corner, clearing people off the mainway, swinging whips at those who stopped to ask questions. *Chugoko is now under curfew*, they announced. *Go home.* Vendors rolled their carts into dark corridors. Shopkeepers swung their shutters. Families cleared their children from the street.

Ugo shoved Danso into an empty stall in the nearby market, and they ducked beneath the storefront, watching the vigilantes come together and form hasty search parties. Kwaga hooves clattered nearby. Dust billowed, and two travelwagons rolled past, packed to the brim with peace officers.

Please be safe, Danso prayed. But he wasn't sure who he was praying for—himself or the others.

In the distance, the gong continued to ring.

18

Lilong

Chugoko
Sixth Mooncycle, heist day

MOMENTS AFTER RUNNING INTO the two guards, Lilong realised she didn't need to expend any ibor after all.

The men were at least one-half bigger than Kakutan was, but that didn't deter her. She moved swiftly and noiselessly, swinging the baton with lightning quickness, jaw locked, eyes bright, excited. Her blows were short thwacks and muffled thuds, taking out a muscle here, distending a joint there. Lilong had not seen the woman fight before, and she was both awed and jealous at the efficiency and neatness of it all.

The two men soon fell, bruised and battered, but not dead. Kakutan gave each a thwack to the head to ensure they stayed unspeaking for a long time.

"There goes your solution for uniforms," Kakutan said, wiping her brow. "Now you're spoiled for choice." She began to strip the nearest man.

Lilong faced the gate and turned her ibor toward it.

Possessing the keylock, as usual, was an exercise in patience, bursts of fatigue nudging at her consciousness. She took her time, trying to make the least noise possible while searching with her consciousness for the iron pins that formed the locking mechanism. Her heart beat faster, anticipating the pressure of a new Possession. Blood rushed to her head as she found the lock and gained access to the iron. She pushed and pushed until she had a firm grip on it. Then she Commanded it to open.

A click. The gate swung open, and Lilong leaned on it, tired.

"Here, here," Kakutan was saying, reaching to support her, before someone barreled out of the holding cell, pushing the gate so that it knocked both women into the wall. Then the prisoner was running down the corridor.

"Moons' balls," Kakutan swore, but didn't wait to ask the question that was on both their lips. She freed herself before the prisoner could round the corner, squinted in one eye, and flung her baton.

The baton struck the running prisoner in the back of the head, who in turn slammed into the nearest wall and fell to the ground, motionless.

"What in Menai's name—?" Kakutan leaned and peeped through the gateway, covertly inspecting the holding cell, ready for another attack. But none came, and she straightened, regarding the fallen prisoner.

"Seems like we found our Speaker's daughter."

The prisoner's face was covered by unkempt hair, but one look at her complexion, and Lilong knew it was Oke. She had rags for under-clothes, as filthy as the underclothes Lilong had on. Fingernails bitten and chipped, some bleeding. Sores beneath her feet. One could be for-given if they'd mistaken her for a beggar in the street.

Lilong rose slowly to her feet, then faltered, swaying. She steadied her-self with a hand on the wall.

"Okay, she can't walk," said Kakutan, trying to wake Oke, to no avail. "That is the roof plan cancelled." She lifted Oke and threw a hand under her arm. The taller woman slumped over Kakutan, groaning and drooling.

"Ah, she's too heavy for the window!" Kakutan was circling through their options too quickly for Lilong to think. "Out through the front, then?"

Pull yourself together! Lilong squinted her mind back into focus, eyed the two men on the floor, and a plan came together in her head.

· ◇ ⋯ —————— ⋯ ◇ ·

The first warden patrol they came across saw nothing but three wardens in uniform—two helping a drunk colleague between them. Kakutan nodded to the patrol without a word, and after a moment's hesitation, they nodded back. The silent understanding was all they needed. Lilong's gamble—that plenty a warden got drunk themselves during the Ochela, and it would be up to their colleagues to ensure they were tucked away to avoid punishment from their superiors—was paying off.

They went past the second patrol in the same way, though at least one of them looked back to watch the three go, unsure of what they were seeing. Kakutan pulled more of the uniform's wrappers over Oke's drooping head, hoping that no one recognised the woman's face—not in this uniform anyway. Even though most of these wardens didn't know each other well—turnover was high due to poor working conditions, according to Alaba's insider information—they would recognise an odd voice within their ranks. It was best they moved as quickly and spoke as little as possible.

They went down the stairs. One last patrol to go.

At the last patrol before the corridor that led back outside, one of the wardens greeted them in a border pidgin.

Lilong froze, as did Kakutan. Lilong could tell it was a greeting from the tone alone, but she did not know the appropriate response for it. She looked to Kakutan, head bowed to prevent recognition. The woman shook her head, short and sharp. She didn't know either. They had all learned Savanna Common in Chabo because it was the most connected to High Bassai, but the belt's wide array of indigenous pidgins had proven too much of an undertaking.

They increased their pace, hoping the warden would shut up. He did not. He greeted them again, but this time, Lilong felt the greeting shift into something with more menace, like how one would say *Welcome* to an enemy.

She squeezed a fist by her side, ready to call for her blade to fly, when Oke lifted her head and groggily answered the greeting. She said something else, shook her head, and spat in the dust. The wardens laughed and let them pass. One even gave Kakutan a friendly thump on the back.

Lilong exhaled, then realised Oke was awake.

"Alaba sent us," she whispered in Savanna Common.

Oke nodded weakly, hair matted to her face. "My head . . ."

"My fault, sorry," said Kakutan. "What did you tell them?"

"Had...too much...to drink," she said. "Hit my head."

"Useful," said Kakutan. "But say no more until we're safe."

They burst back into the main entryway. As Lilong had predicted, almost all the wardens still had their eyes glued to the parade outside. Perhaps Danso had done his duty after all. The main gate was right there, gaping. They rushed for it.

"You!" A voice came after them.

"Don't stop moving," Kakutan whispered. "We only need to cross that gate..."

"You!" Lilong recognised the voice now. It was the warden from the station, the one who had taken her clothes in the beginning. He seemed to be the only person with no interest in the parade, contest, or festival at all, so diligent in his duties.

"Wait there!" he was saying.

"Run," Kakutan whispered, and they pitched forward.

"Stop!" the warden shouted as they ran past the gate and into the entryway. "Stop them!"

For some reason, the guards in the entryway had doubled in number. Now, they were eight instead of the four previously encountered. No way they could make it past these eight as well as escape those now converging on them from inside.

So much for no ibor, said Lilong, then stepped back and let Oke's arm slip, leaving her with Kakutan.

"Go," she said.

Kakutan's eyes widened. "Don't—"

"Go." She turned toward the gate and Drew.

Her blade came flying and struck the pulley mechanism that held the prison gates up. The gates rolled down, iron screaming as it scratched stone, and with a deafening clang, slammed into the earth, trapping the pursuing wardens inside.

Then she turned to the eight in the entryway. But rather than attack her, all eight stood shaken, hesitant, staring. Not at her blade suspended in the air, but at her body. Lilong followed their gazes down and saw what they saw.

Yellow.

Her true complexion was visible where the warden robes allowed—face, arms, neck, feet. Somewhere during the Command of her blade, she had managed to let her concentration slip. Only for a moment, but it was enough.

Now back to a desertlander low-brown, the guards still trying to process what they were witnessing, she had to decide: fight or run. She made quick calculations: time to dispatch all eight; the amount of ibor required; alerting vigilantes and peace officers in the street; being left behind by the getaway travelwagon. Fighting did not seem favourable.

Lilong recalled her blade, clasped it, and bolted away, crashing into the street from the enclosed entryway. She looked left, right, trying to remember what direction Kubra was in.

It was then she spotted Danso, dressed in contestant attire, his hair and makeup like she'd never seen. Ugo stood behind him, along with three other desertlanders she was unfamiliar with. Danso's eyes locked onto hers with some perplexity.

Lilong? he seemed to ask.

Run, her gaze said, then she turned in the other direction and bolted.

A gong began to clang.

19

Lilong

Chugoko
Sixth Mooncycle, heist day

THE DEAFENING GONG FOLLOWED Lilong all the way back to their hide-out. Kubra had appeared from nowhere, out of the scattering crowd, and grabbed her, then suddenly the travelwagon was there and he was shoving her into it. Kakutan and Oke were already inside, warden robes shed, covered in old wrappers, tucked into the floor, blinds drawn. Lilong joined them, and together they rolled in the darkness as Biemwensé drove the travelwagon down the undulating road. She clenched her teeth as every muscle and joint, sore from iborworking, was prodded even more, the gong's continued clanging stirring up a headache, following them home like an omen.

Finally, it was quiet and they came to a stop. Kubra opened the blinds. They were back at the hut, Alaba emerging with the baby Thema in his arms to welcome them.

Once they were all standing outside, it became clear that the party was incomplete.

"Where is Ugo?" asked Alaba, at the same time Lilong asked: "Where's Danso?"

In the distance, the gong pealed.

"What happened?" Alaba started, then he saw Oke lying in the travel-wagon, dazed, semi-conscious. His lips ran out of words, eyes shining with what Lilong decided were genuine tears. He knelt at the foot of the travelwagon door and placed Thema next to her maa. Then he let his body fall over Oke, embracing maa and child, shaking with joy and relief.

Lilong was going to press the question, but Biemwensé rested a hand on her shoulder.

"Give them a moment."

After Oke had been carried into the hut, maa and daughter now under Biemwensé's care, Lilong stood outside with Alaba, Kubra, and Kakutan.

"I saw him," she was saying. "Standing in the street with some people."

"Was Ugo with him?" Alaba asked. She nodded. Alaba bit his lip.

"Think they've been caught?" asked Kakutan.

"I think not," said Kubra, pensive. "Peace officers waste no time. If they knew the yellowskin"—he turned to Lilong—"my apologies—was here, and that they had caught two people connected to you, they would've already flayed them for answers. Danso and Ugo are no warriors—they would offer this location up in a blink. So long as we are still standing, then it means they are still out there, trying to find their way here." He shook his head. "City is crawling with search parties. They must be stuck somewhere." He snapped a finger at Alaba. "Where is the easiest place to hide and the most difficult to find something?"

The two looked at one another and said, together: "Marketplace."

They started toward the travelwagon. Lilong made to follow, but Kubra put out a hand.

"Where do you think you're going?"

"Where do you think? With you, to get Danso."

Kubra shook his head. "You let us handle this one, Snakeblade. You've done your part. You can go prepare for your trip."

"There's no trip without Danso," she said. "Besides, you will need a hand. You cannot fight off all those vigilantes and peace officers alone." She gestured toward Alaba. "And you *will* be alone, because that one cannot skin a goat to save his life."

Kubra chuckled. "Maybe. But he's going because his loved one is in danger, and that is reason enough. I know you care for Danso and want him to be safe, but you have been recognised once today, and we cannot risk another sighting." He pointed to himself and to Alaba, who had taken up the driving seat of the travelwagon. "We two are the only ones that haven't so far been associated with the prison in any way."

Lilong's argument got stuck in her throat. She hated that he was right.

Kubra turned to leave, then stopped for a moment to say: "If you must know, we do not intend to fight. Sometimes, invisibility and stealth, the ability to be nothing, to be forgotten, to blend into the landscape, will get you what fighting cannot. Remember that, Snakeblade."

Oke regained full consciousness within an hour of Alaba and Kubra leaving. She spent another hour holding Thema close to her chest and weeping, then yet another wolfing down copious amounts of food and beverages. Soon, she was aglow, completely replenished. A cold rag bath later, prison stenches banished, she emerged a new woman.

Lilong did not recognise her at first, when Oke came up from the tent to join her at the edge of the thicket, under the dim glow of twilight. She watched Oke approach, noted how she suddenly looked every bit the Speaker's daughter she was. She carried herself with the same measured grace as Alaba did.

She stopped a distance from Lilong. The two women regarded each other.

"You really are his daughter," said Oke. "You look just like him."

Her inflection was remarkably flat, the mainland-ness of her tongue polished away. Lilong considered this dubious. So much of Oke's demeanour was of something wiped clean, an evident *nothingness* where there should have been, well, a *thingness*.

People who wiped themselves this clean always had something to hide.

"I want to thank you." Oke sat on the ground, maintaining the distance between them. "They say you are the reason I'm here." She put a hand to her chest. "Consider this a debt owed."

"What were you doing with my daa?"

Lilong had been wanting to ask this question for so long that it had built up steam in her chest. Seeing Oke sitting there, all languid-like, while chaos raged through her own life—it simply burst out of its own accord.

Oke chuckled. "Ah, I see. Jaoudou wasn't wrong about your patience."

"*Don't you say his name*," Lilong said, closing the distance between them. "Don't you *ever*."

Oke held her hands above her head. "Okay, okay. I won't say it."

"You are lucky you have that baby," said Lilong.

"Pardon?"

"You are lucky you have that baby," Lilong repeated. "That you have loved ones, and that the Gaddos want you alive. Otherwise, Great Winds help me, the moment you stepped out of that tent, I would have put a blade through you."

"Ah." The other woman nodded. Silence fell between them.

Oke chuckled.

"You think this is *funny*?" Lilong snapped. "Our people—*my* people— are out there, people who put their lives in peril for *you* to be here. And all you do is laugh? Is this how indifferent and spiritless you were with my daa? Is this how you got him attacked?"

Oke remained smiling.

"You know," she said. "He said you do that often."

"Do *what*?"

"Threaten. Called you a *raging tempest*. But he said despite all your rages, you still harbour more love than hate in your heart, and that one needs to be patient when it comes to you."

Lilong fought the urge to Command her blade into this woman's chest. Who did she think she was, quoting her daa's words? How dare she act like some sage after everything she'd caused? The audacity!

Oke, watching every emotion play out on Lilong's face, shifted so they faced each other.

"I understand you have some…feelings toward me," said Oke. "And I understand the risks everyone—you, your daa, *everyone*—has taken to bring us to this point. But if you think I have not made sacrifices myself, that I do not understand the gravity of what we are fighting, *who* we are fighting, you are mistaken."

Lilong shifted her weight. *Fair enough.* The woman had seen her share of suffering and sacrifice. But she had still not answered the question.

"What were you two *doing*?" she pressed.

"He didn't tell you?"

"How could he? He came back home unconscious."

Oke looked pensive, sad. "Is he...alive?"

There was tenderness in her voice, like she genuinely cared. No one had spoken to Lilong about her daa this way in a long time.

"He hadn't awoken when I left," said Lilong. "That was two seasons ago." She rolled her shoulders, uneasy. "So...I don't know. Not until I get home."

Oke sighed. "I'm...I'm so sorry." She rose and began pacing. "I really thought we were going to change everything, you know? We had a plan, a *good* plan. But now, all this work, only for us to end up defeated."

"What work were you doing?" asked Lilong. "Where were you even going when you got captured?"

Oke stopped pacing. "You know where I was going, Lilong."

Impossible. Her daa would never.

"Yes, he knew the risks associated with revealing your people's secrets," Oke said, leap-frogging Lilong's thoughts. "But he told me anyway, because he trusted me, because he believed in what we were trying to achieve."

This woman is a crook, Lilong decided. There was no way her daa had told her how to find and cross the Forest of the Mist. Perhaps this was simply a ruse to get her to reveal the secrets herself.

Oke watched her with a sad expression.

"He said if I ever sensed something amiss, or felt we were being hunted, then I needed to follow the Lonely Roads East, find the Forest of the Mist, go through it, and head for the isthmus." She lowered her voice. "He gave me all the directions, taught me how to find the tree patterns in the mist. How to find your secret entrance."

Lilong grew cold. *No, no.* No one knew about the tree patterns. No one knew there was a secret entrance.

This was not the kind of information that could be faked.

She watched Oke pace some more. A simple, regal woman. Broken, but not quite beaten. What was it about her that had entranced her daa so much as to give this information?

Then it came to her: This woman was just like Danso. And just like Lilong had been entranced, swayed, irrevocably altered by one Bassai rebel, one stubborn idealist, so had her daa.

Oke was still speaking. "He said once I had crossed, I must give myself over to the sentries."

The sentries. Another thing that no outsider knew about. No outsider who lived to tell the tale, that is.

"But he said not to talk to the Abenai Elders, not to talk to anyone. He said I must only pass everything I know on to . . ." She trailed off.

"Who?"

"*You*, Lilong. He wanted me to pass it on only to *you*."

Inside Lilong's head, it felt like bubbling soup—scrambled, melting. *What is this? What is happening?*

"Tell me," was all she could say.

Oke inclined her head. Then, without warning, her eyes turned grey.

It happened fast, but Lilong had witnessed her daa's grey iborworking for so long that her heart did not miss a beat. When the fires in the hideout began to dance, even in the absence of wind, Lilong knew exactly what it was. The flames dimmed, so low that all visibility was snuffed out in an instant. All they were left with was the light of the blue moon, Ashu. It slanted over the faces of the two women, cloaking them like beasts lurking in the forest's shadows.

"He taught me how to do that, your daa," said Oke. "Gave me a few pieces even though I didn't ask, even though I never wanted to touch them after I realised how important they were to your people."

Lilong leaned forward, trying to see where Oke's stones were. The woman, understanding what was happening, pulled up her wrappers. In the side of her body was an ugly, ungainly stitch.

"Inside me," she said, answering the unasked question. "Preserved it there in case I was captured. But I was pregnant when they took me, see? So I didn't use it because I wasn't sure how it would affect the baby. Then they took her, and I didn't have that fight in me anymore, didn't want to die without seeing her again. So I've been waiting for the right time, the right reason, to use it again."

The flames in the hideout returned to full burn as quickly as they had dimmed. Oke's eyes were back to normal.

"Your daa believed that this power in the hands of everyday people, people who wanted good for the world, was better than in the hands of a few. That was why he taught me and gave me the stone-bone. That was why he was going to give me your Diwi heirloom." She paused. "That was why he told me about Risisi."

Something about that name tickled a memory in Lilong's brain.

"Risisi, like the children's folktale?"

Oke shook her head. "Oh, Lilong. Risisi is no folktale." She leaned in. "I will tell you a story, and soon, you will learn that your leaders and my leaders are no different after all."

Lilong did not look at Oke when she spoke. She did not want to hear the tale the woman was telling.

Not the tale of a buried city with a surviving ibor deposit, located somewhere on the seventh, uninhabited island of Ofen. Not the tale of a secret society of select Elders in the Abenai League who knew this location. Not the tale of her daa, a member of the league, and also of this secret society.

She did not want to hear why her daa, watching the Great Waters, Great Winds, and Great Lands bite at the seven islands, tried to convince the Elders to lead the Ihinyon off the islands before they sank into the Neverending Sea. When that didn't work, he turned to his secret society within the Abenai: What if they excavated Risisi and benefited of its treasures? What if they had so much ibor that they could place a few pieces in honest and capable hands on the continent, aid them in their quest to combat the empire's power? If they succeeded, the Ihinyon could always find goodwill there if their islands were swallowed.

She did not want to hear why, when the secret society refused, Jaoudou opted to head out on his own, adamant to prove that ibor, if placed in the hands of the right people, could be useful in building a future for the Ihinyon and the rest of Oon. She did not want to hear how he met Oke in the desertlands while seeking those who had escaped the mainland's clutches, who had no designs on power, who were only interested in making things better for all of Oon.

She did not want to hear of his plans to visit this buried city of Risisi and furnish Oke with enough ibor from there to redistribute to allied desertlanders and mainlanders. She did not want to hear how he decided to hand her the Diwi as a show of faith, and how that failed because, unknown to them both, Oke was being tracked. How he was inadvertently attacked at the Weary Sojourner, or the rest of the story that she · was already familiar with: being discovered by an Ihinyon scout and whisked back to Namge before he gave in to his injuries.

All she kept thinking, while Oke spoke, was: *Why?*

Why could he not have confided in her, asked for her help? *Why did he think I couldn't help him?* Why did he believe she would have objected? (She would have, but he should have at least tried.)

And most importantly: Why did he want to be a hero, a saviour? *Why would you try to save the world, at the expense of yourself?*

These weren't questions Lilong wanted answers to. Not anymore. If he was still alive when she returned, she would get her answers. The problem, now, was that everything she knew and believed was a lie.

She had been told fabled legends, growing up. The seven islands were filled with tales of warriors and their larger-than-life feats: the one who dove into the sea in search of jewels and fought monsters of the deep along the way; the blind warrior who was blessed by the Great Waters to command the Neverending Seas and still its monster waves; the one-armed sage who ventured outside the archipelago and became the first scout to interact with the desertlands.

The tale of Risisi was only one of such, so how could it be true? How could the source of ibor be a city buried in a cave in Ofen? If that existed, then why had her family invested itself in protecting an inert stone-bone for so long? Was it all a ruse to sell the story of dwindling ibor supply, to uphold the lie that it was the Great Waters who supplied the stone-bone?

Had she abandoned all she knew to chase a family heirloom that was a decoy, an honour that was a falsity, a duty that was not real?

Had she given her whole life for a lie?

·◦────ꞏꞏꞏ──────ꞏꞏꞏ────◦·

Night had fallen proper when Oke was done talking. The little sister moon stood above them, as dim as their comportment.

"Why are you telling me this now?" Lilong asked.

"You asked," said Oke, quietly. "And he wanted me to."

Lilong shook her head. "What do you want me to do?"

"I don't know," said Oke. "What *he* would have wanted you to do, perhaps."

"Which is?"

Oke shrugged. "I was trying to save my people, and he was trying to save yours." She paused. "Perhaps, with your help, we can finish what he started."

Lilong cast the woman a sidelong glance. "Excuse me?"

"I can come east with you—"

Lilong scoffed. "Over my dead body."

Silence sat between them.

"I was going east when I was captured," said Oke. "I simply want to finish that journey."

"You may go wherever you like," said Lilong. "But you will not be going east. Not if I am walking those same roads. My daa may have been lenient with our secrets, but I can assure you I am not."

Oke let it lie for a moment before she said: "Okay. I hear you. But, I want you to know—I intend to go east anyway."

"I see," said Lilong. "So, what, you will leave your baby behind to go on a treacherous journey to a mysterious forest you may or may not find?" Lilong chuckled dryly. "The sentries will slice you up before you even reach the isthmus."

"I will take Thema with me. And I have the right words to say to the sentries."

"Good luck, then," said Lilong. "If your partners agree."

Lilong turned around to face the bush, the conversation ended. But Oke had one more thing to say.

"If we travel together," she said, "I was hoping to take the time to help you understand the choices your daa made, why he thought it was safer to keep you and the rest of his family away from it all." She leaned in closer. "I know it can be disorienting, learning that the world is not what you thought it was. I felt that, too, when I first read the Manic Emperor's codex, when I first learned ibor was real. I couldn't trust what my eyes saw, what my ears heard. Then I met your daa, and he taught me how to trust again, how to believe in others, in the possibility of good. It's why I know that regardless of all you've said today, you believe in good too. That's why you worked with Alaba and the Gaddos to get me out. A warrior like you—it was not just about the payment. It was duty. Because you believe in people too, just like him."

Lilong hated this woman. She was Danso all over again, her daa all over again. Telling her things she did not want to hear.

"Give it some thought," said Oke, turning back to the hut.

There was a sound in the bushes. Before they could make sense of it, the travelwagon came barreling through the thicket and into the hideout, Alaba in the driving seat. He brought the kwagas to an abrupt halt, so that the travelwagon jerked forward, and through the destroyed, open door, a body fell out.

It was Danso, covered in blood.

20

Danso

Chugoko
Sixth Mooncycle, heist day

NIGHTFALL WAS A BLANKET of desert purple over Chugoko. In the streets, vigilante numbers increased, as did the intensity of the alert gong, which was still going. Peace officers had joined in the search for the prison escapees, extending into crannies, nooks, and corridors, swarming every corner of the city with torches and leopards.

In the marketplace, Danso and Ugo moved from empty stall to empty stall, seeking shadows, ducking behind any awning or facade that offered sufficient cover. The lights and sounds of their pursuers followed. They were now lost in the market's maze with no way to tell their exact location, but at least they were a safe distance away. For now.

Beneath a storefront counter, Danso tucked his legs into himself. Ugo, next to him, counted the numbers until they were to leave this place and locate another empty stall. He leaned an ear toward the lights, eyes darting, alert. He was a far cry from the drunk, clumsy man Danso had met on that first day.

"I want to thank you," said Danso. "For saving me—twice, now?"

Ugo only offered a quick glance. "Mmm-hm." He peered at the lights in the distance, his mind far away.

"You're not scared," said Danso.

Ugo turned. "Hmm?"

"Throughout everything—from the peace officers to the parade to the Chief Warden to right now. You've been so…bold. Tell me: Who are you, really?"

Ugo regarded Danso quizzically. "What do you mean?"

"I mean, how is a Bassai man out here in the desertlands, living freely among desertlanders? A Bassai man who is clearly not a merchant or Idu noble with border crossing rights?" *A Bassai man who only seems graceless and uncoordinated*, Danso wanted to say, *but is in truth equipped and prepared.*

Ugo sniffed and exhaled. "You ever heard of *journeyman?*"

"The children's rhyme? *Journeyman, journeyman, bring me bread*—that one?"

"Mmm-hm."

"Definitely. When I was growing up, the children in the outer wards…" Danso drifted off, surprise taking over his tone. "No…"

"Mmm-hm."

"*You're* journeyman?"

Ugo shrugged.

"How? You're not even—"

"Old?" Ugo shrugged again. "I was about thirty seasons when I crossed. So, more like *journeyboy.* Maybe those who made the song thought *man* sounded better. Or maybe they just wanted to convince themselves that their false tale was really true."

Danso remembered the insistence of the jalis, when he'd asked, that no Emuru had ever crossed the Soke moats. Back then, he hadn't yet grown into arguing with scholars, being fairly new to the university. But he'd always known that the street songs he'd grown up hearing in the marketplaces could not all be myth.

"So you're really the first person to beat the Bassai system." Danso chuckled. "I'm hiding in the market with a legend."

"Don't worry," Ugo replied. "You and Oke can keep your crowns. The fewer people know the truth about me, the better."

He was probably right. Before meeting the Gaddos, Danso had believed *he* was the first Bassai to cross the moats and live to tell the tale. After learning about Oke, and now Ugo, he was sure there had been many more before them, just unnamed. The jalis' saying was right: *No act of resistance is new under the moons.*

He wished those who had gone before could've done more with their newfound freedoms. Brought back truth and liberty and promise and hope to those caught in Bassa's web. Instead, they had all just disappeared, much like Lilong was asking him to disappear with her now.

No matter. Now that he'd joined their ranks, moons willing, he would change that.

The sounds of pursuit drew nearer. Ugo counted down, and they hustled to another stall and settled in again, listening. Danso took the time to recite the rhyme to himself:

Journeyman, journeyman, bring me bread.
Baker first, thief at last, away with his head.
In the Dome he pinched the pearls that hung from the emperor's neck.
He took the jewels, scaled the mounts, and lived in the sand forever.

"Did you really do it?" asked Danso. "Steal the emperor's necklace?"

Ugo did not answer, but Danso did not need to press. If he truly was the journeyman the rhyme spoke of, then whether he truly stole the necklace was pointless. This was Bassa, after all. He'd have only needed to step on the wrong Idu noble's foot to get his name engraved in the minds of generations for the wrong reasons.

Either way, Ugo's escape was a win. Danso had always assumed *lived in the sand forever* meant he'd been caught, killed, and buried beneath the sand, a dishonourable end for any Bassai. But this was just one more way for Bassa to obfuscate the truth in plain sight.

Thank moons for children's rhymes. Simple as they were, there was some truth to them after all.

"Let me guess," said Danso. "You didn't really scale the mountains."

Ugo chuckled. "Went under, just like you. It wasn't the Gaddos running those channels back then, though."

"Did you have to work it off? Like us?"

Ugo nodded. "Price was even steeper back then. That's how I got to travel the Savanna Belt—east, west, up and down the trading route.

Picked up the accents, the fashions, the cultures. I'm not a walking trove of desertland secrets by choice."

You and me both, thought Danso. Nothing about this situation was by choice. It hadn't been his choice to attend the university or become a scholar. It hadn't been his choice to leave Bassa the way he did, to cross the moats the way he had. It hadn't been his choice to dance for desert-landers, to raid a prison, to journey eastward.

All of this was circumstance being foisted upon him. And he was tired of circumstance.

Ugo was still talking. "After paying my debt in full, I've tried not to leave Chugoko. Everyone in my quarter knows me, treats me like their own. It's safer here than out in the wilds."

If by *like their own*, he meant they did not afford him the respect they did to other Bassai—like at the public house, when they had him sit outside with the desertland commoners—Danso wasn't sure that was a good thing.

"But your safety is still tenuous," Danso said. "That's why you're always alert, prepared, wary." He understood it now. "That's why you're with Alaba. For the Gaddos' protection."

Ugo did not answer, did not even look at Danso, which was all he needed to know that though unspoken, this was clearly not a secret.

"I get it," said Danso with a sigh. "Seek safety wherever you can find it, right? That's what I'm trying to do now too. Travel east to hide in the islands' mists." He made a click in the back of his throat. "But that's not really freedom either, is it? Someone else's power covers you anyway; here or there, it's the same. Always someone else's power, never yours."

He shook his head, looked long into the night, wistful. "Maybe, just *maybe*, people like you and I—what we need is not safety. Maybe what we need is *power*. It's the only surety for safety and the only thing that guarantees true freedom."

Ugo had not spoken a word since, but now he turned to Danso and stared at him like he was looking at someone different.

"You know it's true," Danso said, unsure if he was trying to convince the man before him, or himself. "Look at how Alaba and Oke move through the world. Look at the Gaddos. Look at this heist. Look where we are right now, hiding! If we had some power of our own, whatever that looked like…"

The sounds of their pursuers neared again. Ugo gave Danso one last perplexed glance, then darted across the stalls. Danso followed. Soon, they had found another safe stall.

But the sounds of searching did not relent. They intensified, closing in around them, so that all the previous joviality and introspection disappeared from the two men's dispositions. Their nerves stretched taut, bodies brimming with agitation.

"We can't do this all night," said Danso. "We need to find a way back to the hideout."

"Only the mainways lead to the outskirts," said Ugo. "We can take our chances with the peace officers, or we can take our chances with the night predators in the bushroads."

Danso peered at the advancing lights. "You think the others know we're still out here?"

"Of course. Lilong saw us."

"Yes, but do you think they *care*?"

Ugo glared at him, offended. "You think they'll leave me—us—here?" He looked back at the lights. He seemed so small in that moment.

"Oke and Alaba and Thema are probably together right now," Ugo said, quieter. "Happy. Free."

Danso knew what he meant. Lilong wouldn't leave him out here either, would she? But again, perhaps he was a burden, slowing her down. Perhaps she might feel more relief than sadness. Perhaps she might be quick to move on, take the payment from the Gaddos and go east without him.

The lights advanced farther.

"We can't keep going deeper inside. We'll become trapped in this market." Ugo squatted on his haunches, deep in thought.

"We're going to have to brave the mainway, aren't we?" said Danso.

Moments later, they were crawling along the edges of the market, parallel to the mainway, following it eastward as much as they could tell from the moons' positions overhead. It helped that they moved in the dark, without lights, and among stalls. It did not help that the streets were still being heavily patrolled and leopards had a great sense of smell.

Soon, the marketplace came to an end. It was time to join the mainway.

"Just pretend the usual," said Ugo.

"Sahelians," said Danso in understanding, and they joined the wide street.

They were halted and harassed by multiple vigilante parties with faces warped by snarls, but were soon let go after being presumed to be visitors and to not be familiar with the city's language or customs. They managed to move east of the city proper in this way, raising eyebrows but opening no eyes.

Then they came upon a peace officer search party. Even before halting them both, the peace officers had already begun to move in their direction.

"Stay calm," Ugo whispered.

But there was no point. Because as soon as the light of a nearby torch fell on the face of the mouthpiece, Danso knew it was over. The mouthpiece, a youthful man, was squinting in a way that told Danso that he was the smart kind. A beard and some extra hair did not fool this one. He promptly saw beyond the disguise and recognised the jali behind it.

"Dehje," the mouthpiece said.

"Run," said Danso, and pushed Ugo into a side corridor.

Shouts rang from the party. A shrill whistle went off. Hooves followed, then faded away, followed by heavy footfalls. A spear—the short, fast ikiwa—whizzed behind them, thunked into something wooden. Another ikiwa grazed a wall. A third missed Danso's ear, disappeared into the darkness. They kept running blind, crashing into obstacles, righting themselves, going left, right, left, stumbling into backyards, ducking under clotheslines, scaling fences, hedges, animal pens.

Ashu, Danso prayed, panting. *Help! I don't want to die!*

The gong clanged in the distance. Shrill whistles pierced the night air, alerting more search parties of the chase. The footfalls of those in pursuit were louder now, doubled in number.

Then, as if the hen god had been listening, there was light at the end of their corridor, no forces in sight. *An exit!* Danso headed for it.

"Wait—" Ugo started, but didn't finish, as they burst into a wide street—

—into the path of a barreling travelwagon.

The driver pulled the reins, and the kwagas dug in their heels. The travelwagon came to a halt in a cloud of dust, barely a foot away from Danso, who had frozen in the middle of the street.

The driver leaned over the side. It was Alaba.

"Get in!" he screamed.

Danso needed no second invitation. He pitched forward, as did Ugo. The door to the travelwagon opened, and Kubra, hoisting a torch, jumped down, urging them forward.

A spear whizzed out of the corridor and shattered the backrest beside Alaba.

"In, in, in!" Kubra waved frantically.

Danso plunged headfirst into the travelwagon. Ugo fell atop him. Another spear shattered the side of the vehicle, the tip stopping only a hair's breadth from Ugo's eye. Kubra jumped in after them and attempted to shut the door, but the spear held the door open.

Out of the corridor burst a motley group of vigilantes and peace officers.

"Go, go, go!" yelled Kubra.

Alaba goaded the kwagas. They shrieked, barking into the night, then dropped their heads and charged off. Kubra looked out the open door, back at the peace officers in the dust. He turned to Danso, laughing manically.

"Almost!" He wiped his brow and sheathed his curved sword. "Look at us thinking we won't find—"

There was a sound like a whip, the snapping of bone, the squelch of flesh. Blood spattered Danso's face and chest.

Kubra glanced at his chest. The blade of an ikiwa sat in his chest bone, blood dripping from its tip onto the floor.

"Oh," said Kubra, and fell out of the travelwagon.

Danso sat dazed, blood dripping into his eyes and lips, unable to process the empty space before him where Kubra had just been. He did not gather himself enough to move, not even when another ikiwa, and then another, whizzed past the open door. It was Ugo, yet again, who leaned over and pulled him away.

"We have to—" Danso was saying. "Tell Alaba. To stop. We must go back."

"He's gone." Ugo bowed his head. "He's gone."

"We must go back," Danso repeated. "We must go back."

He shrugged off Ugo's pull on his wrappers and leaned out to see Kubra. If he was dead, then Danso wanted to pay witness to his last moments. Kubra deserved that, to not die such an ordinary death, like a fowl. His death meant something, and Danso wanted to hold his eyes and let him know it. He wanted to memorise the face of the peace officer who had thrown the spear, to hold it in anger and spite, to use it as fuel.

But when Danso looked, all he saw was dust.

21

Lilong

Chugoko
Sixth Mooncycle, heist day

"Moons," said Oke.

"It's not my blood," said Danso.

Alaba jumped down from the driving seat, dejected. Ugo emerged from the travelwagon, just as shaken. Oke, spotting them, rushed into both their arms, and they held each other tight and wept silently—for what was lost, for what was found. It felt private, so Lilong turned away.

"Kubra," she said, noting the gaping absence.

Danso was shuddering, face set with pain.

"We were recognised," he said. "Peace officers. Threw a spear."

He looked as shaken as he'd been when he'd lost his own daa. Lilong found it surprising, seeing as he didn't even know the man that well. She who had worked with Kubra felt a small pang of sadness. He hadn't been the most amiable, but he was a solid general and a generally decent person. The Gaddo Company would miss him, as would she.

For Danso, though, this was about something else.

Lilong wanted to ask, but Kakutan came out then, holding the baby Thema, Biemwensé in tow. Oke retrieved the child, and the three lovers gathered around, sniffing together, laugh-crying with their baby. Biemwensé motioned for the others to give them space, before glancing at the blood in Danso's hair, beard, clothes.

"Kubra?" she asked, and Danso nodded. She and Kakutan shook their heads.

"Better him than you," said Biemwensé.

It sounded cruel, but it was true. They had all thought it. But Danso retained a deeply twisted expression. Determined. *Vengeful.*

He turned his back on them and went into the hut. After the reunifications were over, Alaba ushered everyone else to follow suit.

"I'm afraid every moment longer we stay here is a danger," Alaba announced, once they were gathered. "Kubra will already have been recognised as a Gaddo employee as we speak. Danso has been recognised, Lilong has been spotted. It's only a matter of time before one of those tracks leads here."

"So what now?" asked Kakutan.

"We clear this location, go our separate ways."

"Excuse me?" Lilong interjected. "What about my payment?"

"I was coming to that," said Alaba. "Listen, I will not lie to you. After what has happened here, my parents will go into hiding. They will not be seen for a long time, not even by me, not to talk about you. So—" He held up a hand as Lilong made to protest. "*So*, I will do my best to get you all the resources you need to make your trip. But we must all leave this location, *right now*."

"And go where?" asked Biemwensé. "We have nowhere to go."

"Then tell me where you want to go," said Alaba, "and I will get you there."

The two Whudan women looked at one another, the answer already decided.

"What about us?" asked Danso.

"I know you were promised food, water, transport," said Alaba. "I can offer you the rest of the supplies this hideout has to offer—it remains a sizeable amount. There is good camping material here too, strong. Out there are two travelwagons, mine included, even though it's battered. You may take your pick for transport."

"I want what I was promised," said Lilong, infuriated.

"And I understand," said Alaba. He pointed westward. "The alternative is we somehow make our way back to Chabo without being captured, hope peace officers don't trace us there, and wait for my parents to return from hiding so you can get your due." He pointed east. "Or, you can begin your journey tonight, right here and now."

Lilong was shaking her head. *This cannot be happening.*

"And what about her?" she asked, pointing to Oke.

Alaba frowned. "What about her?"

Oke was waving Lilong down, but she paid no attention.

"She wants to come east with us," said Lilong. "I don't assume those supplies will be sufficient for us all?"

Alaba turned to Oke. "You *what?*"

After that, the rest of them left the trio of lovers and their baby in the hut, as anger and consternation swelled inside. Danso changed clothes, and Lilong, with Kakutan's help, gathered all the remaining supplies and loaded the getaway travelwagon with it, pretending not to hear the forced whispers and occasional bursts of frustration.

Either way, it was evident to all what was happening: Oke was doubling down on going east with Lilong's party and taking Thema with her. Ugo, after trying unsuccessfully to play mediator between her and Alaba, had given in and decided to join Oke on this quest. Alaba, furious, walked out on them both, to the edge of the thicket to clear his head.

Once the supplies were loaded, the Whudan women waited for instructions on how they would proceed with heading back to Bassa. Lilong joined them as they packed.

"Thank you," Lilong said to the women. "For everything. You both are the reason we are still alive, in many ways. I wish you luck finding what you are looking for."

"Same here," said Biemwensé. "Go safe."

"Take care of that one for us, will you?" Kakutan angled her head in Danso's direction. "He will be crawling his way through this world for a while."

"Those ones," said Biemwensé, indicating Oke and Ugo, who stood with the baby Thema, arguing softly while waiting for Alaba's return. "May I ask that you let them come along if they decide to?"

Lilong shook her head. "I wish I could. But it is not my decision." It was her daa's, the sentries', the league's. If they wanted to go east, fine, but it would not be under her banner.

Later, Lilong sat near the dying fire, rolling in her hand the pouch of artifacts she'd collected for her brother Kyauta—hopefully, he'd still be there when she returned. She thought about Biemwensé's plea, likely born of the little time she'd spent with the baby. She thought of the story Oke had told her, of her daa's own words—which Oke could have made up, but she knew her daa well enough to know that Oke didn't have to.

I will go to Risisi and bring you ibor, before it's too late. These were his last words to Oke before their fateful meeting at the Weary Sojourner.

Lilong had begun to wonder if he'd gone to Ofen and found the buried city before arranging the failed meeting with Oke, or if he'd planned to go after handing her the Diwi. If he was alive and had now recovered, would he still insist on going? She envisioned him escaping the league's watchful eye, leaving his family behind yet again, chartering a dhow to the uninhabited seventh island. Working grey ibor on the Neverending Sea, beaching at Ofen unsighted.

None of this was impossible, though success depended on a series of slim chances. Knowing her daa, though, that wouldn't deter him. Lilong thought Oke was a bit like him in that way: adamant, hopeful, foolhardy. After all, she'd recklessly plunged into the savanna wilds, alone and pregnant, trying to locate the Forest of the Mist.

Still, the big question was yet to be answered: *Is Risisi real?*

Or, the bigger one: *If we go to Ofen, what will we find there?*

An underground city of ancient stone people and forgotten tales? Buried mountains of whole, pure, untouched ibor? This was once an unbelievable folk tale, still just as unbelievable now. But other questions raised by Oke's tale were not so easy to dismiss. What about the secret society within the Abenai League? What about Jaoudou travelling the desertlands to hand the Diwi over to a stranger? Between Oke, Jaoudou, and the Abenai League, who was the liar here? It couldn't be all of them, could it?

Something had to be true.

The part of Jaoudou's statement that clung to Lilong was: *Before it's too late.* What was going to happen to ibor? Or to Risisi? The stone-bone supply was already dwindling in the islands, and the Neverending Sea drew closer every day. Lilong agreed that ibor and the islands had a role to play in the future of the continent. This would eventually be her burden too. How could the tale of Risisi help?

Lilong poked at the fire with a stick, deep in contemplation.

Her daa had been so invested in this buried city, to the point of recruiting a foreigner into his plans. Maybe he was onto something after all. Maybe the children's folktale contained more truth than she believed.

Maybe she hadn't quite dedicated her whole life to a lie just yet.

She met Oke outside the hut.

"If you wish to come east," Lilong said, "if you wish to finish what he started, you will do as I say, and you will tell me everything you know." She paused. "The child and her care will be your problem, not mine. And whatever happens with you and the sentries, you are on your own. You are not with me."

Oke smiled a wry smile. It was not *yes*, but it was not *no* either, which was fine. Because Lilong knew that if something happened to the islands or their ibor and she had done nothing to stop it, she would never forgive herself, league warrior or not.

Alaba finally returned and went straight to the Whudan women. He had a package for them, with a message and a code of words. He gave them directions for a meeting with a contact in the outskirts of Chugoko, someone who would help connect them with a team that would get them back behind the Soke Pass. The contents of the package would let the team know they were sent by Alaba.

"You are not coming along," said Kakutan, not a question.

"No," he said, sad. "I'm going east."

Everyone turned toward him. He lifted his head, shuffled over to Oke and Ugo.

"I have lost you once," he said. "I will not lose you again."

The family formed a huddle. Lilong ground her teeth, worrying about supplies. One more body on such a long journey was a weight. But the more she thought about it, the more she decided it was perhaps best to have strength in numbers, as her expedition to Bassa had taught her. All three new companions, minus the child, were useful in some way. Plus, the thought of travelling alone with Danso suddenly wasn't so appealing.

Both travelwagons were soon packed, kwagas checked. Alaba drove, while Ugo, Oke, and the baby joined Lilong and Danso inside. The Whudan women took the battered travelwagon.

Before they rolled away in opposite directions, Kakutan set flames to the thatch of the hut.

Ash and smoke, vestiges of this destruction, were all Lilong could see for a distance. She caught Oke staring too, and realised that this must be similar to the last thing she saw before heading east last time. Lilong wondered whether Jaoudou had looked up into the sky too, seen ash and smoke. She wondered if he was still alive.

Chugoko and its gong and smoke faded, became one with the rear horizon, and then the party was into the desert wilds.

The Written Codex of Danso DaaHabba, First Jali of Bassa to Journey over the Soke Borders: Hereafter lie his personal accounts of travels and travails through the desertlands, from the western vagabond colony of Chabo, to the fabled eastern Forest of the Mist.

The Eighth Account: *The Cautionary Tale of the Stone City of Risisi*, as recounted by Oke, daughter of Abuso, Speaker of the Upper Council of Bassa; as told to her by Elder Warrior Jaoudou of Namge and the Abenai League.

LISTEN, THEN, CHILDREN OF the seven islands, for I am going to tell you of a city once prosperous in this archipelago.

Long, long ago, after the sister moons took to the sky, there was an ancient city, called Risisi. It was named for the stones upon which the city was built, and was ruled by leaders long forgotten, swallowed up by the Great Forces as with all trace of this city itself. But it is said that once, Risisi was self-preserving. Its markets were filled with life and noise, its fields green and abundant. This ancient city was known for its cloth, its iron, its brass. But it also had something no one else—not even the other islands—had: *ibor*.

Risisi traded with the peoples of its sister-islands and welcomed emissaries of their governments. It offered all its products and secrets for sale and barter. Everything except for ibor. It was rumoured that the city contained within it a large deposit of ibor buried beneath one of its stone mountains, from which they mined the mineral, discovered its powers, and used of it to build the city and its riches.

But one day, its voices became still. No hands tilled its fields, worked its iron, wove its cloth. No lips spoke its name, and no feet graced its halls. The city died, as the old people say, and became lost forever. All that is left of it today is this warning tale of a once-prosperous city fallen, and how it came to be so.

In a dry, dry land far beyond the archipelago, there lived people who sought to bring all the great knowledge of the world together, so that anyone who wished to learn about everything touched by land and sky and water could have one place to do so. They decided to traverse the continent and collect such knowledge. Their expeditions led them to the archipelago, and for a lack of means to travel on the Neverending Sea, they waited.

Soon, word came to the people of the archipelago of a group waiting to gain passage into their islands. They sent word to Risisi, who provided them with dhows, commandeered by a number of White and Grey Iborworkers—those who had learned to speak to the Great Winds and Great Waters, tame the violent waves of the Neverending Sea, thereby making island-to-island transport possible. The Iborworkers took a party out to meet these strangers in the place we now know as the Forest of the Mists. There, they found the visitors not to be an army as initially thought, but expeditionists.

So they welcomed the party and took them into the islands on their dhows, with one condition: They could go anywhere and learn anything they wished, but they could not go to Risisi.

The leaders of the archipelago islands showed the visitors their cities, their architecture, their technology, and the visitors marvelled and recorded what they saw, swearing to take the good news of the islands back to their people.

But in time, the visitors yearned to learn about Risisi, about the deposit of ibor that resided there. Once again, they begged to visit. Risisi's leaders were against it, but were swayed by the arguments of the leaders from the other islands, who believed that sharing their knowledge would lead to a better understanding of them by others, and therefore a better world.

There is much to do to educate the people out there of our ways, they said. *They may learn about us as we do of them, and we may become a better people for it.*

The leaders of Risisi finally agreed, but on one condition: The visitors could learn everything they needed about Risisi, but were to learn nothing of ibor itself, or its use.

"The three Great Forces that sustain this world—wind, dirt, sea—have handed this power down to us," said the leaders of Risisi. "A power so great must never be shared, in knowledge or stone, without their granting it. It must be protected from hands that cannot be trusted. It will be better for such a power to be buried for all time than for it to fall into the wrong hands."

When the foreigners visited Risisi, they marvelled. They itched to know how Risisi achieved its grandiose feats of development. How did they build walls so high? Carts that moved on their own? Seavessels that succumbed to neither quiet nor monster tide, but sailed even without wind? The answer to all of this, of course, was ibor, but the foreigners were not permitted to learn about its ways.

But as itches are wont to do, the desire to scratch became overwhelming, and despite their promises, the visitors eventually succumbed to their bodily whims.

One night, when no one was watching, they slipped away and went seeking for themselves. After searching for a long time, they stumbled upon the large cave, and within the cave, discovered the source of the secret mineral. Every kind and colour and size present—grey, white, amber, red. They found stories written into the walls of the cave, of the ancestors who had discovered this mineral. They could not interpret what was written, but they assumed them to be stories, warnings, directions, educating the people on how to employ this mineral for their needs.

The visitors drew images, took notes, excited to return to their people with information about this enthralling mineral.

But come morning, there was wailing. The leaders of Risisi, upon discovering what the visitors had done, cried out: "You have killed us! You have angered the forces of this world, and for this, we will all pay."

And pay they did. Before the day was ended, all three Great Forces colluded to punish them in multiple plagues.

First came the Plague of Beasts. The grounds rumbled, uprooting everything from their foundations. Beasts from the annals of myth and history, small and large and long asleep, arose from their depths, ibor tugging at their consciousnesses, a clarion call to Risisi. They trudged toward the city, rampaging and ravaging all they found in their way.

But even these beasts were not spared by the Plague of Fires and Dirt. Out of the mountains burst a rain of fire and clouds of ash. All came down on the city of Risisi with vengeance, until everything they touched turned to ash, and then to stone.

In their wake came the Plague of Wind and Water, a storm weaving through the land. Whatever was left that had not already turned into ash and stone was washed or swept away, and whatever remained was buried beneath mountains of debris. The great city of Risisi, which was once the centre of all, became the centre of nothing.

To this day, no trace of the buried Risisi has been found: not its people, not the visitors, not its knowledge. Many have searched, but have discovered neither form nor sound nor movement that leads them to the leftovers of the city. Whatever was left that the plagues didn't touch crumbled, every bush grew into forest, and every stone person melded with the mountains. This is why we call the stone-faces—those carved by our ancestors into rocks all over the seven islands—this is why we call them *risisi*. They carved those faces to remind us of what happens when we interfere with the gifts the Great Forces have given us.

This is why in Island Common, when we say *risisi*, we mean "stone" or "mountain" or "ground," but also "ancestor."

But this is only a legend, so take with it a grain of dirt. As with all legends, rumours persist until this day. In some corners of the seven islands, it is rumoured that the Stone City of Risisi still lies, that if you scour the islands diligently enough, you may find a hidden cave. This cave, it is believed, is where this shining city once stood. There, you will find hundreds of stone figures, of people working, dancing, playing music. You will find parents chasing children, guards with weapons, rulers making decrees, maybe even the visitors. And you will find ibor. Lots and lots of it, pristine, untouched.

Perhaps it is the will of the Great Forces that this cave not be found. Now we only get whatever ibor is offered up to us by the Great Waters, sufficient for our needs. This is why, to this day, we never go seeking ibor. The destruction of Risisi must never happen again. We will take what is offered and make the best of it.

And never, *ever* again, will we open our gates to visitors from beyond the Forest of the Mist.

nameless

Second Season of the Red Emperor

22

Esheme

Bassa: The Great Dome
Sixth Mooncycle, 13

IT WAS THE AFTERNOON before Esheme was to present herself to the people. The stories, the performances, the reintroduction of the Ninki Nanka—it had all been meticulously planned. The only thing left to be finalised was the royal regalia, which was undergoing daily refitting. Between the toll of ibor from the last trip and the bodily implications of her most recent conception, the emperor's form had shifted considerably since the last time she was in full regalia.

She stood on the dais, surrounded by textile craftworkers, flitting around her with pins, ties, measuring ropes, and rods. Present also was Ikobi, dispersing instructions to the other royal beauticians in attendance: hairdressers, jewellers, makeup artists, whose own attendants made copious records.

This blissful cacophony was soon interrupted by Igan bursting into the fitting room, trailed by the keeper of the royal coop.

"Emperor," said Igan, "you'll want to hear this."

Esheme had never set eyes on the keeper of the coop before. Messages usually came to her through Nem or her advisors. Also, the coop man didn't seem to be carrying a message.

"Leave us," she ordered everyone. Once the room was cleared, she turned to the keeper of the coop. "Speak."

"I beg your pardon, Sovereign," he said. "I was only doing as commanded."

"Doing what? Commanded by whom?"

"The First Consul," he said. "She asked me to keep silent about messages from Chugoko."

Esheme lifted an eyebrow. "What messages?"

"I do not know, Sovereign. I never got to look at them. I only know they were from the warrant chiefs, marked as urgent. I passed them on to the First Consul as I usually do, and that was the last I had to do with them."

"How many?"

"Multiple," said the man. "A flurry of pigeons."

Esheme looked to Igan. "Why is this of sudden importance?"

"Because I just got word from my own people at the border," said Igan. "Something has happened in Chugoko, and unrest is beginning to brew there. Everyone is on hot coals, waiting for the Emperor's response. But for some reason, we never received any message that you should be responding to."

Esheme sighed, shook her head. "I'll deal with this."

She found her maa on the portico, Satti and a few hands in attendance. Below them, the courtyard, and First Ward beyond it, buzzed as usual, unperturbed by the royals and nobles looking over them. Esheme went up to Nem, waved everyone else away, and sat by her side.

"Was it them?" Esheme asked. "Was that why you hid it from me?"

Nem, sipping on a small calabash of wcybo, swallowed her gulp of spirit and said: "Yes."

Esheme put out a hand. Nem hesitated. It was common knowledge that the Red Emperor did not engage in spirits. But times had changed, and Esheme was no longer that person. She shook her hand, urging. Nem shrugged and poured her a small helping. Esheme sipped at it, and it traced a dry heat down her throat.

"I knew that any mention of their names would set new fire to your feet," Nem said. "It was sensible for me to refrain, at least until I could clarify the claims—which, if I may say, are not even substantiated. A prison break, reported sightings by untrained wardens and vigilantes—these are not matters big enough for the emperor's attention. You have an empire to run."

Esheme took another sip. "You should not have kept it from me."

"You almost died." Nem's face was tight, jaw set. "As First Consul, maybe I shouldn't have. But as your maa, I am not sorry I did."

Esheme nodded. The two women drank.

"What is the message?" asked Esheme.

Nem shut her eyes. "Esheme..."

"The message, First Consul."

Nem swallowed. Esheme felt a pang of guilt for employing this particular weapon, for reminding her maa that being a subject of the emperor would always be in contest with any other relationship they had between them. But this was the only way to get the information out of her.

"Two sightings," Nem said. "Him and the yellow woman, separate occasions. Helped by what they think is one of the more organised companies in the Savanna Belt. Likely one with roots in Chabo."

"Where are they now?"

"Unclear. Some say they escaped into the outskirts. The remains of an incinerated hut were discovered, but tracks led in several directions. They could be anywhere."

"But you've thought of possibilities."

Nem shrugged. "Eastward, maybe? If the Forest of the Mist truly contains an isthmus, they'll be taking the red stone-bone back to the Nameless Islands—assuming that's where the yellow woman truly comes from, and that the islands are truly there. They'll be escaping the long arm of the emperor too. Many good reasons to go east."

Esheme nodded. "And the prison break?"

"You won't believe it, but the prisoner was the late Speaker Abuso's daughter, Oke. Stuck there, anonymously, for some reason." Nem chuckled. "See the irony of it? The very person whose search started the journey that brought us here, to this portico at the top of this empire, might just be the same reason its road downhill begins."

"Road downhill," Esheme repeated. "You think I will ruin the empire by going after them."

Nem turned to her daughter. "You *are* going after them, are you not?"

It was not really a question, and Nem was right to ask it this way. Esheme's mind was made up the moment that coop keeper walked into the fitting room. But her maa still was yet to understand why.

She was not going because she hated Danso, even though every mention of his name still caused her a pang of anger and pain. She wasn't going after the islander woman for revenge, as Nem was probably thinking. Revenge and embarrassment were insufficient reasons to abandon her post and head for the Savanna Belt.

No, she was going because she had one arrow right now—the Ninki Nanka—and with it, could strike multiple targets.

She was yet to tour the desertlands, and where better to start than with Chugoko, the largest city in the belt? If she was to gain desertlander trust—or *regain*, since her peace officers had done such a poor job of capturing the fugitives—then she had to show up in person. And what better time to show up than with a Ninki Nanka in tow, a statement of her might and conquest?

"You wanted me to reveal myself to the people," said Esheme, "to demonstrate my aptitude for this role with stories of accomplishment, with this beast at my back as proof. I do that here or in Chugoko—what difference does it make? It has the same effect."

"You are not well," said Nem, with a sideways glance at Esheme's not-quite-bulging belly. "Or in the best shape for travel."

"Don't act like Chugoko's gates are not only a strong ride's day and a half away," said Esheme. "Or like you won't enjoy your time on the elephant throne in the meantime."

Esheme watched her maa's face tighten further. Again, she felt a pang of guilt. But sometimes, Nem needed to be poked to come to her senses.

"I am only going there to offer inspiration, bolster the search parties," said Esheme. "While also showing might, gaining trust, the whole thing we planned. Remember: one arrow, many targets."

"Mmm-hmm," said Nem.

"And yet you still think otherwise."

Nem eyed her daughter. "How many ibor pieces do you have left?"

They had both been avoiding this question. After expending her very last travel pieces in bringing down the Ninki Nanka, there was only one left—the final piece, now installed in her armlet. It was the smallest too, mostly sufficient to keep the Ninki Nanka tethered to her, but not quite for performing any significant feats of iborworking. If she was to remain emperor for long, she had to get her hands on more ibor. It was why she had set the peace officers on the Savanna Belt in the first place. Finding the fugitives was finding the Diwi.

Her silent hope was that this arrow, this trip north, could result in the fugitives being captured, and gaining access to their stone-bone. But she couldn't tell Nem that because it was a hope too far, a foolhardy thing to believe in.

"You can't use it, that last piece," Nem was saying. "It will break you—and moons know if you'll survive another such strain. And once it crumbles, it will be the last ibor you ever have." She glanced at Esheme's belly again. "Likely the last time you'll ever work the stone-bone."

"Even more reason to go, then." Esheme swept her hand over First Ward below them. "How else will we keep hold of all this? If there's a chance we can get our hands on more ibor, we should take that chance. Whether I can use it or not is not the point. *Having* it is."

Nem shook her head, downed the rest of her spirit, poured another.

"You don't keep power by acquiring more," said Nem. "You do it by brokering the one you already have. Did you learn nothing I taught you?"

Esheme put down her calabash and rose. It was time to change into other clothes, preferably ones more suited to a journey.

"As long as Danso and his friends have life and ibor," Esheme said, "they have the same power we do, and the opportunity to broker it too. That is more danger to this empire than any trip I make."

Nem nodded. "Okay." She held up a finger. "But if you go, remember this: Every step beyond this dome increases the chance that you may not return to it."

"Then so be it," said Esheme. "At least you will then have what you've always dreamed of."

She did not look at Nem this time, or feel any pang of guilt, even though she was sure Nem's face would twist as much as her heart did. Rather, she fumed as she returned to the fitting room.

She wasn't as reckless as Nem thought. She would never expend her last ibor piece for anything beyond a life-threatening situation. Having the Ninki Nanka present would be enough. Now that she had no more Soldiers of Red and no ibor to make new ones, she would travel with civic guard squadrons instead, and supplement them with peace officers in the desertlands. Iborworking was not in the plan.

When she'd said she wanted to be free, she did not mean being chained to this Great Dome like her maa. To be truly free was to be able to leave whenever she wanted, to never have to look over her shoulder. *That* was freedom. And she could get there only by gaining the respect and adulation of the continent. It was worth a few tough choices.

Last possible conception. The finality of the physician's words had unlocked something in her, something that since that day had grown into hesitancy and discomfort. For the first time, Esheme did not consider this conception a means to an end, but a possibility all in itself. Perhaps an heir. Or someone she could teach to work ibor for themselves. Her own Little Esheme, who would love her for who she was, who would understand all her sacrifices, who would not question every little decision she made. A Little Esheme in whom she could place her trust, and who could prolong her reign.

So Esheme returned to the fitting room with an impossible task: one arrow, so many targets to hit, and yet no bow to shoot it with. But, by moons, she had done impossible things before. She was the emperor of the world. She would always find a way.

23

Kangala

Tkithnuum
Sixth Mooncycle, 12–14

AFTER TRAVELLING SOUTHWARD ON the trade route for two and a half fortnights, Moy Kangala arrived in Tkithnuum, the sixth port city of the northern trade route, his eighteen champion children and their parties of a dozen warriors each behind him. Together, it was a company of over two hundred persons, excluding camels and dromedaries.

Just like the other villages, hamlets, and towns they'd encountered along the trade route, word of their serpentine caravan had reached the city ahead of them. Whispers had moved from scouts to sentries to clan leaders and tradespersons up to Bassa-favoured warrant chiefs. Even the bandits who usually plied the barren roads that connected settlements took a holiday the moment they learned that the Man Beyond the Lake was coming south.

Though Tkithnuum was the second-largest settlement along the route, possessing the strongest ties to the mainland (bested only by Chugoko), the oasis city prepared just like those before it. Traders, who had never before set eyes upon a caravan of such a size, stocked as many wares as they could, sure to make bountiful sales. The vigilante groups and their leaders prepared fighters—not to protect the Kangala caravan, but in the hope of joining it themselves. Private travellers who hoped to journey south to the border prepared gold and bronze pieces, hoping it could change hands and earn them Kangala's protection.

The warrant chiefs prepared only by holding their breaths, wishing that whatever Kangala had planned would simply pass them by.

Kangala himself had no particular plan. The journey so far had been uneventful. Save for one overzealous hamlet—with which they had quickly dealt and left behind in smoke—their journey had been relatively calm. Kangala simply considered this city an opportunity to gather information. He needed to know what to expect ahead of arriving in Chugoko, and what it would take to cross into the mainland. He needed to know things like how to gain quick and efficient access to the Red Emperor.

Kangala and his company set up camp just outside the city and were immediately besieged by all who had heard of their arrival. Kangala left the business of managing trade to his third- and fourth-born children, and as usual, gathered Ngipa and Oroe and a handful from their respective parties and made way through the city.

Tkithnuum was deficient, a city hung out to dry, ravaged by vultures masquerading as people. The once-sprawling and -sparkling oasis the city had been built around, that which had made it a trading port in the first instance, was now close to completely dried up. Clearly, season-long droughts weren't hitting just the Sahel—they were all over the desertlands.

Kangala surveyed the new wells dug to replace the dry spots in the once-oasis. They were the reason the oasis itself was now under constant guard, vigilantes patrolling to prevent water thieves. The wells looked shallow from a distance—he assumed less than ten feet deep, judging by the lever-and-pail mechanisms they used to draw water. He chuckled at the simplicity of it all. So close to Bassa, the famed centre of all knowledge, and yet they still had not figured out a better way to lift water from a deep well.

This made him more confident that his water-lifting pump would be welcomed by the emperor. In all the region, he was yet to spot a well that employed anything similar to the internal-displacement-with-external-wheel system he'd innovated. His design and method drew more water with less effort, doing so efficiently every single time. It was this very system that had helped propel him from lowly Sahelian youth to the most powerful man in the Sahel—*he* made it possible for Sahelians to dig wells as deep as twenty feet, therefore lasting scores of seasons before drying up.

The group headed into the heart of the city, weaving through corridors of stalls-cum-abodes to reach the offices of the warrant chiefs. Kangala noted that the city was also missing most of its youngest and most thriving population. He asked their guide—a little girl Ngipa had hired, no older in age than his twenty-fourth child—for the reason. The girl explained that most of the youthful citizens had chosen to undertake the journey southward, hoping to get into some form of employ within the new emperor's programs. The growing cost of water had made it impossible for them to remain here.

By the time Kangala arrived at the local government offices of Tkithnuum, there were only two warrant chiefs left. There used to be five, he was told, but two had left much earlier on their own journey southward, and the last one left recently upon hearing of Kangala's impending arrival. The two warrant chiefs left were the most senior: an elderly man with greying hair and a bald woman.

They welcomed Kangala and his champions into their small office and sat. They offered their guests wine and spirits—water for such a large group would be too costly, they explained. Kangala surprised the chiefs by offering *them* water instead. He had one of Ngipa's hands pour them a healthy amount. They gulped it down with gratitude.

"Why you no run too?" Kangala asked in one of the trans-regional vernaculars, the closest pidgin to his Sahelian tongue. Ngipa, who had done more travel outside of the Sahel than anyone else, stood by to translate in case he needed it.

"This is home," the grey chief said, matching Kangala's choice of tongue. "We no forsake it."

Kangala nodded. "I understand. Home…hard to leave."

"Then why you leave?" the bald chief asked. "You wan' tell us where you dey go?"

"Bassa," he said, matter-of-factly, then switching to his preferred Sahelian tongue, and enlisting Ngipa's translation skills, explained the information he sought.

"Oooh." Both chiefs glanced at one another when Ngipa was done.

"Chugoko no good right now," the bald chief said. "Bad things happen there."

Kangala leaned forward with interest. "Bad like what?"

"Prison escape," the woman said. "News say one of the emperor enemies." She pulled forward various notices sketched onto cloth, featuring faces and inscriptions Kangala couldn't read. He passed them to Ngipa, who ran her eyes over them.

"It's the warrior Butue spoke of," she told him in Sahelian. "And the escaped intended."

Kangala nodded, then asked more questions. Ngipa relayed their responses to him:

"They say the emperor has been made aware of the break-out," she translated. "And she has decided to act upon it immediately."

"By doing what?"

"By coming to Chugoko herself."

Kangala leaned back in his chair and began to laugh. He did so until tears came forth from his eyes, until the sound of his satisfaction filled every nook and cranny of the local government offices of Tkithnuum.

Ahh, yes. A new plan had begun to take shape in his mind, one that no longer required him to give up the secrets of his special pumps in exchange for the emperor's favour. There was something else the emperor wanted even more badly, and he was going to give it to her.

Two days later, Kangala set up camp at the edge of the city of Chugoko. Then he sat in his tent and waited for the emperor to arrive.

24

Esheme

Chugoko
Sixth Mooncycle, 14–15

THE CITY GATES AT Chugoko were reminiscent of the Great Dome's at Bassa. They weren't made of iron, and there was no courtyard beyond them, but that did not stop the architecture from mimicking the seat of the empire. The pedestrian openings were the same in number—five. The entrance for drawn traffic sported pillars on both sides that carried Bassai proverbs. Behind them, welcoming every new entrant, stood statues of emperors past, much in the same way of the courtyard of the Great Dome.

Little Bassa to the last.

Something here was different, though—new, set apart. Even though Esheme had never visited before, she recognised what it was long before the welcome assembly stepped forward and presented themselves.

She let them finish their elaborate greeting and introduction. None of the royal company were complete strangers to her—she recognised the warrant chiefs before her, the Elders of the trading union, heads of guilds and vigilante groups. Barring the peace officers and their mouthpieces, whom Igan had appointed themself, everyone else present had attended her coronation and introduced themselves to her. It was good, though, to let them believe that the emperor did not remember because she did not much care to.

In lieu of a response to their greeting, she pointed to the tall figure concealed by cloth at the end of the row of statues. "What is that?"

The welcoming assembly glanced at one another.

"We were hoping to present it to you at a later point, Sovereign," said a warrant chief. "We hoped you would visit under more favourable circumstances, and we would have completed it by then."

"Present it now," said Esheme.

The assembly looked at one another, then gave the signal. The cloth dropped. Suddenly, Esheme could smell the freshness of the clay from which the statue was still being built, the stone and metal that supported it, the oil that caused it to shine. She saw how much taller by design it was than the others. And most importantly, she saw that every part of the head was detailed in bronze and outlined with gold.

She leaned over and whispered to Ikobi: "Is that what I look like?"

Ikobi shrugged. "Close."

It was fine work, in truth, but could have been better if the best Bassai craftworkers had been employed to tackle it. Besides, Esheme couldn't help looking past the beauty and seeing the gift for what it was: a preemptive attempt to placate her anger. This, and the many gifts they brought before her that she didn't need.

"You should paint it red," whispered Igan on her other side.

True, thought Esheme, and nodded to Ikobi, who whispered it to the jali, who announced it to the welcome assembly. Immediately they nodded furiously, as if it were something obvious.

"That is... all?" asked the warrant chief. "The Scion of Moons is... happy with our gift?"

"Oh, no," said Esheme. "The Scion of Moons is not happy. The Scion of Moons will never be happy until all threats to the elephant throne are gone." She pointed at the group. "And you—*all of you*—let those threats go. Tell me: Should the Scion of Moons be happy?"

Heads bowed, and the assembly shuffled their feet. Esheme shook her head, then nodded to Igan. Igan screamed an order down to the back of the royal party. The riders of the last wagon, a long, specially built monstrosity, heard their command and acceded, jumping down and throwing off the clothing used to conceal what the wagon carried.

"Fire of Menai!"

Gasps rippled along the crowd as the people of Chugoko, for the first time, set eyes on the emperor's conquest. The Ninki Nanka wasn't even moving, tucked into the wagon as if asleep, but there was much to be feared from the look of the swamp-snake alone. Iridescent scales that caught the sun in otherworldly ways. The sheer size of its hefty body. The large gashes all over, greying with death.

Chatter spread through the assembly. Before long, it would move like a bushfire, touching every corner of this city, and then hopefully, after she was gone, every part of the desertlands.

Esheme didn't need to Draw or Command to get the Ninki Nanka to wake up. The moment she peered into herself, tickled that layer of consciousness where ibor always sat in wait, the great beast's lids snapped open, revealing red eyes. Awakened, it rose and stood tall, head grazing tree branches, so that those who had not yet fainted or run away had to shade their eyes just to see.

"I have travelled far and conquered many," said Esheme, once the cries had mellowed. "Now, I am here to do the same for Chugoko. But first, I must rest." She pointed to every faction of the welcome assembly before her. "And by the time I wake, you better have a good plan ready."

She waved her hand, and the assembly parted for her to pass.

It was midday the next day before Esheme could put herself together to address the Chugoko ruling council. She had spent the night restless, unable to sleep. Most of the morning was spent battling nausea and attempting to keep down thick corn pap, the only thing she could eat when pregnant. The journey had not been rough by relative comparison, but the early periods of her pregnancies were often the toughest, she'd learned through experience. Her whole body rocked with the vibrations of travel, still trembling from the effects after a day.

Once she was strong enough, she went out to meet the rest of the royal party. As the city did not have a central dome, they had put her up in their largest structure: the city hall. It was a meeting-place with a handful of private rooms in which speakers often prepared. The largest of these had been prepared for her, and the others for the most senior members of the royal party. Everyone else had found a warm corner of the main hall—which had been rid of all its seating—and made camp there.

They were all waiting once she emerged. All heads turned to her as she entered the main hall, and she soon realised she had made a grave error. None of these people had ever seen the emperor in this state before: stressed, tired, fresh from sleep. They weren't familiar with the puffy eyes and slower gait, the nightdress and hair without arches that reminded them that she was only an ordinary woman who had lucked her way into greatness.

Igan, sensing this just as quickly, rushed their posse quickly to cover her, but Esheme knew the damage was already done. There were already worried gazes that spoke multitudes, stares that queried her well-being. She wondered how long it would take for such thoughts to extend into the typical worry about her fitness to run the empire. How long would it take for someone to voice that thought and give it credence? She needed to demonstrate her capacity quickly and rid their minds of such dangerous imagery.

Her first stop was with the beauticians, who soon restored her to the glorious, breathtaking emperor they were more accustomed to seeing. Next was the woman priest whom she had opted to bring along this time, who cracked an egg on her forehead and blessed her with the protections of the mother hen Ashu, then circled her head with incense made of bark shavings and animal blood, covering her with the fiery blessings of the mother leopard, Menai. Then she rode out to meet the ruling council.

With the city hall taken over, the council had set up in the next best place: the open grounds of the city centre, right where the Ochela festival parade had gone through, and only a few steps from the prison centre. A perfect choice, by Igan's estimation. Not only would they get the detailed anecdotes of what had happened and who had been spotted, but they'd be able to visualize it too.

Once announced and seated, Esheme called the first witness: the Chief Warden of the prison. The man appeared with the most senior prison staff and bowed before the emperor, sobbing like a child, begging for mercy. His account of events, his suspicions of those involved—this was all information Esheme already had. She had only one inquiry: of Danso and his companion's role in all of this.

The Chief Warden relayed his interaction with the Ochela contestant, a finding that left her equal parts confused and alerted. Apparently, Danso had no direct role in the prison escape plot, though Esheme believed he'd still been somehow involved. She was perhaps a little proud that her once-meek scholar from Bassa was no longer the naive young man she remembered him to be.

But she tempered that pride with vigilance. Danso and his motley band were clearly strengthening for some reason, and breaking out the former Speaker's daughter was important to it. For them to risk everything and come out of hiding—whatever they were concocting was sure to be a challenge to her reign.

"I told you it was no simple break-in," said Esheme, whispering to her advisors while the Chief Warden awaited her response. "They're planning something."

"Maybe," said Ikobi. "Or just gathering allies."

"Not just any allies," said Esheme. "*Iborworkers.* The real question should be: to do what with?"

Igan and Ikobi looked at one another, and they knew the answer would not please the emperor.

"We have to go after them," said Esheme.

"*We?*" asked Igan, brows raised. "You could barely get up this morning."

Esheme shot them a look. "What do you suggest I do? Let them hurry east and find more Iborworkers and return to challenge my throne?"

"We have no squadron, no hunthands," said Igan. "You have no Soldiers of Red."

"I have the Ninki Nanka," said Esheme. "We can recall all peace officers, have them join us."

"Those will be barely enough, even with my posse added. For something like that, we'll need something close to an army, especially when you're this...vulnerable. And as I explained before, now is the worst time to pluck civic guard squadrons from Bassa and take them on a long trip. Splinter factions of the coalition are running wild in the outer wards—the city will be susceptible with so few members of the guard. Yet, if we travel without those numbers, we will be similarly underprotected—just like we were in the swamps. I can't have you underprotected. Not again."

Esheme was silent because Igan was right. But her thoughts kept coming around to the prison break. How could she prove her competence as emperor if, with all this power amassed, she could not catch a simple scholar and his gang?

She had to find them, find out whatever they were planning. She just *had* to.

"We can recruit vigilantes from here," Ikobi, listening in, offered. "Get the warrant chiefs invested."

Igan shot Ikobi a look that said: *Whose side are you on?*

"No, no Chugoki," said Esheme. She did not trust the way these Savanna Belt folks regarded her. "Even if the recalled peace officers turn out insufficient, I'd rather have fewer people whose loyalty I can count upon. Moons, I'd take a Sahelian over these Chugoki."

Igan remained adamant, shaking their head. "A trip such as what you're suggesting takes planning, time, resources. We can't just wake up and travel the Lonely Roads East." They leaned closer, using their inside voice. "I'm begging you to rethink this, Esheme. You can't win these people over this way. It's not worth it."

Esheme sighed, then matching Igan's quiet tone, said: "Make it happen."

She returned to the Chief Warden. His punishment was swift and simple: to be stripped of his post and imprisoned in this same prison until further notice. His second-in-command was to take over immediately.

The warrant chiefs were the next to be brought before her. They offered little else but supplication, requesting forgiveness for not overseeing their charges rightfully. The rehearsed nature of their performance irritated Esheme, especially because it offered little of note by way of solution. Since they were not primarily involved in the prison, she opted for public flogging, which was carried out immediately while she watched.

Next were the peace officers present in Chugoko, and their mouthpieces, who said they were willing to carry out whatever orders she requested, including honourable deaths for failing to meet their obligations. Esheme surprised them by having Igan and Ikobi shunt them to a separate location to be briefed in secret about the impending journey. They were to be tasked with sending news of the recall and its terms to their comrades beyond the city.

Last came the heads of the vigilante groups, who swore there was little they could have done to prevent the breakout, especially in the middle of the festival. These she simply sent away. Did the elephant have any time for ants beneath its feet?

Once done, she was ready to take her leave, when she was approached by Ikobi.

"There is a man here who has been waiting patiently, seeking permission to stand before you," her advisor said. "He will only say his name to you, but not to me."

Esheme frowned. "Why?"

"Apparently, he doesn't often need to. He is renowned farther up the trade route. People recognise him by his title."

"And what title is that?"

"They call him the Man Beyond the Lake."

25

Kangala

Chugoko
Sixth Mooncycle, 15–16

WHEN MOY KANGALA WAS brought before the Red Emperor, his first impression was that she was taller than he'd been led to believe. Throughout his trip, when everyone had spoken of a youngling on the elephant throne, wielding a power greater than anything Oon had seen in hundreds of seasons, Kangala had imagined her as a small child playing the popular game of broad leaf. The one where they stuck a thin stem through the middle of said leaf, then ran full speed into the wind, causing the leaf to spin, faster faster faster. *Conjury*, the children called it. But any discerning adult eye could tell it was simply the work of nature: It was the very wind that blew against them that caused the leaf to spin. In Kangala's mind so far, everyone had only been watching the emperor's leaf spin. Someone was simply yet to point out the wind.

As he stood before the Red Emperor now, he threw out that whole image.

The part of her that screamed *big* was not her physique, but her presence. She radiated an intensity that swallowed everything within proximity. Her gaze was unreadable yet measured, in a way that told him she was more discerning than she appeared. In fact, he decided, anyone who took this emperor's youth to heart was misguided. This was a young woman who did not end up here by mistake.

"I greet you, Sovereign Emperor and Scion of Moons," Kangala said, bowing low, his hand on the bridge of his nose in the practiced Bassai greeting. Next to him, Ngipa also bowed, rattling off his words from their Sahelian tongue into High Bassai. "I come to you humble, with prayer that you accept my homage and offer me ear."

The emperor nodded. "Welcome, Sahelian. I am told you are some sort of custodian by the Lake Vezha?" Ngipa translated the words.

"Indeed, Sovereign," said Kangala. "My family and I do crossings on the lake, both the Sahel and Idjama side. We have done so for seasons longer than I can remember."

"Ah, so you come from nobility," she said, her gaze trained on him.

Kangala recognised the sarcasm beneath. She was trying to slide the mat out from under his feet, see what kind of man he really was. It would be a tricky endeavour to deny his affluence—he was in good clothing, had a private translator, and boasted a widespread reputation.

So he waved Ngipa to step farther behind him, then embraced the challenge of speaking directly to the emperor—in Savanna Common, however broken—with the hope that more of who he truly was would shine through.

"I may speak in Savanna Common, Emperor?" he asked. "Is the only tongue I can manage to say directly."

The emperor nodded.

"I am no nobility, Sovereign, no," he said. "I come from family of fishing hands. My parents, my grandparents—they fish the lake like everybody. Only after the weather start to change, then we say: How other way to eat? Me, I was still a youth when I start to charge traders to cross the lake, only me with my canoe. A few barter here, a few cowrie there—things grow fast. I am blessed."

"Ah, so a self-made man."

"A man not afraid to work, Sovereign," he replied. "No more."

That seemed to satisfy her. "Fair enough," she said. "Make your ask."

"That is the thing, Emperor," said Kangala. "I no simply come to ask. I come to offer."

That brought her leaning forward. Even her advisor beside her, the one who had helped him gain access to the emperor—she, too, leaned forward. It was the other advisor, the bald one who continued to regard him with what Kangala concluded was deep suspicion, who remained unmoved, eyes never leaving his face.

"An offer of what?" the emperor asked.

"My service," he said. "If you will have it."

"And what service is that?"

"Eighteen champions with each their party," he said. "Total company of two hundred and more, leading by my first child, Oroe. Best commander and most talented tracker the continent ever seen. We camp on the outskirts of the city, but ready to move at your say. We will ride east, pursue your fugitives, if you let us."

The emperor frowned. Not the response Kangala expected.

"This thing you describe," she said, slowly, "sounds like an army."

"No, no, Sovereign," he said, backtracking. "We no soldiers. This is simply my own children, and hands they employ. We no wear colours, and we no swear allegiance to anybody." He looked up to her. "But if you wish, we can swear to you."

"And why would I wish it?" Her frown was deepening and did not look like leaving anytime soon. "I have a swamp serpent ready to do my bidding at a finger snap. I have peace officers, civic guards, the vigilantes of this city—all at the behest of the empire."

"Yes, Sovereign," said Kangala. "I no doubt that your subjects are capable. But my thinking is a company like my own will make pursuit easier on empire. No need to scatter whole city just for this. We go, no change to empire trade, no adjustment to city. Just easy, and all goal achieved."

The emperor regarded him warily, but her frown had receded. She leaned back in her chair. Immediately, the bald advisor began to whisper in her ear. The emperor listened, giving Kangala a long, hard stare throughout.

Kangala imagined what was being whispered. *He is a nobody from nowhere, a foreigner bearing gifts, a person who cannot be trusted.* But Kangala held faith. Everything he'd learned from Butue down to Tkithnuum proved that the emperor desired something from these fugitives. He could wager that she'd be open to any opportunity to find them that came with minimal cost. His gamble was based on this belief: She did not sound like someone who often passed up a good opportunity.

The emperor finally leaned away from her advisor, a palm up to silence them.

"I want to hear what you want your reward to be for this," she said to Kangala, her gaze intense. "And do not lie to me or tell me anything about doing it in service of the empire. I will have you thrown out."

Kangala adjusted himself on his feet. "Independence, Sovereign."

The emperor did not seem to comprehend, turning to her advisors to ask if something had been lost in translation.

"If I can explain, Sovereign," he added, quickly. "We will like your blessing to keep everything our family have since generations, like the lands around the Lake Vezha. Also, we will like your word that everybody who is affiliate to us, whether here or north or south, will have your blessing too."

The emperor lifted an eyebrow. "That is a significant ask. Do you plan to leave the lake anytime soon?"

Kangala thought about lying, but decided against it. "Yes, Sovereign."

This got the emperor's attention. "Why?"

"Look everywhere, Sovereign," he said, gesturing around. "Weather change every day. Rains dry up in the Idjama. Sahel is small and getting drier. Soon, no lake at all, and everyone move south. No lake, no people. No people, no trade. No trade, no business."

"So you are simply thinking ahead," the emperor said, leaning back. "Tell me: Do you intend to move your people southward too?"

Kangala decided against lying again. "Yes, Sovereign. Later."

"And you would like to keep your independence, even when closer to Bassa."

"If we can give our service, now and later also, yes. With your blessing."

For the first time since they began talking, Kangala sensed he was catching the emperor's attention. She turned her head to consult with her advisor again. The interactions were mirrors of the first: the stately, scholarly advisor seemingly in agreement with the emperor's disposition; the warrior-like advisor in intense disagreement.

"I will think about it," said the emperor at last. "Do not consider this an acceptance in any form. But just in case, prepare your company to move out at dawn."

Kangala and Ngipa bowed deeply and left. Afterward, they regrouped with Oroe, out of sight.

"That looked like it went well," said Oroe. "Though I will not lie—I hate to see you bow."

"Respect doesn't equate to inferiority," said Kangala, relieved to return to his native Sahelian tongue. Wading through tongues he was not fluent in often took a toll. But it was a small sacrifice to make.

"Did she agree?" Oroe asked Ngipa. "Are we in allegiance?" Ngipa shrugged and looked to her daa.

Kangala considered the emperor's words. *Just in case.* No one said *just in case* unless they were convinced about the viability of something.

"Come," he said to his children. "Let us prepare for a pursuit."

·⋄·⋯·   ·⋯·⋄·

At the break of dawn, Kangala stood at the eastern junction of the Emperor's Road as instructed, his children and their full company with him. It was a long time since he had been dressed like this, for a fight. He wasn't a fighter in any way, but he dressed like one regardless, complete with a sheathed blade and dense fabric armour underneath his kaftan, a headdress over his metal helmet to prevent the sun from cooking his head in it. Everyone else was dressed the same.

"Sure they're coming?" asked Oroe, antsy.

"Patient bird, fattest worm," Kangala replied. "So stand steady, look grand."

The royal caravan soon came into view. Kangala counted the travel-wagons. Barely a day since the emperor's announcement of a recall of her peace officers, a significant number had descended on the city from the outskirts. They filled the first two travelwagons, about twenty of them, all without their mouthpieces. Behind these came the royal travelwagon carrying the emperor and her advisors, followed by one with a handful of royal attendants.

Behind all of these came a lengthy cart, bearing the giant swamp serpent of lore: the Ninki Nanka. Kangala had never set eyes on it, and could not take his eyes off as it rolled past him. Now, he understood how such a beautiful monstrosity struck fear into the hearts of all. If he also had the power to awaken this beast and wield it to his liking, oh what things he could do!

The caravan pulled to a stop. A stool appeared before the emperor's door, and she descended from the travelwagon, trailed by her two advisors. He'd taken the time to learn their names now. The one who'd granted him audience the day before: Ikobi. The one who continued to stare daggers at him: Igan.

The emperor said something to Kangala in High Bassai, but he could not understand. She frowned and turned to Ikobi, who asked, in Savanna Common: "Where is your translator?"

"Alas, Ngipa is ill and cannot come," Kangala said with a smile. A lie, as Ngipa was not ill, but somewhere deep in the city, seeking any information that could aid Kangala's venture.

The emperor whispered some more to Ikobi, while Igan watched Kangala and his company carefully, eyes resting on Oroe. They bent and joined the royal whispering, eyes darting to the company and back.

"You must select only a dozen," the emperor announced at last, opting for Savanna Common, eliminating the need for a translator. Directly to Kangala, she said:

"We will go on this pursuit. Once this is done, we may discuss other ways your whole company may be of use to me. As for your independence, I have decided perhaps some agency will be granted to you. But only *some*. Bassa will retain prerogative in whatever new establishment you install."

It wasn't quite what Kangala wanted, but it was sufficient for his purposes. He had his foot in the door now, and that was all that mattered.

He bowed in acceptance. "Sovereign."

While Oroe picked out the dozen champions and argued over the number of hunting dogs they could bring along, Kangala inquired of Ikobi what the plan was. She produced two cloth notices like the ones he'd seen in Tkithnuum and filled him in on everything else.

The islander was to be captured alive under all circumstances. The current belief was that she was travelling eastward alone, back to the

Nameless Islands—though how she would cross into islands no one had seen in hundreds of seasons remained a mystery. As for the Bassai escapee, it was believed he had scattered into the desertlands alongside the rest of their helpers. But if he happened to be travelling with her, then even better. Two for the price of one.

Kangala passed on the message to Oroe to pass to his dozen. As they spoke, the emperor returned to the royal travelwagon, but the travelwagon did not turn back like the others. Kangala approached Ikobi.

"The emperor is coming also?"

"Of course," said Ikobi. "The Sovereign would never let her subjects go without her leadership."

Kangala returned to Oroe. "Change of plans. I will be joining you."

His son raised an eyebrow. "You are coming?"

"So is the emperor," said Kangala. "We must follow her example."

"Hmm. Perhaps it is best you come." He motioned toward Igan with his chin. "The way that one has been looking at me, I suspect we will tear out each other's throats before we find those fugitives."

"Cool heads will have to prevail," said Kangala. "Now, send the others back to camp. Let them wait until we return."

"And Ngipa?"

"She will stay behind and help prepare for our return." Kangala mounted his kwaga. "Us, we have a duty now, one that will reverberate in our lineage for seasons to come. We stay focused, find these fugitives, gain the emperor's trust, and claim our reward."

He patted the kwaga absentmindedly, half an eye on the royal travelwagon. "We stay focused, child, and the Four Winds help us, we will preserve our legacy."

26

Lilong

The Lonely Roads East
Sixth Mooncycle, 15–16

"CONSIDER OUR TRIP DIVIDED into two portions," said Lilong, pointing to the map of the savanna they had received from the Gaddos. "There is the open grassland before the Weary Sojourner. Then there is the open grassland after. They're different—you can't cross both the same way. But if we make it, we'll end up at the Forest of the Mist."

The travel group were on their first evening stop in a while, making camp in an elevated spot chosen by Ugo, who was most familiar with the Savanna Belt's terrain. It had been days since they left the hideout, and this was the first time they felt far enough away from Chugoko to have a long rest. Lilong could no longer remember how many sunrises and sunsets they'd seen, all blending into each other in tense, sleepless nights of huddling next to one another in the travelwagon, eyes wide and bloodshot as Oke and Ugo and Alaba took turns trying to quiet the distressed Thema.

It didn't help that Lilong's body, after all that ibor use, had chosen this period to declare its discontent. The rickety travelwagon, tumbling through the savanna, caused aches to linger in her joints for most of the trip, and her throat remained dry no matter how much water she drank. All had taken turns driving the wagon, except her. Her eyes were extra sensitive to light, and she had a small fever. It was taking her much longer than usual to recuperate, as food was being rationed and she wasn't getting the required nutrition to bounce back swiftly.

"I really wish we had a better plan before coming out here," said Alaba, who stood bouncing the baby Thema on his hip while the others crouched in a circle over the map.

"I already know what we can expect on this side of the trip," Oke said, ignoring Alaba's lament. "Few more days of slow travel, we'll reach the Weary Sojourner. We can rest there, gather more information about the second side—the wilds farther east. Then we move again."

"Didn't the Weary Sojourner burn down?" asked Danso.

"The information my parents received says it's been rebuilt," said Alaba. "New owner goes by the name of Madam Pikoyo."

"Won't she recognise us?"

They all went silent. Danso was referring to the public notices, a few of which they had spotted on their way (and immediately removed and burned). They were far enough away from Chugoko to not be easily recognised by the average desertlander, but that did not mean they were safe from the long arms of the peace officers just yet. The notices they spotted had inspired them to get off the well-trodden roads and take a bushroad, which, this far out in the wilds, was not good for the travelwagon's wheels. It also opened them up to bandits and wild animal attacks. So far, they were lucky enough to have encountered neither, but if they kept on this road, it was only a matter of *when*, not *if*.

"I'm afraid it's a chance we must take," said Oke, stabbing a finger at the map. "Grassland after the Weary Sojourner is teeming with feral animals. Trust me, I learned that the hard way." She pulled aside her wrapper to reveal a deep gash, poorly healed. "Leopards can be vicious when yet untamed."

Danso nodded. "I'd argue a lot has changed too since you and Lilong travelled."

A lot had indeed changed. The sun was more brutal than Lilong remembered it, and the heat was unbearable, forcing incessant cries from Thema. Oke and her partners were able to rock the child to fitful sleep for only short moments at a time, before she would awake and begin all over again. A damp cloth remained on her forehead permanently, and even that was yet to solve the problem.

"And that's why we need more information," said Oke, glancing at Lilong. "Don't you agree?"

Lilong looked up at the moons settling in for the evening. "I don't know."

She left them to go take out the camping materials, sturdy tents from the Gaddos, made from woven hemp and tough enough to withstand sandstorms. As she offloaded them, she paused just long enough to look around. She did not recognise any part of the sprawling flat grassland before her. All this dryness, the rolling browns and intermittent greens, short grasses mixed with low-lying shrubbery—none of this looked familiar from back when she had made the journey from her island to the border. Her eyes had been too focused on the ground before her, piecing together her daa's tracks, mostly in the dark. She had not taken time to breathe in the wonders of the wilds. Only when she'd arrived at the Weary Sojourner did she finally look up, and by then, it had been too late.

Oke came over to help with the tents, having divided the rest of their camping labour—Ugo and Danso to gather wood, Alaba to tend to Thema. The two women worked in near silence, driving the pins, Oke only pausing now and then to listen to Thema's coos and cries. Lilong found the ground rocky and hard to work, but Oke seemed dexterous with it all, which was useful now that the winds had begun to pick up and they still had no fire yet. It got cold quickly in the savanna, especially this close to harmattan.

Lilong struck hard at the pin she was working with, frustration giving swing to her arms.

"Easy with that," said Oke. "You want to be able to pull it out tomorrow."

She shot Oke a sidelong glance. Only one word came to her each time she saw this woman: *Risisi, Risisi, Risisi.* The name rang in her head like a warning bell, reminding her of everything it signified: that she no longer knew what was true and what wasn't; that everything she believed about honour and duty was shattered; that she could no longer trust her own league—not with Danso, the Diwi, or any other secret she'd learned.

That *home*, the one place in the world where she felt safe, was not safe anymore.

She shut her eyes and let the thoughts float away.

"Is everything okay?"

Lilong slammed a pin. "Everything is *fine*."

Silence, again. Lilong considered Oke's temperate comportment to be irritating. It was a mask, Lilong decided, a shade over the other signs that, being a warrior, she recognised. The little frown on Oke's face as she focused on a knot. Her constant alertness—in this case, to Thema's every hiccup. The way she reacted whenever she sensed something amiss. The brooding air she returned to once she was satisfied all was fine. It was warrior-like, a natural Iborworker's instinct, the kind the Abenai League spent many seasons honing.

This woman resembled Lilong in too many ways, and Lilong found it unsettling, because she wondered if this was why her daa had chosen to trust her with all his secrets.

"Thank you," said Oke, out of nowhere.

"Hmm?"

"For letting us come with you," she said. "I know we are a burden."

Understatement, thought Lilong, but nodded and forced a smile.

"Ask it," said Oke.

"Ask what?"

"The question you've wanted to ask all this time," she said. "Ask it."

Lilong opened her mouth, ready to say, *Why did he choose you?* It was his own daughter who had sacrificed her life—her childhood, her body, her whole self—to become a protector of their islands, of their family. Why would he not come to her with this?

But the words would not leave Lilong's throat.

"I will save you the unease and answer it," said Oke. "Your daa did not choose to offer up his secrets to me, nor did I choose him for my own purpose. I am a believer in fate, and I believe it is what brought us together—the same fate that has now brought you to me, to finish—"

"—what he started, yes," said Lilong. She struck the pin. "I don't care why you're going east. I just want to go home, and as long as you're not in my way, we are fine."

The sounds of pins being struck surrounded them. Oke paused and squinted into the dark, trying to make out Danso in the distance.

"You know, reading that cursed codex does something to you," she said. "It's impossible not to come out here after. You just *know* that it's up to you to do something with that knowledge, to make change in this world." She turned to Lilong. "But it's not just the codex that does that— it's *all* knowledge. That's why he did it, your daa. The Abenai League might see protection in hiding things, but your daa saw the value in revelation, and so do I. In time, you will come to see it too."

Lilong looked up. The white moon had begun to emerge, the red moon nowhere in sight. A good omen, according to the Bassai. Too bad Lilong did not believe in good or bad omens, or fate for that matter.

Her daa was not a foolish man, she knew. Every decision he'd made, even the seemingly bad ones, must've been done with a goal in mind. If he—and Oke, in tandem—had abandoned all family in pursuit of something grander, driven by nothing but dreams of uniting the continent against a collective enemy, then there was something truthful about that choice, even if only the devotion itself.

But she was not on this journey to continue his path. She was here because there were truths, and there were lies, and she wanted to know which was which so she could decide how to live her life going forward: as an Abenai warrior, or as someone else. But it would start, first, by finding Risisi, and learning what was myth and what was real.

"We will stop at the Weary Sojourner as you suggest," she said to Oke. "But only for a night." Then she went back to building the tent, the matter closed.

⋄———⋄

The next morning saw disaster before they could set out. One of the travelwagon's wheels had finally succumbed and become displaced, the hub nearly falling off. None of them were versed in anything that had to do with travelwagons, which meant they needed help.

"We should abandon it," said Alaba as they stood around pondering. "Find another way."

"Like what, walking?" asked Lilong. "Five people and a child—yes, the odds of us making it through the wilderness are wonderful."

"We could try one of the nearby settlements," Oke offered. "Back then, I stopped by a few to top up on food and water. I vaguely remember them having blacksmiths. I suspect these will too."

"Aren't we supposed to be avoiding settlements?" asked Danso.

"I'm not sure we have that luxury now," said Ugo, examining the wheel. "None of us can ride in this thing—it'll fall off right away, and *then* we'll be in hot soup." He rose, dusted his knees. "Better to fix it now before it's too late."

They all looked to Lilong, waiting for the final decision. Lilong squirmed under their gazes. Once, this was what she craved—leadership, insisting on the right things, avoiding the wrong. But for the first time, she wished for someone else to take the reins, give her time away from this totem of warriorship she had carried her whole life. She was in unfamiliar territory and did not have her powers. She had no clear plan, no solutions to problems that arose, and no idea who she was anymore.

"Nearest settlement," she offered, unsure.

The nearest place was a hamlet with no obvious name, nestled in the thick of tough acacia scrubs. Dwarf fences separated compounds from one another, and mud-plastered, thatched-roof abodes littered each. In the yards, a bevy of livestock—goats, fowls, dogs—ran about alongside unsupervised children at play. It was the best possible kind of settlement they needed at this time—too small and isolated for peace officers to bother with. Officers preferred to stick closer to the cities and towns where their mouthpieces lived. Still, they took caution when they entered, leading the wobbly travelwagon slowly, eyes darting for any signs of trouble.

When the children stopped their play to observe the strangers walking into their hamlet, the adults began to emerge from their huts. All were elderly—Lilong guessed most younger folk would have migrated toward Chugoko or the northern trade route in search of work. They seemed more perplexed than troublesome or afraid, which made sense. Five young people with a baby and a broken wagon did not immediately scream threat.

Ugo walked up to a nearby compound and respectfully greeted an elderly woman. Lilong couldn't make out what he was saying in his rapid Savanna Common, but the woman pointed in a direction, then went back into the house.

The blacksmith was at the opposite end of the hamlet, which meant they had to walk through most of it to get to him. The curious gazes did not abate, and neither did Lilong's discomfort, even though she was wearing a desertlander complexion. Danso, who perhaps felt just as out of place, wondered aloud if they could replenish their water supply from the wells they saw in the courtyards. Oke and her partners seriously discouraged it.

The blacksmith, when they found him, was a small, wiry man with reddened eyes, soot-stained hands, and a complexion darkened by time spent next to fires. He looked them up and down.

"Lost?" he asked.

Ugo shook his head, then pointed to the hub of the defunct wheel. "We need help."

"Ah," said the man, then glanced at the group. "Bad time to be travelling the savanna." His gaze flicked to Thema, then to Oke, who was carrying her. "Hot as a dozen suns."

"That's why we need help," Alaba interjected. "So we can quickly be on our way."

The man crouched to peer at the wheel. "It is bent out of place. You travel the bushroads?"

The group looked at one another. Lilong gave them the eyes. *Nobody answer that.*

"How long will it take?" Oke asked. "And what will it cost us?"

"I will take it out, knock, refix," he said. "Hour, maybe. You have copper?"

The man set to work, while Ugo and Alaba tended to the kwagas, and Danso opted to meander in search of water. Oke went with him to prevent any trouble, which left Lilong alone with the blacksmith. At some point, a helper—a child, really—appeared and joined him. Perhaps a grandchild of his? It reminded Lilong of her own daa, of her being his apprentice of sorts from a young age. She wondered if this child would feel like they needed to become a blacksmith too when they grew up. Anything to continue the work their daa had begun, right?

Danso and Oke returned victorious with a jar of water, though Thema was becoming fussy again. Oke tried to calm her with a quick cloth bath, but it was only a temporary reprieve. Luckily, the blacksmith was almost done.

"Told you is a bad time to travel with baby," he said, grunting as he replaced the wheel. "Dangerous out there. If not bandits, then wild beasts. You hear about the new ones?" When no one asked, he pressed on anyway. "They all over the savanna now, driving native animals out. Nobody knows where they come from, but they travel in packs. You go far enough, you find them near the little hills. Tall as antelope, teeth like a half dozen leopards. They call them *genge*—it's how the children say *monster*."

Danso chuckled. The man shot him a glance. "Something funny?"

"No...?" He glanced at Lilong, who was frowning at him. *What are you doing?*

"Well, you laugh now, but I tell you—you see those isolated hills out there, you run." He paused. "I did not ask—east or west?"

"Sorry?"

"Where are you going—west to Chugoko, or east to wilderness?"

"West," Oke interjected, too quickly, so that any discerning ear would know it was a lie. But the blacksmith was focused on finishing up the wheel.

"Then the genge are not your problem," he said. "Worry about the Red Emperor's peace officers."

Now *that* raised concern. Lilong rose, and everyone else perked up.

"Are there...peace officers out here?" Oke prodded, cradling the child to her body and bobbing up and down.

"Oh yes," said the man, rising and dusting his palms, done with the task. "Not *here*, but they ply these roads today, all of them headed west. The travelling youngsters say there is an edict, say the Red Emperor has sent pigeons and recalled every peace officer to Chugoko."

Lilong blinked. "The Red Emperor is *in* Chugoko?"

"Holding court after some disturbance," said the man. "They say she arrive with a monstrous beast—fearsome, just like the genge, but ten men tall and serpent-like." The man shook his head. "First we hear of undead soldiers, now we hear of fearsome beast. Whatever she gathers these brutal elements for, it can never be good." He shaded his eyes, glanced at the sun overhead. "You leave now, maybe you are fifty, a hundred paces behind the last officers that passed."

If we were headed west, thought Lilong. Heading east—they would be running *right* into the next cohort.

Lilong was already moving, as was Oke, who pulled out copper pieces to pay the man. "Thank you for your service," she said, gesturing toward Thema, who continued to protest, "but we have to get her somewhere cooler."

The travelwagon was sturdier than Lilong remembered it, when they crammed in and Alaba took the reins. But she wasn't thinking about its sturdiness. She was thinking about if she was strong enough to wield ibor. She flexed her consciousness to test, see if she was replenished. The ibor in her arm responded, eager, but her teeth chattered in disagreement, her body closed to such power.

Too late, thought Lilong, as they charged out of the hamlet.

Ahead, the Lonely Roads East were no longer lonely. A pillar of dust, tall enough to be seen from afar, clouded the horizon. And in front of that cloud, through the high noon haze, Lilong counted three figures on kwagaback.

27

Lilong

The Lonely Roads East
Sixth Mooncycle, 16, same day

THEMA BEGAN TO CRY.

"Ready your power," said Lilong to Oke.

The other woman's eyes narrowed in disagreement as she tried to calm the wailing child. Alaba, in the driver's seat outside, leaned over to speak into the wagon.

"What's the plan? Should we turn around?"

"They've already seen us," said Lilong. "We'll just have to prepare." She returned to Oke. "Your power—we're going to need it."

"Mine?" Oke asked. "What happened to yours?"

"I'm not replenished."

"Can't you use the blade without ibor?"

The cloud of dust had thinned, but only because the peace officers had spotted them now and had slowed. Their kwagas remained spread across the width of the road, blocking off all paths. They clearly intended to get the travelwagon to stop one way or another.

"No mouthpiece," Ugo said suddenly. "If they stop us, they will not be asking the usual questions."

True, when they looked, Lilong saw that it was just the three peace officers travelling alone. Whatever thoughts their group had of explaining their way out of this were gone. They had one choice, and that choice was to face the peace officers head-on. If they were to survive, there was no room for hesitation.

Thema's cries filled the wagon.

"Ready. Your. Power," Lilong hissed at Oke. "*Now.*"

"I'm not..." The Bassai woman suddenly looked timid, a look that did not fit her at all.

"What?"

"I'm not ready."

"*What?* What does that mean?"

The peace officers were close enough for their features to be in view—tall, even on kwagaback. Well armoured. Well armed.

"I never learned how to *combat*," said Oke. "Jaoudou, he never got around to teaching me that."

Lilong couldn't believe her ears. "So you're only a Grey Iborworker for *tricks?*"

"They're almost here," Ugo was saying.

Lilong glanced at her single blade. Five people and a baby. She'd never make it. She could choose to protect just herself and Danso, but it would weigh on her if something happened to the others. Especially the baby. But she had to do *something.*

She gritted her teeth and gripped the hilt of her blade. *I guess I'll just have to take my chances.*

The peace officers were already upon them, their sewn lips, bloody and swollen, visible from this distance. They had still not given way for the travelwagon to pass.

Lilong gripped the hilt of her blade, knuckles shiny.

"Pull aside and stop," Oke said suddenly.

"What?" all in the wagon chorused.

But Oke was already slamming the roof, yelling the instruction to Alaba. Then she turned the jar of water she and Danso had just fetched and emptied its contents onto the floor.

"What are you *doing*?" Lilong whispered, aghast.

"Trust me," said Oke, then paused. "You *do* trust me, yes?"

Absolutely not, thought Lilong, but it was too late, because the wagon was slowing down and pulling aside.

The peace officers responded accordingly, slowing to a stop just as their travelwagon rolled to the roadside. Then they stalled, seated atop their kwagas as if waiting for them to make the first move. Alaba, outside, did not move either. Lilong imagined he was trying his possible best not to look at them, not to invite a question or, worse yet, an action.

"Crouch low, cover your head," Oke said to Lilong and Danso. "Sheath your blade, stash it. No one speak a word."

With that, she pushed open the window and poked her head outside, then began yelling, greeting the peace officers.

But at the same time, she lifted Thema ahead of her, into the sun that was now angling into the travelwagon, so that it shone in the baby's face. Thema burst out in fresh tears, straining her lungs and coughing.

"Water!" Oke was shouting over Thema's cries. "Water! My baby—she needs water, but we have none. We are looking for the nearest settlement, but maybe…maybe you could share some of yours? Maybe you could… help us?"

This woman will get us killed! Lilong, who had begrudgingly stashed her weapon, now searched for it in the dark on the floor. *This was her plan—asking for help from peace officers? From peace officers!*

There was a thud, the crunch of boots on the ground. Lilong could not look up, her head covered. But she felt Oke flinch. Everyone in the wagon felt it too—Ugo retreated farther into the corner in which he sat, and Danso wrapped his wrapper tighter, covering his complexion.

The smell of dust and sweat flooded the travelwagon's interior. Then came darkness, as a shadow blocked the ray of light streaming into the wagon. Lilong's hand, which had just found the hilt to her blade, stilled.

The man standing there was not looking at Oke or the crying baby, even as they blocked his view. His eyes were fixated on the inside of the wagon, flitting from Lilong to Danso to Ugo. He leaned back and looked up, presumably to Alaba in the driver's seat, then his eyes returned to inside the wagon.

Lilong's fingers wrapped around her blade. She dipped into her consciousness, trying once again to touch ibor. It responded, but her body recoiled, anxious at the promise of injury.

Thema screamed bloody murder into the peace officer's face.

"Water, sir," Oke was saying, the empty jar now in her other hand. "*Water.*"

The man looked at Lilong, cocked his head so he could see her face properly. She half turned away, offering a choreographed nervous smile, mimicking a shy bride, hoping it paid off. It seemed to, as he turned his face toward Danso, who, luckily, sat farther inside the wagon and behind Ugo, so the complexion of his hands was not as visible.

"Water, sir," said Oke, shoving the jar into the man's face. "*Water.*"

The man stepped back and swung an arm. Lilong almost moved, before the sound of the jar tumbling on the ground outside told her what had happened. She looked up, and the jar was gone from Oke's hand.

"Hmm," the man said, then turned and walked away. A moment later, the sound of hooves filled the wagon, and dust filtered in. Then all was still, and everyone could breathe again.

Except for Thema, of course, who was still crying.

"Oh shhh, dear one, shhh, I'm sorry, I'm sorry." Oke held the child close to her body. Ugo quickly snapped out of it, reached for a previous damp cloth, which was already drying, and handed it to Oke.

"Maa promises never to use you like that again, okay?" Oke was saying to her baby, who was beginning to quiet down. "I promise, I promise."

The travelwagon rocked as Alaba came down and opened the door. His hands shook, but he worked hard to contain it.

"Everybody fine?" he asked.

"Hearts in our mouths," said Oke, "but good."

"That could've gotten us all killed," Lilong said.

"We survived, didn't we?" Oke said. "That's all that matters."

Alaba, after retrieving the discarded jar and handing it to Oke, climbed back into the driving seat. The Bassai woman's eyes flared grey, and the water on the floor of the travelwagon rose in stringy drops and made its way back into the jar.

Lilong scoffed. "So *that* you can do."

Oke wrinkled her nose, then began to sing quietly, rocking Thema. The travelwagon got moving again, slowly this time. After a moment, Oke leaned toward Lilong and whispered:

"You never answered."

Lilong frowned. "Answered what?"

"Whether you trust me or not."

I don't trust anyone, thought Lilong. *Not anymore.* But to Oke, she said: "Try anything like that again, and you're on your own."

28

Nem

Bassa: The Breathing Forest
Sixth Mooncycle, 23

THE GHOST APE WAS twice the size of the heftiest among the hunthands that encircled the cage, sticking spears in to keep it calm. The spears had the opposite effect, causing it to lunge into the iron bars instead, rattling the cage, quaking the ground, jarring Nem's teeth. But that was not what caused her agitation. Each time the ape touched something, its colours— the salt-white of its fur, the grey of its eyes, the pink of its underbelly, the yellow of its teeth—all *rippled*. First they became a rainbow, a crashing wave of every colour imaginable, a sight that turned the eyes and the brain. Then, they changed, became one with the iron, so that the Ghost Ape and the iron bars and black floors melded into one and became indistinguishable. Blink, and one wouldn't even know the Ghost Ape was still in there, camouflaged, invisible. Not until a hunthand poked in its general direction, and the beast roared back into being, all white rage and snarling yellow teeth.

An ape that was also a chameleon. Nem had heard the legends, but never in a thousand seasons would she have thought she'd ever see one in the flesh.

"I cannot believe I'm saying this," said Elder Yao the scholar, placed in temporary charge of security assignments in Igan's absence. "But it seems the emperor's giant serpent may be the least of our problems."

"Perhaps," said Nem. "But tell me this isn't why you brought me out to the edge of the Breathing Forest? Because you already know the answer to this question." She pointed to the furious ape. "That thing can't make it into the city. Not while all is so...unbalanced right now."

"Yes, I know," said Yao. "But—there's more."

He led her away from the clangor and towering bamboos, toward another part of the forest threshold, accompanied only by both their Seconds. As they went, he filled her in on how a hunthand posse had happened upon the beast. Apparently, while chasing an unrelated bounty, each hunthand they had sent in this direction, they had lost. When the rest finally arrived here, they were sure none of the previous men had made it into the forest, because all their weapons were found at the edge. So they had sat in wait for a night, and only then did they finally spot the Ghost Ape appearing from within, bathed in Menai's fiery light and no longer invisible to the naked eye. It had been attempting to go somewhere, cross the city, but had hesitated, perhaps fearful of running into people.

It was hard work, capturing it. Several people had been wounded in that affair. But the men soon learned that the beast, although strange, was not responsible for the disappearance of their comrades. There was something even more menacing at play.

Yao finally arrived at an area of the threshold away from the bamboos, this one populated by plantain trees. Or at least it looked like there used to be bamboos, but the plantains had somehow taken over.

"Show her." He gestured to his Second.

The young woman—recently promoted to Potokin—hesitated before placing a hand into her wrappers and producing a small agama lizard. She placed the lizard in the grass and let it wander toward the trees, which had begun to sway gently.

"What's this?" asked Nem.

"Just...watch," he said.

The agama, glad to be free, headed for the forest cover. As if sensing its approach, the trees around it began to sway even more, broad leaves excited.

It took Nem a moment to realise there was no breeze against her cheek.

The trees were *moving*.

Not with limbs, or roots, but with a shamble, a slow sideways shift as if on hurt buttocks. Nem saw the farthest of them drag earth in their wake, slinking forward like earthworms, not quick in any sense of the word, but not particularly slow, especially for the unsuspecting.

"What—"

Then she saw the bones scattered in the grass. Disparate but unmistakably human—thighs, arms, fingers, toes, a skull. All clean of flesh or tissue, white and unstained by blood, as if buried for a long time and then exhumed. Except they were still fresh, as evidenced by the flies gathered about them. Beside them lay the weapons Yao had spoken about: two blades, a spear, one shield.

The lizard, unperturbed, climbed over the shield, over the bones, and continued to make its way forward. Then, just when it was a few feet away from the nearest tree, it stopped.

Perhaps the lizard felt the same way Nem did: eyes peeled, hair raised, awaiting any sign of movement.

In a flash, the plantain trees opened up, and they were no longer plantain trees, but an endless mass of thorns and tentacles and teeth, green and red and black, hissing, lunging. The lizard dodged the first stem that came at it, slipped past the second, but was not fast enough, not far away enough. The third tree caught it in a vise grip with a stem extending from its broad leaf—spindly as rope, strong as an arm—and plucked it from the grass. The lizard, wriggling, disappeared down a black teeth-lined throat, and the tree closed up slowly, trembling, digesting. Every other tree near it did the same, and soon all was back to stillness, and the threshold before them was filled with ordinary plantain trees again.

"Fire of Menai," Satti whispered.

"Remarkable, isn't it?" said Yao, who seemed to be enjoying this. "Apparently, they started out somewhere within the forest—there's a trail of bones behind them that, if we follow, can tell us their initial location. But somehow, they've migrated this far, as if, like the Ghost Ape, they're *going somewhere*."

In reply, the tree that had just swallowed the lizard shuddered, then opened up the throat in the middle of its stem and spat forward small, uncrushed bones: a head, a tail, ribs, a spine.

Nem remained fixed, her mind spinning like a textile mill. Her hands shook. She clasped them together. *What is happening to this land?* Gigantic beasts, trees that ate people, the natural order of things turned on their head. What else was next?

"Speak no word of this," Nem said, but Yao was already shaking his head.

"Too late. The hunthands have told the families of those who died by it, and they in turn have spoken to neighbours, friends. The Ghost Ape we can hide away, but this one—"

"The ape dies *today*," said Nem with finality. "Moons, you people cannot be the death of me." She beckoned to Satti to push her back to the travelwagon. She did not want to stay here for one moment longer.

"Any panic?" she asked as they went past the ape's cage. "From those who have learned of this?"

"Not so far," said Yao. "It still sounds like myth and legend to them, I think. But I heard the hunthands talking, and they say many believe it is the emperor's actions that have angered the moon sisters. Now our land is being punished, becoming hard to live in."

Nem sighed. If only they were right—but also, if only they were wrong.

"Destroy it, all of it," said Nem. "Let us return to what is important."

"And for those who have learned of it?"

"They will forget. It is myth, after all."

Yao put a finger in his ear, squeezed. "Perhaps it is best to get in front of this—"

"And show them what, an empty throne?" Nem shook her head. "Just do your job. Get the best civic guards from every ward down here and let them all stand there until you cut down every single one of those barbaric monstrosities. Then you burn it all, you hear? I don't care how long or how much it takes, but you make sure they're all dead. We cannot lose control of our land to just about anything that tries to take it."

Yao lifted a finger. "A problem with that, First Consul."

"What?"

"The emperor, before leaving, allocated most civic guard resources to the porous portions of the border. To stem the migration tide, Igan told me, but also to aid the fixing of areas in disrepair. If I pull the best available here now, civic guard numbers in the city proper will be...thin."

"Then just recruit more," said Nem. "Do I have to explain your job to you?"

"A small matter there, too, First Consul. It seems not as many are as interested in working for the guard as they once were. Whispers have proliferated about the emperor's trip, how detrimental it has been for the civic guard squadrons hand-picked to follow. Many now consider the role of civic guard quite dangerous, and are not as keen to join. We simply don't have the numbers—and we sure don't have the time to train them."

Nem shook her head. This was just unending, wasn't it?

"Fine," she said. "Reallocate some from border to here. For now."

"Are you sure?" asked Yao. "Several locations are in mid-repair. They will become vulnerable if we do."

"Does the border sound like a priority to you right now?" Nem asked, exasperated. "Elder Yao, if you can't do this job, just tell me so, and I'll find someone else to do it."

"Yes, First Consul. I'm just concerned that—"

"There will be no border to be concerned about if we all get eaten before then," she said. "Get to work." She started to roll away, then added: "And once you're done with these monsters, you keep those civic guards here. I want them standing watch, day and night. Nothing leaves that forest and makes it into this city, you understand? *Nothing*."

She returned to the travelwagon, riding all the way back to the Great Dome in silence, engrossed in her thoughts. She recalled Esheme's stories from her journey south, the capture of the Ninki Nanka. And now, this. Whatever this was, it wasn't happening just here—it was happening all over the continent, and it was moving fast.

Worst possible time for an emperor to be away from her empire.

Back in the Great Dome, she immediately headed for her private workchamber and sent for Basuaye. Soon, there was a soft knock on the door, and the gaunt man bowed in.

"Rough outing?" he asked.

"Understatement." Nem waved him to a seat. "Where are we on dialogue with the factions?"

The old man sighed, shook his head. "Trying my best. Networks are not what they used to be. I find more people these days are sceptical of anything that looks like a friendly hand." He leaned forward. "But I have heard…things."

He told Nem of eavesdropping on Mawuli, Ebrima, and Inyene's conversations about their respective merchantry, farming, and craftworking guilds. Apparently, whispers had made way to their ears that, for some reason, a flurry of hinterlanders had begun travelling northward and entering Bassa through Fifteenth Ward. After what Nem had just seen in the Breathing Forest, she had an inkling about what the reason might be.

"They say the new splinter factions are welcoming them with open arms, convincing them to join their cause," said Basuaye. "Your advisors fear that with numbers bolstered, and with discontent rising so, they could rebel, try to feed the emperor her own hand and do what she did: march on the Great Dome."

They wouldn't dare, Nem wanted to say, but thought: *Why wouldn't they?* The emperor wasn't even here.

"We are running out of time," Nem said, leaning back in her chair. "We cannot wait on the goodwill of those factions anymore. Either they meet with us now, or we make a proactive move."

Basuaye angled his head. "I would say it'd be unwise to push too hard."

"This is not about pushing hard. New forces arise every day that may destabilize this empire, by action or inaction. We continue like this, and this Great Dome will not last until the emperor's return." She leaned forward. "We must find a way to corral whatever's kindling in the outer wards and douse water over it, or it will sooner burn us all down."

Basuaye nodded. "Okay."

"Take whatever you must, find whoever you must," Nem ordered. "And don't come back until you've succeeded."

29

Basuaye

Bassa: Fifteenth Ward
Sixth Mooncycle, 24

Basuaye emerged from the travelwagon, shut his eyes, and inhaled deeply.

With this came the smells and sounds of Fifteenth, all of which he could still recognise, despite being away for so many mooncycles. After-work sweat and roadside urine. Beans and rice fried in palm oil. Call-and-response music accompanied by foot stomps and hand claps.

"Wait here," he said to his Second, a wiry page assigned to him from the Great Dome. The boy—a Yelekuté—frowned.

"I beg your pardon, Elder, but I was advised that in the absence of civic guards, I am to ensure you are—"

"I am *advising you*," Basuaye said, "to do as I say. If you don't understand why I have not brought civic guards along, then you're not worthy of this conversation."

He turned to the four people behind him: the two Tombolo Elders and two hinterland Elders that Nem had recently sworn into the Great Dome's court alongside him. After learning about the incoming hinterlanders and coastlanders warming up to the factions, Basuaye had decided to bring them along. He suspected their presence might make a difference, persuade the faction leaders that not everyone was on the side of their cause. Weaken their resolve before putting forth the First Consul's propositions.

"No speaking," he said to the four in Mainland Common. "Not even when asked."

"So we are wrappers?" one asked. "Put on to make you look good?"

"No speaking," Basuaye repeated. "Starting now."

As they headed for the meeting point, Basuaye went over his preparations to meet this leader of the largest splinter faction. After the murder of his generals, then his capture and imprisonment, the coalition lost all its appeal. Each leader who tried to revive it failed, causing it to splinter further. There was no enemy to fight anymore, because its very purpose—returning to the days of emperors—had been achieved.

But this new leader had somehow created a new purpose, and many flocked to it.

Basuaye knew nothing about him. All he had was a name given by his informants—Ifiot. None of his old connections could offer more information, other than that Ifiot and his followers were not as confrontational as the original coalition, and had so far organised nothing public. But each informant had been very clear about one thing: This new resistance group was irate and unpredictable, and seemed ready to take on anything they deemed detrimental to their progress. Even the emperor herself.

As they went on, he noticed that Fifteenth had indeed changed much. More people and languages than he remembered, and the ward now seemed to have sprawled into what was once the outskirts of Bassa. Even the housing styles were different, with more ramshackle abodes and fewer built with an eye on permanence, no doubt influence from the incoming population.

A member or two of his group attempted to extend greetings to a fellow hinterlander or coastlander they ran into, but Basuaye stopped them short.

"Focus!" he said. "The people we are meeting are discreet and dangerous. We do not want to announce our presence before we arrive."

He navigated densely packed streets with the group, wrapper cloaks draped over their heads to avoid recognition. Recognition would be bad—it would mean his return being perceived as some sort of homecoming, flying in the face of his mission here. It did feel odd, he would admit, to be on the other side of the fence, fighting for the once-enemy. But at least he wasn't concerned with destruction. Of most interest here was diplomacy, which thankfully left everyone alive. In a way, in fact, he was doing the same thing he had been trying to do as coalition leader: making sure everyone got what they sought.

Soon, he arrived at the establishment in which he had been instructed to wait. It was a public house, but was not yet open for business at this time of evening. A peek inside showed him it was mostly empty, and no music played.

He went in with his group, and they sat down. A couple of people sat around and chatted, waiting for the place to open up. None paid them any attention.

After a short moment, the housekeep came over to Basuaye, laid down a piece of cloth, and walked away. Basuaye read the message, rose, and followed the directions: *past the counter, through the back door, into the corridor.*

A man stood in the shadows. Upon sighting Basuaye and his party, he began moving away. Basuaye followed, familiar with this pattern, one he had in fact designed himself. He couldn't help smiling, proud of his achievements.

After a few turns, the man disappeared under some thatch. Basuaye and his people followed, and soon found themselves squeezing through a narrow yard and a doorway.

A door slammed behind them and pitched the room into darkness. A spark struck, a char cloth set aflame, and a lantern was lit.

There were six people in the room. Basuaye took in the faces: three men, three women. All youthful, all bearing accusatory gazes, all wearing the pomp of their passion like blades. The man who'd led him here disappeared into an inner room.

One of the women—an Emuru, from her complexion—stepped forward. She was the only one who hadn't been seated, perhaps being the only armed person in the room, a long spear strapped to her back. She wore her hair short, much like many in Fifteenth, but kept the decorations of cowrie and beads regardless, sewn into individual dangling plaits. She also wore a healthy amount of facepaint. Looking at her, Basuaye decided she was not a fighter at all. She was a regular citizen who did not forget to look well-dressed and presentable, and who possibly had a gift of speech much similar to his.

"I am Ifiot," she said.

Basuaye frowned. "I was told—"

"You were told wrong, Cockroach," said the woman.

"Ah, my sincere apologies," he said. "I would introduce myself, but it seems you already know who I am."

"Not only do I know who you are, Cockroach," Ifiot said, "but we all knew you would come."

Basuaye nodded. Perhaps he had been hasty to attribute her charged aura to that of passion mixed with inexperience. What she really was was zealous, which was its own thing, and even more dangerous.

"May I sit?" he asked, pointing to a nearby array of chairs. Before she could answer, he sat and waved his group to do the same. He crossed his arms, his way of reminding himself—and them—who was in control of the meeting.

"You look well-fed and rested," said Ifiot, "for someone who was only recently let out of prison."

"Our people say: *A bird that perches on an anthill is still very much on the ground.* I have only perched, my dear Ifiot. The ground that supported me before my capture is still there, only now it is an anthill."

"That should be the last time you call me *dear*," said Ifiot. "If you do it again, you will not have a tongue with which to speak."

Basuaye cocked his head. "Again, forgive me, I mean no disrespect. I came here with the understanding that we would engage in friendly camaraderie."

"That word, *friend*, does not exist between us," said Ifiot. "You are a coward who abandoned your people in their time of need. And now you come back here, dressed in the colours of the enemy."

"There are no enemies in Bassa. Only parties with competing priorities."

"You use their language too, don't you?" Ifiot chuckled, and everyone else in the room chuckled with her. They stopped when she did.

"At least the new emperor does not mince words like you do," Ifiot continued. "She is clear with her aims in the same way we plan to be clear with ours."

"And what are those, your aims?"

"Your ears are not worthy," said Ifiot. "We will only speak them to worthy ears."

"Like?"

"Like the emperor herself."

Basuaye chuckled. "I hate to disappoint you, but the emperor will be out of earshot for quite a while. I am the closest thing to an audience you get."

Ifiot smiled a wry smile, unstrapped the spear from behind her, leaned it on the wall nearby, and finally sat down. Now Basuaye felt like he was making progress.

"Perhaps you judge us by the same indicators you have judged yourself," she said. "This is the first place you are wrong, Cockroach. You failed, during your time as leader of your coalition, to gain the attention of the Idu and their cohort. Yet that is all you were—an attention-seeker. We have bigger ambitions."

"How so?" asked Basuaye. "No one knows who you are or what you're doing. No one knows you."

"Again, you only perceive through the lens of attention, of performance. We do not aim to perform. We aim to *do*."

"Do what?"

She shrugged. "What else do a downtrodden people fight for? We no longer want to be the grass upon which the elephants trample. We want to be the elephant."

"How are you downtrodden?" asked Basuaye. "Any sensible lips would proclaim that, in fact, the Red Emperor has liberated us all. She fought for this empire under the banner of the very same coalition you claim to represent."

"There you sit, wearing the finest wrappers, telling us, who sit over here in wrappers that cannot keep the cold away at night, who is downtrodden and who isn't." Ifiot scoffed. "You call us liberated, but look around this ward. Have our abodes changed? Have our occupations? Have our circumstances? You look at us and still see Emuru, look at people like your Second and think: Potokin, Yelekuté." She pointed to the Elders he had arrived with. "You stand with them at this meeting, but do you stand with them outside this room? Is there a soul in this city, you included, who will welcome hinterlanders and coastlanders and swamplanders, who will let them mingle in the city with us?"

Basuaye wondered how she knew what his Second looked like. They must have had him followed for much longer than he'd thought.

"Not a soul," Ifiot pressed. "But *we* will."

Basuaye frowned. "You will what?"

"Welcome them," she said. "Once we destroy the Great Dome and rid this continent of its artificial divisions: wards, protectorates, fences—all of it."

Basuaye blinked. "You cannot be serious."

Ifiot blinked back. "Dreams are serious things, Cockroach. We dream of a republic of nations, succeeding together with mutual respect, trade, and development. We hope to achieve this dream. And we do not need a redeemer to lead us there. We will do it as we plan to rule it—by council."

"And what council is this?"

"Does it matter? We will not have a name, because we do not need one."

"Listen," said Basuaye. "You are but a few. You will need hundreds more to join you before the emperor gets wind of your activities and sends any one of her forces after you: beast, Soldiers of Red, peace officers, civic guards—take your pick."

"Well." Ifiot rose and cocked her head. "Our ancestors say: *You do not wash your hands with spittle when you lie by the stream.* We have chosen to wash our hands in the stream."

A strike, and the brief brightness of a char cloth flame lit up the inner room. The doorway, which had been dark all this time, became illuminated once the lamp was lit. Then the man who had led Basuaye emerged, and after him came another figure.

The sheer height of the person caused Basuaye himself to rise. Basuaye was a tall man, but this person was at least a head taller, and not as lanky. When Basuaye had looked in the room and seen youthful zealots, he had deemed them unable to grasp the extremes they might need to go to in order to achieve what they wanted. These children had never killed a person in their lives.

The man standing before him had. Basuaye was sure of it.

He was dressed in clothes that Basuaye had never seen, and his skin was darker than the darkest Idu Basuaye had ever set eyes upon. Judging by the decorative marks etched into his face and the large pieces of jewellery hanging from his ears, this man had never seen this side of the mainland before either. He stood barefoot, two hands folded behind him, and it was clear this was a person who understood power in all its manifestations, and knew exactly how to use it.

"Who…" Basuaye, for the first time in a long while, found words failing him.

"Perhaps I should offer you another wise word from our ancestors," said Ifiot. *"Do not start a fire in a dry forest, because you never know what may catch."* She pointed to the man standing in front of them. "Your emperor, upon deciding that every land the sun touches is hers, ventured into the delta swamps and started a fire by capturing the Ninki Nanka. The *one* beast who, for decades, was revered by every swamplander for being the reason the seas did not overrun the swamps and all who lived there. But she wanted power so much that she took away the one thing that kept all the peoples of the delta settlements in the swamplands. Kept them from leaving, yes, but also kept them from dying. Now, thanks to your emperor, the swamplanders must find a new home, before the seas find them." Ifiot cocked her head. "You know what this means, yes? For the first time in hundreds of seasons, the peoples of the delta settlements have been given reason to venture inland. And venture inland they have."

Basuaye glanced over the man, his heart rate increasing. *A swamplander? In Bassa?*

"You are…from the delta settlements?" he asked the man.

"He doesn't speak our languages," Ifiot said. "And we will not be translating for you because your ears are of no use to us."

"Just tell me what you want. We can always find a way to discuss this."

"I *have* told you. Were you not listening?"

"You can't seriously want to gather warriors from all over the mainland and bring them to Bassa?"

"Why not? Your emperor seems to think it is a winning strategy." She pointed to the Tombolo and hinterland Elders beside him. "Are they not from your court?"

"Yes, but—" Basuaye breathed deeply, calmed himself. "You do not want to start a war with Bassa."

"No, we do not," said Ifiot. "We want to start a funeral for the empire."

Basuaye felt all the fight slowly leave his body. Now he understood what he had been told. These were not people to be reasoned with. These were people driven by something that could not be satiated by dialogue. These were, as he had been truly forewarned, people driven by rage alone.

"Okay, okay," said Basuaye. "I will take your message back to the emperor. Is there anything else you would like me to tell her?"

Ifiot smiled, clicked her tongue, and the swamplander moved. Not a lot of steps, but enough to reach the spear leaning on the wall. He grabbed it, and in the same swift motion, turned and hurled it at Basuaye.

Basuaye did not feel pain when the spear impaled his chest, or drove him into the wall and pinned him there, in the corner of the room. All he could feel was the pounding in his ears, his vision failing, his senses straining to catch what they could. His heart beat faster and faster, trying to keep him alive. Blood welled up in his throat, and he coughed it out, pouring over his lips, his tongue struggling to translate what it was tasting—*metal? salt? bitters?*

Ifiot went over to the alarmed Elders and spoke to them. Basuaye, senses failing, could catch only snatches of the words: *tell your people . . . something big . . . us or Bassa . . . no in-between.*

Then Ifiot turned to him, sidling up to where he was pinned. He could only see her out of what was left of his peripheral vision, fading as fast as his heart. She leaned in close, so that her breath was like a flame in his ear.

"As I said," Ifiot whispered, "we do not speak to ears unworthy. But if you must give the emperor a message when she joins you in the skies, tell her this: We want her to know that it was the Nameless faction that did it."

30

Lilong

CAMPING IN THE OPEN savanna at night was a perilous endeavour. There was always something seeking a next meal, and not all of them were afraid of people. Ugo, who had spent some time with animal trainers in Chugoko, explained that the wild leopards were the least of their worries, as they didn't attack people except when their usual prey became scarce. The most dangerous animals here, Ugo said, were not predators, but insects like mosquitoes and pilferers like hyenas.

Regardless, Lilong insisted on barricading the party—travelwagon on one side, kwagas on the other—to form an enclosed camp. But even then, it was impossible to sleep soundly. The savanna mosquitoes, almost nonexistent during the day, intensified tenfold at night, buzzing about with menace. A bite from one meant severe fever and dehydration—and on the road, that was sure death. Alaba had packed some repellent oil, but between the five of them, it finished quickly. Luckily, Ugo knew a recipe of the eucalyptus leaf, and that tree thrived in the savanna.

A pack of hyenas found their camp a few nights after the peace officer encounter. They did not come close, but watched from afar in coordinated groups, eyes lit, waiting for whoever was on watch to doze off. When Danso and Alaba, both on watch, dozed off at the same time, the hyenas converged. If not for Thema, who awoke then and fussed, causing Ugo to wake and raise the alarm after spotting red fiery eyes prowling the camp, all their supplies might have been stolen.

Upon hearing the alarm, Oke rose, and her eyes turned grey instantly. She pulled from the dying fire and batted the beasts back. The hyenas scattered into the grass, laughing into the dark, embers trailing after them. A quick assessment showed that they had done little more than rummage through storage and pilfer some smoked meat.

"Is this whole journey going to be like this?" Danso, ruffled, asked.

"This is nothing," said Oke. "Wait until we get to the real wilderness."

So far, they had not run into any new predators, save for the night Ugo had spotted a puff adder slipping through the grass, chasing after a rodent.

"Blacksmith was right," said Ugo. "We should be seeing all these animals, yes, but not all in the same place, and not all at once."

"You think we'll see—what did he call them, *genge*?" asked Danso.

Ugo shrugged. "Maybe we look out for the little hills he spoke of. As a precaution."

For Lilong, surviving wild animals was the easier part of the trip. She was yet to recover from the peace officer encounter, and found herself irritated by Oke and her partners' behaviours. The three always found new ways to bicker, and Lilong couldn't tell if it was worse that the arguments were never really bitter or aimed at inflicting harm. Just expressions of frustration here and there in the manner of many romantic relationships. It raised tension among the group, and everyone was forced to sit in the negative energy they left behind, like pigs in shit.

Then, in the same manner of many romantic relationships, they would reconcile and return to good relations by nightfall. That, in fact, became the most annoying part of it all for Lilong, because said apology and good relations would then lead to, well, *really good relations*.

Nightfall today, for instance. They had come upon one of the safest campsites they'd found in a while—higher ground—and could finally let off their guard for a bit. After Oke and Alaba had largely ignored each other the whole day due to the ever-present argument that Oke should never have dragged her partners on this trip, Ugo ended up playing peacemaker. After said mediation was over, Oke came over to Lilong and attempted to hand Thema over. *Just for a moment*, she said.

"Why?" Lilong snapped, eyeing the squirming child. "Because I'm a woman or what?"

"I'll take her," said Danso, writing nearby.

Afterward, the three partners commandeered the unhitched travel-wagon for the specific purpose of vigorously exploring their bodies. It was not their first time having sex on the road, but those had been too-short moments stolen under sleeping packs, attempting to whisper their moans so as not to wake Lilong and Danso (it never worked—Lilong always heard them). Tonight, however, they had given up all discretion and invested time and energy in the act. Which was how it came to be that Lilong sat with Danso, squirming child in his arms, while behind them, the unhitched travelwagon rocked gently.

"They could have waited a few more days," Lilong was saying. "They could have had a proper bed and better privacy at the Weary Sojourner."

Danso shrugged. "Sometimes, the body just wants what it wants."

Lilong raised an eyebrow. "Ah, so your new best friends have confided in you, have they?"

"Best friends?" Danso snorted. "Wait—don't tell me you're jealous?"

"Jealous? What am I—a child?"

"No, jealous because you have no friends."

Lilong winced, but Danso didn't see it.

"Besides," he continued, "bodily desires don't go on holiday just because our lives are in peril. Haven't you heard the saying that in war-time, all soldiers think of is sex and death? All I'm saying is that it's nothing to be ashamed of."

"Well, this savanna must be making me hear things," Lilong said, "because the mighty jali of Bassa did not just defend sex on the open road."

Danso laughed. "I'm just saying! Not everyone can be emperor of restraint like you."

For the second time, something he didn't mean as an insult stung Lilong anyway. She shifted in her seat.

"Is that what you really think of me?" she asked. "That I suppress myself?"

Danso looked up from the child. "No, Lilong, I mean—" He pursed his lips, searching for the right words. "I know you have your particular way of…being. I just wonder—when you bear the weight of responsibility for so long, it does something to a person, you know? Easy to forget to listen to your body and mind when you put yourself under so much pressure."

"So, be like you, then. Go wherever my nose points."

"Harsh!" he said, laughing. "But—I don't know—is that so bad?" He adjusted in his seat. "Okay, like this—when last did you think of someone you'd like to, you know…" He angled his head. "Rock your travelwagon."

Lilong had indeed considered this, starting back in Chabo, where there was no shortage of charming young men eager to take off her wrappers. But no—her restraint was not because she did not enjoy relations or companionship. It was because so much of her was still not…*hers*. She had given all of herself over to something else, and now that foundation was crumbling. She couldn't *also* give herself over to a person. Not until this was over. Not until she knew who she was.

"Contrary to your smelling opinion," said Lilong, "I know what it is to be loved."

Danso's eyes widened. "No lie?" He grinned. "Do tell!"

Lilong shook her head, thinking of Turay back home. When she had conceded defeat, distanced herself from him, and chalked up what they had to youthful infatuation, these actions had ended up searing deep marks in her heart. And though both of them had remained friends and continued to be around each other, she believed Turay's heart carried those same marks. Something permanent had shifted between them.

Or maybe it was only permanent in her mind. Unlike her, Turay was not quite the kind to bury himself so deeply into something that he couldn't be extricated from it. With him, a door was always open. She wanted to believe—and a part of her truly did—that somewhere in Namge, Turay was still there, waiting for an answer from her.

Lilong sighed. *It's for the best*, she'd once convinced herself. But as Danso said, sometimes, it was okay to go where your nose was pointing. So right here, right now, she thought: *If I get a second chance, if we get home safe, if that door is still open—maybe I'll walk through it.*

The travelwagon stopped rocking. A moment later, Ugo exited, glancing at them sheepishly. Lilong and Danso snickered. Thema, laughing with them, hiccuped, and a quarter of her last meal spilled from her mouth and all over Danso.

"Moons!" Danso leaned over. "Hold her a moment while I get this off."

Lilong received the child. It was her first time holding Thema, and the girl felt smaller than expected. Warm too. Comfy. She babbled, as if happy about the mess she had caused. Lilong chuckled back at her.

"What about you?" Lilong asked Danso as he wiped his wrappers. "I've never heard you speak of anyone you fancy. Anyone outside of, you know, *her*."

He tilted his head. "I..." He stopped wiping his wrappers for a half moment, then continued. "It's complicated."

Lilong did not press. There had to be some damage done to anyone who had to endure being the intended of one of the most ruthless emperors the continent had seen. She wouldn't fault him if he never again wanted to look at another person with interest.

Ugo came over and offered to relieve Lilong of the baby. Lilong looked at Thema, now drifting into sleep, face tucked into the crook of her arm. Warm. Comfy.

"Not yet," replied Lilong. "Just a little while longer."

⋄ ⸺ ⸺ ⋄

The next day, they did not go far before spotting the first little hill. It was an isolated cleft outcrop, whipped into shape by fierce, dry winds. It stood out in the grassland like a thumbs up, surrounded by a clump of vegetation that seemed greener than everything else around it.

The group stopped, crouched in the grass, and waited.

Danso was the first to spot the pack of genge lazying about the little hill. At first glance, they looked like the blacksmith had truly said: tall as antelopes, darker than leopards, ears like a kwaga's. But that was where all the normal ended, and the ethereal and otherworldly began.

They were spindlier than any four-legged creature Lilong had ever seen. Velvety skin shimmered with each movement, but they weren't hairless—in lieu of fur, numerous strands of *skin* extended from all over their bodies, sticking out like a cat's whiskers, swaying of their own accord, *sensing* the environment like a cockroach's antenna. The animals themselves moved in a manner that was similarly confusing—slow and stately at first, then in quick bursts, as if spooked, then slow again, each time iridescent.

Their mouths, when they opened them, were traps. There were more teeth in there than Lilong believed any animal should be allowed to have.

"Magnificent," said Danso, when they first spotted the pack. He reached into his wrappers for a stylus to draw with. Lilong put a hand over his and shook her head slowly.

"They're hunting," she said.

Indeed they were, and their target seemed to be a wildcat, a predator in its own right. But the genge did not look like they understood or respected the natural order of things. One genge, slightly bigger than the others, paced back and forth, shooting the group glances whenever it could. The others followed suit, prancing as it did.

"That's a dominant," said Ugo with conviction. "Looks like a hunting vote."

"How do you know?" asked Danso.

"Pack animals. They're all the same."

The dominant genge sneezed. The rest of the pack—about eight in total—sneezed back in unison.

"Well," said Ugo, "sorry to that wildcat."

As he said it, the pack rose and charged at the wildcat, which first attempted to stand its ground, then turned tail at the last moment. But it was too late. The genge were faster than anything Lilong had ever seen run. They didn't even all need to chase the wildcat—they simply seemed to enjoy doing so, as if toying with it. But toying or not, soon, the wildcat was between those trap-like teeth, and then there were only blood and intestines left.

"Where could they have even come from?" Alaba wondered aloud. Oke, next to him, baby strapped to her back, was lost deep in thought.

"I don't know, but they surely don't belong here." Ugo pointed to the little hill. "You know why they gather there? Stone hills like those have crevices that trap water from the rainy season. Or at least when there was still a proper rainy season in these parts." He massaged his chin. "These animals expect this place to be green, maybe like it was back, I don't know... four, five hundred seasons ago?"

"You're saying they're from the past?" asked Danso.

Ugo shrugged. "I'm saying they think nothing has changed."

They gave the little hill a wide berth, and Lilong thought they had put the matter of the genge behind them. But at their next stop to switch wagon drivers—Alaba for Ugo—Danso had a thought.

"The Diwi," he said, cornering Lilong at the rear of the wagon, where she was sorting rations for the forthcoming evening meal. "Is your offer of practice still up?"

Lilong frowned. "I feel like I won't like where this is going."

"No, listen." He sounded inspired. "We should go back. Get one of them."

"Get one of who?"

"The genge."

Lilong stopped sorting. "Explain *get*."

"You want me to find my way back to iborworking, yes? So, instead of some harmless critter, we get the biggest predator in the savanna. Imagine capturing one of those, Possessing it, Commanding it." His tone had become breathless, enchanted. "We use it to protect us, like the Skopi. We make camp wherever we want, sleep however long we like. We cut through any predator, any peace officers. We get back on the open road, we cross the savanna in no time."

Lilong put away the rations and stared at Danso. Whoever this was, it wasn't the young jali she'd called out to for help in that Bassai barn seasons ago. This was someone who said things like *cut through* when they meant *kill*. This was someone who'd been so racked by anger and loss that he couldn't see how it was slowly chipping away at who he used to be.

"I'm not sure we need a genge for... that." She tried her best to be gentle. "We can handle ourselves."

"Oh, can we now? Is every band of peace officers going to fall for the baby-in-your-face routine? We escaped by the skin of our teeth!"

"I'm replenished now. I can handle them."

"At best, you're still one against many, and that is still insufficient. At worst, it means we *die*, Lilong. Enough people have died already, don't you think? I don't want to die, Lilong. Not today, not on this journey, not ever."

He was sweating. She realised, now, that his situation was worse than she'd thought. He seemed to have been doing all right since before the heist. Something must have happened to take him back to this place of gloom and recklessness.

Ah. It dawned on her now. *Kubra.* Witnessing such a brutal death would leave a mark on any person.

"Kubra's death was...unprecedented," she said. "That will not happen to anyone on this trip. Not while I'm here. I promise."

"And if you aren't? What then—we become helpless?" He shook his head. "I've been helpless for too long, Lilong. I can't do it anymore. I need...*something*." He pointed in the direction of the isolated hill they'd left behind. "That's *something*."

Before he turned to leave, he said: "If you won't help me, fine. I'll ask Ugo, and we'll take a stab at the next pack we see." He paused. "Don't try and stop me. I've already made up my mind."

31

Danso

The Lonely Roads East
Sixth Mooncycle, 27

UGO AND DANSO ROSE before daybreak and prepared to hike back to the isolated hill they'd left behind, to see if the pack of genge was still there. The night before, when Danso had broached the subject to Ugo, he had nodded solemnly, squinting like a sage older brother, before simply replying, "Say when."

Under the twilight of dawn, they gathered every conceivable weapon they could find without waking up the rest of camp. Danso felt underprepared regardless. These were no ordinary beasts after all. He'd been of a mind to steal the Diwi from Lilong and take it along, just in case. But the pouch at her hip remained glued to her body, even when she was asleep.

They were about to head out when Lilong suddenly appeared and stood before them, bright-eyed, fully dressed, blade at the ready. The stone-bone pouch was with her.

"I told you I don't want anybody to die," she said. "And I meant it."

They set out without waking Alaba and Oke, instead leaving a message in the sand: *Gone hunting nearby, will be back before noon.* Then they began their trek.

The genge were still there when they arrived at the spot an hour later. Or *a* genge—just one, lying in the grass and soaking in the early morning sun. The rest of the pack was nowhere to be seen. It was unclear if they were nearby, or if this one had been abandoned.

The trio surveyed the resting genge for another hour, lying in the grass a distance from the outcrop, waiting to see if others came to join. Nothing.

"If this isn't a sign from the moon sisters, I don't know what is," said Danso. "Best we strike now while the iron is still hot."

Lilong, the dregs of her previous hesitation still lingering, sighed. Danso had never seen her this reluctant to use iborworking. How could one have access to something so great and be so hesitant about employing it for a good cause? Now he realised how silly he must've looked all this time, rejecting this power in favour of... what? Sitting in a dark room and moping?

"It's as I said," she said finally. "I go alone. You two wait here."

She didn't even didn't need to go too close to the genge. After finding a good vantage point behind a nearby naboom plant, she shut her eyes and unleashed her power.

The blade flew, clean and true, and sliced through the neck of the animal. But it didn't stop there. For assurance, she Commanded it to strike certain spots: skull (in case it had a brain), upper torso (in case it had a heart), all four knees (so it couldn't walk even if it lived), face (as a precaution). It was bloody, messy, and efficient.

All was silent in the savanna afterward, as Lilong trudged back to where Danso and Ugo waited. She untied her pouch, retrieved the Diwi—still wrapped in cloth—and handed it over to Danso.

"All yours," she said.

Danso and Ugo approached the animal together. (Lilong opted not to go. *Seen enough death already*, she said.) Up close, the genge was much larger than he'd thought, almost kwaga-sized. Ugo knelt next to it, plucked dry grass, and wiped the blood off the beast's snout.

"What a waste of something so beautiful," he said.

"At least we can still get some use out of it," said Danso, rolling the bundle from one hand to another. "You've... never seen this, have you?"

"Seen one resurrect a deceased being? No, I can't say I have."

Danso chuckled. "You might want to join Lilong. It's not... pleasant."

Ugo surprisingly agreed, leaving Danso to slowly unwrap the stone-bone. When his fingers brushed the bare ibor, it felt so cold, so smooth, so old. Somewhere within his body, once-dormant senses arose, but only in a trickle. The responses felt strange but familiar, like reuniting with an old friend. This was the first time he was touching it since they'd emerged from the Soke mountains, and it returned to him a sense of confidence and control, a welcome feeling he'd sorely missed.

He knelt in the grass, gripped the Diwi tight, and placed a palm on the dead genge.

The stirrings of power within him began, but soon he realised something was amiss. That was all they were—stirrings. They did not grow into a rush of power as he'd expected, or overtake him and bring him into being one with the animal. When he opened his eyes, nothing had changed. The genge remained cold and dead in the grass.

He tried again, and again, and again. Nothing. He stared at the stone-bone, surprised, then rushed back to where Lilong and Ugo lay in wait.

"Something is wrong," he said, troubled. "I think the Diwi's been stolen." He handed Lilong the heirloom. "I think this is a fake."

Lilong received it with a frown and examined. "No, it's the same."

"Then why isn't it working? I did everything like usual."

Lilong looked from him to the stone-bone to the animal in the distance. "I don't know."

"I can still feel the power and everything, but it's like . . . it's too far and I can't reach it."

"Or too small and you can't grow it," said Lilong.

"Exactly." Danso paused. "Wait, so you know about this?"

Lilong gazed wistfully into the distance. "Not *this*. But I've seen something . . . similar happen to warriors back home. A broken connection between an Iborworker and their stones."

"What was wrong with the stones?"

"Not with the stones, Danso. With the Iborworker." She peered into his eyes. "With *you*."

That gave him pause.

"No," he said. "No, no, no. We can't have done this for nothing." He stepped forward. "How do I stop it? What do I need to change?"

"Nothing," she replied. "In every situation I've witnessed, the disconnection was always because something else was broken within the person. Something else they needed to fix before the power could find them." She shrugged again. "The only way to surmount it is to try and try again, until you find your way there."

Danso could see that Lilong was doing her best to be gentle. Once, he'd have appreciated that. But now, he hated it. He did not need anyone's pity. He just wanted to have some damn agency. Moons, was that too much to ask?

"We should head back," Ugo interjected. "The others will be getting worried by now. And that dead beast will attract other predators and pilferers, if not the rest of the pack itself."

"Then we take it with us," said Danso. He turned to Lilong. "Try and try again, you said, right? That's what I'll do."

"That is one heavy beast," said Ugo. "I'm not sure we can travel lightly with that."

"Lightly, slowly, what does it matter," said Danso. "We won't make it to our destination anyway if we don't have better protection."

Lilong was still silent, pondering. After a moment, she said, "Ugo is right. We shouldn't take that with us. But I understand what you are going through, and I understand that there could be benefits to this. It is reckless, foolhardy. It is going wherever your nose points." She paused. "But maybe sometimes we need that. I can't say if this is one of those times, but I'm willing to take this chance. For you."

Danso was unsure if to say *thank you* or *fuck you*.

"Consider it a favour," she said. "Perhaps the last one I'll do for you in a while."

Fuck you was more like it, then.

· ⋄ ⋯ ———— ⋯ ⋄ ·

The genge, when they'd successfully lugged it back to camp, surprisingly fit into the spacious rear of the travelwagon. Alaba and Oke were at once alarmed and fascinated by what the group had brought back, and were a bit surprised it was not meant to be food.

They rejoined the road, with Ugo driving and Alaba occupied with

Thema. Danso finally had something new to enter into his codex, and was in the process of doing so when Oke brought everyone in the travelwagon to attention.

"I've been pondering," she said. "About where the genge came from. And I think—I finally have a theory."

"Go on," said Lilong.

"Remember the Risisi plagues? From the tale?"

"I remember." Though he didn't need to, Danso flipped through his codex to the place where he had documented *The Cautionary Tale of the Stone City of Risisi*, as told to him by Oke over their trip. He scanned the pages and read out the plagues in question for their benefit.

"Plagues of dirt, fire, wind, water, and beasts." He paused, his eyes lighting up. "*Beasts.*"

"Exactly," said Oke, conviction in her tone. "I think something has happened in the seven islands."

"Like what?"

"An event. A *catalyst*."

Lilong sat up at the same time Danso did.

"I think someone has set off the plagues."

By late evening, Ugo had found a suitable campsite. They set up quickly and went straight to nighttime arrangements. Danso spent most of the time in deep conversation with Oke. Both were equally frenzied by the possibility that the genge were Risisi's plague of beasts come to life. What did this mean for the islands, for Bassa, for Oon? What did this mean for their trip, for Jaoudou's plans?

He found Oke to be a delightful intellectual companion. For the first time in a while, he felt like a jali again, like he was back at the university chatting with a fellow scholar—postulating, projecting, scribbling. None of the others responded in a similar manner. Ugo maintained a workmanlike, practical demeanour, while Alaba became deeply invested in worrying about their fates. And Lilong—she simply curled in a corner of the wagon, lost in her own head.

After Ugo and Alaba had put Thema to sleep, Oke made her way over to where Danso was writing in his codex, and they continued their discussion. Lilong emerged from the travelwagon, bleary-eyed. She sat next to them, at first saying nothing. Then, after a while, she cleared her throat.

"So," she said.

Danso and Oke looked at one another.

"So," Oke replied.

"It's time," she said, staring at Danso.

Danso blinked. "Time for what?"

"To show her the..." She angled her head.

"Oh. Are you...*sure*?"

Lilong turned to face Oke. "Did he trust you?"

"Who?"

"My daa. Did he trust you?"

Oke offered a wry, sad smile.

"He took hold of your family heirloom and rode for days to meet me at the Weary Sojourner. I would say that takes trust."

"And you trusted him too?"

"As much as I could."

Lilong gave her a long look, then turned to Danso and nodded.

Danso shrugged, then reached into Lilong's pouch, which he now wore around his body. He pulled out the bunch of rags tied with strips of cloth. Unwrapping them took a moment, but once done, he set the Diwi carefully on the ground.

Oke's eyes lit up. Danso took this to mean that the woman recognised the chunk of red stone-bone, even if she'd never seen it before. Lilong's daa must have described it to her at least, and it had not changed much— still chipped, still lustrous, still retaining much of its character.

"Does it...work?" was her first question, once she had regained her composure. She reached forward and made to grab it, then stopped herself at the last moment, realising that touch possibly came with consequences.

"It does," said Lilong. "On some people." She motioned toward Danso.

Oke's eyes widened. *"You?"*

Danso shrugged, grinned.

"Tell me more," she said.

"Here," said Danso, handing her his codex. "It's all here."

They waited as Oke read silently, leaning into the light of the fire. Danso watched her digest his accounts of everything before Chabo: Lilong on the mainland, crossing the Breathing Forest, the Skopi, the discovery of red iborworking, the dalliance with Whudasha, the great escape in the Dead Mines.

By nightfall proper, when her two partners had fallen soundly asleep, Oke had learned about Esheme and Oboda and the Whudasha Youth and Zaq and Habba.

She shut the codex and lifted her head. Her eyes were watery.

"Now you understand," said Lilong.

Oke nodded. "I understand."

Lilong rose. "Maybe, now, you will think of me less harshly, and know that I'm not stupid, or unfeeling. That I am simply..."

"Afraid," said Oke.

"No," said Lilong. "Tired."

But to Danso, watching her closely, her eyes said: *Yes.*

32

Biemwensé

Bassa: Outskirts
Sixth Mooncycle, 23

ON THE MORNING BIEMWENSÉ and Kakutan left the tiny homestead outside of Bassa in whose barn they had been hiding for half a fortnight, they donned wrappers over their heads and bade goodbye to the owners. The couple, two men—one mainlander, one desertlander, just like the Gaddos—were familiar with the entails of living on the outskirts of the Bassai Ideal, literally and figuratively. The younger of them, who came from merchant blood, had invested his privilege of land ownership in the Gaddo Company, becoming one of various waypoints connecting the otherwise wilderness between the city and the border.

They offered the women a travelwagon, but Kakutan refused. She thought it would attract too much attention, especially if they ran into any overeager civic guards. In lieu of that, the couple furnished them with a pack of supplies—food, water, medicine, two short blades—and sent them on their way.

Walking to the fringes of the city was arduous and time-consuming, lasting the better part of the day. It was no match for their earlier trip, in which Alaba's directions had led them from Chugoko to a small vigilante outpost and to the contacts they sought. Then they had taken a circuitous route through a circumspect portion of the border, a little ways east of the Pass itself. They did not go under like last time, as it turned out the border was more porous than usual because large parts of it were in various states of disrepair.

The paucity of civic guard patrols continued once they'd entered the mainland, and also now, as they headed for Bassa. That didn't make their trip any less challenging, though. Entering Bassa from the outskirts meant that there was an equal chance of arriving at Sixth Ward as there was arriving at Tenth. The women had little intelligence on how to ensure they entered closer to Fifteenth than not. As it stood, their plan was like a blade thrown by a blindfolded person: equal chance of being completely deadly or completely useless.

Both women trudged on for the better part of the day, keeping well out of sight. So far, they'd only come across lone travellers. There were no notices out for their capture like Danso and Lilong had, so they were at little risk of being identified except by the Red Emperor herself, the only person who had set eyes on them. But it was best to be cautious than caught unawares, so they wrapped away every measure of skin to prevent their complexions and likenesses from being easily deduced. Beneath the folds of cloth, sweat ran slick down Biemwensé's armpits and settled in the folds of her belly. The sun had doubled its heat, become angrier.

Soon, the architecture of the city loomed before them. The heights, designs, and relative cleanliness of the buildings ahead were sufficient evidence that they had arrived at a ward much closer to the Great Dome than intended.

"We could go around," said Biemwensé to Kakutan.

The younger woman wrinkled her nose. She had not spoken much throughout their journey and had spent much of her alone time deep in thought. Biemwensé would give a cowrie to learn what plagued the woman, but she sensed it was the same thing that plagued her. Both of them, independently and together, had failed Whudasha, and they wanted to correct that. But they both feared that they would die or be captured before being able to.

"Night comes too early these days," said Kakutan. "It'll be unwise to camp in the open this close to the city." She spat in nearby shrubbery. "Perhaps we can find somewhere to hide until morning."

Rather than step into the mainway that ran through the ward, they slipped into its corridors and hugged the shadows. There were more Idu and Emuru using these backways than Biemwensé's foggy memory remembered were allowed. Between the heavily starched wrappers, face-paint, and the size of the courtyards they went past, Biemwensé took a guess and decided they had landed somewhere between Fifth and Seventh Wards.

She also sensed something amiss. There was much serious chatter—not gossip, but the kinds people huddled in a corner and whispered. Everyone: nobles, mainlanders, immigrants, even the few civic guard patrols they came across. Biemwensé attuned her ear and tried to grasp the discourse but fell short of the exact words. She came away with only the overwhelming feeling of anxiety and impatience gripping the city.

They circled the corridors covertly for two hours until darkness met them there. Still, they were yet to find a compound with an open barn or stable into which they could slip and spend the night.

"Perhaps it's time to try our luck with the mainway," said Kakutan, after they had surveyed their umpteenth barn and found it fortified against entry.

"Wait," said Biemwensé, pointing. "Listen."

A small distance from the barn behind which they hid, a trio that looked like farmhands offloaded a large cart. They tucked bales of cotton and bags of what seemed to be kolanuts into storage in other equally secured barns in the compound. They worked quickly, and as they did, spoke a rapid-fire combination of Mainland Common and some kind of border pidgin.

"What are they saying?" Kakutan's Mainland Common was not as good as her Whudan.

"The tall one says they need to be quick so he can get back home for evening food," said Biemwensé. "The other two are laughing, saying Fifteenth is not that far away."

Kakutan nodded. "They're heading back there once done." The woman eyed the wagon. "A tight squeeze, that'll be. I don't see how we can hide in there without at least one of them spotting us."

"I wasn't planning on hiding," said Biemwensé, then stepped out.

"What are you—?" Kakutan started, but Biemwensé was already gone.

"Dehje!" she greeted, loud enough that it startled all three farmhands. "Dehje!"

They soon relaxed once Biemwensé pulled her cloak over.

"I...lost," she said, wearing her Old Woman Voice like a wrapper. She repeated the words in a random border pidgin, then in Mainland Common, then in Savanna Common, hoping the men would latch on to at least one.

It worked. One of the laughing farmhands, who looked like the most experienced and therefore with most authority, relaxed. His body language shifted from that of fear to concern.

"Are you okay?" he asked, matching her Savanna Common. "Are you looking for somebody?"

"Yes, yes, thank the Four Winds, yes!" She paused and bent forward, feigning breathlessness. The man put down his bale of cotton and stepped to her, waving his colleagues to continue with the offloading.

"Who do you seek?"

"My son," she said. "My son. Sent to Fifteenth Ward, they say. We are trying to find him."

"*We?*" the man said, then looked up, and anxiety returned to his posture again. Kakutan's shadow loomed over them both.

"This is my sister," said Biemwensé, "who has come with me from our small town along the borders." She put a hand over her mouth as if she had said something wrong. "Oh no, I should not have—I should not have said." She looked at Kakutan. "I am so sorry, sister. I forget sometimes." She turned to the man. "Please, do not report us, I beg you. We are not trying to cause any trouble. We are simply trying to find the boy and take him back home to his family, where he belongs. We have walked for days—" She shook her head, slowly. "He is only a small boy, all alone..."

"No, no, maa," said the man. "No, we will not report you." He placed his hands akimbo. "You don't have to worry, I understand. Family is everything, yes? I came to this land just like you, without the blessing of the elephant throne. You do what you need to for family." He gestured toward his colleagues. "You are just in luck—we are going to Fifteenth. You..." He glanced at Kakutan. "You can come with us." He turned to his colleagues. "Yes?"

The other two looked at one another and nodded.

Biemwensé let them help her into the wagon. While the farmhands went on to finish their offloading, Kakutan came and sat beside her.

"Well, that was reckless," she whispered, her lips registering minimal movement. "They could have easily been pro-Bassa. Then we'd be in hot soup. You should always wait until we have a clear and reliable plan."

"One former Supreme Magnanimous to another," said Biemwensé, "your plans are often shit."

"That's not true."

"We are here because of your last plan."

"That was *your* plan."

"Yes, but only the parts that *worked*."

Kakutan clicked the back of her throat. "With this your coconut head, it's a wonder they didn't kick you out of the Youth earlier."

Biemwensé went silent.

"Oh, I'm . . ." Kakutan sighed. "Sorry, that was too far."

"Yes, it was," said Biemwensé. "You have no respect for elders."

"I think I'm just . . ."

"Afraid?"

The younger woman looked at her. Even without the light to see, Biemwensé knew her eyes were moist and honest.

"Me too," she said, and placed a hand over Kakutan's.

She did understand. Afanfan and Owude were not her real children, in the same way the Whudans were not really Kakutan's family. But it did not matter. They were leaders, and their job was to lead. Biemwensé had failed at hers twice—at the large scale of the protectorate, and at the smaller scale of her home—with nothing left to salvage from either. Afanfan and Owude, and the children who had come before them, had been the only ones willing to give her a chance, an opportunity to lead again. They had come willingly, looking beyond the stories that denounced her as a madwoman. *Lead*, their eager gazes had said, *and we will follow*.

She had obliged, and so had Kakutan, in her own way. They had failed, yes, but they had the chance to do it over. Fear was natural, but so was courage.

The farmhands had finished offloading.

"Do we need to hide?" asked Kakutan, once they all climbed on.

"Hide?" said the lead farmhand, then chuckled. "Ooh, no, maa. This city has bigger problems than two women from over the border." He leaned toward them, conspiratorially. "And if you ask me? This is just the beginning." He looked up, breathed in a chestful of air, and exhaled.

"Big things are coming," he announced to no one in particular. Then he goaded the kwagas.

The wagon rolled out of the courtyards and joined the mainway.

Biemwensé

Bassa: Fifteenth Ward
Sixth Mooncycle, 24–26

Biemwensé and Kakutan spent their first day in Fifteenth Ward at a public house, gathering courage. Kakutan, being the more agile of the two, eventually went out and mingled, garnering as much information about the Whudans as she could. Once they had sufficient information on where to locate the Whudan quarter they sought, they headed there the next morning.

Much like on the night they had arrived under the cover of darkness, Biemwensé could sense something impending. An incessant crackle and pop of excitement filled the air. Biemwensé noted that she did not feel endangered by it, only flummoxed, things moving faster than she could keep up with. The myriad manners of speech, the variations in manner of appearance, the frenetic pace of hustling for an everyday living. If not for the climate and the darker inclinations of most complexions, she could have sworn it was Chugoko by another name.

At least she appreciated being able to move freely for the first time in a while. Kakutan shared this sentiment. For the day's sojourn, both women had forsaken their layers and opted for the lightest clothing they could get. Kakutan was back in what was closest to her appearance as a Whudasha Youth—cowries and weapons excluded. Biemwensé stuck to a simple Bassai wrap.

"Yaya!"

The two women had barely ventured down a nondescript street before running into their first Whudan. Biemwensé startled when the name reached her ears, sending tremors down her body. She had not heard that word in a long time, and the memories that came with it doused her in equal levels of apprehension and excitement.

But she did not recognise this person hastening to catch up to them: a young woman, twice the age of the children she sought. Kakutan seemed to be having the same difficulty recognising her, but as the girl neared, it became clear she was Whudan. As soon as she spotted Kakutan, she immediately put a hand to the bridge of her nose.

"Dehje, Supreme Magnanimous," she said in Whudan, out of breath. "Oh, I—I can't believe it! You—I saw you and I just—I knew. Oh, thank moons, you're alive. We heard you all died!"

After such a long time away, hearing Whudan from someone else's lips other than Kakutan's tickled Biemwensé's ears.

Kakutan nodded, accepting the girl's greeting. "I can assure you we are very much alive, er..."

"Mudoro," said the girl with a shy smile. "But everyone calls me Rudo."

"Rudo." Kakutan smiled back, in a way Biemwensé had never seen her do before—all nice and warm. "You are indeed blessed. Thank moons, we were not dead, only lost."

"Thank moons, indeed!" said Rudo, her eyes shining. "I can't wait to take you to everybody."

Kakutan smiled that smile again. "We would want nothing more. We have travelled far to find our way back to you."

"This way!" the girl said, excited, tucking her arm beneath either woman's and leading them forward.

Biemwensé frowned at Kakutan across the girl, and Kakutan frowned back. *What?*

You are indeed blessed, Biemwensé mouthed, mimicking her. *We have travelled far to find you.*

Kakutan laughed, and Rudo glanced, inquisitive. Kakutan smiled at the girl. When she looked away, Kakutan mouthed back at Biemwensé: *Leadership is performance sometimes. Deal with it.*

The Whudan quarter, when they arrived, was more well-to-do than Biemwensé had expected. The ramshackle houses they often built on the coast weren't as many, and their abodes were now larger and made of sturdier material, with some even going as far as decorating their walls with paintings. Unsurprising what a people could do with more resources at their disposal, even in the buttocks end of the city.

Rudo led them through the quarter, screaming, "The Supreme Magnanimous has returned! The Supreme Magnanimous has returned!"

Many came out as Biemwensé and Kakutan passed through, unsure of how to react, especially once they spotted Biemwensé by Kakutan's side. Some bowed in greeting, excited to see their old leader and the promise of new direction she might bring. Some stood rock-solid in defiance— likely those who did not take kindly to being led to their almost-deaths, and who wanted nothing to do with the Whudasha Youth ever again. Others nodded toward the duo, as equals.

None of the discontent was surprising. Biemwensé and Kakutan had discussed the possibility of it during their journey. Their people had survived another near-extinction attempt on them, and had been given an opportunity at a new life, even though under Bassa's watchful eye. Most would not welcome a return to old ways—especially those who had always thought of moving from Whudasha to Bassa as progress, the end-goal of their existences.

Discontent was fine. It was malevolence Biemwensé was worried about.

Kakutan, enjoying the attention, bent to embrace children and the elderly, exchanging greetings, as if reuniting with a long-lost family. Not Biemwensé, though. She was here for one specific family, and she hadn't found them yet.

She grabbed the girl Rudo and took her to a side.

"I'm looking for two boys," she said. "Young, twenty-three, twenty-four seasons when I last saw them. They'd be older now and might no longer be small. Their names are Afanfan and Owude."

"Oh, I know those two," said Rudo. "They work with the Nameless faction."

"The what?"

"The Nameless." She angled her head. "Come, I'll show you."

Biemwensé tried to get Kakutan's attention as the girl pulled her away, but the woman was too busy enjoying the affections of her people. Someone had found a colourful wrapper and draped it over her. She was beaming and, in Biemwensé's mind, had completely lost focus as to why they had come here in the first place.

She let Rudo lead her away.

As they meandered through the Whudan quarter, Biemwensé marvelled at how even though the people had been transplanted, their way of life had not changed much. Most homes still had shopfronts for their facades, and internal trade was still the primary means of sustenance. Biemwensé suspected that the Whudans must have tried to trade with mainlanders, but could imagine how well that went.

They arrived at a nondescript house, smaller than most.

"Here," said Rudo. "They don't seem to be home, but you can wait. I will look around, see if I can send them your way."

Biemwensé sat on a low stool out front. The neighbouring abodes, just as small, contained inhabitants she didn't recognise. In the boys' abode, there were telltale signs that young men lived here—the clothes hanging on the line, for instance. There was a whetstone for sharpening tools, or weapons. From the arrowhead-shaped stones tossed around, she figured it was the latter. She'd completely forgotten that Afanfan had always wanted to be an archer.

As she sat there, a chorus of cheers went up among the people around her. A wagon cantered past, to which celebratory strips of colourful cloth were tied. In the wagon was a person-shaped thing, covered in cloth that was now wet and stained with pepper and tomato seeds. As it went past, they pelted the body with rotten fruit and screamed *cockroach* and *betrayer* at it. The driver, who was not Whudan but a mainlander, they cheered for, throwing flowers and sweet-smelling herbs their way.

All of this Biemwensé found odd. Why were her people cheering a Bassai person and desecrating what increasingly looked like a corpse? What had this person done to draw such ire that could unite Whudans and Bassai?

She was pondering this when someone said her name: "Yaya?"

Afanfan and Owude came down the street, eyes bulging at the sight of her. At first, Biemwensé did not recognise them, how poor her eyesight was now. But also—how big they'd grown! The two seasons between now and when she'd last seen them felt like an eternity. Afanfan, who was the skinny but tall one, had accumulated an amount of muscle that did not match his boyish face, showing signs of stubble that arrived with a coming of age. Owude, the younger and stockier of them both, still carried a childlike disposition, but with the way he walked, had clearly begun to understand the social expectations of his manhood.

"My children," said Biemwensé, and opened her arms. The two ran into them, and they embraced, tight. The children smelled of sweat and dirt and something like stale water. It was the best thing Biemwensé had smelled in a long time.

·⁃◇⁃⁓⁓⁓⁓⁓⁓⁓⁓⁓⁓⁓⁓⁓⁓⁓⁓⁓⁓⁓⁓⁓··⁓⁓◇⁃·

The day wore into evening. Biemwensé sat back and let the boys take care of her. She watched them cook and chatter, asking questions about what happened to her while simultaneously filling her in on what happened to them. She told them just enough to satisfy their curiosity, but was more interested in how they had fared since that night at the Dead Mines.

Turned out that the emperor's forces had lifted them out of the cave, but prevented any of the young ones, them included, from returning to Whudasha. Most of the elderly opted to return, even if the protectorate was practically a ghost village now, and every single Whudasha Youth left had been imprisoned. The rest had taken the option of Fifteenth Ward.

There was much to be sombre about in that account, but Biemwensé was content with listening to the music of their voices. Afanfan's had broken and had an unnerving quality to it, an assurance she did not quite know he'd always possessed. Owude chattered away—she had forgotten how talkative he could be. Both laughed a lot. They seemed much more at home here than they had ever been in Whudasha.

Afterward, they had one of her favourite meals—boiled plantains soaked in pepper soup—though they used grasscutter meat instead of the usual catfish. As they ate, she asked them about the corpse wagon she'd seen earlier.

"Oh, that's the Cockroach," said Afanfan. "The Great Dome sent him here to scatter our plans, but the Nameless faction killed him. They are sending his body back to the Great Dome as a message."

Biemwensé remembered what Rudo had told her. "This is the same Nameless faction you work for?" Afanfan nodded. "Who are they?"

"Resistance," said Owude.

"What do you mean *resistance*? And who was this cockroach person?"

"Former resistance," said Owude.

"He was the old leader, but he betrayed them," said Afanfan. "New leader is different—she helps us. Helped us build this house, helps us get food, makes sure nobody treats us Whudans anyhow. So we help them back."

"Help them how?"

"With anything they want," he said. "Like, today, they asked us to dig. That's why my clothes were rough when you came. But I don't know what we're digging for."

Something about this put Biemwensé at unease. She made a mental note to discuss this with Kakutan once she saw the woman tomorrow. For now, she just wanted to spend some time with the boys.

Once they were done with dinner, she raised the question she was there for.

"I will be going back to Whudasha as soon as I can," she said. "You can come with me if you want. Forget the emperor's command—if you come, you can stay with me. I will protect you."

The boys looked at one another.

"Is Whudasha not empty?" asked Owude.

Fair point. "You could say that."

"Why would we want to go back to an empty place?" There was clarity and assertion in Afanfan's tone, one that said he'd thought about this already.

"Because it is quiet, it is safe, and I will be there."

Owude lowered his gaze, upset at the idea of her leaving so soon.

"Why don't you stay here with us instead?" asked Afanfan. "This way, we can still be together, but here."

"Why would you want to stay here?" asked Biemwensé, perplexed. "This isn't home. This is just a prison Bassa doesn't want you to leave."

"But so is Whudasha."

That caught Biemwensé off guard. But Afanfan was right—it was simply one prison for another, wasn't it?

"I can't just leave the Nameless," Afanfan continued. "You say this isn't home, but . . . it is for us. The Nameless has made it so."

There was a part of Biemwensé that agreed with the boys, that understood they didn't *have* to be with her or in Whudasha for their lives to be better. In fact, she knew, now, that all of this had been a selfish endeavour, a quest to satisfy her own yearning for meaning. Things had gone wrong, yes, but Ashu had shined on the boys, and they had turned out fine. Better, even, than whatever life they'd had in Whudasha. She was trying to cook a meal that was already done.

But this business about the Nameless—it rubbed her the wrong way. What sensible person would risk such young lives in a battle with Bassa? Someone so tactless as to murder a Great Dome messenger and parade his body in the ward with the most defenceless population? It reeked of recklessness, and she did not like that the people she cared about were being made accessories to this. They were already easy targets for Bassai ire—this would just make that worse.

"Okay, enough upsetting talk for tonight," she said. "I will stay for now, and we can talk about this later."

Before drifting into sleep, Biemwensé made another mental note to speak to Kakutan about possibly meeting the leader of this Nameless faction or whatever they called themselves. If someone was roping the Whudans into a fight with Bassa, it was best for the Supreme Magnanimous—nay, the Supreme *Magnanimouses*—to have a say.

But Biemwensé would not have to wait long for that.

Hours before dawn, an explosion rocked the house to its foundations. Pots shattered and shelves fell. Biemwensé rose from sleep, groggy, heart pounding. She called out the boys' names, but neither was anywhere to be found. Their beds were empty, lightly slept in, the fine dust of dislodged mudbrick sweeping over the abandoned beddings.

Biemwensé dressed, picked up her stick, and ventured into the Whudan quarter.

34

Ifiot

Bassa: Fifteenth Ward
Sixth Mooncycle, 24–26

THE SAFE HOUSE HAD an odour. *Salt-air* was the description that came to Ifiot's mind when she stepped into the dark living room. After a long night of drinking and celebration, she had left the smells and sounds and lights and laughter of Fifteenth behind. Making her way through the corridors had been by feel alone, because she knew every corner of the ward that had been her home since birth. And though it was only a few mooncrossings ago she'd begun to use this safe house as a private abode, she knew every corner of it by feel too. Every piece of furniture, every sound made when they scraped the floor, every smell in the house.

The salt-air that greeted her was alien to this place. She had encountered something similar to it once before: back when she still had work as an Emuru hand, loading and offloading travelwagons at the border, just enough day's wages to keep her belly full. Upon return, travelwagons carrying salt mined in the desertlands smelled like this. But those odours were fresher. This smelled stale, something left too long to absorb moisture, become damp.

Someone was in the safe house.

It was dark inside. Ifiot prodded the space ahead with her foot, angling into the room with her shoulder. She approximated the distance between her and the corner across the door, where she knew one of her spears leaned. *Twelve steps*, she counted, then took one. *Eleven*. Another. *Ten*.

Ifiot did not consider herself a fighter. Not in the sense that those who sought out her faction envisioned. They all approached the Nameless with lofty dreams of a *Saviour-with-a-Spear*, as they'd taken to calling her, since very little was known about the secretive faction. She hadn't called it Nameless by mistake—she'd been inspired by the Nameless Islands, that place of myth (or was it?) that no mainland eye had seen or set foot upon (or had they?), that existed only in minds but maybe also in reality (or did it?). She liked this idea of either/or, of invisible visibility, of being something that transcended time, space, reality.

Those privileged enough to meet the coalition weren't always as enamoured—neither fellow Bassai nor immigrants nor outer mainlanders now hauling into the city's fringes by the wagonload. But most of them stayed because they wanted the same thing: someone to fight and win *with* and *for* them. Much unlike the past coalition, which did little but use everyone for its selfish goals of revolution, only to leave them in the dust after, right back where they started.

She angled her body to slip past a stool she knew was there. *Five steps*.

They were disappointed, too, once they met *her*; once they realised she was much better with her words and strategies than with her spear, and most especially, when they discovered she was not the man they'd sometimes been erroneously told she was. But they were wrong about that too. She was a woman now, yes, but in times before, she'd been raised to live as a man, a life she'd quickly found detrimental, insufficient, scant in its embodiment of who she truly was.

It was the same with the spear: She could wield it as capably as any hunthand out there, but found violence alone deficient in problem-solving. Only in combination with ears that listened close, lips that spoke carefully, and a mind that strategized conscientiously did she find violence effective. Ifiot knew that she could fight anything using that combination and *always* win. Especially when it came to protecting what was hers.

She was three steps to the spear when the second odour hit her. Something akin to rotting eggs, although not quite. Only then did she stop, sigh, and shake her head.

"You should really change out of those clothes," she said.

A flint struck, and the lamp next to the only chair in the room lit up. In the chair was seated Hakuoo, the man from the swamplands.

Ifiot willed herself to settle. The tall stranger's presence still put her on edge. It didn't help that, with the room now lit, she could see her spear wasn't actually in this corner, but had been moved to a different one. Hakuoo did that often, repositioning weapons. Keeping them within reach so they were still there if truly needed, but not as reachable by reflex. She hated that, but she could understand it. No stranger came into the home of a resistance leader and slept easy.

He lifted his two hands, then signed: "What did you say?"

She chuckled, signing back: "Swamp stink gives you away."

He chuckled too, then sniffed at himself. He did not jerk his head back as she expected, but instead signed: "I smell fine."

Fair point, she thought. It was she, after all, who was a stranger to the smells of the swamplands. Everything about him would be different to eyes trained to see the Bassai way: his garments of woven jute and bushrat skin, crocodile hide for heavy chest armour; his hair that had never seen a blade; the tribal marks etched into the skin of his cheeks and temple. Hakuoo was as different from her as night from day, and in more than just complexion.

Thankfully, the one thing they shared was the only thing of importance: They could communicate despite not speaking a word of each other's language. Their sign languages were different—hers, she perfected while growing up near the Soke border, learning to communicate across various pidgins and without verbalized language; his from practicing the silence crucial to hunting in the swamplands and living to tell the tale. Luckily, they mostly understood each other, which was the only reason he was still sitting here unharmed since his unannounced arrival in Fifteenth.

"A drink?" Ifiot signed, abandoning her quest for the spear and heading for her gourd of weybo. She poured two calabashes and handed him one. He frowned at it, so she laid it down on the table and set herself on the stool.

"Have you not just been out drinking?" Hakuoo asked, signing.

"I have been *with* people who were drinking," she said. "Different thing."

He picked up his calabash and sipped at the spirit, then gazed out the window, into the darkness, at the two moons in the sky.

"You seem calm for a person who only just murdered a Bassai noble," Ifiot signed.

Hakuoo smiled, put down his calabash. "I am not calm."

"Best not to be. You do not know Bassa like I do. What they can do."

"Yes," he signed. "I do not know your fear of this place. In the deltas, we fear greater things than a woman with a dead serpent." He took another sip of weybo. "If you must fear something, do not fear death. Instead, fear living with nothing but fear."

His manner was direct in a way that Ifiot appreciated. It kept her on her toes. It was why the day he had appeared in the city, and then in her home—man from nowhere, sitting in a corner in the dark of her living room, repositioning her spear, calmly asking questions in sign language—she'd known he was worth her ears. So she had sat through the smell of garments soaked by days of swamp travel and listened.

What a listen it turned out to be.

So much had changed in her life, and in the outer wards, since that day. Sure, it had taken a lot to convince her faction, and then the representatives sent by the hinterlands' interested clans. Few thought Hakuoo and the swamplanders to be a good addition to the faction's plans. They considered his presence threatening and suggestive of imbalance. Even earlier tonight, after demonstrating his commitment to their cause by killing Basuaye with his own hands—this way, everyone else could deny involvement—there were a few who were still yet to be won over.

She understood, though. She would give them time to come around. The hinterlanders and Bassai folk and immigrants and Whudans would soon come to see that, just like she had done the painstaking work of gaining their trust and pledging allegiance to an uprising if it ever came, they would need to do the same with the people of the delta settlements that Hakuoo represented. It was the same hand of Bassa that had touched them all, after all.

"Have you decided when you will you return?" she signed. "To gather your people?"

He nodded, signing: "Soon."

"How soon?" she asked. "Will you be here when they come for us?"

He shrugged. "Why wait?"

She didn't understand this expression. She repeated her question. He clarified, signing slowly: "Why wait for them to come to you? You should go to them."

Ifiot leaned back and took another sip. "We are not ready to strike yet."

"Perhaps you are using a lacking approach." Hakuoo sat up. "Or you have your sights set on the wrong targets."

Ifiot regarded the man. "You have ideas?"

He angled his head. "*Knowledge* more than ideas. One does not become the leader of a hunting settlement without learning a few things about hunting."

"Is that what we're doing?" Ifiot signed. "Hunting?"

"You seek to bring down something many times larger and stronger than you are," he signed. "You do it with one wound, two wounds, three wounds, until they bleed and stop moving. That is hunting."

Night animals called in the distance. Ifiot took another sip of weybo.

"Tell me," she signed.

"No need." Hakuoo rose. "Let me *show* you."

‧◇‧⋯⋯━━━━━⋯‧◇‧

When Hakuoo presented the swamp gas to Ifiot, she recognised the smell as similar to that which clung to his clothing, but did not understand what it was. When he described the method of collection—siphoning the gas over rotting and decomposed vegetation in the swamp—she wondered why he considered the smelly contents of his gourds any sort of gift.

In demonstration, he lit a tiny flame over the top of one of the gourds.

The gourd exploded into pieces, producing a burst of flames large enough to swallow a face whole. Only then did she realise that Hakuoo had just gifted her a power even the Red Emperor herself did not have. Not a power that could command the dead, yes, but one that could ensure they stayed that way.

Hakuoo showed her to a storeroom in her safe house where, while she'd been out all night celebrating the Cockroach's demise, he had safely stacked a significant number of these gourds, away from any fire and light. His plan had been simple: If they come for you, here's how to defeat them. But now he was asking her to do something else.

Strike first.

By dawn, Hakuoo had left for the swamplands, promising to gather and return with as many warriors and as much swamp gas as possible. In the interim, Ifiot called an impromptu meeting of the Nameless council.

An idea had come to her during her morning bath, borrowed from the very city she was trying to take hostage. Bassa had held power for hundreds of seasons by digging its moats deep and keeping a wall behind them to protect its resources. To keep Bassa's hand at bay would require something similar. She could find something Bassa desired, barricade it from reach, and force the emperor to negotiate for its release.

Death by many wounds, as Hakuoo had said.

She presented this at the meeting of the Nameless council. It was immediately refuted. Once the leaders learned of the swamp gas, a direct attack on the Great Dome was favoured instead.

A direct hit to the Red Emperor, they argued, *will serve us better*. Especially one that could take out her Ninki Nanka—or even better, the woman herself—before any response could be fashioned. They proposed lying in wait for her return from Chugoko before striking.

But Ifiot was stuck on Hakuoo's words. *A lacking approach, wrong targets*. They did not need the emperor's presence to take over Bassa—if anything, her absence was crucial. As far as Ifiot was concerned, there was only one important question:

How and *where* could they dig a moat, uninterrupted, in under a day?

Luckily, impossible feats galvanized Ifiot more than they inhibited her. After the meeting, she consulted in secret with other stakeholders, collecting information about various means of approach. She sat with allies from nearby wards, including some Whudans, who now made up a significant number of said wards. All thought, as usual, that she was a bit too hasty, too ambitious. *Such choices will only annoy the emperor*, they said, *and then we'd be doomed*.

But Ifiot *wanted* to annoy the Red Emperor. Angered people made rash decisions, and rash decisions got them in difficult positions, which would be a boost for the Nameless faction. If her plans brought the emperor back into the streets and out of that Great Dome where she'd remained hidden for many mooncycles—that would be another boost.

So, on the twenty-sixth day of the sixth mooncycle in the second season of the Red Emperor, Ifiot set off the biggest explosion Bassa had ever seen.

35

Nem

Bassa: The Great Dome
Sixth Mooncycle, 25–26

NEM'S LATE AFTERNOON MEAL was interrupted by urgent, heavy knocks on the door to her private chamber. She groaned, dipped her last mound of cassava into the bitter-leaf soup, then stuffed it in her mouth. Meals were the only time she got alone other than when asleep—which was why she ate in her chambers and not the large dining hall where even the emperor rarely ate. Why couldn't they just leave her alone for one moment? She was not the emperor, after all.

"Come," she said.

Satti was the visitor, and her face had lost all colour.

"What?" asked Nem.

"You need to come see," said Satti.

Nem washed her hands and let Satti push her down the hallways, winding past hands and officials and everyone who had a word for Nem that she didn't want to hear. Soon, they were in the dining hall, the very room Nem had been avoiding. But it wasn't empty—all members of court were there, save for the hinterlanders and Tombolo Elders.

One person lay on the table, dead.

Basuaye—or at least, his body—was covered in waste, reeking of a range of nasal assaults from wastewater to urine. Face and clothes still splattered with dried blood. A smattering of cuts and bruises on his arms, legs, neck, forehead. A fleshy red hole gaped wide open in his chest, his chestbone crushed, shoulder disjointed, hanging loose. From her sitting position, Nem was at just the right angle to see through his broken ribcage and make out his cold, dead heart.

The best way to describe the corpse was *molested*.

"How?" was all Nem asked.

"Second says they found his body in a wagon in a corridor in Fifteenth," said Elder Yao. "Apparently, Basuaye took the outlanders and went to go parley with one of the breakaway factions."

Yes, I did send him on such an errand, Nem wanted to say, but elected to delay that crucial piece of information. Instead she asked: "Do we know which faction?"

"No."

"Where is the Second? And the others he went with?"

"Second is in hospice." Yao shuffled on his feet. "The four Tombolo and hinterland Elders . . . nowhere to be found."

Nem looked to the rest of the court and saw the vindication in their gazes.

"If you love your tongues, better hold them," she shot at them. "This is not the time for gloating." To Yao, she said: "The Second—what has he said?"

"Not much. Said Basuaye refused to tell him anything useful. Almost harmed himself with a blade, too, after delivering the body. Said he'd rather punish himself than be on the receiving end of the Great Dome's wrath."

Nem sighed. "And you all—you have nothing? Not even from all the fingers you have in this city's pots?"

The advisors all looked at one another.

"We believe the factions are becoming braver because of help from the hinterlands," said Ebrima of the farming and hunting guild. "Even from the Tombolo hamlets. In fact, we hear whispers of swamplanders now arriving in the outer wards."

"We hear stories, of strange beasts emerging from forests beyond the confluence, driving the people here," said Elder Inyene, of the craftworkers.

Nem angled her head. "And you're only telling me this now?"

"We did not want to distract from—"

"Get out, all of you," Nem turned her gaze toward the body. "I need a moment alone."

Satti rolled her chair closer to the body, then helped usher everyone else out. Nem sat there, looking at the rictus expression plastered on the dead man's face. *Battered.* She hadn't been particularly close with the man—they had always been business partners more than anything. But no one deserved to die like this, not even him. Nem felt a tinge of guilt knowing it was she who had brought him out of the frying pan into this fire that had now consumed him.

She might not be invested in a personal quest for revenge, but she sure was invested in the empire's integrity. He was a member of the Court of the Great Dome, after all. It could have been any of the other advisors— it could have been *her*. This deserved a response, fast.

She called everyone back in.

"We will address this attack immediately and quickly," she commanded. "By the emperor's return, everyone involved must be one with the humus, or we will have a much bigger problem on our hands."

Nem doled out the instructions. Basuaye was to be discreetly incinerated and sent to the skies without ceremony, seeing as he had no living family anyway. Oluodah would take care of that. Yao was to send word to every civic guard captain, and Mawuli was to do the same to the leaders of the hunthand guild—the Great Dome needed the best of their best. Ebrima and Inyene were to engage their whisper networks once more, find out everything they could about this faction and its leaders and members.

They had until dawn.

By the time Nem returned to her room, her food had grown cold. She asked for it to be taken away, then asked for a bath and to be put to bed early.

All she could think about during the bath was that it was perhaps best that she was the one here when all of this was happening. Though Esheme did not give a grain for Basuaye, she imagined her daughter's response would be to gladly burn through the whole city just to find the perpetrators. The Bassai knew their emperor well and would expect that kind of response, would welcome it, even. The only problem was that Nem, after so long in the trenches, fighting to gain power—she was no longer that person. She could not be her daughter for them.

In bed, before she slept, Nem prayed for the first time in a while. *Dearest Ashu*, she thought, *please let all this pass us by, and let peace reign.*

She had chased power for so long that when it finally bought her the freedom she sought, she did not want to let that freedom go. Not freedom *from* fighting, but freedom to choose *when to*, which, these days, was more like no freedom at all. It had taken Nem watching her daughter rise to the highest level in the land, drink of this forbidden cup, and let it fill her with even more ravenous hunger—for stone-bones, for beasts, for the destruction of her loved ones, her subjects, even her own body—to understand that she, herself, did not really want power like this.

No—what she really wanted was *peace*. But the kind of peace that power bought was peace without harmony, which was no peace at all.

Dearest Ashu, Nem prayed, *let this be solved quickly.*

Prayer, as she would soon learn, was a fork with many prongs. And one of such prongs came to bear soon when, hours before dawn, she was stirred in sleep by a thunderous boom. Far, far away, so she did not awaken.

Soon, though, urgent knocks besieged the door to her chamber. Groggy, Nem sat up and called the knocker in.

This time, Satti wasn't alone. Elder Yao was with her, and both looked ashen.

"What now?" asked Nem.

"An explosion," said Yao, flustered. "Eighth Ward."

36

Ifiot

Bassa: Eighth Ward
Sixth Mooncycle, 26, same day

THE EXPLOSION WENT OFF on mainway eight.

The choice of location was not random. Extensive plans had identified three matters of high importance to the success of a blockade campaign, the first of which was its location.

Fourth Ward had been the initial choice, a transition ward between Emuru and Idu. Ifiot had argued against it, citing that it was still only a lateral division between two kinds of mainlanders. Eighth Ward was the definite caste divider, she offered, because it separated most mainlanders from most immigrants. Mainway eight was where Emuru citizens gave way to Potokin and Yelekuté, meaning more immigrants would be protected behind the demarcation than lost beyond it.

But that wasn't all. The outer wards' farms, being farther inland and closer to the rivers, produced the most crops in the city—even if they weren't owned by the ward dwellers, only operated by them. These farms contained tuber, bean, rice, and nut crops the nobles needed for sustenance, but also cotton for textile and thatch for building and craftworking, two of Bassa's most useful resources beyond gold and other ores. This made mainway eight the most important roadway for Bassa's goods.

A blockade across mainway eight would cripple the city in more ways than one.

The explosion went off with a blinding flash, so bright that at first, some inhabitants thought the sun had risen much too early. A rolling tremor followed, like a stampede of elephants, rippling across Eighth and adjacent wards. Next: a cloud of dust and ash, sweeping over the ward, so that all manner of vision was lost. Debris rained from the sky, and the acrid stink of burning sand was sharp enough to bleed noses. Citizens ran out of their abodes, screaming about the sky falling on their heads. They were quickly greeted by a crier's gong and loud announcements commanding them to return to their abodes, until all was assessed and it was deemed safe for them to venture out.

Timing had been the second matter of import. Ifiot planned for this to happen long before the farmhands awoke for their trip to the farms, but close enough to dawn that the blockade would be up and functioning just as daylight broke. The ward dwellers would be asleep in their homes and unlikely to come to harm. She had no interest in harming those for whom she was fighting.

Explosion completed, Ifiot and her faction rolled out to the site. The next stage of the plan was to examine the pits formed, ensure they were of satisfactory depth. Ifiot had learned from Hakuoo to bury the gourds of swamp gas shallow enough to make sure the explosion from their ignition did not destroy buildings, but deep enough to ensure it created pits that carts carrying goods or travelwagons carrying civic guards could not go through. So deep that even people on foot would be unable to cross without the aid of a bridge.

A moat, in essence.

A cursory survey of the ash and dust told Ifiot that the pits were deep enough. She waved her people over, and they moved forward with their carts, began the task of building a short wall. A pit was just a pit. Ifiot's thinking was that, with the right fortification—not even necessarily a high one—a pit became a barrier, a border, a blockade.

They dumped all gathered material onto the outer side of the pits. Mostly dirt, loads and loads of it dug from the forests in secret. Within an hour, anthill-high lines of dirt stood along the pits that cut across the ward from bushland to bushland. Before the smoke fully cleared, the faction added other objects atop their hills of dirt, a haphazard combination of throwaway material. Sticks, metal, old tools, weapons. Carts and wagons broken down to pieces. Palm fronds. Bones. Whatever they could find.

By the time the sun rose on Bassa, the blockade was an insurmountable hill of tightly bound rubbish. Eighth Ward and beyond came under the control of the Nameless faction. Then Ifiot and her people planted themselves behind the blockade and waited for Bassa's response.

Waiting in silence was by design. Ifiot learned from her time growing up in the armpits of Bassa that it was never the strength that one possessed that made one feared, but the appearance of it. So they set up sentry points behind the blockade, with sight holes that betrayed neither their faces nor their few numbers. Hakuoo had painstakingly described this, explaining that it was the way he and his ancestors had kept their settlements safe from intruders, human and non-human alike. Depriving the enemy of sight and sound was a performance in itself. It made the Nameless faction a difficult enemy to approach, made it so that if they were ever forced to speak, they could do so with voices that made them seem larger than they really were.

Ifiot herself sat behind one of these sighting holes, watching the Bassai citizens on the other side of the newly created moats gather and wonder what was happening. On her side of the blockade, a mass of confused citizens had formed as well, a growing buzz of murmuring. Members of her faction had tried to drive them off, but Ifiot advised against it. *Let them see us fight,* she said. *It will convince them to join us more than anything else.*

One of her advisors, a woman named Sileya, came across to inspect the sighting holes. She stopped before Ifiot's and shuffled on her feet. She was the youngest of the Nameless faction's leadership, but was one of the few people who had the effrontery to take Ifiot to task.

"Out with it," Ifiot said without taking her eye off the hole.

"Are you sure about this?"

Ifiot shut the hole and frowned at the woman. "What do you mean?"

"There is uncertainty among the faction," said Sileya. "They believe we are no longer taking orders from you, but from a stranger from the swamplands."

"And what does it matter where the ideas come from?" Ifiot asked. "Have we not in the past implemented ideas drawn up at council?"

"Yes, but—"

"But nothing," said Ifiot. "Nothing about what Hakuoo has said is new or revolutionary. This is but a common strategy even the little snake in the forest employs. A small predator does not tackle larger prey in a contest of strength. It does so by slinking swiftly in the darkness, taking its target by surprise, delivering a thousand bites laden with poison." She opened the hole and peered out again. "This blockade is only the first of many such bites. We will keep biting until our enemy lies in the understory and stops moving."

Sileya stood there for a lengthy moment, then nodded. "I will tell these words to them."

"You do that."

It wasn't long after Sileya left that the first party of civic guards appeared. They were surprisingly fewer than Ifiot had expected, few enough that her people could take them all in direct combat if they wished. They were also all from Eighth Ward, judging by the captain who arrived with them. Perhaps word had not yet reached the Great Dome?

The captain got his guards to push the crowd on the outer side back, surveyed the moat, then descended into it himself. He walked to within shouting distance of the blockade.

"This is Captain Jantar of the Eighth Ward civic guard. In the name of the Scion of Moons, Sovereign Emperor of Bassa and all of Oon, I command whoever put up this monstrosity to emerge and speak."

Silence. Murmurs rose on either side of the blockade, something only those peering through the sighting holes could experience. From a nearby stack, Ifiot grabbed one of the shorter, lighter desertland ikiwa spears designed for throwing.

"I must ask again—are we sure?" Sileya, who had returned to her side, whispered.

"Is there a choice?" Ifiot replied. "A thousand bites must begin with one."

The captain, opposite the blockade, cleared his throat again. "I repeat, in the name of—"

Ifiot opened up a larger portion of the blockade and flung the spear. It travelled fast across the short distance, then planted itself into the chest of the captain. He took one step backward, two steps, then knelt in the dust, cradling the spear, before falling to the ground. It was a quiet death, ensconced by the hushed silence of those who witnessed it.

Nobody moved. Not even the civic guards, who looked at one another, unsure about what to do in the absence of a command. Attack? Delay? But that hesitation only lasted for a moment, after which one civic guard stepped forward, an air of authority having gathered around him. A second-in-command, Ifiot guessed.

This one did not announce himself. Rather, he lined up the few archers in their party and prepared to shoot into the blockade.

Ifiot dropped him with another spear before he could finish the command. Then she called on *her* archers, who shot arrows at the feet of all who remained before the moat. Citizens and civic guards alike scattered in every direction.

"Put out the signs," Ifiot ordered.

They climbed ladders and placed wooden signs across the length of the blockade. Ifiot had painstakingly overseen their preparation and did so again for their lengthwise placement, all boards together making a coherent statement. Large enough to be read from afar, clear enough to declare intent, menacing enough to institute action.

Our demands are thus, the message read in High Bassai, so they knew it was serious. *Independence from Bassa, or we deprive this city of food and resources until it crumbles. No negotiations. We will speak only to the emperor. Attack in any way and suffer the consequences. We have more where this came from.*

"We are missing the last board," Sileya said to Ifiot, after the message was in place. "The one with our name."

Ifiot checked, confirmed it was missing, then snapped her fingers. "Give me a fresh one."

Handed a new board, she dipped an oxtail into ochre and scribbled hastily across it. Then she ordered them to place it at the end of the line.

Signed, it read, *The Nameless Republic.*

Biemwensé

Bassa: Fifteenth Ward
Sixth Mooncycle, 26, same day

DAWN CAME OVER THE Whudan quarter like a mistful blanket. Most of its inhabitants were already up and about, awoken by the same disturbance that had shaken Biemwensé from sleep. They meandered like spooked fowls, babbling questions at everyone within sight. Biemwensé easily found Kakutan among them, slipped neatly into her leader role, calming the flustered and ushering them back into their homes until she could find out what was happening. The girl from before, Rudo, was there, shadowing her.

"Thank moons you're alive," Kakutan said when she spotted Biemwensé.

"The boys are gone." Biemwensé went on to explain everything that had happened since they'd last seen each other.

"Said they were working with the Nameless to move dirt," she concluded. "I suspect that's where they are, but I don't know where that is."

"I hear wagons have been carrying dirt from here to the middle wards," said Kakutan, turning to Rudo. "You know where?"

The young woman nodded. "I hear somewhere between Seventh and Tenth."

"Maybe we visit this dirt site, see what's what," said Biemwensé.

"I agree. These people deserve some answers." Kakutan looked around. "But we'll need a ride." Her eyes lit up and she snapped her fingers. "Our old friend!"

Their old friend's name was Mpewa, and he was just hitching his kwaga onto his wagon when Rudo arrived with the two at his house.

"Ah, the Supreme Magnanimous!" he said when he saw them. "Why did you not tell me who you were on the night? I would have been honoured."

Kakutan shook her head. "Can never separate enemy from friend in the dark."

"Indeed," said Mpewa. "In the daytime too."

"We're trying to get to the middle wards," said Biemwensé. "See what caused that thundering."

"Oh, that happened in Eighth," he said. "One of my comrades with an early delivery got turned around it. There's a blockade there now."

"A *blockade*?"

"Yes, maa. The Nameless faction has constructed a moat and wall across the mainway. No goods or people crossing Eighth until they speak with the emperor."

Biemwensé looked to Kakutan. "That's where the boys went. To help."

Kakutan turned to Mpewa. "If you can't cross, how come you're you still going?"

The man gestured toward his wagon. "I still have an employer, don't I? If they put in a complaint to the local government, they're not going to hear that I couldn't do my job because someone was protesting. I'm going to try my luck with the corridors. That's what most of us are doing."

"We will come with you," said Kakutan.

"Me too," said Rudo.

Kakutan frowned at the girl. "It could be dangerous."

"I know," she replied.

As the three clambered on, Biemwensé caught Kakutan's creased brow, the one she often wore as Supreme Magnanimous. She was indeed getting her fill of being back where she belonged, a leader of her people.

Biemwensé couldn't help but feel a little jealous. She had only just gotten her boys back, and now they were gone again.

Please be safe, she prayed as the wagon pulled away. *Please.*

◦ ⋯ ⋯ ◦

The trip to Eighth took longer than it was meant to, the wagon meandering through masses of people migrating toward this new blockade. Anxious chatter from the crowd filtered through to Biemwensé: Most people wondered what future this new development bade for them. Interspersed with this general concern was Mpewa's own chatter, offering accounts of other recent woes in Bassa. Biemwensé only half listened as he spoke of strange beasts emerging from the Breathing Forest, and how the Nameless faction chose the wrong time to divide the city. Despite these distractions, her thoughts remained with her boys.

Once they reached Eighth, the crowd became too thick to pass through with a wagon. The women and the girl got down and bid Mpewa goodbye as he opted to try his luck with the corridors. They pushed their way to the front of the crowd until they came face-to-face with the blockade.

The monstrosity before them was a giant earthworm that had wriggled through debris and collected everything in its way. Now it stood as a wall of rubbish separating the outer wards from the rest of Bassa. On this side of the wall was a small but diverse group of armed guards—the Nameless faction, Biemwensé guessed. From the tongues and inflections she was picking up, they seemed to contain people from various parts of the continent, not just the city. A few members of the faction milled about the wall, peering through gaps in it to see through to the other side. The rest were tasked with convincing everyone gathered here to return home and await further instructions. The gathered citizens offered them a few choice words in return.

Biemwensé scanned the crowd for Afanfan and Owude, but her eyesight was not very helpful. She grabbed the girl Rudo instead.

"Can you see them?" she asked. "Point for me."

The girl squinted, looked around, then pointed. "There."

Biemwensé pushed her way through in that direction, until she heard someone say: "Yaya?"

It was Afanfan, armed with his bow, sweaty and smeared with dirt. Owude stood glued to him, looking the same. It occurred to her, now, that she'd never asked them if they were related. She had always assumed they were brothers or cousins, and they had never bothered to furnish her with the details of their relationship. Perhaps Afanfan had only appointed himself protector of the younger one, much in the same way she had appointed herself protector over them.

"What are you doing here, maa?" Afanfan's voice had a nervous quality to it, as if he was afraid someone would hear. "Come, come away!" He pulled her and Owude to the back of a nearby shop, a small shed whose owner—tomato seller, judging by the baskets around—had never opened for the day due to the events. The front of the shed was filled with onlookers attempting to stay out of the sun while keeping an eye on proceedings. The rear was vacant.

"I heard the thundering," Biemwensé was saying. "Awoke and didn't see you two. I thought you were in trouble."

"Sorry I didn't tell you we were leaving," Afanfan said hastily, leaning to glance elsewhere, as if watching for someone. "I did not want to wake you. Can I—explain later? We are working."

Working? Biemwensé thought, but before she could make sense of this, Rudo had found them.

"Ay, you are there," she said. "Supreme Magnanimous is asking where you went. She wants you to meet somebody."

As she said it, Kakutan emerged from the crowd and was immediately followed by a younger Bassai woman with soft features, but with an air that told another story. She wore her hair short, with a few plaits adorned with cowrie. Her facepaint remained immaculate, even though she was sweating beads above her lips.

"Ah," said the woman, speaking first. "This is this the infamous Yaya, is it?" She greeted in the Bassai way, a hand on the bridge of her nose.

Biemwensé frowned at Kakutan, who looked almost sheepish, but stood firm, demonstrating clearly that this was not a chance happening.

"Who are you?" she asked.

"I am Ifiot." The woman smiled, but it did not soften Biemwensé's demeanour. "I lead the coalition here. Your boys have spoken often about you." She reached forward and draped an arm about Afanfan and Owude. The boys looked down at their feet. Not scared, not giggling, just…comfortable.

Something bitter clawed at Biemwensé's insides.

"Coalition leader," Biemwensé repeated.

"That's right."

"I remember meeting one such leader recently," she said. "In a wagon. Dead."

"Ah." Ifiot's smile had not left. "Well, you know what they say about desperate times and measures."

Biemwensé turned to Kakutan. "What is this? What are you trying to do?" She paused. "So you lured me here, is it? Pretended you cared about the boys, about helping the Whudans."

"I apologise for the clandestine nature of things," said Kakutan, "but we both know how stubborn you are, and that I couldn't have gotten you here otherwise. But don't you for one moment believe I don't care—why am I here otherwise?" She had put her Supreme Magnanimous voice back on, something Biemwensé had not heard in a long time. "Maybe if you can climb off that throne you're sitting on and listen to her speak? She has some interesting ideas." Kakutan waved a hand behind her, at the blockade. "This one is just the first of many more to come."

Biemwensé regarded the coalition woman again, taking time to study her eyebrows, her skin, the spear strapped to her back. She was lovely looking, slightly muscular yet maidenlike at the same time. Back in Whudasha, she would not have been deemed appropriate for the Youth. Too languid. She seemed adept anyway, like she knew how to be in charge. *But*, Biemwensé thought, *there's already one such person occupying the highest seat in the empire. Look how well that's going.*

Ifiot, knowing she was being weighed, angled her head.

"This is not a great time to become acquainted, I admit," she said. "But I hope we can call on your support, seeing as you and the Supreme Magnanimous have worked together a long time. The Nameless Republic will be grateful to have your experience and expertise on our side."

Republic? Side? What was this woman talking about?

"Your people are eager to be of aid to our quest," Ifiot continued.

"Stuck here as they are with the rest of us, they could do with some guidance like that which you have given your boys." She pressed the boys closer to herself.

Biemwensé's eyes narrowed. She did not like this woman, and she did not like whatever this talk was. She did not dignify Ifiot with a response, but instead turned to Kakutan, betrayal brimming in her eyes.

"One day with your people," she said. "Just *one* day, and you could not hold back. Could not take time to hold them, love them, care for them. *One* day, and you're already out here making deals on their behalf, selling them out to renegades."

Kakutan, whose role so far seemed like it was to placate, turned sour.

"This *is* care," she shot back. "I am here *because* I care, because it is my duty to make things better for them." She stepped forward. "The people chose me to make decisions on their behalf, and that is what I am doing."

"By what—making them soldiers in a fake war with Bassa?"

"It is not a fake war..." Ifiot started, but the look Biemwensé shot her dripped with so much poison, the woman swallowed the rest of her words.

"Tell me—what is this, really?" Biemwensé asked Kakutan. "Because I refuse to believe you have chosen to stay here, in a foreign land, to fight behind a blockade made of litter and waste—one that the emperor will sweep away with a wave of her hand. So tell me—*why?*"

The flick of Kakutan's eyes toward Ifiot did not seem intended. The moment was fleeting, but it was clear. Something passed between them, a softness that Biemwensé often found absent in Kakutan's demeanour. She turned to see Ifiot, who still wore a smile of amusement, brushing away her dangling plaits.

"Menai strike me, for I must be dreaming," she said. "You are selling your people just to crawl into this woman's wrappers?"

"*Ooch,*" said Ifiot, placing her hands over Owude's ears. "There are children here."

"If you speak again!" said Biemwensé, a finger in Ifiot's face. She lifted her stick. "Go on! Try me! Speak and try me!"

She hadn't seen the people standing in the wings, watching the group like vultures. The moment she raised her stick, they descended, and suddenly the group was surrounded by a small armed guard.

Ifiot held up her hand before they could do anything. "It's okay." She shuffled aside, away from the children. "You're right. I shouldn't speak. This looks like something…private." She ran a hand over the heads of the boys, winked at Rudo, then beckoned to her guards.

After they had left, Kakutan turned to the older woman and shook her head like a disappointed parent. "Now look what you've gone and done."

"Me? *I* have done something wrong?" Biemwensé laughed dryly. "I can't do this. I can't." She beckoned to the boys. "Come. We're leaving."

Kakutan put a hand on her shoulder. "Wait."

Biemwensé looked at the Supreme Magnanimous's hand. "I give you until the count of five…"

"You can't leave yet," said Kakutan. "The blockade is not going to be opened for anyone. Not here, not in the corridors, not anywhere in the ward. There are Nameless everywhere to ensure that."

"Ah, so we're prisoners," said Biemwensé. She turned to the children. "You hear that? A resistance, they say, but still oppressors, yes?"

"We're not prisoners." This was Afanfan, head still slightly lowered to show his deference. But there was firmness in his tone. Images of the young, ruffled orphan boy who once came seeking food in her corner of the protectorate, kneeling in the sand at her door to ask for an onion to eat, flitted through her mind.

"We are not prisoners," he pressed, "but we are not leaving." He did not look Biemwensé in the eye when he said it. Owude, to his side, turned away too.

"Look at me," said Biemwensé. She could feel them now, all the tears she never cried when she lost everything—family, status, the respect of the protectorate. Creeping out of her eyes, threatening to run down her cheeks.

The boys did not look.

"Everything I have done, I have done because I want you to be safe," she said, lips trembling. "You are not safe in this city. You are not safe with these people."

"We will be fine, Yaya," said Afanfan.

"Will you?" she said, then pointed to Kakutan. "Because *she* says so?"

"Ifiot says she will take care of us," said Owude.

"*I* will take care of you!" Biemwensé had never screamed at them before. She couldn't even recognise her own voice.

"Okay, that's enough," said Kakutan, pulling Biemwensé away. She pointed to the children. "Wait here."

Biemwensé let Kakutan pull her out of view and earshot of the children. She did not want them to see her cry.

"What is wrong with you?" asked Kakutan.

Biemwensé could not find the words. Kakutan gave her a moment to wipe her tears and collect herself, then said: "You say you do everything because you want them to be safe. That is a lie."

Biemwensé looked up. "Excuse me?"

"It's a lie, because you and I have been doing the same thing—avoiding the truth that we're just empty shells trying to fill up with . . . something. It is why you planted your feet and helped Danso and Lilong back in Whudasha, even when you knew it was foolhardy. It is why I believed I could lead *a whole protectorate* beneath the Soke mountains. It's why we're both here, trying to fill up our empty shells again."

Kakutan sighed. "For once, we should stop thinking about ourselves and start thinking about what *they* want. I have listened to the chatter in Fifteenth—no Whudan wants to go back to an empty protectorate. Here, there—what does it matter? We're still all under Bassa's thumb. But *now* . . ." She pointed toward the blockade. "They have something to fight for, and they want to fight for it. They need a voice at the table. So yes, I'm happy to be that voice because I *am* listening. Are you? Listening?"

The incessant clamour of the crowd around them filled the silence. Many in the streets had begun to depart, trying their luck in the corridors like Mpewa had done. If Kakutan was right, they were going to encounter similar barriers elsewhere.

"I can't stay here," said Biemwensé. "I just . . . can't."

"I know," said Kakutan. "Which is why I will ask Ifiot to let you go."

Biemwensé peered into her comrade's face. She wasn't joking.

"No one is looking for us right now," said Kakutan. "There are no notices with our names. So you're free to go wherever, but I say go to Whudasha. Start afresh, become someone other than who you used to be. Do not stay in Bassa. It will be dangerous here for a while." She exhaled. "But the boys have chosen to stay, and you must respect that. I know it will be lonely, travelling all the way back alone. I will ask Ifiot to get you a travelwagon."

"I will go," said a voice behind them, piercing the moment. It was Rudo.

"What are you—"

"I want to go back to Whudasha. I don't like it here."

Finally, thought Biemwensé. *Someone with sense.*

"And your parents—what do they have to say about that?" asked Kakutan.

"I have no parents," said Rudo flatly. "But my great-uncle is alone in the protectorate." She swallowed. "I don't want him to die alone."

Biemwensé looked at Rudo's eager eyes, alight with anticipation in a way the boys' no longer were, in a way that rekindled her own fires. Perhaps Kakutan was right. Perhaps this was truly an opportunity to start afresh, become something new.

"Trying times are coming," Kakutan was saying, stepping forward. "Even more trying than now. Whudans, here or in the protectorate, deserve guidance, a leader to help them navigate." She placed her hand on Biemwensé's shoulder. "I can take care of those here. But those in Whudasha need a Supreme Magnanimous too."

Biemwensé's eyes widened. "What are you doing?"

"As Supreme Magnanimous of the Whudasha Youth," said Kakutan, "I hereby bestow upon you, sister, an equal claim to leadership. As the moons are my witnesses above, and young Rudo my witness below, I bid you: Go forth, serve your people."

Biemwensé blinked at Kakutan, unable to find words. The other woman kissed her on the cheek.

"Don't worry," she said. "I will keep the boys safe. You have my word."

Biemwensé stood there, leaning awkwardly into her stick, struggling to process the barrage of emotions that washed over her. Then slowly, surely, she leaned forward, into Kakutan's arms. Kakutan held her close, warm, sure. It was a long time since Biemwensé had last embraced someone like this.

"Be careful," Biemwensé whispered.

She took Rudo by the hand and turned away. She did not return to say goodbye to the boys. She could not bear for them to see her face. But she was sad no longer, angry no longer, only hopeful for the future and all the possibilities it promised.

38

Kangala

The Lonely Roads East
Sixth Mooncycle, 20

"A FAMILY, TRAVELLING EASTWARD in a wagon," Igan was saying. "The men did not say how many, but they spoke of a baby. Said a woman put the wailing child in their face."

The emperor, whom the advisor was regaling with this tale, blinked her understanding. The caravan had stopped early to camp because their numbers had swelled by up to three-quarters beyond the initial, thanks to peace officers heeding the emperor's call and joining up with them along the way. The Sahelian-to-peace officer ratio was now one-to-one, which meant the caravan now required an extra hour to set up camp, forcing all into closer quarters than usual.

The emperor's own camp, built around the royal travelwagon, frequently changed position for safety reasons—today, they had chosen the edge of camp. Which was how Kangala's daily meditation became interrupted. He'd opted for shade and discreetness behind a towering naboom plant on the edge of the location, but had now ended up an accidental eavesdropper on the emperor's conversation.

"Put a child how?" the emperor was asking.

"Like…" Ikobi, the other advisor, pantomimed lifting something. "Into the man's face. Said he was trying to look into the travelwagon, but the woman was asking for water, and the baby was crying. Said they were in a hurry to come join us, so they just left."

Daylight had begun to wane, and the sky above melded blue with orange. Kangala considered revealing himself, but decided against it when it became clear that neither emperor nor her advisors or guards noticed him.

He kicked a nearby dead rat away and settled in, crouching lower. This was the second bushrat he was seeing that had nibbled its way to death by ingesting the naboom plant's milky, poisonous sap. Even *he* couldn't attempt that. Skin irritations, blindness, death—those were givens. Both bushrats showed signs of having clawed at their eyes and flesh before succumbing to death.

If the animals in the desertlands could no longer survive the harsh conditions, what hope did he and his family have?

"Did they spot him? Or her?" The emperor's voice was soft, out of character. She adjusted the small armlet on her arm, the one she always wore everywhere, even now, while she sweated from the exhaustion of the day's travel. Kangala thought she looked pale, and wondered why she had insisted on coming on this journey. The savanna did not seem to agree with her.

"No," Igan said, chewing on a blade of dry grass. "But putting together the Chugoko wardens' descriptions of the prison escapee, I believe that baby-thrusting woman was Abuso's daughter. Has to be. I hear she bore a child in prison. Can't say there are many women out here with a child, headed east in a travelwagon."

Kangala agreed. It was their fifth day of pursuit, and they had followed the trail of campfires and travelwagon tracks that Oroe had picked up from the razed hut discovered in Chugoko. There was no easy way to tell if each new campfire they encountered was the product of the fugitives they sought, but not many walked the Lonely Roads East and made campfires in the open—and definitely not such a motley group as Igan was describing. Though the tracks disappeared and reappeared at will, erased by fierce wind, the campfires offered footprint evidence as well. Oroe had counted at least five people in the party, enough bodies to contain the emperor's fugitives. Igan's assessment was more right than wrong.

"Hmm." The emperor's eyes were distant, unfocused, the information received absentmindedly. "Why did they say it was a family?"

"*Looked* like a family," said Igan. "I'm almost sure that if Abuso's daughter is going east, then at least one or two of those who aided her will be going east with her. And if one of those is the yellow woman…"

They left the sentence hanging, but Kangala knew what this meant. The fugitives—and they, their pursuers—were headed for the Forest of the Mist, that storied place, which Kangala had so far only regarded with amusement. But the seriousness of Igan's tone made him reconsider that position. If they truly believed this pursuit would lead them there, then so be it. He was open to being wrong.

"At least this means we're going in the right direction," said the emperor. Seemingly satisfied with this information, she reclined into the cane seat she often used outside the travelwagon, the matter closed.

Kangala had earlier seen a group of peace officers being punished—stripped of their officerhood, relegated to hand status, shunted to the rear of the caravan—for a reason he didn't understand at the time. Now he realised they must have been the ones who brought this news to Igan.

Kangala was a bit disappointed that the emperor was yet to display the ruthlessness she was famed for. The complete absence of her rumoured Soldiers of Red was conspicuous. Though there *was* the Ninki Nanka—the undead beast's motionless, unbreathing sleep unnerved Kangala even more than the animal's size, or the stories he'd heard of what it could do, how just a drop of its spittle could peel a man's flesh off his bones. It had taken him a while to get used to travelling alongside it, and always ensured to keep it at arm's length.

But all the beast had done so far on this trip was sleep. For some reason, the emperor was not interested in meting out brute force. Even when they had faced danger—say, on their third day in the savanna, when they had come upon a herd of feral elephants, and the lead elephant had trumpeted at them, refusing to leave the path. He'd expected the emperor to rouse the Ninki Nanka and scare them off. Instead, the caravan ended up killing time by using loud noises to scare the herd away.

Kangala was not a superstitious person, and did not really believe in or pay reverence to any gods in the desertlands or mainland, but he knew one thing: A beast of this nature did not come under a person's control without a significant amount of power of some form being expended. Which begged the question: If one harboured such power, and one was the most powerful figure in the whole continent, why would one refrain from exercising said power?

There was only one answer: The power was finite, and was being conserved.

The emperor, as if responding to this discovery by Kangala, emanated a sudden long groan, jolting Kangala out of his thoughts. He made himself smaller behind the naboom plant, watching Igan and their posse encircle the emperor to cover her from sight. But not before Kangala, who was close enough, noticed the emperor place a hand on her belly and wince.

Slowly, recognition dawned on him.

He'd heard that groan intermittently before, during the ride—most of the caravan had. Everyone simply pretended it did not come from the emperor's travelwagon. But he had seen, with his own two eyes, which mouth the sound had come from, and what it signified.

The signs had been there to see all along. The emperor's swings between periods of extreme boisterousness and extreme tiredness, so that she was missing for large swaths of the trip, asleep in the royal travelwagon even in the daytime. Her growing pallor, her slower gait, her increased asocial demeanour. It made sense now.

The emperor was with child.

He managed a peek from behind the naboom. The cane chair was empty, emperor and advisors nowhere to be found. The door to the royal travelwagon was shut.

Kangala crept away from behind the plant and went in search of Oroe.

· ◇ ···   ··· ◇ ·

That night, while all of camp was asleep and only the peace officers on watch were out, Kangala awoke and prayed.

"Four Winds," he whispered into the dark, night breeze caressing his face. "If there is a sign, show it to me sooner than later."

Once, while attempting to investigate why Oroe's champions' rations

had been suddenly reduced (*all* of the caravan's rations had been shorted
to make up for an unplanned shortfall), Kangala had discovered that it
corresponded with an increase in the emperor's rations. He'd wondered
why one who felt such ravenous hunger would subject themselves to
travel through the wilderness. Now that he knew her pregnancy was the
reason, it raised even bigger questions.

Who were these fugitives, and why were they so important? What did
she seek of them that made this sacrifice worth it?

He knew only what Butue had told him, what the public notices
offered, what gossip he'd gleaned. An invader, yes; a former intended, yes;
a deceased politician's living daughter, yes. But there seemed to be something deeper here than just prison escapees and enemies of the crown.

He rummaged in his pack, dug out and unwrapped the cloth tales his
daughter, Ngipa, had handed to him before they left.

He and Ngipa had developed this secret messaging—one even Oroe
did not know—for situations such as these. Stories told in fabric, strips
of cloth with thread woven through in very specific patterns only the
weaver and the receiver understood. She'd handed him a stack of them
before the journey began, informing him that it was all she had learned
from her sojourns into the city in the few days since they'd camped outside Chugoko.

Now, Kangala held the strips of cloth between his fingers, positioned
them just like Ngipa had taught him, so that every finger was equidistant
from the other in the pattern of the weave. Beneath each weave was a
knot of thread, pinprick-like, easy to miss if one wasn't feeling properly.
One knot followed the other, each knot a sound, each sound a word, each
word a small part of a longer message. He shut his eyes, settled in, and
began to read.

◇ ⋯ —————— ⋯ ◇

Ngipa's report began with a retracing of the steps of the prison escapees,
from every location they were deemed to have been spotted, back to the
prison. She learned about the constant visitors to the escaped prisoner—
two men, who had been given the baby she bore in prison. Few knew
much about the men—even after she'd visited the public houses, no one

was willing to speak. So she returned her gaze to the woman, and was surprised by what she uncovered.

Her investigation asked deeper questions than the wardens had dared to. *Why now?* Why did the emperor's greatest enemies leave hiding after all this time, show up in the one city with the most allies of the empire, break out a prisoner, then escape?

She began to seek out wardens, searching for one of those who had set sight on the yellow woman that day, whether they had interacted with her or not. She finally bribed her way into a drink with one of the wardens on duty at the prisoner's gate during the escape. He was still limping from the beating by baton his knees had taken, and had a bandage wrapped around his head.

"I have not work here long, see?" the man said. "I just join a mooncycle or two before the attack. Only thing I know is that the prisoner is Bassai, and she don't talk plenty. She just sit there and sing sometime. A long song, maybe like a story, I don't know."

Ngipa wanted to know what the song was.

"A foreign language, I don't know it, but I can say what I hear. Maybe it is correct, maybe it is not."

Ngipa asked him to sing anyway. It indeed was a foreign language, sounding like the gibberish the warden thought he was singing. But that was only because it was not one language: It was many braided together. High Bassai slipping into Mainland Common twisted into Savanna Common chopped up with various border tongues. A tale hidden by its own telling, so that only a person blessed with multiple lips and multiple ears could unravel it.

Unluckily for this clever weaver, Ngipa was such a person. And so, as the man began to sing, Ngipa began to translate:

Listen, then, children of the seven islands, for I am going to tell you of a city once prosperous in this archipelago.

⋄⸺⸺⸺⸺⋄

When Kangala lifted his head, both moons had taken to the sky. He put away the cloth tales and rose. It was a bright night, but the two peace officers on duty did not seem concerned with him. He shuffled across camp, greeting the two watchmen, pretending to seek a spot to piss in. The tent he sought stood opposite his. He slipped into it silently.

Oroe was already waiting in the dark, awake.

"How many peace officers can each champion kill before they are killed?" Kangala asked.

"Eh?" Though he couldn't see it in the dark, Kangala was sure Oroe's eyes widened.

"How many can they kill," he repeated, "before they go down?"

"What are you planning?" Oroe asked.

"You know what," was Kangala's reply.

"She is only pregnant, not indisposed," said Oroe. "One wrong move, and she rouses that beast. We won't last half a moment."

Kangala paused, then said: "I know why the fugitives are headed east, and why the emperor is *really* going after them."

He told Oroe of the tale of the buried city of powerful minerals he'd learned about from Ngipa's story, a tale that spoke of the power to rouse dead beasts and move mountains. A city beneath islands filled with peoples that may or may not exist—people like this yellow woman the emperor spoke of. A tale that told him what said power was: not a blessing from the moon gods, not an ordination of person, elevating them to supreme being.

It was all a little stone. A little stone that could be taken away.

Oroe was shaking his head, even after Kangala finished his explanation.

"Ngipa should know better, filling your head with this nonsense," said Oroe. "A dozen peace officers and a great beast aside, there is also the Second's posse. We cannot possibly defeat them all?"

"No," said Kangala. "We cannot, and we should not plan to. To achieve our goals, we do not have to defeat them all, or all at once, or all in the same manner."

"What are you planning, daa?"

"I don't know yet," Kangala said, "but I know it is possible." He straightened. "How many, Oroe?"

Oroe was silent for a moment, then said: "Two."

Kangala nodded in the dark. "Two is a good number. It is more than one." He rose. "Stay close and stay ready. Opportunity may arise at any time."

Oroe's breath was audible. "And the beast?"

"Haven't you heard the old saying *The bigger they are, the harder they fall*?" He chuckled. "Leave the beast to me, son."

Kangala slipped out of the tent and back into the cold night.

39

Lilong

The Lonely Roads East
Sixth Mooncycle, 28

BACK ON THE ROAD, Lilong opted for driving duty, hoping for some time alone to settle the tempest raging in her mind. She had not driven a travel-wagon such as this before, but she took to the reins anyway, absent-mindedly receiving Danso's navigation instructions. The sun was at its most violent by the time she climbed into the driver's seat, and the lonely roads were unshaded. After applying sun-butter to her face and arms, she pulled large wrappers around herself and wore her large straw hat, then began to steer the kwagas with difficulty.

The plagues of Risisi have not been triggered. There is no plague of beasts. Danso and Oke must be wrong. We don't even know if Risisi is a real place!

These and other denials had filled her mind throughout last night. But the more she thought about it all, the more she realised not everything could be a lie. The genge were proof. These were no ordinary beasts, so *something* had to have triggered their arousal from slumber. Maybe ibor had something to do with it; maybe not. But something *was* happening.

She just couldn't bring herself to believe that the Ihinyon or the Abenai League could be involved in this world-affecting change. Or worse: her own daa. If this buried city of Risisi was truly real, and someone had uncovered it—and in so doing, unleashed plagues onto the world—her daa was the only one who had the knowledge, access, and will to do so.

Did this mean he was still alive? Did this mean he had somehow found a way to uncover this city and its secrets? Did this mean that the ibor scarcity in Ihinyon was over?

As if sensing her disconcertment, the kwagas drawing the travelwagon kept disobeying her commands. She manoeuvred them back into place, suddenly aware of the discomforts of this job, like the bare wood of the seat digging into her buttocks. Regardless, this felt revitalizing, distracting enough to lighten her mind and heart. Driving the travelwagon gave her a sense of purpose and direction, a conviction that she was *doing something*, as Danso had put it.

And indeed, she had decided she was going to *do something*. Witnessing Danso's strange new desire for iborworking made her realise that maybe her daa and Oke had it all wrong. Power like this—it rotted insides. It turned the most well-meaning people into predators. And if her daa had truly discovered a buried city full of power, what was she—an Abenai warrior, sworn to protect her land and people—to do?

She couldn't turn her back on it all. Not with all the knowledge she'd gained, especially if it turned out to be true. She didn't even have anywhere else to go—she had been to the world out there, and it wasn't exactly welcoming. If Risisi was truly real, then there was no running from it. She might escape the plagues of fires, dirt, water, wind, and beasts, but she'd never escape the plague of human greed and desire.

If Risisi's reopening didn't destroy the world in plagues, then someone would eventually gain access to its immense power and become a problem for all of Oon.

No, she couldn't turn away from this. Her very responsibility as a warrior—the only thing she knew how to be—demanded that she *do something*. So yes, she was going to do what was required to protect everyone from Risisi and its plagues.

And maybe the best protection from a city that was going to implode on itself was to ensure that, this time around, it finished the job.

⋅◇⋅⋯⋯⋯⋯⋯◇⋅

They were coming upon a wooded area, one of many such areas they had marked on the map and planned to steer clear of, as these were notorious for travellers getting waylaid by bandits. If she remembered Danso's instructions correctly, Lilong was to turn them off the lonely roads and onto any of the various bushpaths that circled the area.

She steered the kwagas conscientiously, and they went down one of the requisite paths.

A bang came on the roof of the travelwagon. Someone was calling for her to stop. She pulled the reins, and the kwagas reluctantly obeyed.

Danso's head poked out of the window. "Where are you going?"

"Hmm?" Lilong looked around, frowning. "You said take the path."

"Oh for moons' sake, I said *do not* take the path."

"Oh," said Lilong. "I thought we were avoiding woodland?"

Oke, Alaba, and Ugo emerged from the travelwagon, looking around. "Where are we, even?" Alaba was asking.

"We're avoiding woodlands, yes," said Danso. "Except *this* one."

Lilong retrieved the map he'd marked and squinted at it. In the high sun and without her reading stones, she couldn't see anything useful.

"The Weary Sojourner is a half day's ride," Oke was explaining, balancing Thema on her hip. She pointed behind Lilong, in the opposite direction. "*That* way. So we should be going *through* the woodland, not away from it."

"Oh," said Lilong again, looking sheepish.

"Why are we not avoiding this one again?" Alaba asked.

"Because it's not real," Ugo offered. "Set up by bandits so that travellers avoid it, take these paths instead, then run into their waiting ambush."

"Ah," said Alaba, chuckling. "So that means—"

A fizz, a *thwack*, and there was an arrow sticking out of Alaba's side.

The blood did not come immediately, but in slow motion, spreading over his garment. Alaba stared at the arrow, confused, before falling to a knee, and then to the ground.

"Everybody down!" screamed Lilong, and Drew as two more arrows flew past them.

Six figures appeared from nowhere—two on foot, four on two kwagas. They were fast, even the two on foot, closing the distance in a quarter moment. They were dressed head to toe in singular robes, veils over their faces, and hands wrapped so that their skin could not be seen. Almost Gaddo-like.

But Lilong knew, at once, that this was no company. There was no order to their approach, and no strategy to their assault. They simply charged toward the group, misjudging their constitution—two women, a baby, three men who didn't look like fighters—and thinking them there for the taking. Their eyes, the only parts of them she could see, were not even assessing the dangers, as if they expected no threats.

She had not harmed anyone in a long time, and she was not keen to return to doing so. But one look at these bandits, and she knew that if she did not move fast, arrows would be sticking to them the way one stuck to Alaba right now.

Lilong Drew as they approached, and did not bother to swing a blade in anyone's direction. Instead, she sent it toward the ground, whirling it before the kwagas in wild, whipping motions. The beasts, spooked, barked and reared to a halt, pitching their cargo—including the archer, whose bow snapped as they fell—into the dust.

Those on foot headed straight for Oke. Lilong could see the plan: hold on to the most vulnerable of them and use that as leverage. But Oke saw it too, and she Drew. Water hurled from inside the travelwagon and smacked the first bandit in the face, sending them down. The other was close—too close. Oke was pulling the water back from the other bandit, now in the dust, but it was a slow and arduous process.

Lilong did not think. Her warrior training took over, and she Commanded the blade without hesitation. *Go.*

The hilt arrowed straight into the back of the bandit's neck, knocking them from behind and off balance. The bandit staggered, dagger a hair's breadth from Oke's face. Oke stepped out of the way as the bandit fell forward—

—and crashed their jaw into the edge of the travelwagon.

There was a jarring *pop*, and the bottom half of their face separated from the top, veil tearing off, clinging to the white bone and bloody flesh that landed in the dust. The bandit rolled over, nose and upper teeth drooping, eyes wide. Where the rest of their face should have been, flesh dangled, and blood spurted. Oke turned away and covered her baby's eyes.

Time stopped, and not just for Lilong. Even the remaining bandits—three of them—paused, suddenly putting together what they had witnessed:

Lilong's moving blade, Oke's Commanded water, their fallen comrade, the wounded Alaba, whom Oke and Ugo were now kneeling beside.

Lilong found that her throat was dry, watching the wounded bandit jerk in the dust, saying a silent prayer that they were still alive. This was not something she had done before—praying for the well-being of someone she had just attacked. When last had she even attacked someone this way? Not even as Snakeblade of the Gaddo Company, and not even during the prison break. The last time, if she remembered correctly, was at the Dead Mines, when she had hurled her blade at Esheme, or before then, when she had fought Oboda in Whudasha, or Nem in Bassa. *Those* were deserved. This? Not so much.

She was a warrior, yes, trained as such. But more than anything, Lilong thought herself a protector. Not an aggressor or attacker. Not a *killer*.

The wounded bandit stopped moving.

She turned around to face the three still standing. One of them, the only archer left, had their bow taut, arrow aimed straight for Lilong's head only a short distance away. Their hands shook. Watery eyes darted toward the bandit on the ground, then to Lilong's discarded blade, then back to Lilong.

"Put it down," Lilong said, calmly lifting her hands. "Put it down, and you can take your comrades home. Survive." She angled her head in the direction of the wounded bandit. "Especially that one."

The archer looked at their comrade in the dust again, then to the others who had been knocked unconscious when they fell from the kwagas. Behind, the other two looked unsure as well.

"Down," said Lilong. "Do it now."

The archer's eyes brimmed with tears. Their arms relaxed, the string slackened a tad, and the bow lowered just a pinch.

Behind Lilong, Alaba groaned. From the corner of her eye, she saw Oke compressing the wound, having removed the arrow. Danso knelt next to her, Ugo on the opposite side, trying to keep the stricken Thema calm. Lilong wanted to turn around to see if Alaba was okay, but feared that the bandits would do something rash with that opening.

"How is he doing?" she shouted over her shoulder.

"Not good!" Ugo screamed back.

Thwack.

Perhaps it was nerves, or poor training, but the bandit let go. Lilong was sure she'd seen the resignation in their stance, was sure that they wanted to put it down. But a taut arrow was primed to fly, and fly it did.

Fortunately, Lilong had been prepared for this too. As soon as the arrow left the bow, she Commanded her blade.

It struck the arrowhead exactly where she'd wanted it. The arrow diverted, but only slightly, whizzing too close by her ear, the tail slicing her cheek. She did not hear a *thunk* behind her, or a scream of pain, so knew it did not hit anyone or anything, and therefore was still flying into the wilds.

A stinging pain bloomed on her cheek. She lifted a finger, touched it. It came away wet and sticky.

The bandit, eyes wide, fell to their knees in the dust. Then their shoulders heaved, and tears wet the veil, causing it to droop. Now she could see the face: a young boy—too young.

"Brother," he was saying in what sounded like a savanna pidgin. *"Brother."*

The other two bandits did not pull back their veils, but Lilong peered now and could finally see they were all young. She turned around to see the bandit without the face, and decided that one was similar too.

Children, she realised. *These are all children.*

In that moment she registered Danso rise from beside Alaba and disappear behind the wagon. She felt for her pouch, and remembered that Danso had it, with the Diwi inside. Then she realised why he'd run to the rear of the travelwagon: The dead genge was there.

"Danso!" she called, trying not to turn her gaze away from the bandits. "Danso!"

No response.

"Danso!" she called again. "Don't! They're just children!"

Slowly, tentatively, Danso appeared from behind the travelwagon. His eyes were fiery red, a tumultuous blaze. In his hand: the Diwi, to which he was completely given over.

Oh no, thought Lilong.

The bandits panicked at the sight of him. A foolhardy bravery took over the face of the lead child, who now stepped forward, ready to advance on Danso.

"No," Lilong said in the child's direction, then to Danso: "Put that away!"

The bandit advanced farther.

Lilong stepped in to cover the distance, gesturing toward Danso. "I said move—"

A buzz like a giant bee filled her ear, and with it came sharp air. An arrow whistled past her and struck the back of the travelwagon, next to Danso. She shot around to find the archer reloading the bow.

"Stop!" she screamed, running over to Danso, blocking him with her body. She grabbed the Diwi from his hand, praying that the genge had not already been activated. Thankfully, it was still in the back of the travelwagon, yet to move.

She returned her attention to the bandits.

"You have a choice," she said. "Turn around now. Take your injured comrade and go. I promise you will come to no harm. You have my word." Then she flexed her mind, and her blade rose and swung in circles before her, raising dust. "Or you can stay and meet your end. You have my word on that too."

After what seemed like an eternity of pause, the archer finally lowered his bow. The other two quickly stepped forward, pulling back their unconscious comrades, and then their wounded one. Soon, they were on kwagaback, retreating, dust in their wake.

Lilong exhaled with relief and turned to Danso. "Are you all right?"

He was staring at his hands. "It still didn't work."

"And thank Great Forces for that," said Lilong. "You were going to let that thing murder *children*."

"They tried to murder *us*."

"And *so what*? They're still *children*! Did you ever stop to think that somebody *trained* them to do that? Did you ever think that maybe they never had a choice?"

She saw that Danso knew she was right, but was too consumed by anger to back down. After glaring at one another, fuming, she tempered tensions by putting the Diwi back in his hand.

"Put that away," she said. "Now."

Alaba's groans cut through their quarrel. Conflict suspended, they dashed for him. Alaba whimpered with pain as Oke pressed down on his wound.

"I can dress that," said Danso, dashing to the travelwagon for medicine. He returned with a pack, giving instructions—*chew this, spit that here*—while Alaba's lips emanated sounds of agony. Even after wrapping the wound in herbs and a bandage, the pain did not seem to abate. And when he sat up, it resumed bleeding.

"Can we get to the Weary Sojourner before nightfall?" Danso asked. "He needs to lie flat, get some rest, maybe even a strong drink."

"If we ride hard," said Oke, and climbed into the driver's seat.

They tried to make space for Alaba to lie in the wagon, but the genge had taken up so much that there was little left for them all.

"We have to get rid of the beast," said Lilong to Ugo. She glanced at Danso. "Unless you object."

What that look in his eye was, she wasn't sure. A sort of twisted anger, maybe a little of it directed at her, but most of it wasn't *about* her. It wasn't even *about* those child-bandits. It was something else, something she didn't have time for right now.

"I said do you object, Danso?"

He shrugged. "You do what you have to do, Lilong, and I'll do what I have to."

She kissed her teeth, beckoning to Ugo. "Brother, help me get this thing down. We'll drag it under that naboom plant there. And then let us ride for the Weary Sojourner with everything we have."

40

Danso

The Weary Sojourner Caravansary
Sixth Mooncycle, 28, same day

THE WEARY SOJOURNER, WHEN the party arrived, did not look like a formerly burned-down establishment to Danso. Before them was a quaint little compound with an entryway, a main building with one storey, and scattered adjoining huts. At said entryway was a conspicuous sign that read in as many languages as it could: NO ARMS. Beside the entryway was an array of wooden chests, some open, some nailed shut. Likely where all the disarmed weaponry was stored.

"What if we don't want to leave our weapons?" Lilong asked aloud.

"Then you fit to be on your way," said a voice in Savanna Common.

A woman emerged from the main building. She was stout and hard-faced, yet had a matronly air about her. She held a gourd of water, and a rag hung from her shoulder.

"You must be Madam Pikoyo," said Danso.

"Indeed I am," said the woman.

"We have a wounded," said Oke. "And we need aid."

The woman tilted her head. "Bandits, yes? You no hear about taking the woodland?" She observed Lilong's sheepish expression, shaking her head. "And what this business about keeping your arms?"

"We have just been attacked," said Lilong. "You can't now be asking us to give up the only thing that ensures we do not suffer an attack again?"

"I can, and I will," said the woman. The rag and gourd made her seem very ordinary, but Danso knew that no ordinary person built an establishment in the middle of the savanna, to talk less of insisting upon disarming as a rule.

"Okay, okay," said Oke, casting panicked glances at Alaba, who still lay bleeding in the wagon. "How will we keep safe while we're here?"

"Safety is no worry at the Weary Sojourner," said Madam Pikoyo. "This establishment bear allegiance to nobody. Whoever you are out there, in my house you are neutral party. No enemies here."

"What if we get in there and someone chooses not to follow your rules?"

Madam Pikoyo offered a wry smile. "I say *you* can't have arms. I don't say *I* can't have arms."

Lilong and Oke glanced at one another.

"It's okay," said Lilong, then unlatched her blade. "Oke and I don't quite need it anyway." She dropped it in one of the open chests. Oke and Ugo, who both had daggers of their own, did the same. Danso held up his hands to demonstrate that he had nothing.

It was then Madam Pikoyo spotted the baby strapped to Oke's chest.

"Oh, my, my, my," she said, flummoxed. "Why you carry a child into this kind life so?" A formerly missing earnestness had suddenly crept into her voice, as if she were scolding a member of her family. The party looked at one another.

"No just stand there," she said, tucking a hand into the crook of Oke's elbow and leading her away. "Less get you and that baby clean."

"My partner, wounded…" Oke was saying, but Pikoyo whistled. Out of nowhere came a number of young people of all genders.

"They will take your wounded upstairs," she said, beckoning to Ugo to lead two helpers to where Alaba lay in the wagon. Another helper goaded Oke forward with the baby, pointing her toward some place of comfort. Others helped unhitch the kwagas and take them out to the back where they could rest and replenish.

Pikoyo turned to Danso and Lilong, left behind.

"Well, then," she said. "Welcome to the Weary Sojourner. We have whatever you are willing to buy. Food, drink, beds, comfort." She leaned forward. "*Comfort.*"

As she said this, one of the helpers approached Lilong and Danso.

"Same or separate quarters?" the young man asked Danso.

"Separate?" said Danso.

"Separate mean one of you stay in my quarters and the other stay alone." He smiled invitingly at Danso. "I choose you. But if you like, us three can stay together."

"No," Lilong and Danso chorused.

"Fine," he said, walking away. "That just mean you two stay together in the same quarters." He shook his head. "Boring."

A stone scrub, a long soak, and a trim of his beard later, Danso felt brand-new. Dressed in fresh wrappers and with the cleanest hair he'd had in a while, he felt like the jali he was meant to be. Lilong, who had been waiting out of his way as much as he'd been ensuring to keep out of hers, took her things to the washroom as soon as he emerged.

Danso dressed, deciding it was impossible to spend the rest of the night within proximity of her. He gathered his manuscript and charcoal stylus. Maybe later, he'd go to the main building and see if he could find a drink and some stories for his codex. But he needed to do something first, and that meant checking on Alaba's health.

The compound, as he crossed it, was a loose collection of buildings with no particular style. Each hut surrounding the main building had its own character, built to represent the personality of its inhabitant. The young woman whose quarters Lilong and Danso currently inhabited had told them that each person here was from a sacked community, displaced by peace officers gone wild and drunk on the Red Emperor's backing. Unable to live on the trade route or under the ham-fisted rule of big cities like Chugoko, most survivors of such communities ended up here, seeking a safe haven. Madam Pikoyo had offered each new arrival materials to build their abode, and the opportunity to make a living working at the Weary Sojourner in exchange for sustenance and the protection of the neutral establishment. And just like that, the public house had grown from the singular housekeep into a community of desertlanders who did not fit anywhere else.

Upstairs, Danso heard Alaba's room before he saw it. The door was shut, but Oke's familiar voice carried through.

"You are staying, and that is *final*," she was saying.

"You don't get to make decisions for us." This was Alaba. He did not sound like someone in pain at all. Madam Pikoyo had assured them that there were good healers in the community, but Danso had thought it best to confirm for himself. Turned out he needn't have worried after all.

"This is not the time to be stubborn, Aba," she said. "You have risked your life enough for me already—you *both* have. I cannot have your demise on my hands, don't you understand? I cannot *live* to see you die. I cannot—"

She choked, and then there was silence, filled only with blubbering, unintelligible sounds Danso could have sworn Oke was incapable of making. Then someone was saying in a calm, placid voice: "It's okay, it's okay. Don't let Thema hear you—she'll cry too."

"You have to make him stay, Ugo," Oke said through sobs. "You have to make him. I don't care if you have to stay and do it—make him stay."

Danso thought he heard footsteps coming in his direction, so he walked away. But Oke came storming out the door and saw him anyway. He turned to her, pretending to have randomly stumbled upon the room by chance, but her glare quickly sliced through the act. She looked offended, as if he had just caught her in a bad act.

"Tell Lilong we leave tomorrow," she said. "Just us three." She paused. "And Thema."

She breezed past him and went downstairs to the main room. Danso watched her order a drink and take a seat in the empty space—there were no travellers in sight, save for them.

He watched her for a moment longer, assured that she'd registered that she'd seen him with his codex. Then he slipped downstairs, to the backyard, where the kwagas—now separated from the travelwagon and being tended to—were tied.

A stablehand stood there, refilling the water troughs. Danso beckoned to the young man, reached into his wrappers, pulled out a copper piece or two, and handed them to him. The young man's eyes widened with appreciation, before his brows furrowed in confusion.

"If anyone asks," Danso said, unsure if the young man understood his Savanna Common, "I'm inside there, writing in this." He pointed toward a nearby stable, then tapped the codex.

The man nodded. Danso plopped the papers, stylus and all, in the young man's hand.

"I want you to hold on to these for now." He pointed to the kwagas. "Prepare one of those for me."

The genge was still there, under the naboom plant, when Danso arrived.

He'd only half expected to find it. Current conditions in the savanna meant every animal was roving in hunger. He wouldn't have been surprised if another pack of genge had simply eaten one of their own.

He descended from the kwaga, tied it at another nearby naboom tree, then dragged the dead animal a little ways away so as not to spook the kwaga when it awoke.

If it awoke.

He knelt in the dry, prickly grass, reached into his wrappers, and pulled out the Diwi. He lay his other hand on the fallen beast. Then he shut his eyes tight, inhaled a lungful of the night air, and *hoped*.

"I have done everything I can," he said into the quiet night. "I have done all I've been asked, and yet I come away with nothing. With only pain, regret, ashes." He swallowed. "So I will stop. I will no longer do what I have done, what I have been *told* to do. Today, I will *do something else*—I will no longer be a victim. I will no longer be the basket that collects the rain, or the vane that the wind swings any way it wishes. No—I will *be* the rain. I will *be* the wind."

The genge remained unmoved. The disquiet of the open wilderness, punctured only by chirping crickets, answered him back.

"I want to live," he said as he felt the power of red ibor begin to coalesce at the bottom of his belly, build up into his lungs. "If I must help those I care about—the oppressed, the underserved, the invisible of Bassa and beyond; *my* people—then I must live. I cannot perish like those who have come before me, like those who I've loved but who were not strong enough."

His voice took on an edge, sharper, angrier. "I could not protect them, and I cannot protect myself. But if I must live, then I must be safe." He inhaled, ibor rushing into him, filling every crevice. "So *rise*, old beast. Rise and protect me. Rise, and aid my quest."

Somewhere, the stirrings of something familiar—old and angry and ready—began. He leaned into it, wished its journey along, pushed its trajectory onto that of the animal beneath him.

Consuming power rushed forth—lively, eager, foreboding. Memories circulated through his consciousness: lightning striking the Bassai hunt-hands near the Peace Fence; the Skopi attacking various hunthands in Whudasha; Zaq burning at the pyre, his screams rending the air; Habba bleeding on the ground in the Dead Mines, blade in his shoulder; Habba, engulfed in fire, burning.

The kwaga, tied to the tree, barked and snorted.

The memories cleared. The genge stirred.

Blood-red eyes opened.

Danso felt the prickle of the grass on the animal's side where it lay. He rose, and the beast rose with him. Now one with the beast, every single motion of its was his: every straining sinew; every tired knee; every nerve ending tasting the dusty water droplets in the air and perceiving the sweat of the petrified kwaga in the distance.

Danso drank it in, laughter escaping his lips. The genge was a majestic beast to look at, but even more majestic to *feel*.

When he had drunk full of this feeling, he returned to the kwaga. The animal, sensing something new about him, remained perturbed. He reached out a hand and calmed it until it allowed him to mount its back again.

Then he turned it around, faced the direction in which the bandits had gone, and cantered off.

The genge, eyes brimming red, followed its master.

41

Danso

The Lonely Roads East
Sixth Mooncycle, 28–29

IT WAS EASY TO find the bandit camp. Danso had added so much to the original map he'd started out with that he now had a better idea of the savanna's patterns. He knew where one might end up if they followed certain roads, if they tracked certain vegetation, and whether possibilities for settlement existed. From their direction of escape alone, he'd surmised the most feasible location for a base of operations and was unsurprised to find them there.

It was a small camp, semipermanent, with one large tent orbited by a few smaller ones. Telltale signs of a nomadic lifestyle abounded: Livestock—sheep, goats, a singular camel—were scattered around the camp. A fire burned in the middle, and another near the edge of the large tent. The children—the bandits from earlier, he guessed—were crowded near that tent, morose and whispering to themselves. Around the fire sat a group of three adult men, enjoying a drink, some meat, and a lot of laughter and camaraderie.

Danso did not wait or hide. He Drew and Possessed the genge as soon as the kwaga was close enough to be noticed, sending the unsightly beast ahead of him. The genge was a silent monster, slithering silkily through the grass unnoticed until it was right upon the morose children.

The children looked up at the shadow that fell upon them—and screamed.

The men by the fire rose at the same time other men emerged from the darkness. Danso, still atop the kwaga, counted six, all dressed like the children had been earlier but without the veils. They had their weapons at the ready: bows, swords, spears. They recoiled, stricken, when they saw the genge, and their confidence faltered. But they stood forward anyway.

"Who is you?" the closest to him asked in Savanna Common. "Talk!"

Danso's heartbeat increased at the sight of blades, but he willed it to slow down. *Be like Ugo*, he told himself, channelling the legendary journeyman who was always the embodiment of calm in every chaos.

Instead of panicking, he Commanded the genge: *Go.*

The animal did something. Danso couldn't say what that *something* was because it happened too fast. One moment, the genge was standing next to him; the next, it was standing next to him again, a lump of bloody flesh hanging between its teeth, dangling from the sides of its mouth, painting its chin in red.

The man who had spoken looked down at his sword, lying in the grass, bloodied at the handle. Still gripping the hilt was a hand—*his* hand, missing a few fingers. He lifted his arm to his face, and where there used to be a wrist, there was a fleshy, bloody stump leaking blood.

The man made a deathly noise that rent the night air. Then he promptly collapsed. The rest of the party went white, from children to adults.

The genge spat out the fingers and licked its bloody lips, primed for another Command.

"Put down your weapons," said Danso in Savanna Common. "Or your heads will be next."

The bandits slowly acceded, lifting their arms after letting down their weapons. From inside the tent emerged one more adult, unarmed, carrying a bloody rag. He followed suit.

Danso descended from the kwaga and strutted through the grass to where the genge stood. He ran a hand over the animal's velvety body and teased one of its skin-antennae between his thumb and forefinger.

"You hurt someone I care about," he said. "You sent children to kill us just for a few cowries. And now you sit here and banter as if nothing about the world has changed." He was looking at the adults. "Do you ever think that each time you do what you do, people lose more than their goods? Did you know that *everything* changes for them?"

He was breathing heavily in a way that terrified the camp.

"*Please*," the nearest man said. "We no do anything. Just take what you want."

"You think I'm a *thief*?" Danso felt insulted. "You think because your life is driven by greed and murder, mine is too?"

"No, sorry—"

Danso Commanded the genge to stand in front of the man, so close its antennae touched the man's nose. The man yelped, knees shaking.

"I am not a killer," Danso said. "Or, shall I say—I do not intend to kill. Not tonight. But you have done a bad thing to good people, and for that, you must pay."

He pointed to the men. "I will not ask this more than once. I want you to turn around where you stand and start walking."

The men looked at one another. "Where?" one asked.

"Away. Away from these children, from these desertlands, from good people. I want you to wander the desertlands until your feet ache and your throats peel from thirst. I want you to be so delirious from sun-stroke that you drink of the naboom plant and see visions and scratch out your own eyes."

The men gulped.

"Please," the nearest man said. "The child in there—is hurt. We repair face. We must take care."

Danso stepped forward, pushed aside the tent canvas with a finger, and peeked inside. The wounded bandit child from earlier lay there, asleep or unconscious, their face wrapped in cloth bandages, leaving only their eyes visible.

"Please," the man repeated. "*Please.*"

Danso returned to stand beside the genge. He flexed his mind and gave the genge a Command: *Maim*.

He did not look at what ensued. What needed to be done needed to be done. The only thing important was that the man yelped and choked in the grass as the genge stomped on him and bit him in places that were sure to leave scars, and that the camp watched all of this, horrified.

By the time the genge finished and returned to Danso's side, the man in the grass could only make small motions, covered in blood, cuts, and bruises, but very much alive to feel every single one of them.

"Make me repeat myself again..." Danso said, leaving the rest of his statement hanging.

The men did not need further invitation. One by one, they turned around and began walking, away from the light of the camp and into the darkness. One man tried to grab a torch as he went, but Danso sent the genge after him. The man ran.

All was quiet at the camp afterward, save for the crackling of fires and the billowing of tent canvas. Danso, satisfied, turned to go.

That was when he noticed the children, standing there, grasping each other in a huddle, whimpers and shudders passing along them, one to the other.

"You find some way else to better yourselves, you hear me?" he said to them. "You leave this life of banditry behind. If I hear that you robbed someone else in these desertlands again..."

He returned to the kwaga and mounted it. After a moment's thought, he added:

"Your comrade is in your care now. You take care of them, nurse them back to health. You are all you have. Remember that."

He turned around and rode into the night. The genge lingered, then followed.

·◇·⋯ ⋯·◇·

When Danso returned to the main room of the Weary Sojourner, codex and stylus back in his hands, a couple of the Weary Sojourner workers sat around, but the place was otherwise empty. Oke was still there, drinking, but did not notice him enter. However, Ugo, who sat next to her, joining her in drowning sorrow and anger, did. His eyes followed Danso over the rim of his calabash, never leaving even after he went upstairs.

Not that Danso cared. He'd done what no one else was brave or powerful enough to do—bring order and safety back into the desertlands, one bandit troop at a time. *This* was what power was meant to do: help the weak and defenceless. The bandits had thought he and his people were weak and defenceless, and he'd shown them that they were not. Going forward, moons willing, he was ready to show everyone just the same.

This had been Lilong's daa's dream—to put power in the hands of ordinary people who could use it to protect others around them. Danso agreed with that dream. It had taken him a while to come around, but now he was sure: That was also what he wanted.

Do something—well, now he had. Never again would anyone take something or someone he loved. Not if he could help it.

He opened the door to his quarters—

—and bumped into Lilong, emerging from inside. His codex, map, and stylus fell to the floor.

"Oh—sorry." She grimaced, bent, picked them up, and handed them back to him.

"Thanks." He hustled inside before she could smell the fresh dust of the savanna on him. But as he went in, her eyes followed him.

"What's that?"

He stopped, lifted an eyebrow. "Hmm? What?"

"That." She pointed to the side of his tunic.

He looked down. Across the lower right was a stain on his clothing, a smear that went past the cloth and onto his skin itself. A *red* smear.

"Is that... *blood*?" Her tone was accusatory.

The two stared at one another in elongated pause. Lilong's gaze prodded, the cut on her cheek still blooming red. In that moment, Danso realised just how different from one another they were. Foreigners, in all senses of the word.

A part of him prepared to lash out, to say, *And so fucking what?* She'd be infuriated, but who cared? They were already strangers. They might as well become adversaries too.

But he remembered the little matter of needing her good word when they arrived at the islands, without which he might not fare as well, Red Iborworker or not.

"Ah," he said. "That must be Alaba's, from earlier."

Lilong's gaze did not falter, her eyes asking the unspoken question: *But did you not just take a bath?*

"I came to get my things," Danso said, changing the subject. "Think I'm staying with Ugo tonight." He trudged through the room, picked up his pack.

On the way out, he said: "Oke says the men are remaining behind. Ugo will stay to nurse Alaba back to health. So it's you, me, her, and Thema for the rest of the journey."

Lilong did not respond, gaze unwavering. He slipped out the door as he had come in. Her steely gaze followed him all the way, and even after crossing the compound, Danso could still feel her eyes piercing holes in his back.

He found Ugo still drinking in the main room, Oke having returned to check on Alaba. Danso took a seat next to him, put down his pack, and ordered a drink—a jackalberry spirit like Ugo's. Ugo, on his own part, was discreetly eyeing the bloodstain on Danso's side.

"I'm staying with you tonight," said Danso.

Ugo nodded. "Do I even want to know?"

"No."

"Okay." Ugo sipped at his drink. "But if I may?"

"I would prefer that you not *may*."

"If I *may*," Ugo pressed. "You don't have to tell me anything. We all have our secrets, our demons, our haunts. But—" He held up a finger. "The hope is that they don't consume us. And it is my hope that yours, whatever they are, do not consume you."

Danso's drink arrived. He gulped half of it down in a long swallow. His hands shook.

"I've heard you," was all he said.

"Okay, then," said Ugo, and the two men, in silence, drank jackalberry spirits for the remainder of the night.

⋅◇⋅⋯⎯⎯⎯⎯⎯⋯⋅◇⋅

The parting of the trio of Oke, Ugo, and Alaba the next morning was a heartrending scene. Alaba, now able to stand with some help, draped one arm around Ugo, the other around Oke, and together—just like they did at the hideout—they wept.

Danso stood from a distance and watched, nursing a slight headache from the night before. Lilong was also there, but her eyes were not on the scene. Her eyes were locked on Danso.

"I will come back for you, I promise," Oke said between sniffles, accepting Thema and strapping her to her chest.

Alaba smiled. "Stay alive, you hear? Don't eat cockroaches."

Oke laughed. Danso had not heard her make that sound in a long time.

"I never ate cockroaches," she said.

"Well, I hear prison makes you do mad things." Danso thought Alaba sounded quite jocular for someone who only recently had an arrow stuck in their side. He realised, now, that Alaba had ingested a significant amount of pain herbs, which meant he was slightly inebriated.

"I will not eat cockroaches, and I will be back." She smiled at Ugo, the more downbeat of the two. She kissed his forehead. "Thema and I will be fine, I promise."

Ugo smiled back weakly. "Nothing about this is safe."

"I know."

"You can stay. We can all stay." He paused. "We should be together. We only just got reunited. We should never leave each other's sight."

"I know."

His eyes were watery. He wiped them.

"I will come back," said Oke. "But I need to do this. The world needs it. *We* need it." She kissed his forehead again. "You want us to be together? This is the only way we do so freely. We give *everyone* the opportunity to be free, and *then* we can be the family we desire."

"I don't know," said Ugo. "If we must be the ones to sacrifice."

"It has to be somebody," said Oke, "and fate chose us."

Afterward, the men each kissed the baby affectionately.

"You know she can stay with us," Ugo was saying. "I will never let her out of my sight."

"I know," said Oke. "But she's my reminder why I'm doing this. She's my reminder to stay alive." She clicked her tongue. "Also, insurance, maybe? I reckon the Abenai League will be less threatened by a woman with a baby."

She kissed both men on the lips, long and hard. Then she adjusted the baby wrap and went into the travelwagon. Afterward, Lilong said her goodbyes to the men with light embraces. Danso clasped Alaba's hand and nodded. When he clasped Ugo's, the other man held firm.

"You thanked me, once, for saving your life," Ugo said. "If you ever wish to repay me . . ." He motioned toward the travelwagon with his head. "Take care of them?"

"I'll do my best," said Danso. "Promise."

Afterward, Danso got into the driver's seat. Oke, their primary navigator, was saddled with Thema, which meant he was on driving duty until they arrived at the Forest of the Mist.

Lilong busied herself with retrieving their weapons. Or so Danso thought. But suddenly, there she was, standing beside him, looking up into the driving seat.

"Hand it over," she said.

She didn't need to say what *it* was to know she was asking for the Diwi. Even before bumping into her at the doorway the night before, Danso knew she would ask for it at some point.

But what she was truly asking in this moment was for him to pick a side: her side, or the side of ibor, of agency, of *power*. And as much as he respected her, as much as he owed her his very life, he simply could not choose her. Not this time.

"I left it for you on the seat inside," he said.

A charged silence passed between them.

"And the genge?" Lilong asked.

Danso let the question hang for a beat before asking: "What genge?" Then he turned his face away from her.

Someone had to do something to make the world better. An emperor as ruthless as Esheme on their tail, a smouldering empire in her hands. His stories alone were insufficient for this fight—that much he'd learned in Chabo. This trip was about bringing salvation—to himself, and to as many others as he could—but also retribution.

His maa. His daa. Zaq. Kubra. All perished at the hand of powerful forces who cared nothing for the weak or defenceless. No more. Not if he could help it.

They rolled away from the Weary Sojourner. Danso set the kwagas into a trot, his mind turning. He would speak no more of his thoughts—not to Lilong, not to Oke. He would do everything as directed—cross the Forest of the Mist, go to Ofen, find Risisi. And when they got there, Lilong could do whatever she wanted to her heart's content. But moons so help him, he would not leave those islands without taking with him whatever Bassa needed to be saved.

This was it. The lines in the sand were drawn. There was no going back.

Kangala

The Weary Sojourner Caravansary
Sixth Mooncycle, 30

OROE'S CHAMPION YANKED THE sleeping hand out of bed. The hand, a young man, hit the floor before his eyes opened. There was a click where he landed with his shoulder, and the boy yelled. But Oroe's champion did not stop. He grabbed the boy to his feet, put a boot to his buttock, and shoved him out the door.

The boy dropped to his knees in the dust of the compound outside, where Oroe was patrolling, his voice loud enough that every soul in the Weary Sojourner could hear.

"We seek the abouts of Red Emperor fugitives," said Oroe in broken Savanna Common. He slapped one of the public notices containing the fugitives' faces on a nearby wall. "Everybody of this parlour—come out! Kneel before the elephant throne!"

Kangala watched from an archway near the entrance as every worker and guest in the caravansary was pulled from their room and forced to their hands and knees in the compound, heads bowed. Each doorway was a mouth, offering screams from the huts within. A new person or two or three was rushed out of each and put to their knees, until every single abode was emptied.

Kangala did a quick scan and could at once tell that the fugitives were not among this lot. No one here looked like a traveller.

But the fugitives had been here, he knew it. The caravan had stopped here at the emperor's insistence—she had some history with this place Kangala could not quite deduce—but a cursory check was the extent of her suspicion. She did not know what Kangala knew about these fugitives, where they were going, what they were after.

They must have stopped here. He was sure that if he dug around this establishment carefully enough, he would find evidence of this.

Once every abode was emptied, the compound filled with whimpering desertlanders, Igan stepped in with their long axe strapped to their back, flanked by their posse: jaws set, shoulders locked. Next came Ikobi, announcing the Red Emperor's string of titles. And lastly came the Scion of Moons herself.

Kangala took the time to observe the Red Emperor again as she floated in, surrounded by a gaggle of hands and an army of peace officers. Stripped to mere travel clothes—roomier ones than usual, he noted, to conceal her ailments and changing body—her entrance did not carry as much gravitas as the more ceremonial clothing she'd worn when he'd first met her. All this regardless, she looked every bit as exquisite as all her representations and likenesses suggested—fullness of cheeks, a twinkle in her eye, the stride of a youngling who knew they had many days ahead of them. Every gaze in the room was drawn to her.

The Ninki Nanka slithered in behind her, raising every head, even bowed ones. Gasps came from every corner of the compound, murmurs of shock, fear, discombobulation.

Kangala took this as his opportunity and slipped into the first nearby hut.

Inside looked like he had expected—ramshackle, unkempt, banal. He scanned quickly, moving into the next hut when he didn't find anything. The next was the same, and the next, and the next. Ikobi's voice droned on in the background, speaking on behalf of the emperor, asking where the housekeep of the establishment was, if she had fled. No one was answering.

The huts on the ground floor offered nothing, so he crept up the stairs, scurrying in the dark spots between torches, pushing open the doors to the upstairs rooms. He took off his shoes to move more quietly on the wooden flooring, bending below the banister. His knees popped and his back protested, both reminding him of his age, but still he pressed forward, nudging open room doors, swiping their mats and curtains aside to peer inside.

After looking into the last room, in which he'd found nothing noteworthy, he was already turning away when he heard a squeak at the end of the hallway. He headed for it, and even before he got there, saw what it was: hinges, attached to a trapdoor masquerading as dislodged flooring. And peering from between trapdoor and floor were a pair of eyes, frozen with the panic of being discovered.

The missing housekeep, he realised. Kangala reached a hand forward silently, finger over his lip.

"Come," he said in Savanna Common. "No harm."

The trapdoor opened further to reveal the face of a woman only slightly older than himself. It was dark inside, but Kangala could see she was alone, evaluating the situation, considering if giving in without a fight was worth it.

"Is okay," he said. "Come."

Finally, the woman swung the trapdoor open. Kangala took her hand in his, then silently led her down the stairs.

·◦·˙˙˙———————˙˙˙·◦·

"Where they go?" Oroe was asking. "Tell us now!"

Extracting Oroe from the mass gathered in the compound had not proved challenging. He had been all but forgotten after doing the grunt work of rounding up the inhabitants. But no matter. While the rest of them were out there putting on a spectacle and poking empty crannies in search of the housekeep, Kangala was out here with Oroe in a small alley in the back, tucked between huts and hedges, doing the real work of extracting information from the most important person in this establishment.

"I don't know," said the housekeep, her jaw set. She was no longer the scared figure Kangala had surreptitiously led down the stairs, allowing her to think him an ally, asking her for a hidden location, her showing him this nook, him asking her to wait while he got more help. But that *help* turned out to be Oroe, whose voice she recognised the moment he spoke, and her face had hardened ever since. She knew, now, that he was no friend or helper, and was furious. Not that Kangala cared—he had done his task.

Kangala put a hand on his son's broad shoulder, nudged him aside, smiled in a manner he believed was friendly.

"We just want to know why they stop here," said Kangala. When her eyes moved too quickly, betrayed her concern about what he already knew, he pressed on. "Yes, the emperor know they stop here. We see the baby shitcloth—nobody have baby here, yes? Then blood bandage in same room. One of them wounded, is it?"

Indeed it was Oroe's hands who had discovered this, and not the emperor. So far, only the Sahelians were aware of this find, but the housekeep didn't know that.

"Nobody wounded," the woman said. "The wounded people are others, gone."

"Oh." *So the group has separated*, Kangala mused. *But who has gone where?* He knew the scholar and the yellow woman were the emperor's greatest interests. Could those two still be together, and were they still travelling east?

"They go east?" he asked the housekeep. "Or west? Maybe even north?"

The woman glanced at Oroe, as if she wasn't even listening to Kangala. He realised, now, that she was sizing him up. Hopefully she did not do anything stupid. Oroe was equally stupid when anger got the better of him. Putting two goats into a fight never ended well.

"Listen, maa." He made his voice softer. "The emperor just want to know if you hear anything, see anything, notice anything. Even just tiny little—anything you can tell is fine." He made a show of glancing toward the enraged Oroe. "Better you tell fast also, because this one is no patient."

With those words, the woman's expression changed into something Kangala found discomforting: A twinkle arose in her eyes. She'd had him worked out, realised he was pretending to be the kindly alternative to Oroe's brutish manner. She had realised, now, that it was *him* who wanted the information, and not the emperor.

"Take me to the emperor," she said, a turn in her demeanour. "Anything you want to hear, I tell you there."

"Now, now," Kangala was saying. "No need to put you in danger for nothing. I help you already, not?"

But she wasn't listening. She was eyeing Oroe again, and this time, Oroe was looking right at her when she did.

"What you looking at?" he growled.

Kangala saw it as late as Oroe did—a flat blade, crude, emerging from the folds of her garments. She'd timed it perfectly too, waited until Oroe was too close to dodge. Her assessment that he was the greater threat was correct—Kangala would be an easier target after getting rid of him.

She lunged forward and her hand came around, going for Oroe's throat. But Kangala, rearing back, defensively pushed against her. This knocked her off balance, so that her blade missed Oroe's neck and instead angled toward his face.

Steel slashed through Oroe's right eye. He reeled, clutching his face, yelling.

Kangala, from his sitting position, gaped at Oroe's bloodied face, red lines drifting through his fingers, down his elbow. The woman, too, was frightened by Oroe's furious howls and knew in that moment that she was dead if he caught her. The way behind her was blocked, and Oroe was standing at the one opening she had to get away.

Don't do it, thought Kangala, eyeing the space she needed to slip through.

But the woman didn't seem reality-prone. She scurried forward on hands and knees, frazzled by fear, clattering into every bit of junk in the alleyway. She would have made it too, so close the space was to her. But Oroe had only one eye impaired. The other worked just fine.

Oroe reached out and grabbed her hair as she went by. He whirled her around, and in the very same motion, slammed his other fist into her temple. The woman went limp instantly, but Oroe did not stop. He turned her around and slammed her forehead to the ground. A *crack*, but that was not enough for him either. He raised his fist, pummelled the back of the woman's head once, twice, thrice, until not even her limbs were twitching anymore.

Kangala rose as his son did, standing over the dead woman.

"What a waste," he said, shaking his head.

There was movement at the top of the alley. Igan stood there, bald head shining, axe strapped to their back, silent, watching.

◦ ⋯ ⋯ ◦

Back in the Weary Sojourner's compound, Kangala and Oroe stood before the emperor as Igan recounted what they had seen: the house-keep of the caravansary being beaten to death. Kangala, when asked, filled in the details—with truths that were really lies, of course. They had found her (true) and she had attempted to escape (true) by attacking Oroe (true), who then killed her in self-defence (also true). When asked what they had been doing in the alley, he simply said that was where they'd found her (lie).

Igan, who did not seem convinced, pressed the matter. So Kangala was forced to reveal some other truth: the discovery of the bloody bandages and the baby shitcloth. He braided it with another lie: The house-keep had hidden these things away in a trapdoor upstairs, trying to conceal the fact that the fugitives had in fact landed here. All the better that she was dead, wasn't it?

This, coupled with the deep gash across Oroe's eye, now bandaged, seemed to convince the emperor enough. She waved them away, asking to be prepared for bed. She looked completely spent, and not just by the journey. Her eyes drooped, her words slurred, and she seemed unable to hold a conversation for long.

Perhaps this was the perfect time, then, to hold one.

"Sovereign, can I?" Kangala said, stepping forward so that he was past Igan, blocking the advisor from the emperor's view. "Before she try escape, the housekeep say something."

The emperor turned. Bags settled beneath her eyes, like rotten fruit weighing down a branch.

"Anything useful?" she asked, only half-interested.

"She say they split into two, when they leave," he said. "One escape go east, other one go west, north, I don't know." Another lie that was not really a lie.

This gained the emperor's attention. "She said that?"

Kangala nodded. "Say if you ask them, they can tell you where." He pointed to the establishment's occupants.

"She could have been lying," said Igan, stepping out from behind to face him. "*You* could be lying."

Kangala made a great show of taking offence. "Why I lie? What I gain? We go on wild kwaga chase for nothing—how that help me?"

He was addressing the exact counterpoint Igan had been ready to follow up with, and he could see from the way their eyes narrowed that they knew he was doing just that.

"Go on, then," said the emperor, motioning toward the caravansary's hands. "Ask."

A short moment later, they had the information they needed. Three men and two women had come here with a baby, one of the men wounded. They had stayed a night, but only the women, the baby, and one man had left for the rest of the journey. The other two had remained behind for the injured one to recover, but for some reason—as if they had known the emperor was coming—had hastily packed up and left not too long after their comrades. Whether they went in the same direction as the others, no one knew, but they were all at least a day's journey away from here by now.

Once shown the public notices, the hands were emphatic: The scholar and the yellow woman ("She was no yellow when here," one of them insisted) were among those who had left first. The woman with the baby and the two men were not present on these notices.

The emperor was wide awake by the time this information gathering was concluded. Igan and Ikobi briefed her in low tones, keeping Kangala out of the discussion as usual. He had a mind to go closer and listen as he'd done back at camp, but decided it was better the emperor continued to think of him the aloof Sahelian.

To his surprise, Igan came over to him, looking triumphant.

"She has new directions for you," they said, and didn't wait for a response before leaving.

The emperor's gaze was measured but welcoming when Kangala approached.

"We are splitting the caravan into three," she said. "As we may be looking in the savanna for a while, we will keep this caravansary as a base of operations—a waystation of sorts. One small group will remain here under Ikobi's command." She nodded toward her advisor, who nodded toward Kangala. "Another will go in search of the escaped men, and yet another will continue east." She tapped Igan, flanking her on the other side. "I will continue east with Igan, and you will go . . ." She waved her hand. "West, north, I don't know. But your task is to find those men and bring them here." She cocked her head. "Should be easy, no?"

Kangala's head spun. This was not the plan—everything had gone completely wrong! He realised, now, that this was the reason for Igan's smirk. They had probably convinced the emperor of this exact decision.

But slowly, he realised this was not a failure. As with most things, it was an opportunity in disguise.

He cleared his throat. "My family and I most willing to serve however Sovereign wish." He cleared his throat again. "But if I can?"

The emperor nodded her go-ahead.

"Why waste time, energy, chase people who go in opposite direction? Now we all know—your biggest enemies go east. Forest of the Mist, you say? I don't know of you, Sovereign, but I think that say *danger*. Ambush, attack. You need men, army, fighters."

Igan's smirk began to crumble as the emperor seemed to warm up to Kangala's points. He pressed quickly, before the advisor could jump in.

"I say you select best-trained warriors here." He pointed to Igan. "Your general and their people. Oroe and his best-best champions. Then maybe one, two peace officer, the ones that fight well. The rest? Some can stay here, some can chase men. No loss. You still have army with you for hard east journey."

"That's enough." Igan rose from their seat. "You were asked here to receive instructions, not to give—"

"Igan," said the emperor calmly. The advisor looked at her, then glared at Kangala, before sitting. The emperor returned to him.

"Turning down an easy job," she said. "You must have a good reason for wanting to go east. And don't tell me some kwaga shit about *service*. I know you don't give two nuts about service to me. So tell me: Why?"

The emperor was poking him, seeing what underlying motivations would emerge. He could not deny that he was gearing for something—that would unearth him as a liar. He could not tell her of his *other* plans, of course. So he opted for the best weapon in his arsenal: a half-truth.

"I hear a story," he began, "of old underground city. They say if you cross the isthmus, and you meet the Nameless Islands—which is call *Ihinyon*, by the way—they say you can sail to the smallest island and see this city, which is call Risisi." He paused. "You ask why I come? Is because if your fugitives are going there, then I want to see this city with my own two eyes also."

Silence gripped them all once he was done. The emperor's expression had turned still. Not angered, but curious, a bit surprised, maybe even some admiration.

"Who told you that?" she asked.

"My daughter, Ngipa," he said. "She hear story in Chugoko, gossip. Can be fake story, who knows? But I want to see, Sovereign, if you will allow."

The emperor was contemplative. Ikobi, who had been quiet all this time, said: "Taking the strongest fighters east sounds sensible."

Igan, on the other side, shot back: "What kind of advisor takes suggestions from a stranger?"

"I am stranger, yes," Kangala jumped in. "And yes, no take my advice if it no help. But emperor ask me why I really want to go, and I be honest and say why."

More contemplation. Finally, the emperor sighed. The tiredness had returned to her eyes.

"Half your party," she said. "You and your son inclusive. The other half stay." Then she rose for bed.

Kangala thanked her as he wandered off, his mind brimming with ideas. Of course he did not give a flying fowl about buried cities or hidden islands. Sure, the stones of power existed—he knew, now, that they did, and that the emperor was using one, which was why she was always wearing that armlet, never taking it off, even at night. But just because they existed did not mean that he needed them to gain the kind of power he sought.

The emperor herself was a good example why. One look at the way she was shrivelling up like a dried date, and he could tell it was more than just that child in her belly doing that. That was what such power did, and the story, real or fake, had not been unwise to warn against it. Power, Kangala had learned, was not always a mallet for striking. It was also a glove: to be eased into, its fit ensured, before being used to take hold.

Half his party, she'd said. *Six men.* He'd have to think of a way to carry out his plans with this few. But the emperor would have fewer at her disposal too—a posse of five, a handful of peace officers.

Two, Oroe had said. *Before each champion is killed.*

Six men was more than enough.

Kangala glanced over his shoulder. Igan was still there, eyes locked on him, suspicion so strong it bore holes into his back. No matter. That one, he would handle as well. He would handle them all, just they wait.

43

Danso

The Lonely Roads East
Sixth Mooncycle ends; new season begins

THEY WERE NOW A day away from the Weary Sojourner, but none of the three had spoken a word to each other. Oke, still reeling from the loss of her loved ones, withdrew from everything, throwing herself into doing little other than caring for Thema and keeping her eyes on the road ahead, only interested in the reason she was here: getting to the seven islands. Danso and Lilong gave her the space she desired, but walked circles around each other. At camp the night before, they had exchanged watches with nothing but simple grunts of acknowledgment. When passing food or items, they ensured their fingers didn't touch.

It was afternoon of the second day, and Danso remained glum on driving duty. More little hills had begun to creep up, just as Ugo predicted based on the blacksmith's assessment. They stuck out even more here, the landforms and vegetation changing as they ventured closer and closer to the coast. More isolated woodlands flung across the wide open grassland, thick with clumps of acacias and baobabs.

They avoided both cleft outcrops and woodlands, but then were unable to avoid other obstacles. A small herd of elephants, for instance, frustrated with their failure to find water. They trumpeted loudly at the travelwagon, but luckily trundled off. The other attack came at night, from an unlikely source: a trio of massive scorpions that tried to find cosy spots in the travelwagon. One got really close to stinging baby Thema, but Oke set fire to it with an aggravated scream, burning it to a crisp, and then to ashes, and even then, kept it burning until Lilong had to stop her, remind her of the effects of expending too much ibor.

On the third day, Danso was the first to spot the pack of genge. It was a large pack. They seemed to be moving with purpose, migrating some- where, which explained the absence of a little hill in sight. Eight or nine, he struggled to count.

He stopped the wagon and came down.

"We can't go around them," he said to Lilong and Oke, who had also emerged. "They seem to be headed in the same direction as us."

"We can wait them out?" Oke asked more than said.

"Too slow," Lilong said, her mind elsewhere. "I'm more interested in why they're here."

"Hunting?" Danso offered.

Lilong nodded slowly. "Seeking prey." She paused. "And now they've found one." She angled her head. "Well…two."

One genge had turned in their direction and spotted them. Or per- haps spotted the kwagas, which seemed like more juicy prey than puny people. The dominant genge made a sound, abrasive and guttural. The rest of the pack stopped, turned.

"Back in the wagon," Lilong said. Her eyes blazed amber and her blade rattled.

The dominant began to prance, shooting glances at the kwagas.

Oke unstrapped Thema from her body, handed the baby over to Danso. "Whatever you do," she said, "stay in that wagon."

The dominant sneezed. The rest of the pack sneezed back. Then they charged at the travelwagon.

Danso slid in with Thema and shut the door behind him. Oke climbed into the driving seat, and the travelwagon jerked into motion. Lilong, outside, jumped onto the vehicle and held on, her blade whistling through the grass, weaving ahead of the kwagas.

The blade caught the dominant first, slicing its paws as it lunged for- ward. The beast rolled away, howling. The commotion spooked the kwa- gas, who began to bark and flop, whipping away from the direction Oke was steering them in. Instead, they swung toward a wilting thorntree, the last standing vestige of a once-woodland. Oke turned away at the last moment, grazing the edge of the tree, tearing apart some of the wagon's covering.

"Do something!" Oke was calling out to Lilong.

Thema began to cry.

Lilong's eyes flared amber. Danso saw her blade aim for the dominant, which had shaken off its injury and was leading the pursuit. The blade went through its neck and emerged at its back. The beast buckled in the grass and fell, writhing, then twitching, then still. Blood stained the parched grass.

The rest of the genge, not giving up, bore down on them easily.

The travelwagon tumbled into grassier fare, giving the worn wheels a hard workout and slowing their escape. Now compromised, the travelwagon fared badly in this new terrain. After advancing a small distance farther, the travelwagon eventually yielded and ground to a slow halt.

Lilong called back her blade. When it ejected itself from the genge's body, the movement infuriated the others even more. They howled, an eerie sound like a deep-throated giant bird.

"They're too many," said Lilong, blade whistling before her.

"I can do something," said Danso. He stretched out a hand. "But I need the Diwi."

Lilong recoiled at the suggestion, but the genge were much too close to argue. She grabbed the pouch and tossed it to him reluctantly. Danso handed the baby to her, extricated the Diwi, gripped it tight, and Drew.

Somewhere in the distance, a genge in stasis, which had been following the travelwagon out of sight, awakened. Its eyes flared red, and it sailed through the grass, moving like the wind. From its throat it called out to whichever nearby pack could hear.

The genge pack jerked to attention, startled, ears pricked.

Danso flexed another Command, and the genge called again, louder, this time a challenge, a call to a battle of strength and wits.

This call—one that promised victory, and therefore food—the pack could not resist. One by one, they turned around, and they headed for the beast as it headed for them.

"On the kwagas, quickly," Lilong said, and helped detach them from the wagon. She helped Oke clamber onto the kwaga, clutching Thema, then grabbed the closest pack of food and slumped it over the beast. Then she climbed on the second one.

"Come on!" she yelled to Danso.

But Danso was skin-deep in the Possession. He felt everything as the other genge finally caught up with his and pounced upon it. Danso twitched as their teeth and claws tore at his skin, ripping it to shreds. The beast's antennae ensured he experienced it all: the prickly grass, the smell and texture of the blood, the hot breath of each attacker.

Lilong descended and ran to him, caught him just as he fell, just as the beast succumbed and he pulled out of the Possession, disconnected forever.

"I've got you," Lilong said, dragging him along. She helped him onto the kwaga, weak and heady. Then she climbed on herself, wrapped her hands around him, and together, they escaped.

· ◦ ⋯ ————————— ⋯ ◦ ·

None of them three slept that night. They did not light a fire, and all three stayed up, keeping watch in the dark. Danso spent most of it recovering from his use of ibor, taking in the food and water required to bounce back. Lilong did not ask him about the genge, and he did not offer an explanation. When Oke broached the topic of what he had done to call the pack away, he answered her with silence.

Sometime during the night, Danso realised Lilong had silently whisked the Diwi back into the pouch around her waist. He did not ask for it back.

The next day, they set out again on kwagaback, their journey moving faster now. For food, they found wild millet and sorghum to pair with their roasted meat. The water rations they'd replenished from the Weary Sojourner thinned quickly, Thema taking up the most of it. They resorted to only a few sips per day, and thankfully, this did not form the basis of another quarrel.

For their spare time, they took to solitary activities. Danso filled in the gaps in his codex, especially keen on documenting the tales told he'd learned from his travel companions. The first, *Why the Wind Howls: A Desertland Tale*, was from Ugo, offering insights into the beliefs of the savanna folk, along with some information about the northern trade route and the port city of Tkithnuum, which was as far north as he'd travelled. The other was a recount of Oke's time in prison, which, as soon as he began writing it, he decided was too despondent to pass on. He opted for Lilong's tale, one she had told back in Chabo, when they were still friends: *How the World Came to Be: An Ihinyon Tale*.

He recalled it with genial feeling, loathing the fact that things had soured between them so. After the tale was done, he documented every-thing she'd so far offered about the seven islands—for posterity, yes, but also for the purposes of keeping abreast of the peoples of his destination.

She'd spoken about what each island was known for and why. Hoor for its calm, because whenever storms came—and they did every hundred seasons or so—all inhabitants of the seven islands moved there for safety. Edana and Ufua for their green fields and rice plantations, and for being the trade centres for the Ihinyon. Ololo and Sibu-Sibu for their advocacy toward a tougher Abenai League, wanting to go out and wage war rather than hide behind the Forest of the Mists. Ofen, for being nothing—but if the story of Risisi turned out to be true, for being everything.

. ◦ ⸱⸱⸱ ⸱⸱⸱ ◦ .

On their fourth day since the Weary Sojourner, after the mooncrossing that marked the coming of the rainy season, they ran into their first traveller.

The three stopped and prepared themselves for conflict. But it turned out that this was simply an ordinary traveller indeed—alone, unarmed, nonplussed. Oke, who had the baby and seemed the least menacing, interacted with the person.

"Seems we're close to a few hamlets," she said, once the traveller was on their way.

True to the traveller's word, a couple of such settlements began to appear by the next day.

"We must be so near now," Oke said, when they stopped to consider replenishing their water supply at one of the settlements but decided against it. "Can't say if I'm relieved or tense."

"Isthmus seekers." Lilong was gazing over their heads, obviously not responding to Oke. "Tried to find us a long time ago and failed, so they just…stayed." She glanced at Oke, as if to say: *This is what you were, once.* She turned and gave Danso a look, but one that said something different.

Not long after, the wind picked up. Far, far from the travelwagon, there was the sound of something grand and monstrous moving.

"Coast is here," said Lilong, to no one.

Danso inhaled long and hard. A silty breeze washed over him. It was like being back in Whudasha, standing on the edge of the steep drop. He exhaled, and it came out in short, ragged, anxious breaths.

The Written Codex of Danso DaaHabba, First Jali of Bassa to Journey over the Soke Borders: Hereafter lie his personal accounts of travels and travails through the desertlands, from the western vagabond colony of Chabo, to the fabled eastern Forest of the Mist.

The Twelfth Account: *The Crab-God and the Gourd of Wisdom: An Ihinyon Tale*, as recounted by Lumusi of Namge, a tale which she has always known and in which she firmly believes.

THIS IS A TALE of the Crab-God, and how we became imbued with different wisdoms.

In the land of wisdom and plenty and fruitfulness—which is to say, the land of Gods—the Crab-God was the one most blessed with wisdom. After all, she had ten legs, and with them, could fashion almost anything she wanted. She taught the Spider-God how to spin webs, the Octopus-God how to fashion a house out of coconuts, the Scorpion-God how to see in the dark. She moved slowly, because she contained wisdom great enough for the world.

After distributing all the wisdom she could to the land of Gods, the burden of wisdom was still too much for her to bear. So she chose to spread this wisdom to the land of people. She asked the Spider-God to build a web for her, which would extend from the sky down to our world. Once done, she took a clay gourd, put all the wisdom she could gather into it, strapped it to herself, and began her descent into the land of people.

Now, a man who had been working on his farm saw the spider-web from the heavens and thought it a curse on his crops. So, he took his axe and split the web.

The Crab-God was almost at her destination when the web unravelled and she fell. Luckily, she fell into the water. But the gourd did not. It fell on land and shattered into many pieces. The wisdom contained within floated into the wind, the water, the soil, the plants, and eventually, into people.

But though the wisdom spread equally into every element, it did not spread so into people. This is why, today, some of us are wiser than others. This is why we have different talents, abilities, and understandings. This is why some of us can naturally use ibor, but some cannot. We of the seven islands of the Ihinyon archipelago understand this, which is why we revere the Great Lands and the Great Waters and the Great Winds: for the three Great Forces are wiser than us all.

We hear the Crab-God is still searching for her gourd. Sometimes, you will find her descendants crawling on the beach, seeking the place where the gourd has fallen. This is why we do not eat crabs. Just as we do not wish to anger the Great Forces, we do not wish to anger the Crab-God. Have we not intervened enough? Let us leave the Crab-God be. Let us leave it all be.

risisi

Third Season of the Red Emperor

Nem

Bassa: The Great Dome
First Mooncycle, 1

THE BLOCKADE AT EIGHTH had now been in place for eight days, and Bassa was beginning to feel its effects.

First came the shortages, especially of nuts, produce, and trade crops. Afterward came a dwindling of craftwork. Bribes were steep, even for the affluent who could pay them and were willing. But the Nameless Republic, as many had caved into calling them now, were firm in their demands: They speak with the emperor, or remain silent and keep hurting the empire.

The Great Dome, too, was in disarray. Not a single pair of feet stood at rest, as everything that drew breath scurried in response to Nem's directives. Over the first two days, she prepared for war on the blockade, pulling resources from everywhere and anywhere she could: the civic guard, the hunthand guild, private Seconds who were up to the task. Every last available kwaga was saddled, their handlers standing ready. But even by the sixth day, she was still yet to move on the blockade, because there were matters that needed settling before she could.

Discontent flared in the wards. Nem met with Idu nobles, guild leaders, and respected community Elders to quell worries about the Great Dome's ability to handle this insurrection in the wake of an absent emperor. But the more she learned about this Nameless faction and its spearhead—someone named Ifiot—the more she realised that this was an operation that did not seem so simple beneath the surface. Behind that blockade was a coterie of dissidents who had no love for Bassa or its emperor—immigrants, Whudans, hinterlanders, swamplanders—all mixed in with bona-fide Bassai Emuru. One wrong move, and Nem could end up slaughtering her own people. She did not want to be the First Consul who led a Bassai massacre. That would be the final dagger to the heart of the Red Emperor's rule.

So she trod carefully, attempting to win crucial support before going in. But by day eight, she was still yet to convince those that needed convincing. The emperor's absence continued to be a bone in her throat. The hunthand guild leaders had decided to wait until the emperor's return before joining in any fight, as they wanted assurance that they would be rewarded after the battle was done. They knew to play this hand because they had seen how spare the city had become now that most of its civic guard was either at the border or at the Breathing Forest.

So Nem was forced, yet again, to remove more civic guards from the border to compensate.

"If Igan were here—" said Yao.

"But Igan is *not* here," Nem fired back. "*Nobody* is here. It falls on me to make the decisions, and it falls on you to *follow* them." She turned from Yao to the rest of the advisors, who all stood before her in the great hall. "*All* of you."

After she had dispersed them with instructions for the civic guard captains, Nem beckoned to Satti.

"Help me up to the elephant throne. I will address the captains from there when they arrive."

The corner of Satti's eye twitched nervously. "Are you sure, maa?"

"I am the final word in the emperor's absence, am I not?" said Nem. "If there was ever a day to look like it, it is today."

Satti acknowledged and beckoned to two nearby hands for aid. They rolled Nem to the throne and helped her onto it.

Nem wriggled herself into the massive seat. *Too large*, she thought immediately, her spine unable to meet the backrest, her bottom finding no purchase between armrests too far apart. The hardwood pushed back against her tailbone, and even though she had lost most feeling down there, this she could feel enough to declare it uncomfortable.

But the elephant throne was not a seat, she knew. It was a symbol, a performance, a tale. It was not made for comfort, and rightly so, because no buttocks, no matter how wide, could find purchase here. This seat was made to be uncomfortable because power required one to shift position at any given time, angling this way or that to suit whatever new purposes arose. Power was discomfort and discomfort was longevity, and longevity was the key to freedom.

Perhaps this was the thing that bothered her the most. She had always thought of herself as seeking freedom. But that was freedom *to*. Now that she had that, she ached for freedom *from*. And though both were two sides of the same blade, maybe what she wanted was not the blade at all. Maybe after living for over a hundred and ten seasons in this city, all she wanted was peace.

But there would be no peace for her as long as she lived in Bassa. There would be no peace as long as Esheme was emperor.

There would be no peace as long as Bassa existed.

"Help me down," she said. "I've changed my mind."

After her address, Nem returned to her chambers, but declined to send Satti away as usual. Instead, she beckoned her Second over and patted a seat for her to stay.

"What did you think of my speech?" she asked. "You think it rallied them enough to commit the numbers?"

Satti made a show of looking over her shoulder, as if Nem was addressing someone behind her. Nem clicked her tongue.

"Stop that, woman," she said. "We've known each other too long for theatrics."

Satti studied her hands where they rested on her thighs. They were small and veined, the hands of a worker. Deceptively strong, deceptively tender—just like the woman.

"I thought your speech was marvellous. I also thought it didn't matter," she said, flatly.

Nem leaned forward. "How so?"

"I believe the people already think what they think, and will act accordingly regardless. Civic guards are a part of the people too, you know. Their captains cannot change what they think."

"And what is it that they think?"

Satti lifted her head. "That the emperor is young and hot-blooded and delusional. That she is cursed and has transferred that curse onto the city and the land. That she will send this empire to its grave if something doesn't change soon. That perhaps it might be best if she does not return at all."

Nem frowned. "Careful there, now, old woman. You sidle so close to treason. Remember you are speaking to the First Consul."

"Oh, I am simply repeating the chatter of the corridors," said Satti. "Besides, I was of the belief that I was speaking to my old friend and protector MaaNem, the woman who brought me from nothing, took me under her wing, and elevated me to a status I could never have once dreamed of. That I could speak freely and truthfully."

"You can. I am still that woman."

"Maybe," said Satti. "Maybe more of that woman than you have ever been."

Nem squinted at her Second. "Are you trying to tell me something?"

"You do not want all this," said Satti, waving her hand across the room. "Or that." She waved an arm toward the window that overlooked the city. "Every day since you have lived in this city, you have carried weights on your shoulders. What you really want is to not have to carry those weights anymore."

"Hmm," said Nem. "I must confess—I did not envision that the task of this seat would be so...labyrinthine."

"Then why not simply leave it behind?"

The question gave Nem pause. Not the directness of it—that was simply Satti's way—but the fact that she had never considered it before. Or more like *let herself* consider it. Moons knew she had indeed felt, at various points, like she simply did not have the capacity to juggle the tasks of keeping her daughter in check, keeping the matters of court from disintegrating, while keeping her sanity intact. Perhaps once, back when she was still a strong, healthy woman. But that fall from that window two seasons ago had taken its toll in more ways than one, and she was no longer as given to such weights.

So yes, Satti was right: She wanted nothing more than to be rid of these burdens. But what did that—*leaving it all behind*—even look like? Where would she go, and to whom? There was no place for her in this city, and there was no place for her outside of it. Power was all she had worked for, and Esheme was all she had lived for. If she abandoned both, what else would she have?

For the first time in a long time, Nem was afraid, because she realised that though she finally had everything she wanted in life, she, in fact, truly had nothing.

"I could never step down as First Consul," she said to Satti. "Not while she's still emperor."

"I do not think she will be emperor for very long, MaaNem."

Nem shot her Second a fiery glance. "That's getting too close, Satti."

"I apologise," said Satti. "I do not wish MaaEsheme death—in fact, I do not think her that easily given to it. She is like a beetle—a stomp alone will be insufficient. She will return, all right, and will likely set her wrath on this faction. But it is not just nameless rebellions and blockades to contend with, is it? Dwindling crop yields, drying rivers, people-eating trees, Ghost Apes. All Bassa needs to crumble is simply one more crack in its wall. And no one—no matter how strong or blessed—can be emperor of rubble."

Nem knew she was right. She had thought the same ever since seeing the trees on the edge of the Breathing Forest move. There were simply forces on this continent bigger than anyone could handle, not even the great power that was Bassa. But did that mean she should just abandon everything? Abandon her own daughter?

"I should have made you an advisor instead of those cocoyam heads out there," Nem said. "Even if I know you'd just argue with me half the time."

Satti laughed. "I'm not one for the kind of politicking such a role requires."

"Indeed," said Nem. "Perhaps which is why I come to you." She sighed. "The world is a dangerous place. We all need people we can rely on." She massaged her knee, only half feeling the touch, the response distant and ephemeral. "Esheme relies on me. And I'm not ready to leave her to face the world alone just yet."

"I reckon she's facing most of whatever the world has to offer right now," said Satti. "May I also point out that, so far, she has had no problems leaving you?"

"No, you may not point that out," Nem snapped. She was beginning to regret having this conversation. She had called Satti here for comfort and camaraderie, not to get hard truths thrown in her face like a calabash of cold water.

"I apologise if I was too forthright," said Satti, not really an apology. She rose. "I will be outside if you need me."

At the door, she paused, turned.

"If you ever decide to go," said Satti, "I have a plan. For two. Just say the word." Then she was gone.

45

Danso

The Forest of the Mist
First Mooncycle, 1

THE TREELINE OF THE Forest of the Mist turned out not to be difficult to find. It was not the only forest within sight, but it was easily recognisable. Whoever named it had not been joking about the mist. Long before they even arrived at the threshold, mist had begun to envelop them. Now, upon arrival, the treeline of palms and hardwood was prefaced by tall, unwelcoming grass, soaked in low-lying mist that swallowed everything above their heads.

They stood and stared at it awhile, drowning in feelings of the sublime, the mist settling on their clothes, making them heavier.

Having abandoned the kwagas close to a nearby settlement for a lucky person to find, Lilong and Oke began to walk along the edge of the forest, looking for a point of entrance. A particular one, it seemed. Whatever they found that marked this particular entrance, Danso could not tell, but as soon as they found it, they stepped into the leaves and were immediately swallowed by the forest.

Danso paused at the edge, willing his feet to cross. Memories poured into him in a jumble, past and present commingling, so that he swayed from the rush of it all. He was back at the Breathing Forest, his kwaga stomping at the edge, Zaq with Lilong on his shoulder, Danso urging him on. He kept expecting the ground beneath him to rumble and undulate, the wind to howl, the Skopi to appear from above and screech at him.

Lilong re-emerged from the forest.

"Are you fine?" There was a shadow of concern in her tone. Danso was a bit relieved that there was no malice.

"I'm okay," he said, and ventured forward.

The mists were more like clouds, as if they had opted to swing low at this very point and blanket the forest, turning it into a camouflage of green and white. The forest itself, inside, bore an ethereal presence. It was impossible to see beyond the next row of trees, and movement was only perceptible by how much mist swirled around a body. Luckily, the terrain was predominantly flat and the understory milder than that of the rainforests Danso was used to, which meant they didn't have to worry too much about stumbling. But it was much easier to get lost in this forest—the mist closed around them so tightly that when Danso looked back, he couldn't see the way they had already come. It would be impossible to retrace their steps now. Bodies and trees and mist interwove, slipping through one another like ghosts.

"This is so surreal," Danso found himself saying. "I feel like I am in another world."

"You are," said Lilong.

The temperature dropped considerably the farther into the forest they went. They stopped to put on some of the thicker wrappers and cloaks Lilong had brought along. Oke strapped Thema to her back and put an extra wrapper over her head.

Danso looked up. He couldn't even see the canopy. Or the sun.

"Are you sure we're going in the right direction?" he asked.

"Yes," Lilong and Oke answered at the same time, then glanced at one another.

"He taught me the system," said Oke. "The... tree spacing." She pointed Danso to the treeline. "You see the space between those?"

Danso looked at the tall tree in question, its trunk disappearing into the mist. He shrugged. Oke pointed at another. "Okay, you see those?" Another set of inconspicuous trees. Danso nodded.

"If you look closely, from pattern tree to pattern tree, it's in almost in a line. You can't see them all at once because of the mist, but if you follow one tree to the other, the next one appears. We follow it, and it'll lead us directly to the isthmus—the land bridge to the islands."

Danso observed the tree in question. It had scaly bark, yellow leaves in eights, and branches with arms up like a worshipper. Green moss and budding, colourless flowers on its body. It was the most unremarkable tree he'd ever seen.

"So you can recognise every single one of these in this whole forest?" he asked.

"It is not a native of this forest," said Lilong. "It grows farther inland. Our ancestors brought it here because it was one of our most recognisable trees—every islander can recognise the pattern tree. They planted them as a guide for all islanders. And because it doesn't grow anywhere else on the continent, no mainlander can recognise it and know what it stands for."

Danso wondered if the story of Risisi were true, if it was the survivors of that disaster who had made this decision. He made a note to ask Lilong about this later, when animosity did not exist between them anymore.

They resumed moving. As if on cue, something spectacularly white appeared in the understory, revealed by the mist in that moment. It shone against the contrast of the grass, and Danso recognised it for what it was and shivered: *bone*.

"Perhaps one of many mainlanders who have tried to find us," said Lilong, and Danso thought maybe she was enjoying scaring them a bit too much.

The mist did not let up in thickness. Everything was wet and slippery, always dripping but without becoming spongy. Danso tried to see if he could recognise the plants, trees, and flowers they came across, but only a handful looked familiar. Again, he wanted to ask Lilong for their names, but decided against it.

"How far out are we?" he asked. "Any idea?"

"The spacing," Lilong and Oke said together again. This time, Lilong took the reins.

"Space between the pattern trees tells us," she said. "The closer we are to the land bridge, the smaller the distance between them." She pointed. "With what we have now, I'd say we get there long before twilight."

"And then?"

"And then . . . we surrender."

Danso frowned. "To whom?"

"Sentries," said Oke, looking to Lilong. "Jaoudou told me if I said these words"—she said some words in what Danso assumed was Island Common—"they would not put an arrow through me. At least not immediately."

Lilong smiled a half-smile, like a proud parent.

"They will not hesitate to put us *all* down," she said. "I was never a sentry, but they tend to be the meanest of all the Abenai warriors, especially because they don't even need to be Iborworkers. They just need to be willing combatants. When I was leaving, it was them I worried most about. If they had caught me, I might have even gotten worse punishment than I'll likely get now."

"You still think you'll be punished?" Danso asked. "Even after bringing us, and showing them . . ." He gestured toward the Diwi in the pouch on her waist. "Even after all you've done?"

"*Especially* after all I have done." She swallowed. "But I no longer care what they say or do. I just want to be home, see my family."

They continued for a while before stopping to rest, but without making camp. The mist had begun to soak into their clothes, and they risked intense cold if they stayed too long in one spot.

Danso couldn't stop looking around, however. So much of this experience reminded him of the Breathing Forest.

"There are no animals, so you can stop worrying," Lilong said.

"What do you mean?"

"No Skopi, no beasts, no predators," she said. "Just your ordinary snakes and bushrats."

The mosquitoes, however, seemed not to have received the message of *no predators*. They descended on the group with almost a fury. One of them bit Thema and she began to cry. That was their cue to resume their trip.

True to Lilong's word, the spacing between the pattern trees began to shrink. Soon, they were able to see three in the same line, despite the mist not letting up. Then that number increased to four, five, and soon, the trees ended.

"That's it?" Danso asked, when they were at the last tree.

"No," Oke said. "Look."

Across the last three pattern trees, the thick of their trunks conjoined, having grown into one another. The last curved trunk disappeared into a sprawling thicket that covered the area before them and seemed completely impassable.

Lilong's eyes flashed amber, and her blade floated forward, disappearing into the thicket. All was silent for a moment, then—

The thicket began to part. Except, it was not a thicket at all, but a woven net of vegetation made to look like so. Behind this thicket was the forest line that gave way to the coast on the other side.

"Welcome to *our* great wall," Lilong said with pride.

Ahead of them, as they emerged from the forest, was what Danso had come to understand as the Neverending Sea. Spread in every direction as far as the eye could see, just like back in Whudasha. He wondered if this was the exact same body of water that was at Whudasha, going around to meet the continent on the opposite side. Mind-blowing, if it was.

Then the mists shifted further and he saw it—the isthmus, the land bridge.

It was not easy to spot if one wasn't looking. But there it was—a thin brown line of dirt in the overdose of blue. Dry and wide in some places, wet and so thin in some that Danso wondered if a wave could carry them as they walked past.

It was, in the simplest of words, beautiful.

They stood there as if it was the end of their journey, watching small waves crash at the beach. Even Thema had stopped crying and was so silent that Danso forgot she was even there.

"Jaoudou told me this tract of land used to be wider," Oke was saying, softly. "Said the Great Waters have become less kind, and now one can only cross in a straight file."

"All of the continent is less kind, now," Lilong said, looking up. "Skies too, even."

The clouds looked fine to Danso. The waters too, as much as he didn't want to go in there, looked fine. Everything was fine.

Something flew past his eyes. *A mosquito*, he thought, but it was too fast, gone before he could see its shape. Then a gasp, beside him—before he saw the blades.

They were similar in form to Lilong's. Longer than daggers, shorter than swords, showy at the hilts and grips. All of them floated in the air, circling the group, aimed for their eyes, necks, hearts.

Then, out of the mists, figures emerged slowly, eyes blazing behind fearsome masks.

Thema began to cry.

46

Lilong

LILONG DID NOT SEE much of the sentries. Their faces were covered with woven masks, as was the practice. She did not bother to ask questions and raise problems at first instance—especially if she wanted to ensure no one was harmed. She got down on her knees and put her hands over her head. Her companions, seeing her, did the same.

The sentries, unspeaking, blindfolded them all immediately, as was the practice—not that sentries often got an opportunity to blindfold intruders. They, too, understood that much, and began to whisper among themselves, unsure of what the next step should be. They seemed confused by the mismatch of the group.

Lilong did not recognise any of their voices. Perhaps she had been away too long. But one thing she could do was prevent them from doing anything rash.

"I am Lilong," she said in Island Common, the comfort of her home tongue like a rush of warm honey in her mouth. "Daughter of Warrior Jaoudou, member of the Abenai League. I have returned home with the Diwi, and I have brought along the comrades who helped keep me safe on my journey. Please take us to our Elders."

There was a lull, then, whispers farther away, faster, faster. Lilong craned her ears, and the wind blew their words her way. They had heard the tales. They knew who she was. They were angry that she had brought outsiders.

"The Diwi is alive," she said, the only way to get their attention. "You have not seen its work, but I promise you it is alive and bonds to one of us here. The Elders will need my companions to understand how it works." She pushed the authority she knew she had into her voice. "I say again— take us to the Elders!"

Another lull. Then arms began to pull them up.

She didn't need to see as they crossed the isthmus, the sand beneath her feet all but sufficient, memories accessible in every step. When they crossed back onto dry land, into grass, onto stony paths, onto wooden platforms, into the darkness of a house and a door click, the land spoke to her feet all the way, and it said but one word: *home*.

—·—···—···—·—

When the blindfold came off, Lilong was in an empty room, lit by nothing but a single oil wick lamp that spat out smoke like a bad cough. The warrior who took off her blindfold did not speak. She did not recognise the young woman, and the woman left too quickly before Lilong could make any inquiries. *So many new recruits already?* Lilong wondered how much else had changed in her absence. Just like the sentries, this woman had not spoken outside of offering directions, which Lilong found surprising. As a warrior, she had always been interested in what the scouts had to say when they returned from their mainland excursions. Perhaps this was more about her own adventures being unsanctioned. Or perhaps things had changed much more than she knew.

She wasn't tied up, which meant she wasn't a prisoner. Not yet. There was a door to the room (not mats or door blinds, she noted). Both it and the windows were locked. Sunlight cut the room through a thin gap in the window that let in a ray. She tried to peek outside through the gap, but couldn't see anything useful.

She didn't need to, though. Locked door and windows could mean only one thing: She wasn't in a person's home. She was in the house of assembly.

It was the only place in Namge with multiple rooms that each had their own door and windows that locked from outside. Useful for when the citizens of the island or representatives from other islands met with the Elders and leaders. Sometimes useful for engaging in proceedings out of the public eye—like an errant islander returning with strangers from the mainland. Situated in the quarter that stood at the axis of proximity to the beaches, the Forest of the Mist, and the island's busiest parts. It made complete sense.

She reckoned her fellow travellers were locked up in this same building, in rooms such as these. She wondered about their well-being, especially the baby Thema, who she, for the first time, remembered to count as a part of the group.

But the more she looked around, the less was familiar about the place. She had attended a few of these assemblies herself. But this was empty— no stools, chairs, or tables, nothing but spider-webs and rags abandoned in various corners. It was as if the assemblies themselves had dried up.

Lilong began to think back now to their long walk here from the forest, stripped of sight. She could not remember hearing voices or sounds of activity other than Thema's constant crying. No people whispering about her return, no one pelting her with words or rotten fruit. Lack of reprimand aside, she also did not smell anything. Not cooking, not fires, not the sharp smell of spirits or tobacco leaves being smoked. Not the earthy smell of the clay the children used in the centres of learning, which they had to have passed by on their way here because it was only a few buildings away. The sands beneath her feet had felt familiar as they walked, but the more she looked around the room, the less everything else felt like home.

She did not have to wait long to know the answer to these questions, because the door opened then, and a man walked in.

"Welcome back, coconut head."

Lilong stood frozen for a moment, blinking not only at the shock of a friendly face and voice, but the welcoming sound of Island Common being spoken. Then she was flying across the room and into the speaker's arms.

"Turay." She said his name with soft breath, like a good dream awoken to. And he *was* a good dream, now that she stepped back to look at him. Put on a good bit of muscle, had he? She'd felt it on her cheek, soft against the meat of his shoulder. His face was lean and spare, beardless jaw angled just so. Had he grown taller? Probably not. But for some reason, he suddenly looked much more attractive than she remembered. Perhaps the saying about absence and desire was true.

Not that it mattered right now, because she realised Turay did not return her embrace, arms hanging limply at his sides as he glared at her.

She stepped back. "What's wrong?"

"You *left*." His tone was icy, bitter, sharp.

Lilong swallowed. "I—"

"You said you'd never want to leave," he said. "Said you'd never break the promises you made to the league and the islands. And then you left, *alone*."

It was pointless defending herself because he was right. She had rejected him for wanting something beyond the walls of home, and then had gone and wanted those things for herself. It was cruel, in retrospect. So Lilong bowed her head and waited for him to finish, to let it all out.

"I can understand why you didn't tell anyone, but *me*?" He beat a hand against his chest. "*Me*, who was going to run away for you, who I thought you cared about."

"I'm sorry, Turay," she said. "I just . . . it was something I had to do."

"And put the whole of the seven islands in danger?" He was raising his voice. "What is wrong with you, Lilong?"

"Okay, now, that's too far," she said. "Berate me all you want because I left without you, and I can accept that. But don't you dare tell me what is dangerous or not for these islands. You know nothing of what I know and what I've seen out there. You think I'd be back here if I didn't think it was important?"

He seemed shocked by her rebuttal, cold water poured over his anger. Turay was never one for big outbursts anyway. He was more of the passionate kind, insisting on the things he believed in, and simply walking away from that which he didn't. But he had not walked away from her yet, not even now that she was a poisoned fruit returned from the land of heathens outside. Did that mean he still believed in her? Did that mean he still cared?

"I'm glad you're fine," he said softly, answering her question. Then he shut the door and motioned for her to sit.

Lilong sat. The apology she had prepared for him—for her family, for everyone—it stuck in her throat. The reality of return hit her now, a weight lifted yet replaced by a new one. Home: solace, but also dissonance.

"Are they—" she started, but could not bring herself to finish it.

"Your comrades are fine," he said. "Though they will undergo fiercer scrutiny than you, I suppose."

She held his gaze, until he understood.

"Oh, you meant your family," he said. "They're...fine. I passed by Ma Guosa on my way here, and she was with Kyauta and Lumusi, doing some work outside."

The names of her family members from his lips made reality strike even harder. Each of her choices felt even more laden. Leaving, surviving, exposing the islands. *Abandoning.*

"I have pressing questions for you." Turay said this like an elder brother, rather than a sentry, or a man who once proposed to be joined to her. "Why in the name of all that is kind and wet would you bring strangers—*from the mainland!*—into our home? What have they seen? How much do they know? The league will surely have even more pressing questions and some stiff decisions to make."

She did not have an answer to his questions either, or rather she had answers too lengthy to begin to explain now. So instead, she just looked at him. Turay held her eyes for a while, then sighed and shook his head.

He understands, she told herself. It was why she was sitting here in this room, hidden away, rather than sitting in front of the league Elders. It struck her, now, that this was his own act of rebellion, his rejection of the league's expectations, of the Ihinyon Ideal. Just like allowing herself to look at him again, desire welling up inside her, was also a rebellion of sorts, a culmination of all the small rebellions she had cultivated on the trip. This was her finally beginning to rewrite her story, and there was someone here whose hand she could hold while she did so.

But first, she needed to know a few things, and until she did, she would hold back everything she knew that he didn't.

"Those sentries are my people." Turay had dropped his voice to a conspiratorial volume. "I convinced them not to speak to anyone, and that might work while we're still here, but I don't know what will happen once we get to Hoor. Luckily, the league has not sat for many moons. There are matters more pressing right now than whatever questions they might have."

"You didn't mention my daa."

Turay frowned. "Pardon?"

"When you spoke of my family," she said. "You did not mention him." And now that she thought about it, he did not mention Issouf, her elder brother, either.

"Ah, well." Turay looked around. "Perhaps we should make this place comfortable. This one will be long."

Without warning, his eyes flashed white.

White Iborworking was the most silent of all four. Where fire and water often arrived with ferocity, and the other shades of ibor needed solid objects or bodies to operate, white ibor and the practice of wielding it often occurred in stillness. Unless the Iborworker wanted it so, neither light nor wind announced their deed until it was already far too late, when the deed was already completed.

It happened this same way with Turay. All Lilong felt was a gentle pull on the parts of her body she didn't always know were there: eyelids, eardrums, the hair on her arms. Then, as if the sun had been drawn closer to the ground, the room was suddenly three times brighter than the wick lamp could ever offer. The lone ray of light piercing the room was gone, as if it had been diffused and spread. A barely perceptible breeze filtered through the gap in the window, a movement she was sure was completely absent before.

"I forgot how good you are with this," said Lilong, finding herself smiling and—*at ease?*—for the first time in a while.

"Your daa is gone," said Turay.

Lilong went cold. Her jaw locked and she couldn't find purchase in her limbs. She tried to swallow, but her throat was too small, too tight.

"He left with Issouf," Turay was saying. "Nobody knows where, but we have our suspicions. He had barely recovered when he began to talk about the islands being in danger."

Palpitations in her heart. Lilong blinked.

"He was speaking of some magical buried city or something. I remember the league visiting, warning him to stop scaring everybody by telling anyone who could hear that the islands will be swallowed by the Great Waters. But he paid little heed. The league said he was not quite well, that an attack from beyond the Forest of the Mist had taken a toll on him. But I'm sure they had plans to arrest him once he'd fully recovered, and I think he knew it too. Because one day, we all woke up and he was gone."

Lilong managed a swallow.

"Ma Guosa and Kyauta said they heard him whispering to Issouf about taking a dhow. The league sent some warriors in pursuit, but no one saw them at the twin islands. Which means they have either already succumbed to the waves, or passed unnoticed." He leaned in. "But Lumusi told me, personally, that she thinks they're going to Ofen."

"No." It escaped her lips before she could hold it back.

"There is a lot we need to unravel, but we have no time," Turay was saying. "Perhaps your coming is a blessing in disguise. If we can find your daa and Issouf before the storm, we can still save them. But if we cannot find them before they make landing—"

"Wait, wait," said Lilong. "What do you mean *storm*?"

"You didn't feel it?" Turay said, rising. "Storm is coming."

<hr />

The cloud watchers had looked to the sky and made their calculations. The storm was to be one-of-a-kind, nothing like they had ever seen in the seven islands in their lifetime. There had been no prior warning from the weather stone. One day, they had woken up, and there it was—a change in the cloud patterns, in wind movement, in the thickness of the air. A different swing to both string and stone. This was not the rainfall anomalies they were used to, no. This was an omen.

There were no clear patterns yet, no awareness of how the storm planned to move. But those who watched the clouds understood stillness more than they understood movement, and the long tails they saw above told the tale of what was to come. They informed the leaders of the islands and the Abenai League of what they knew. Whatever was coming was *big*. Big enough to destroy huge swaths of each island—Namge included—if not even big enough to swallow a small island whole. The tiny island of Ofen, they declared, isolated out there at the rump end of the archipelago, was most at risk of disappearing completely.

Lilong had only ever witnessed small storms in her life, here one day, gone the next. But she had heard the last big one discussed in passing. Her parents and other older Ihinyon sometimes chatted about how one *felt* it long before they saw it. They talked about the stillness that came before, the absolute lack of motion, the quiet before the panic. The thinness of the air, sharp enough to cut the hair in one's nostrils. The petrichor that lingered for days before the storm made landfall.

They spoke of how every island evacuated its people to Hoor to hide in the rock formations until the storm passed, then returned to assess the damage and rebuild. It hadn't always made sense to Lilong that Hoor was the one island where emergency resources were permanently stored and periodically updated. She had always thought it was to ensure there would be enough supplies to cater to the other islands if Namge was ever taken by forces from the mainland. But Hoor was simply the only island in the archipelago that was set apart from the wind's path, and therefore tended to receive the least damage from storms.

Forces from the mainland, it turned out, were now the least of their worries. For Lilong and her friends to receive any sort of punishment, they would first have to stay alive.

According to Turay, everyone—Elders, children, youth—was at the west beach right now, headed for Hoor. Namgeans designated to oversee and facilitate these transfers and welcome arrivals from the other islands were the only ones left behind. That included him and his teams of warriors, tasked with ensuring the Forest of the Mist was still protected. This was why Namge was devoid of sound, of soul.

It was the first day of the rainy season. Storm was coming.

47

Danso

Namge
First Mooncycle, same day

THE ROOM THEY WERE kept in remained dark throughout. Sentries entered every now and then, but no light came from the door whenever they did, which led Danso to believe that they were deep within a building. Neither he nor Oke could tell what time of the day it was. The only window in their room was shut tight and was too high up for them to peer through it.

Even without the light, he could make out most of the sentries' features. Many had the same yellow complexion as Lilong, but a handful looked just like a regular Bassai or even desertlander. In fact, though he couldn't be sure, he swore he saw at least one person that looked exactly like him: a Shashi. This was the big lie of Bassa's myths, he realised: The Ihinyon weren't all yellowskins, and simply possessed a range of complexions like everyone else.

"Keeping us in the darkness like this has to be by design," Danso announced to Oke, who had so far spent all her time ensuring Thema was comfortable. "I presume so we can't see their faces—that's why they covered them in the forest and blindfolded us, right? Or they just want to drive us mad, make us desperate to spill our secrets."

"Or prevent us from fomenting thoughts of escape," Oke said, rocking the baby, who, mostly faced with the dark, spent much time sleeping.

"They did this to us quite a bit back in prison." There was a bitter undertone to her words whenever she spoke about her time there, if she even spoke of it at all.

The sentries came intermittently to offer water, cleaning cloths, and some sort of mashed, starchy food for the baby. None for the adults, except water. Like the times before, none of them spoke, just offering the items and leaving. Hours passed this way. Danso couldn't be sure how long they had been there. Half a day? Two? His stomach rumbled from hunger, but he had other things on his mind.

"You think Lilong is okay?" he asked no one in particular, placing his ear to the door. "You think they are torturing her for information?"

"Unlikely," said Oke. "They don't seem like the kind to attack their own."

The door opened suddenly, pushing Danso back, and the first ray of light cut through the room.

Lilong walked in. Relief washed over Danso, but he tucked it away quickly, remembering that both of them were not quite back to being friends. Not yet.

"Are you harmed?" Lilong asked them both, though her eyes were fixed on Oke and the sleeping baby. "Are you fine?"

"We are okay," said Danso, observing her to confirm the same. She looked unharmed, and they had returned her blade too, which meant all was well. He noticed, however, that she did not have her pouch containing the Diwi with her. That one must have remained confiscated. He wondered if they'd retained that to keep him at bay. He wondered if she'd told them about what he'd done, what he could do.

"What is happening?" Danso peeked over her shoulder at the sentries outside, who seemed to be paying little mind.

"I want you to meet someone," said Lilong. She leaned through the doorway and beckoned. A young man entered: muscular, yellow like her, dressed and armed like the other sentries but with none of their edgy demeanour. He wore a soft smile and had a boyish quality to him, but his movements were just like Lilong's: measured, practiced, a warrior's gait.

"This is Turay," she said. Something tugged at the edge of her lips, a softness Danso did not always witness resurfacing. But as she was wont to do, Lilong hid it quickly.

Ah, thought Danso. *That Turay.*

Turay nodded at the group, then said in High Bassai just as crisp as Lilong's: "Welcome to Namge."

Danso glanced at Oke, who looked just as perplexed. "*Welcome?* We are not...prisoners?"

Turay cocked his head. "It is...not that simple."

"You—*we*—are not prisoners," said Lilong. "But we—*you*—are not *free*. Not yet."

"Ah," said Oke. "So, like Bassa, then."

"What does this mean for us?" Danso asked.

"We will be presented to the Abenai League, eventually," said Lilong. "But that will be delayed, because a storm is coming and they are all the way over at Hoor."

She said *storm is coming* with a pointed look at him and Oke. Danso didn't get it at first, but when he turned and saw understanding in Oke's eyes, he realised what she was referencing.

First, the Plague of Beasts. Now the Plague of Waters? He shuddered. Something was *definitely* happening in the seventh island of Ofen. *Oh moons. Risisi might be real!*

If Turay, standing next to her, knew anything about that, he did not betray it. Danso realised what the other half of her look signified: Turay did not know what they knew about Risisi. She hadn't told him. Yet.

"We have a bit of time to prepare some sort of argument before sailing over to meet them," Lilong was saying. "Preferably one explaining what we've discovered about the Diwi and red ibor. But I plan to delay that trip for as long as possible until we can make our strongest argument. Because if we don't..." She shrugged.

"That's...comforting," said Danso.

Turay placed a hand around Lilong's shoulder in a way that seemed quite affectionate to Danso. Even more noticeably, Lilong did not growl or ask him to remove it.

"You will stay with Lilong's family for now," Turay said. "When it is safe, you will join them in sailing to Hoor."

"And you?" Oke asked Lilong.

"I have...other plans," said Lilong.

Danso perked up at this.

"This plan," he asked. "Is it to abandon us? Perhaps to go *somewhere* and *do something*?"

Lilong winced at the word *abandon*, but her disposition did not falter. Turay whispered something to her in Island Common, which from his body language Danso gleaned meant something akin to *Why not just tell them?*

"Is it . . . your daa?" asked Danso.

Lilong hesitated, then nodded. "He's . . . gone." Oke's face fell, but Lilong quickly assured her. "Not *dead*. He's left for Ofen with Issouf, my older brother." She waved a hand, as if deciding it was all too complicated to explain. "Listen, there's no time. You need to get to my family's before they leave. They've been helping get people across the channel to Hoor. They will find a way to help you cross and keep you safe. Safer than the Elders will allow, at least."

"And what will you do?" asked Oke.

"Wait until my daa and brother return. Then I'll join you."

"And probably be arrested alongside us."

Lilong shrugged. "Probably."

Silence fell between them all. Danso did not think, at all, that Lilong wanted to simply rescue her family. She cared for them, yes, but she had other plans. She wanted to find Risisi all by herself. Or worse, do something with it long before anyone was the wiser.

"I will go make arrangements," said Turay, and left.

⋅◦⋯━━━━━━⋯◦⋅

Outside, it was late evening. Save for a few sentries milling about, whose faces were still covered, there was no one around. Lilong had quickly updated them about the storm and the ongoing evacuation to Hoor, as well as other matters of interest, including what to expect when they got to her home. Now she stood chatting with Turay, who nodded and then passed on some instructions to his sentries. He seemed to be some kind of leader, and Lilong seemed to trust him without restraint. Danso had never seen her do that with anyone else.

The island before him was not much different from Whudasha in the way its sand and plants looked, the way the breeze moved, the way the air smelled. He couldn't quite make out the architecture, as the building they stood in was set apart from what looked like most of the settlement, far ahead in the distance. But what most struck Danso was something else: an abandoned wooden structure in the distance. It did not look like any of the abodes he had seen so far—or ever. More like a travelwagon, but if three were stacked one on the other, and if its sides were curved.

Is that...?

He stepped farther out on the veranda, squinting to make out the structure. Three to four persons tall, curved like a cocoa pod if split open in half. Ugly, hasty scaffolding barricaded it in, but did nothing other than declare the structure as the real prize. Stilts propped it up to ensure it balanced properly on a wooden raft of loose logs beneath. From the layout, it looked like the raft was what allowed it to be moved from place to place once the scaffolding was removed.

Danso had heard of *seavessels* and seen some drawings at the university library, but he'd always thought of them as ancient structures from another time, when people were foolhardy enough to venture out to the Neverending Sea and its monster waves. Even when Lilong had spoken of *dhows*, he'd imagined them to be like the canoes he'd heard of from those who followed the Tombolo up to the fishing hamlets on the coast or watched fishing happen on the Gondola back when it had not dried up. But neither description nor drawing had prepared him for what stood before him: the largeness of it, the grandiosity, the *beauty*.

"One of many victims of the Great Waters," said Turay, who had returned from his conversation. Danso marvelled again at how crisp his High Bassai was—although unlike Lilong, Turay seemed to speak it with much reluctance. Whatever these Ihinyon scouts were doing— bringing in pieces of the outside world, ensuring their people kept aware even though they remained sequestered—what a fine job it was.

"Don't know how something so magnificent could be a victim," Danso replied, gesturing grandly at the structure. Oke, who had also come forward to look, gasped in appreciation. Turay beamed, glad that something so mundane could spark such joy and surprise.

"That one is under repair," he said, almost disappointed. "Wait until you see the fully functional ones at the beach. They're glorious." Then, just as quickly, his smile vanished, as if he suddenly realised he was not supposed to be friends with them.

"How will you get us to the house?" asked Danso. "I mean—we are going to walk across the quarter, yes? And the sentries who caught us—won't they talk?"

"We do not speak of activities in the Forest of the Mist to regular folk," said Turay. "Don't want to scare them with tales of intruders and whatnot. As for being seen, don't worry—hiding things is my specialty."

As he said this, his eyes flashed white, just like Lilong's did with amber. Danso felt a tingling in the air, like a breeze but without noise or sound or movement—only the individual particles of air responding to a Command.

A White Iborworker!

Oke did not seem to notice—perhaps she hadn't seen. And unlike the other ibors, nothing physical had changed or moved. But Danso had the pertinent feeling of a sheen surrounding him, a cocoon of protection—but also of imprisonment.

He tapped his manuscript, tied fast to his body in his wrappers. So many parts of this place the world deserved to see. Stories, but also other kinds of knowledge. He just had to survive long enough to make it happen.

If, of course, the plagues did not get them all first.

48

Lilong

Namge
First Mooncycle, same day

THE ISLAND HAD CHANGED.

It was not just the emptiness that unsettled Lilong as she made her way past a route that her feet had begun to remember. It was the way the buildings themselves had changed. The way the coast had edged much too close to the housing line, and how the settlement seemed brighter, more light and breeze from the sea weaving in.

It took Lilong a moment to realise why. Houses in Namge were built in threes before a road, like the one they were on, separated them from the next. The first, the house closest to the road, was the tallest, a facade. Citizens of greater means—those who could afford to pay powerful Amber Iborworkers to move heavy stones—built theirs to contain more than one floor. This was farthest from the coast and therefore would be least susceptible to the waves as they edged closer and closer inland. The middle house was smaller, but sometimes even better decorated, as it was where Namgeans received guests. The last and final house was the small-est, built like a hut, with the crudest material. Mostly used as storage or a workspace, and often contained a household's least precious items. Things that could be sacrificed to the sea if need be.

When Lilong walked past, she saw only two rows of houses on most sides, many of the storage huts missing. What would've been the middle houses were precariously close to the sea. *How could the sea move so fast?*

"Storm did this?"

Turay, walking beside her, said: "What? No. That's just, you know, normal creep."

"Creep doesn't happen that fast."

He angled his head. "You've been gone a long time, Lilong."

Turay had not been joking when he said the island was empty. There was not a single soul in sight, and most of those they came across were fellow warriors like him. Turay nodded at a few as they went past. Thankfully, his Command of light was still in effect, so it was impossible for them to see even the footprints of the group he was leading, so long as they didn't bump into anyone or anything.

"How many new recruits did you lot get while I was gone?"

"Many," said Turay. "It became important to grow our numbers. We didn't know what was going to happen after you and your daa had gone out there and, eh, showed yourselves."

"You were preparing for...war?"

"We were just...preparing. We didn't know what for. We still don't."

"And somehow, they made you leader of them all."

Turay snorted. "What shit leader? All of us warriors here right now got stuck with the job of sentry or shepherding folks to the beach because we did something or the other the league didn't like. Mine was for sticking my neck out for you—and I got assigned here by my daa, no less!"

Lilong smiled wanly, a mix of guilt and appreciation. She remembered how his daa, an Elder old enough to be her own daa twice over, looked at her often. Like a cartwheel detached and run off on its own. He wasn't wrong, and he was likely glad he'd been proven right. But she'd always thought of him as a thorn better to avoid. He didn't quite know about her past with his son, but he still must have been incensed to hear him defend her leaving.

She observed the warriors some more. "Are they all from here?" It occurred to her now that more of them were yellow-complexioned than not, which suggested recruits from places like Ololo, where almost the whole population was yellow, than, say, Namge or Hoor, where each family had a majority of yellows but almost never all—about three in four.

"Most of the new ones are from Ololo and Sibu-Sibu," said Turay, confirming her suspicions. "The Elders at Edana and Ufua were only enthusiastic enough to lend a hand toward anything that would improve commercial activities, which they say war does not. They sent only a handful. Most are in Hoor right now. These ones are likely here because they offended someone in the league."

No wonder they had been so hostile even after she'd introduced herself in the forest. Sure, the Ololo and Sibu-Sibu warriors were renowned for such aggressiveness, but the others were likely only rankled because they'd been assigned the most irritating league task possible: herding wayward people.

They rounded one junction, then another, and soon arrived at Lilong's home.

Lilong stopped. Tears formed behind her eyes.

The front face of their house was beautified in the way only her daa could have done—paintings, colours, swirls of the sea. Just like all the others they had passed, emergency items in different stages of packing were spread across the front yard—gourds of water and wraps of non-perishable foods and herbs for medicine; a few tools and weapons, likely for clearing debris after the storm. It all seemed so alive, yet so dead.

"I swear I saw them out here not one moment ago," said Turay.

"They'll be in the backyard," said Lilong, feet carrying her forward, muscle memory doing its job. She swung the mat over the doorway aside and walked into the house like it was not her first time returning in three seasons. The roof felt too low, the house too dark, too musty.

In the backyard were three people, their backs to her and Turay as they entered. Ma Guosa was the first to turn around, before Kyauta and Lumusi did the same.

It was her sister whose eyes widened the most, who screamed and ran, flying into her embrace. Lilong caught her and they twirled. Ma Guosa looked just as astonished, her eyes twinkling. Lilong embraced her next, while Lumusi chattered, rotating questions like a cartwheel.

"Welcome home, my daughter." Ma Guosa pressed Lilong against her soft body. "Great Forces have kept you safe. Oh, I wish your daa were here to see this!"

Lilong embraced Kyauta. Her brother blinked and blinked and did not do much else.

When they had sufficiently examined her, touched her new scars, asked a basketful of questions she could not answer, and basked in the euphoria of her return, Lilong opened her pack and presented the gifts she'd brought back. Lumusi got one of the paintings Lilong had made back in Chabo, while Kyauta got a pouch of interesting pebbles and shells collected from the mainland and desertlands. Lumusi held hers above her head and began to run about the backyard. Lilong laughed. Kyauta received his wordlessly and blinked and blinked.

"You get it, at least?" Ma Guosa was asking her about the Diwi. Lilong nodded.

"Turay and the sentries took it," she said. "To return to the Elders for safekeeping, now that…" She trailed off. She did not quite yet know how to talk about the current situation with her daa with Ma Guosa. Though she was the only maa Lilong had ever known, and she had been nothing but a good maa to Lilong, she was still not hers. Not really. And they had never learned to talk about the hard things because there had never been a hard thing to talk about.

"Turay tell you about the storm?" Ma Guosa asked. Lilong nodded again. "Good," said the woman. "Because we have waited long enough. We may have to leave Jaoudou and Issouf and go to Hoor. Then maybe… maybe he will meet us there."

Lilong smiled. "It's okay," she said. "Let us worry about that another time. But for now, come and meet my friends."

⁘

Lilong brought her friends into the front house and introduced them to her family. Ma Guosa immediately took to Oke, helping relieve her of the child and ushering them inside for some rest. Danso and Lumusi seemed to hit it off, Lumusi raising questions in High Bassai that ended up in a conversation that looked like two scholars arguing. Of the four children in the household, Lumusi was the one who had picked up High Bassai the quickest, after Lilong had learned it from her daa and begun to practice at home.

Out in the front yard, one of Turay's warriors ran up to him and whispered in his ear. Turay frowned, and Lilong caught him stealing a glance or two back at the house. Then he dispersed the warrior and came into the house.

"Some business to attend to," he whispered to Lilong. "I will be back." He motioned toward Danso. "Make sure they stay here and out of sight as agreed. No leaving this compound until we're ready to take them to Hoor." He leaned in. "I mean it, Lilong."

"I'll keep them here," she said. Then he was off.

While Danso and Lumusi continued to chat, Lilong noticed Kyauta had disappeared. She distinctly recalled him not returning the greetings from her comrades. She went into the back house, past Ma Guosa and Oke trying to communicate as best they could via hand gestures (Ma Guosa had no interest in learning High Bassai, "the language of evil," as she put it). Outside, in the backyard, Kyauta was at his packing duties again.

"You're angry," she said.

He did not respond.

"I'm sorry," she said. "For leaving without telling you. I didn't want you all to worry."

Kyauta had not grown much taller in her absence. Only two and a half seasons would bring him to around thirty seasons old now. Young, still. But she could see the strain in his neck, the sinew of his small biceps. He had not grown *up* in her absence, but sterner, and she heard it in his voice when he spoke.

"And yet," he said. "And yet."

"I had to do it, you understand?" She edged closer. "I had to save our family name, our legacy on these islands."

"And yet," he said, this time turning around, fury written all over his face. "And yet you ended up throwing our name in the mud."

"I—" Lilong stopped. "I'm sorry."

"For which part?" His voice began to rise. "For leaving us to the mercy of the league? For leaving daa when the pain and shame of his attack and mistake was at the highest? For causing him to continue to worry instead of healing? For causing him to convince Issouf and take him to his death?"

Now that he said it like that, Lilong's belly sank even farther. He *was* right. What exactly was she apologising for?

"All okay?" Ma Guosa was standing at the backyard door. "Kyauta—you disrespecting your sister after her long journey?"

"She is not my sister," he said. "Not after what she has done."

"What did you say?" Ma Guosa stepped into the backyard. "If you have two heads, repeat what you just said."

"It's fine, maa." To Kyauta, she said: "I'm sorry I disappointed you." She turned to Ma Guosa. "All of you."

"Never mind him, my dear," said her maa. "There is time yet for redemption. But first: survival. And some food, to begin with."

49

Esheme

The Forest of the Mist
First Mooncycle, 1, same day

THE ROYAL PARTY STOOD at the edge of the Forest of the Mist.

They'd found the fugitives' travelwagon after two days of travel from the Weary Sojourner. Their trail had been easy to follow, showing signs of struggle, an attack of sorts—predators, probably. They'd found the abandoned travelwagon that finally confirmed their postulations. The kwaga tracks had been easy to follow, leading them to where the kwagas themselves had also been abandoned. The mist had been visible from there.

Now that they stood here, Esheme saw why there was little attempt to protect the location of this place. It was impenetrable, mist winding tightly around trees that disappeared into what may have been clouds descended too low. No sensible person would go into this place unguided.

Which was why Esheme decided to go first.

Not *her*, just her eyes: the Ninki Nanka. She would send it ahead, clear a safe pathway for the caravan to go through, deal with any predators in the way, or any traps set up by the yellow woman's people. She just needed to do so without hurting herself more than the trip already had.

Esheme disembarked from the royal travelwagon and stepped forward, held upright only by the force of sheer will. She was the most fatigued she'd ever been in her forty-some seasons in this world. But too much was at stake for her not to try.

Igan, beside her, remained silent and stone-faced. They had not yet recovered from Esheme taking Kangala's advice to split the caravan, leave Ikobi and a squadron of civic guards at the Weary Sojourner, and send half the Sahelian company in pursuit of the escaped men.

But what Igan didn't know was that Esheme had no intention of doing anything here, whether crossing this forest or the land bridge after it. Not in this state. Her time at the Weary Sojourner had finally brought her to see sense: The savanna was a harsh foe, and travelling through it had depleted her in more ways than one. Bodily, and numbers-wise, she was in no place to lead her people into this forest, where they could easily be swarmed by people with far superior numbers.

So, no, she wasn't planning to go into enemy territory unprepared. In fact, she had all but given up on capturing these fugitives, and instead began to think of them as her map, a pathway to greater glory. Because on the other side of this forest and land bridge was a land teeming with ibor that was more than just one tiny piece. She only needed to find that land, and that was all that mattered.

At some point in the future, she would return, replenished, and get everything she wanted.

She stood near the treeline now, mist dropping low enough to settle between the trees' branches, wrap around their trunks, touch their leaves. A truly mesmerizing sight. But beautiful things could be dangerous too, which was why Igan and their posse continued to scan for threats. None, so far. Not that there were many threats out here that could easily get to Esheme before the Ninki Nanka snapped them in half or spat them into a puddle of flesh. She might be physically weak, but she was still the most powerful woman this side of the continent.

She Drew, and called for her beast.

Her mind wandered as she did so, envisioning how she would finally discover these Nameless Islands and return to her people with knowledge that no other emperor had been able to gain. She would claw back respect, not just for herself, but for the institution that was the Bassai empire. Show them that she was more than just the young woman who had spent most of this trip as a passenger. The leadership she hoped to demonstrate, she could start now, show that she was capable.

It took her a moment to realise the Ninki Nanka was not there, in the place at the back of her consciousness where her connection to it usually nestled. She had Drawn, but there was nothing on the other side for the ibor to Possess. No sting in her belly that told her the connection was complete, no waning consciousness or desire to vomit. Simply...*nothing*.

She shut her eyes, strained, called again. *Rise.* No response.

"What is it?" Igan was asking, but then there was a moan of pain and discomfort behind them.

The first civic guard dropped to the grass, scratching at his face—his eyes—then at his body, clawing bits of flesh from his arms. Then just as suddenly, his body began to jerk. Milky foam spurted from his mouth, and his eyes seemed to lose their blackness, giving way to whites alone, and the red from where he had clawed at them.

He stopped moving, dead.

The peace officer next to him, stepping forward to check on the fallen man, had barely taken two steps before stooping to hold his own belly. He fell to a knee and retched. Milky-white spew poured from the edges of his mouth, bypassed the stitching holding his lips shut, surged between threads. He fell, groaning, scratching his eyes, then screamed, clawing at his skin, peeling off the brown to show the whites underneath that quickly became blood-red.

One by one, the royal civic guards, peace officers, attendants—all dropped to the ground, clawing at their bellies, their eyes, their skin. Stricken, demented, dead.

"Protect the emperor!" Igan's rallying cry came. Their posse, the only ones who hadn't fallen, stepped into a protective circle around Esheme, readying their weapons. But there was no enemy to fight, nothing beyond watching their comrades writhe in the grass, go mad, and die.

My serpent, Esheme was still thinking, lost in her own consciousness. *Where are you?*

The Sahelians, eyes wide, were the only others yet to fall. They gathered to themselves, led by Oroe, Kangala nowhere in sight.

"A curse!" Oroe was saying, as they whispered to one another. "We have been cursed! Retreat! We have been cursed by the Forest of the Mist!"

It took Esheme a moment to realise he was speaking Savanna Common, and not his native Sahelian, even though he was talking to his own people. Igan, casting her a glance, realised this at the same time. He wanted to be heard, to be absolved of whatever hand had caused this. Because it *was* indeed a hand.

This was no curse. It was poison.

Igan, arriving at the same conclusions as Esheme did, wore a rageful expression.

"The water!" they said. It clicked into place for Esheme, then. That was why only the guards and peace officers and attendants had died. They drank the common supply, separate from Esheme's own supply, and Igan and their posse had a separate supply. The Sahelians drank from the common supply too, but had not been affected. Which meant...

"Your beast, Sovereign," Igan was saying, crouching, ready. "Where is it?"

Esheme strained, pushed her consciousness. Nothing.

"Where is your leader?" Igan screamed at the Sahelians, now clustered on the opposite side of the camp. "Where is the Man Beyond the Lake?"

"Here," said a voice, and Kangala stepped out from behind the royal travelwagon.

Head to toe, the man was covered in black blood. In one hand, he held an axe, short-handled. Bits of flesh fell off its blade.

In his other hand, dragging along the ground because it was so heavy, was the head of the Ninki Nanka.

Esheme's chest sank inward. She took in a sharp breath. Her knees wobbled.

"Interesting thing about death," said Kangala. "Dying things do not know they already dead. They want to live, hold to things of old." He tossed the head of the Ninki Nanka forward, letting it roll into the grass that separated both groups. "Sometimes, you remind them. You tell them the bad news: You already nothing. This is your fate. Accept it."

Esheme stared at the crux of her power lying in the grass before them. She had never envisioned it, that such great power—*her* great power—could be so easily defanged. Now she saw that she had been foolish, naive. The beast was already dead. *Of course* it could be killed again, while it was in stasis, asleep, unable to wake or alert anyone while its head was being cut off.

She took a tentative step forward, anger brewing into a monstrosity of its own. She Drew, filled herself with power that was useless. The head in the grass called to her, and she had a mind to run to it now, touch it, reawaken it. Deal out justice on this savage man.

But even from here, the coldness on the other end, the lack of a response, told her it was a pointless venture. Heads did not walk on their own, and headless bodies did not have eyes. Separation of undead head from undead body meant one thing, and one thing alone: The Ninki Nanka was gone forever, and Esheme had nothing.

Oroe and his group had stopped their acting. They gathered behind Kangala, Oroe smirking at Igan, who huddled with their posse, surrounding the emperor.

"Snake," Igan hissed. "I knew it from the day you set foot in Chugoko."

Kangala cocked his head. "Then why you keep snakes close? Is common sense not to, yes?"

This only enraged Igan more. "You poisoned the emperor's people! Good people!"

Kangala snorted. "There are no good people here. Only opportunists. Me, you, all of us. Even your fugitives. You know why they here, yes? Looking for power. Myth city in this myth islands, big and small stones with power, make impossible things possible." He chuckled. "You look for power, I look for power, they look for power. Maybe they have cross already, who knows? But us, only one of us will cross."

He reached into his garment and pulled out a piece of greenery—part cactus, part leaf. The naboom. He sniffed it, broke it in two. Milky-white sap dripped from its insides.

The two groups faced off. Six Sahelians, eight counting Oroe and Kangala. Igan and five members of the posse, not counting the emperor.

Esheme swallowed, found her voice.

"Is that what you want, Sahelian?" she asked. "The power of ibor?"

Kangala grinned. On his blood-splattered face, it was a crazed smile.

"No," he said. "I am waiting."

"Why?"

"Kill your guards, take you prisoner."

"Try," Igan growled. "Six of us, eight of you. I dare you to try."

"No, not eight," he said. "Thirteen."

As he said this, there was a clatter of hooves. From the lonely roads, a cloud of dust rose, giving way to more Sahelians on kwagaback. Six, to be exact. The same Sahelians meant to be in pursuit of the Weary Sojourner escapees, now headed for them, coming from the general direction of the fringe settlements they'd passed by earlier.

Igan's face darkened as Esheme's spirit sank. She had been completely fooled, outsmarted by a former fisherman and canoe paddler. A nobody.

Without warning, Igan plucked a spear from a posse member and hurled it at Kangala. But Oroe, who had been watching Igan all this time, relishing a fight, shoved a spare champion into Kangala. Kangala bundled over, and the champion collected the brunt of the spear in his shoulder. Then Oroe was charging at Igan.

"Get to the treeline!" Igan screamed, pushing Esheme backward before flying out to meet Oroe. Esheme fell on her buttocks, pain shooting up her tailbone. Feet charged past her, and the screams of battle and clatter of weapons began.

Esheme, dazed, lost somewhere between helplessness and despair, crawled forward, toward the only thing she could recognise in this chaos: the head of her animal. She ran her hand over the beast's scaly head, its now finally shut eyes, its exposed dead tongue. But then she was suddenly yanked up, dragged over ragged ground. She looked up and saw it was Igan, hauling her with one arm, swinging their axe with the other, blade finding flesh. Bits and pieces of someone flew all over Esheme. A Sahelian crumpled and bled a foot away from her.

"Get up!" Igan was screaming at her. "Run for the forest!"

Esheme rose, but her feet buckled. She fell and vomited in the sand.

Igan suddenly let go. Esheme rose to her hands and knees and began to crawl toward the treeline, dodging swinging weapons, dirt kicked up, blood, brains, spittle. The treeline seemed to grow smaller, farther, the more she gained ground—if she was gaining ground at all.

I don't want to die, she kept thinking. *I don't want to die.*

As if in answer to her prayer, a strong arm grabbed at her and picked her up, onto their shoulder—Igan. And then they were running.

The royal travelwagon grew distant in Esheme's sight. Kangala stood there, hands tucked forward, nodding. A lizard, a snake. Around him, a battle raged, Igan's posse getting overrun, falling one after the other, but Kangala remained unmoved, eyes holding Esheme's, inviting her, over and over, to witness the destruction of everything she had built.

Oroe, fresh from pummelling down one of Igan's posse, turned and spotted them. He shouted an order in a Sahelian tongue, then began to give chase.

Igan did not stop running, did not stop to put Esheme down, not even once they'd crossed the treeline and ventured into the suddenly cool air of the Forest of the Mist. Esheme's joints and teeth and fingernails rang in her ears, ibor screaming too loud, mourning the severed connection, protesting her weakening body. But then the mists swallowed them, every last trace of their enemies snatched from sight, and Esheme was left with nothing but the darkness ahead.

50

Esheme

The Forest of the Mist
First Mooncycle, same day

TIME IN THE FOREST was an imperceptible, immeasurable quantity. No light, no warmth, nothing but grey and green and brown, stifling them. They went on and on until the green seemed too far-flung for any direction to hold any promise. Only once they couldn't tell where or *when* they were, and that Igan had decided their pursuers were no longer nearby, did they finally stop running.

Esheme lay down, listening to Igan's heavy breathing. The hastiness of it contrasted the stillness of the forest, the pause of everything. The quiet before a pot began to boil.

"Why did you do that?" Igan was asking. "When I tell you to run, you run."

Esheme touched the armlet that held the ibor piece strapped to her arm. Still there, but now useless. It struck her, now, how little she knew about anything—about ibor, about what lay on the other side of this mist. Were there beasts in here too, that could become undead under her touch? Could she fight them and win? Was she now *prey*?

"I told you," Igan was saying, half to themself, half to the forest. "I told you he would try whenever he got the chance. I told you we had to act first or he would."

Esheme knew Igan was right. In her physical weakness, she had let her mind succumb to laxity and had ignored every part of it, denounced it as constant bother over nothing. She was the Red Emperor of Great Bassa, the Scion of Moons. *Surely he wouldn't?* She'd believed so much in might—the might of the beast at her back, the might of ibor, the might of her loyal and ferocious peace officers, the might of the greatest city on the continent awaiting her return. She was too mighty to be conquered.

Not once had she ever spared a thought for who she was without these things. But Kangala had, and he had waited for that sliver of a moment when none of it mattered, and slipped through the crack. He had won, because here she was, nothing but a lost woman in a strange forest, directionless. The only thing standing between her and death was her lover-advisor-Second. And the only thing keeping her sane was the life that still thrummed within her belly.

"I'm scared," said Esheme, words she had not said or thought in a long time. "And I'm sorry." It was a declaration: to the world, to Igan, but mostly to herself.

Igan frowned and shook their head.

"I'm sorry," Esheme repeated, a little louder.

"No, that's—" They shook their head again, as if to clear their eyes. "Something is wrong."

"What?"

"I can't see," said Igan, blinking profusely. "I can't—"

"You're bleeding," Esheme said, the wet metallic smell hitting her now. She lifted the edge of Igan's garment, and there it was: the blade of a spear, embedded just to the back of their right ribcage. The handle had broken all the way off, and the blade itself was completely in, so that there was no purchase left, just a living, gaping wound with a faint glimpse of black metal, blood pouring all over it.

"Oh," said Igan, then their eyes rolled back, and they dropped into the understory.

⋄⸱⸱⸱————————⸱⸱⸱⋄

Esheme did the best she could to stem Igan's bleeding, which included padding the wound with her own wrappers, then ripping what was left of the cloth and tying it tightly across their stomach. Afterward, she lay with Igan in the understory, her head over her lover's chest, listening to their distant heartbeats and praying to whatever god was listening that the faint rises and falls never stopped, and that those who sought them never found them like this: alone and helpless.

Nothing in the Forest of the Mist was what it seemed. Light, like time, moved independent of the demands of day and night. Every stream that pierced the canopy and cut through the mist took the shape of whatever lay in its way—tree or person or animal. Esheme had not seen any of the latter two in—*hours, days?*—save for a few lizards, a lone frog, and a few birds and small tree animals above. When there was any perceptible movement, she envisioned it was the Ninki Nanka, her big obedient child, returned from the dead to save her. Once, she saw its head, floating in the mist, but when she flexed her consciousness, tapped into the stonebone in her arm, there was nothing. Just mist.

Sometimes, it was the Sahelians, their feet crunching in the understory as they bounded over to recapture her. But then she would wake up and realise that aside from the continued rise and fall of Igan's chest—a rise and fall that grew weaker by the moment—there was little else of harm or merit within the vicinity.

Stirrings in her belly were the other thing that kept waking her up whenever she drifted into troubled sleep, fatigued by the latent pressures of iborworking and escape. She couldn't tell if it was hunger or ibor or something else—*someone* else. She kept having short, fitful visions—dreams?—of things being taken from her: her power, her empire, her... child? Each dream was awash with despair and impotence, an overwhelming sense of having things happen to her over and over again, and being unable to do anything about it.

In her mistdreams, the faces of her tormentors were warped, unrecognisable, but they all said the same thing. *Look at you*, they crooned. *Emperor of nothing.* They reached out to touch her, first in supplication, but when their fingers met her skin, they were rough, hardened by squalor and seasons in the dirt. She recoiled from them, folded into herself, drowning in the despair of her loss. When she looked up, the tree was so tall, so far away, and she was but a tiny being who had fallen to its roots, a long fall from grace.

What is left to live for? they taunted, the voices. *What is there?*

She tried to remember. People who cared about her, back in a faraway place called home. But she couldn't picture it, couldn't remember their names. Everything swirled in the mist.

Igan's chest had stopped rising and falling. Or perhaps not. Esheme leaned forward and put a finger underneath their nose. A hint of air exhaled. But was that a sign of life, or a sign of the coastal winds?

"Help," she whispered, the word getting caught in her throat, a housefly stuck. Igan's motionless body stared back at her in response.

There is nothing, said the voices in her head, in the mist. *Nothing.*

She was so tired. Hunger clawed at her belly. Her will to resist had vanished.

She nodded. "Nothing."

Perhaps it is time to go. She nodded again. "Perhaps." She reached for Igan's axe.

Then, she remembered a name. Someone who wasn't far away, someone who was with her, right now. Not Igan—Igan was dead (or were they?). This person was here, but not yet in the world, not yet privy to its sufferings.

Little Esheme. The one to whom she gave life, and who had given her power in return. She might no longer have power, and therefore had nothing to give in return, but moons help her, she had life to give, and she would give it.

She would live. She would live, if it killed her.

She put down the axe, rose, and began walking.

How long and how far she walked, she would never know. Her feet and hands bled, cut by thorny and snapping things in the understory. Her clothes, damp from the mist, clung to her body. She shivered, but pressed on. Mosquitoes bit into her once-immaculate skin and drew blood, leaving red welts behind, but she did not slap at them. Signs of life flashed by, but she did not turn around.

Little Esheme was all she kept thinking. *Little Esheme.*

When the sentries found her, her vision had blurred so much that she could not tell what they were. Faces covered, giving them a fearsome and ghostly quality. Some yellow from head to toe, like the spirits-of-the-forest stories she had grown up with. Others: black, high or low, ordinary. When they ordered her to stop in a language she did not recognise, she did not stop, because the stories said that when a spirit in the forest ordered you to stop, you did so to your detriment.

But they had Igan.

Igan lay in a hastily made stretcher, hauled between two of the sentries. They lay motionless, but their face looked peaceful. Esheme stopped then, faced the carriers. Perhaps these were no malevolent spirits at all, no—these were saviours. These were sent by the moon gods, who would never forsake their scion.

Then she saw the ropes, the bindings, Igan's wrists, elbows, and ankles fused to each other. This was the thing that broke her, the sight of someone she loved now a captive. But what broke her even more, drained all will left in her body, was the thought of the other body, the one within her, still yet to meet this cruel world, yet already doomed to captivity as she would now be.

Knees weak, she sank into the understory.

"Why?" she asked, but they did not answer because they did not understand. Rather, they took her by the arms, bound her wrists, and led her away.

51

Lilong

LILONG WAS MIDWAY THROUGH a snack of fried plantain balls and regaling Ma Guosa and Lumusi with tales from her sojourn when Turay returned, a deep frown plastered over his face. They all stood in the kitchen, warming up pepper soup and boiled cocoyams for the new arrivals. Turay took Lilong away from the stinging peppers to the backyard.

"Something has come up." He sounded angry, as if at her.

"What?"

"I can't say," he said. "I have to show you."

He led her back past the house and outside, then cloaked them in darkness and set off quickly, not bothering with an explanation. Lilong, perplexed, wanted to inquire some more, but decided Turay had trusted her judgement so far. It was best to repay the favour.

Half an hour later, they were back at the place of their prior imprisonment—the house of assembly. Seeing as it was now near midnight, there was no one here but a handful of sentries scattered within distance.

"Okay, Turay, you're scaring me," she said once they were outside the door. "Time to explain."

"I have to show you something," he said. "Well...*someone.*"

Lilong pricked up.

"You did not come through the mists alone."

Even before Turay filled the inner room with unnatural light, Lilong knew what she expected to see. From the moment the blacksmith who fixed their travelwagon had mentioned the emperor collecting peace officers, Lilong surmised it could be for only one reason: The emperor had figured out who the prison escapee was, or worse, who had helped her escape, and had come in pursuit. The blacksmith's warnings had lingered with them for the whole trip, which was why she had insisted that their stay at the Weary Sojourner be limited to one night, and had not been quite in favour of Oke's lovers remaining there.

Despite that, nothing prepared her for what she saw. Instead of a young woman in a crown and flowing wrappers, the person in the dirt looked like a vagrant thrown up to the rocks by the sea. Her hands and feet, bleeding and bruised, were bound to a chair.

There she was: the Twenty-Fourth Emperor of Great Bassa, the Red Emperor, fallen from grace. Weak, unconscious, and at her mercy.

Without warning, Lilong Drew and Commanded her blade. It flew, heading straight for Esheme's heart. It was only a moment away when Turay's eyes flashed white. A quick, sharp gust cut across, flurrying Esheme's wrappers. It blew the blade off-course, causing it to stab the chair's backrest, a knife's edge from Esheme's head.

"Are you mad?" said Turay. "You can't *kill* her!"

"What do you mean?" Lilong said. "You know who she is, yes?"

"Maybe? But we don't know for sure! She hasn't spoken or awoken, so we wait until then before jumping to conclusions." He cocked his head. "And look...she's pregnant."

Lilong squinted, saw the slight bulge of her belly, recognised now the tenor of her skin, bearing both shine and pallor. It was easy to mistake the effects of one for the other, iborworking and pregnancy. They both took from the body in ways that gave something back. But for Esheme, it was obvious to Lilong that the weight of both coincided to leave behind the husk of a woman sprawled before her.

"And so what if she is?" Lilong snarled.

Turay's face clouded. "What do you mean *and so what*? You're willing to murder an innocent child?"

"What do you mean, *innocent*? Nothing coming out of *that* can be innocent."

Turay shook his head. "What happened to you out there, Lilong?"

Lilong thought of Thema, of Oke's confidence that her child's presence would easily get her out of trouble. Had Esheme thought the same, brought her unborn child here knowing most would be reluctant to attack her in this state? Because what else would possess someone to sacrifice so much and travel so far in this condition? All for what—even more power than being the leader of the only empire on the continent?

This is why Risisi cannot be allowed to fall into the wrong hands, she told herself. *Or any hands at all. Look at the lengths they will go!*

The gust of wind and their elevated voices seemed to have woken Esheme up. She groaned, head lolling. Lilong walked forward and slapped her hard across the cheek.

"Tell us how you got here! Tell us who came with you!"

"Enough, Lilong." Turay pulled her back. "We found two others, but we're not sure if they were with her. One was a hunthand-type desert-lander, armed, like a warrior. Fought the sentries, so they killed him in defence. The other was already unconscious, wounded by a spear."

The slap, apparently, had not been enough to fully wake Esheme up— she looked spare, like she had been working ibor and had not taken the time to replenish.

"Red ibor," said Lilong. "Did you find any on her?"

Turay retrieved an armlet from within his wrappers. It was Bassai design, bronze hoop, gold centrepiece, with space to hold a precious material, often coral or other gems. But in the middle of this one stood something she recognised: a shattered piece of the Diwi.

"You know, the scouts have been bringing back stories," said Turay. "Undead soldiers, undead armies, undead beasts. We knew she was doing things, but we weren't sure how. All this time, she'd found a way to awaken red ibor, something we've been trying to do here with no success." He shivered at the thought of its power. "Maybe Ololo and Sibu-Sibu were right after all. Maybe we should not be escaping a storm, but planning for war." He juggled the armlet in his hand. "Maybe this is a blessing in disguise. How else would we have learned about the powers of red ibor? The elders will be pleased—maybe even pleased enough to forgive you for leading her here!"

Lilong had been contemplating telling him about Danso's power, but suddenly realised there was opportunity here: Esheme could bear the brunt of this development.

"How did she end up alone in the Forest of the Mist?"

Turay shrugged. "That's what I want to know. Hopefully she awakens soon and tells us, because those sentries out there are getting impatient. Two sets of intruders, both with pieces of an Ihinyon heirloom—it's unprecedented. We waste too much time, and the word will be out on the next dhowload to Hoor, and the league will know. *Then* we'll be in real trouble."

"So, we wake her," said Lilong, and set about it.

When the Red Emperor of Bassa awoke, she did not seem surprised to see the two islanders before her. She did not even seem panicked or angry or fearful. Instead, she looked inquisitive, peeking at her belly, as if to check that her child was still there.

Once she could speak, she asked only one question.

"Igan?"

Lilong and Turay regarded one another.

"What is that, High Bassai?" Turay asked Lilong in Island Common so Esheme wouldn't understand.

"I don't know what an *Igan* is, and I don't care," she said, stepping forward to face Esheme. "Listen, *Sovereign*. We have questions. Either you give us answers, or you die. Choose."

Esheme's sunken, dark eyes met hers. For someone so bent on pursuing her, Lilong realised she had met this woman up close only twice: at Danso's barn, and in the Dead Mines. Now that she looked at her, she was just a scared child, unlucky enough for the moons to align and place power in her hands. Sure, she had bartered and murdered her way there—she was the daughter of a fixer after all—but once she'd had it, she did not know what to do with it. So she had reached for the next best thing all with power always did: asking for more. But *more* always led to disaster. *More* was how a whole emperor ended up on a hidden island alone, captive and defenceless.

"Igan," Esheme said. "Then I talk."

"We don't know no Igan," said Lilong. "Everything here is what we have found."

"We killed a warrior man," said Turay in High Bassai. "I don't know if he was yours, but if this is who you are asking about, he is dead. He fought the sentries and did not win. The other person we rescued is with a healer. We cannot say at this time if they will survive or not."

Relief seemed to settle in her, though she retained some disquiet. Then she said: "Water."

Turay fetched it, and she drank something close to a bucketful. She asked to be released from her binds. Turay was soft to it, Lilong violently opposed. So they met in the middle and loosened the ankle binds only.

Then Esheme began to speak.

Lilong had never heard the woman speak at such length, but as she listened, she began to see what Bassa saw in her. This was an extraordinary woman who was like the face of the Neverending Sea, each wave reflecting something different when the sun shone on a new side. She spoke of her learnings in Chugoko with pride, triumph in her voice when she spoke of her recruitment of a Sahelian called the Man Beyond the Lake. Lilong took in a sharp breath when she told of their time at the Weary Sojourner, then calmed when she learned of the escapees.

Esheme's shoulders began to slouch as she narrated the events of a battle at the edge of the Forest of the Mist. This explained not just where the murdered warrior in the forest had come from, but the tales of her undead beast, and why it wasn't here now.

"This Kangala," asked Turay. "He is still out there? On the edge of the forest?"

"I don't know," said Esheme. "I assume he'll try to find the isthmus. It's what I would do."

"Because he believes there is ibor here, like you do."

Esheme shook her head. "Not like me, no. He spoke of something else—a city underground, filled with ibor. I reckon that is what he might seek." She held Lilong's eyes. "He knew things about you and your island, things even I did not know."

"Underground city?" Turay chuckled. "There is no such thing. Only children's rhymes and old people's tales."

But Esheme had caught Lilong's expression, the discomfort in her posture when the buried city was mentioned.

"Is it, now?" said Esheme, smirking. "Perhaps you want to have a chat with your comrade here."

Turay glanced at Lilong, and it was too late for her to hide her expression of intense concern. His eyes widened.

"What is this, Lilong?" he asked in Island Common. "What have you done?"

Lilong was shaking her head. "Listen, Turay, it's a long story. I didn't—"

"I knew it!" Turay clapped his hands, frustrated. "I knew you didn't just come back because you cared—for your family, or your people, or *me*. You came because, like always, you desired something. And as usual, you hid it from me."

"I did not hide—"

"You're always saying *my daa this* and *my daa that*, but you are just the same. You say you want to help, but you just make things worse for all of us."

The accusation stung Lilong more than she'd expected. Anyone else could believe this about her, but not Turay. Not the one person who was not her family that she might actually care about, whose well-being she was now concerned about—not just because he had put himself on the line for her, but because he made her want to put herself on the line for her family, for her people, for *him*.

It was for *him* that she wanted to do something about Risisi. *Destroy it* if she had to. That life he dreamed of, the one free of imprisonment on an island and tenets of the league and invasion by Bassa—they could have that. But only if Risisi was never there, never accessible by people like Esheme or this Kangala man, or even the Abenai League.

Turay could see his words had had an effect. He cooled down.

"I did not mean to—"

"You are right," she said. "I have made hasty decisions, and they have cost me, cost others. But I can do better, and I want to do better. So just give me a chance and listen, will you?"

Esheme, who had been watching their back and forth, chimed in.

"Might I say," she said, her tone brightened by the chaos her words had sparked, "now is a good time to speak of how you may return me to my people?"

Turay frowned. "Return?"

"For a reward, of course," said Esheme. "It is in your own best interest. Once the whole continent hears their Red Emperor is missing, and the news spreads—and it *will* spread—that Kangala has found the Forest of the Mist that leads to ibor, your sentries will not be able to hold the barrage of power-hungry people soon to appear on your doorstep." She smirked again. "But if I return, only I have that secret. And your reward, among other things, is that your secret remains safe with me. Perhaps, even, somewhere along the line, we can come to an agreement, your people and mine. We can make Oon the greatest it has ever been."

Lilong stared at the woman, befuddled. Then she laughed dryly, long and hard.

"Foolishness must run in the waters at Bassa," she said, once done, "because that is the only explanation for why you believe yourself to be in a position to bargain."

"I am still alive," said Esheme. "If you were going to kill me, you would have done so already. So, as long as I have life and can speak, I will bargain."

Lilong shook her head slowly, then crouched to Esheme's level.

"Make no mistake," she said. "You *will* die. It's a matter of when and how, and whether it is by my hand or others, but you *will* die. Just like the many lives you have taken from this world, you will never see your land or your people again. That, I promise you."

Lilong rose and beckoned Turay outside. Once on the veranda, Turay paced, near frantic. Lilong, however, had already decided what she was going to do.

"We must go to Ofen," she said.

Turay stopped. "Say what?"

She told him the story of Risisi—the *true* one—and the story of her daa's plans with Oke. She told him of the league's lies and secret society, the truth of where her daa had taken Issouf to. She told him everything.

When it was over, Turay was as still as the morning. He gazed up, into the sky, as if trying to find his place in all this mess, trying to answer the same questions Lilong had been trying to answer all this time. He had no response, just like Lilong had had none, just like it had left her deflated and lacking in will.

But now, she had a will, a plan, something to put an end to all of this. Something to give them both the freedom they sought.

"It's all the answers we want and need," said Lilong. "We find my daa and Issouf, find Risisi, find out why the league lied to us."

"And then what?"

Then we destroy it, she wanted to say, but decided against telling him this part. Disillusioned as Turay was, the thought of destroying a treasure trove of ibor would hit too close to home for him. He would try to talk her out of it, and he'd never help her get there if he knew her true plan.

"Then we see," she lied. "But at least we will know all the truth of what really exists."

He thought about it. Honestly too, Lilong could see, because then he said: "Maybe being out there so long, you've forgotten that Ofen is the last island in the archipelago. We'll never make it back before the storm hits."

"Storm has been threatening for what, half a fortnight now? You said it yourself—even the cloud watchers don't know when it'll arrive. Plus, we have you, right? You can get us there safely. Oke can help you—you'll show her how to work the waters. And when we find my daa, he'll help her too." She grabbed Turay by the shoulders. "*We can do this.*"

Turay shook his head. "I—I can't, Lilong." He gestured toward the house of assembly. "What am I going to do with…*that*? What am I going to tell the Elders? They've already been looking at me with side-eyes—I can't give them more reason."

"That?" Lilong waved her hand at the house. "We leave her there."

Turay's jaw dropped. "You can't be serious."

Lilong was dead serious.

"You said it yourself—we should not lay a hand on a woman with child. But you of all people know that we cannot let her leave that room, let her mingle in this population, or in any population whatsoever. That woman in there might be no danger to us now that she is without red ibor, but make no mistake—she will poison anything she gets the chance to. We leave her here, lock her in the lower levels. Let the storm get her."

Turay shook his head. "I don't know about that. I was thinking she might be a good bargain, especially in our inevitable audience with the Elders. We can pretend you returned with her as your prisoner!"

"Maybe," said Lilong. "Or we can ensure, here and now, that no one ever gets harmed again."

"I don't know..." said Turay. "She might be cruel, but that is not who we are."

He was right—they weren't cruel people. And because of that, the emperor had thought she could come here and take their ibor. Her Sahelian friend thought he could do the same too. Even the Elders had taken them for granted, lied to them for ages about Risisi.

Cruelty was awful, yes. But it was the cost of freedom.

"How about this?" said Lilong. "We leave her in the lower levels, locked in with nothing but food and water. Let the Great Forces choose her fate. She survives, and upon our return, we take her to the Elders, to trial by the league. But if not, then the Great Forces have decided, and not us."

Lilong knew the argument would work because she knew Turay well. When she went in, Esheme noted her upbeat temperament, and knew it meant nothing good for her.

They did not speak as Lilong carefully removed the ankle binds and ushered her into the lower levels, blade on her back the whole time. Once in a locked room, she laid down the bowl of food Turay had packed—fruits, roasted cocoyams, bread—then snuffed out the only lantern left. Esheme sat, unmoving, watching her, and she in turn gazed at the emperor in the scant light that made it into the level.

"I once promised your maa I would kill her," said Lilong. "This will suffice."

She swung the door shut and bolted it.

Danso

AFTER BEING INTRODUCED TO Lilong's family, Danso had a lot of questions. Like, what was the history behind Lilong and Issouf being of the same daa but different maas? And Ma Guosa was Lumusi and Kyauta's maa, but not Lilong's or Issouf's? By his calculation, that involved some kind of rejoining of people previously joined to other partners—or who simply had children of their own—and making a new household out of that. A fascinating concept, which he noted for his codex. Was this kind of free-range approach to family an islander thing, a Namge thing, or just a thing with this family? But his attempt to get an explanation only earned him blank stares.

To take his mind off the oddities and other matters swarming him, Danso followed Lilong's younger sister, Lumusi, to the backyard, so he could help them pack and prepare for transportation to Hoor. But between the dagger stares he received from Kyauta and Ma Guosa's constant intimations in the two High Bassai words she was good with—*Go rest!*—he abandoned them and wandered to the beach at the edge of the compound, looking out to the darkness beyond the shore.

So much was familiar about this moment. The last time he had stared out at the horizon, the waters of the Neverending Sea leaving behind a wet wasteland of castaway things, Lilong had been there too, though lying injured in Biemwensé's hut. There had been the euphoric sounds of children at play, just like there were those of people at work now. The breeze felt the same, the night just as thick and pressing. Ihinyon, just like Whudasha, felt like home if he closed his eyes and believed.

But Danso did not close his eyes. He had been a fool once. No longer.

He was not welcome in Bassa, he was not welcome in Whudasha, and he definitely was not welcome here. If he was ever to be welcome somewhere, he would have to make that place home, to make that place *free*. And the only way to do that was to make *every* place free, to provide the power needed to stand up against the bullies of the world.

He had tried to give them truth. Now, he would try to give them power. And with each in either hand, maybe they could finally be free.

It was a dream, yes. A big one. But dreaming came with risks, and Danso, unfortunately, was doomed to be a dreamer.

"What are you thinking?"

Danso swung around to find Lumusi standing behind him. She had somehow peeled away from her packing duties and now stood curious from a distance, looking every bit the child of twenty-two seasons that she was. Now that Danso found some time to look at the girl clearly, he marvelled again at how much darker than Lilong she was—yellow, still, but not in the same shade. She had let her hair grow into a large brush atop her head. Eyes larger and neck longer than Lilong's. And despite all this difference, they were more family than any other family he'd ever seen.

"You are missing home?" Lumusi stepped forward, sensing his disquiet.

So far, he had never had cause to engage with anyone outside of his age group. Staring at Lumusi right now, he realised he was yet to find proper ways to respond to her and her questions. Partly because he didn't really know the answer himself.

He smiled wanly. "Somewhat. Maybe. Not really."

She frowned. "That makes no sense."

Danso chuckled, disarmed, then tried on the bit of Island Common Lilong had taught him back in Chabo: "No, it not."

"No, you say: It *does* not." Lumusi stepped forward again, then proceeded to sit by him.

"It *does* not." Danso repeated her Island Common and sat by her too.

"You like it here?" she asked, indicating the sea bed before them, now vacated by low tide.

"Somehow, yes," he said, then hesitated before trying Island Common again: "But here no want me."

"Here *does not* want me," she said. "Maybe we speak High Bassai so you don't cut your tongue and spoil our language at the same time."

Danso chuckled. "Fine, okay."

"You say here doesn't want you. Who here?"

He gestured around. "Sentries, your Elders, the Abenai League." He paused. "Maybe even Lilong."

"You don't know that," she said. "You have not even spent half a moment here. Maybe think again when we get to Hoor?"

"Nobody here wants mainlanders."

"Nobody here wants mainlanders *who want to destroy us*," she said. "But you are not that."

He smiled. Cute of her to think the world was simply this way. He'd once been like this too. He ached to tell her now that their Diwi had chosen him, a foreigner, but another piece of this very same stone had *also* chosen someone else—the vicious emperor who was the very reason he was here in the first place. But that would be too complex for her young mind, he thought, so he just nodded.

"Abenai does not choose who stays or who goes." She picked up a rock and tossed it over the sloping edge, into the sea bed below. It didn't tumble far before getting caught in the sand. "The Great Forces do."

Danso gazed at the girl for a moment, then chuckled. "Okay."

She frowned, and in that moment, she did not look like twenty-two seasons anymore. He could see all of Lilong in her mannerisms: perceptive, quick to challenge, slow to retreat.

"You mock our belief?" she asked.

"No, no, not at all. I just—"

"Don't believe them?"

He shrugged. "I am not one of you. You can understand that I don't understand?"

"Why? Sister Lilong says you are a storyteller of a kind."

"I am."

"Storytellers always understand," said Lumusi. "We see the stories in everything, and in telling them, we learn to understand even if we do not believe. That is what my daa says."

"You are a storyteller?"

She shook her head. "But I want to be. I will join the League of Chroniclers once I become of age."

"You can tell me?" said Danso. "A story?" He pulled out his codex and a stylus.

Lumusi smiled a wry smile, then told him the tale of the Crab-God and the Gourd of Wisdom.

· ⋄ ··· ··· ⋄ ·

After Lumusi's tale was done, and Danso had written everything he needed, he gazed out to the waters. The sounds of the tide returning to shore had begun.

"Now you see?" asked Lumusi.

He couldn't say for sure that he did *see*. But he understood. He understood that there were things in this world bigger than them all, forces and connections too incomprehensible to contend with. Ibor—how it became, where it was found, how it worked—this was one of such things.

"You know the tale of Risisi?" he asked, going out on a limb.

Lumusi frowned. "The playground song?"

Danso shrugged. "That is all it is, yes?"

There was a twinkle in her eye as she regarded him, as if she was onto his plan.

"I told you, I believe things," she said. "Maybe even things sister Lilong does not believe."

"So you believe your daa and brother are out there trying to get to this mythical city of ibor?"

"My daa says, *Myths are simply truths woven with lies to hide their verity*," she said. "I don't know if a city of ibor is true or not. But I believe my daa is trying to do something good."

This warmed his heart. If she believed it, then yes, he, too, was doing the right thing, regardless of the twisty, backyard manner in which he was going about achieving it.

"Do you think the islands will ever let you leave?" he asked. "Do you ever want to leave—like your sister and your daa and the scouts?"

She thought about it and shrugged. "I don't know yet. I know I don't have to leave to tell my stories. The stories are enough for now. Maybe when they stop being enough, I will want to leave."

A bundle of contradictions, wasn't she? This turned over the last thing she'd just said, reminded him that his stories, whether he liked it or not, were just as powerful all on their own. A sliver of doubt crept into him then. Maybe he didn't need to go to Risisi after all. The tracts had not worked in Chabo, but maybe they would work if they came from somewhere else, from someone else?

But Lumusi believed in her daa, and Danso wanted to tell her, *Yes, I believe him too, and I believe in what he's doing. I want to achieve the same dream he has, but your sister will not let me.* But that would be putting too much on her young shoulders. She didn't deserve that.

"Lu," a voice called behind them. They turned around, and Kyauta stood there.

Now *that* gaze, Danso found familiar. It was the same one he got in Bassa, the one that screamed *outsider* without words. Kyauta's shoulders hung square and locked. He was but a boy, only a few seasons older than Lumusi, but looked like someone who had hardened too fast, been shuffled toward manhood too soon.

"Maa wants you," he said in Island Common. He kept his eyes on his sister, refusing to even acknowledge Danso's presence. But in High Bassai, clearly directed at Danso, he said: "Sister Lilong is back. She has news."

"What does maa want me for?" asked Lumusi.

"Why not go and find out?" Kyauta hissed.

Lumusi reluctantly gathered herself, dusted off her clothing, and was about to leave when Danso called to her. He gathered up the sheaf of papers that made up his codex and handed it over.

"Fill it with all the good stories you know," he said. "I don't know what will happen to us on this island, but I want to know this is in good hands." He paused. "And if anything happens, you have my permission to share it as far and wide as you can."

"Are you sure?" She beamed, but Danso could also see she looked concerned.

"It's okay," he said. "I think I've found a better way to make change." He chuckled. "Plus, do you know I can remember everything I read? Same with what I write."

Lumusi smiled. "Sister Lilong has always known good people. Maybe now you just need to believe, too, that you are good."

The only sounds after she left were those that marked the final return of tide—waves and wind that snatched words, and the birds that called after them. In the time between, Kyauta stared at Danso with nothing but the sounds of the sea between them.

"She is mistaken." A whisper, but firm, the anger behind it hard and flat. Kyauta said the words in High Bassai because, Danso believed, he wanted him to know.

"She is mistaken," Kyauta repeated, "because you are no good. You are just a mistake."

53

Kangala

The Forest of the Mist
First Mooncycle, 1–2

OROE WAS LOST IN the Forest of the Mist through the night and for the most part of the next day. There were times when Kangala feared the worst: his most formidable son killed by the emperor, or her quite able Second. Or worse: that Oroe had killed her, and that they would have to return to Chugoko, by way of the Weary Sojourner, without the emperor as leverage.

As the day wore on and he sat alone at the treeline, surrounded by the stink of blood and bodies and rotting parts, he began to wonder what would come next. How was he to be welcomed in the emperor's absence? What satisfactory tale could he tell to her devotees? What would be their response?

There was more killing to be done, he decided. Not because he wanted to, but because it simply had to happen. Which was why he needed Oroe to return. Because he, too, knew that his power only came from something else, not from a thing he himself possessed. His children, his well-pumping secrets, his wealth—these were all things that could be taken, like he had taken the emperor's.

It was a tight corner he was stuck in, but Kangala was very good at shaking out of tight corners. He *was* going to win, eventually. But he needed everything at his disposal.

After emptying the royal travelwagon of its resources, he set fire to it.

The flames blazed high into the evening, casting light over the blood on his clothes. He wrapped a blanket around himself, sat beside the fire for warmth, and waited in the smoke.

·—◇—····————————····——◇·

It was night when Oroe did indeed emerge from the Forest of the Mist, without the emperor or her Second in tow. Instead, they had lost at least one champion to the forest. Not to attacks of any sort, but simply because he had lost his way. The rest of them had to string their garments together and form a train in order not to get lost, a situation that made it very difficult to move adequately through the thick forest, delaying their return. Only after hours of wandering aimlessly in the general direction in which they'd entered did they finally spot the treeline ahead of them.

Once they had caught up, Kangala ordered the champions to gather the bodies—the Ninki Nanka's included—and add them to the great fire. He stood by the smouldering flames with his son, watching them rise into the night sky, the smells of blood and burnt meat washing over them.

"What now?" asked Oroe.

Kangala pinched his teeth with a stick until his gums hurt and bled. He was a man of opportunity. Impossible situations were his cocoyam and oil.

"My guess is you did not find the land bridge?" he asked.

Oroe shook his head. "Who knows if it even exists?"

"You think they travelled all this way for a lie?"

Oroe shrugged noncommittally. "From the notices, I can't say these fugitives are known for rational pursuits. Much like the emperor herself."

"Maybe," said Kangala. He pointed to the burning royal travelwagon. "What do you see, when you look at that?"

Oroe frowned, confused.

"Empty," said Kangala. "An empty travelwagon, an empty crown, an empty throne. And where there is emptiness, there is opportunity."

Oroe gasped. "You want to sit on the elephant throne?"

He had thought about it carefully in the time since. He was a Sahelian, and therefore not a man that would be accepted as emperor of Bassa. But he did not need that acceptance.

"Not quite," said Kangala. "We cannot find this island or its buried city of power. Not on our own and without direction. So we find the next best thing: an empty throne. Then we make sure no one sits on it, even if we don't plan to."

All Kangala wanted was the exact thing he wanted before leaving the Sahel: freedom to build his ventures, expand and trade without oversight or intrusion. Where and how he did it—mainland, desertlands, the Lake Vezha—it did not matter. All that mattered was that he got what he wanted.

"What do we tell them happened to their emperor, when we return?" Oroe asked.

Kangala swung his arm around. "Lost in the Forest of the Mist? Drowned after slipping at the land bridge? Attacked by strange people wielding strange powers? Attacked by a pack of vicious beasts? Take your pick."

"No one will believe any of that."

"The Bassai will not, yes," he said. "But they are not who we have to convince."

He had thought deeply, since, about why the Red Emperor had accepted his proposal. Even he had expected it to be thrown out, and the Second, Igan, had rightfully thought the same. Only when he realised the emperor had not selected a single desertlander to follow on the trip did he realise why: because they hated her, and she knew it.

She did not trust them, and rightfully so, because they did not trust her either. All Kangala needed was a seed to plant in that already fertile soil. He was from the same side of the border as them, after all. He was no more foreign to them than the emperor was.

"What about those stationed at the Weary Sojourner?" Oroe asked. "How do we go past them?"

Kangala shrugged. "If we have to raze the Weary Sojourner to the ground again, so be it. Otherwise, we can simply avoid its path."

"And when we get to Chugoko?"

"An army," said Kangala. "Isn't that what they already think us? Perhaps it is time to live up to that expectation."

"And fight who?"

"Anyone who stands in our way. Or—" Kangala held a finger in the air. "Maybe we do not need to fight at all. At least not in the beginning. Maybe what we must do is weed the farm, purge it of the binders that prevent everything else from thriving. Then, we may open the eyes of those who wish to see, who will follow us into conquest." He jammed a fist into his palm. "And *then*—we conquer."

His son sighed. "I don't know. This sounds...risky."

Kangala clamped a hand on his son's shoulder. "This is the path we have been gifted, Oroe, and at its end is an opportunity for gain. If we wish to survive this harsh existence, then we do what we must: We make way through the Soke Pass, through the Great Dome, and into the mainland and the riches it contains, and take what we need for our future generations to flourish."

Oroe nodded, then left to prepare the party for the return journey.

Kangala leaned back and looked at the sky. It was a post-mooncrossing night, and the stars were invisible, obscured by the overwhelming shine of the combined moons.

A good story is what I need, he thought. *Ngipa can help with that.* Then, he would do what he did best: put on a good performance.

54

Lilong

Namge
First Mooncycle, 2, dawn

LILONG GATHERED EVERYONE AND broke the news slowly: She was no longer waiting for Jaoudou and Issouf to return. She was going to Ofen *now.* And she wanted them to decide if they were going to come along.

First, she would need a dhow, which Turay had grudgingly volunteered to steal from his daa. He would captain it, navigate, wield the wind, and help them remain invisible so they could not be spotted when they passed by each island. And though Oke was no Grey Iborworker, if she decided to come, she could help gentle the violent waters and make them easier to cross—under Turay's guidance, of course. And Danso…

To Lilong, his coming wasn't really an option. First, she had sworn Turay to secrecy—they would tell neither Danso nor Oke about the emperor they had just imprisoned below ground. Not until they'd returned from Ofen. But Lilong knew that leaving Danso here would run the risk of him finding this out. And seeing as the Diwi was currently being stored in her house—though hidden away by Ma Guosa as soon as Turay handed it over—it was too risky to have Danso there. Who knew what he would do if he laid his hands on it? Especially if he found out about Esheme's presence?

No, he was coming with. He had to be where she could see him.

Oke, at first perplexed, took little time in coming around and accepting the invitation. Danso was slower to this, suspicious that things had changed so swiftly only after Lilong and Turay had gone off somewhere alone. He grudgingly accepted.

Ma Guosa, in typical fashion, did not oppose, but did not give her blessing either. She was glad, however, to take Thema in Oke's absence. Her biggest concern, it seemed, was that if they did not return, Thema would have to grow up without a maa. She made sure not to say this in front of Oke.

Lumusi, nose buried in Danso's codex, did not even acknowledge the news. Kyauta, on the other hand, did not say much during the announcement, but once the family had dispersed, he came up to Lilong, and in a surprising move, held her tight. His arms were skinny against her midriff, and his breath came in short gasps.

"Thank you for going to help them," he said. "And thank your friends too."

He was about to leave when Lilong asked: "Did you, by chance, hear anything of their plans? Anything that may help us?"

He wrinkled his brow, thinking. "Yes. I wanted to tell you." He paused. "You know how we say *risisi* when we mean *stone*, but also when we mean *statue*? Those rocks with the faces carved into them, the ones the ancestors made?"

Lilong did indeed remember the songs. It was the reason the story never made sense to her in the first place. *A buried city of ibor named after stone statues?* she'd thought. *Really?* There were such risisi all over the islands, sculpted by ancestral hands, going back generations, many seasons before even the current Elders were born.

"That's how Issouf kept saying it, when he and daa were talking, whispering," said Kyauta. "When I heard *Ofen*, I kept wondering how the two connect. After they left, that's when I remembered." He wore an intense expression she'd learned to take seriously. "Ofen has only one risisi. The oldest statue in all of Ihinyon, and the only one on *that* island."

He was right. Lilong remembered being taught that the statue had survived all of Ofen's storms and quakes because it was carved out of the very stone that formed after the mountains erupted. Ihinyon ancestors on that island had figured out a way to carve it. It was easily the most recognisable thing about the small island, its black, polished body glinting in the sun and reflecting the sea, the only non-greenery visible from a distance.

"That's where they went," said Kyauta. "I'm sure of it."

Lilong hugged her brother.

Turay soon returned with good news: His family's dhow was still in its shed. He could cloak it and ride it out to the outer beach ("Best to go around the far side of the island, avoid the packed Hoor beach," he'd said). All he needed was a Grey Iborworker to help get it into the water.

"Take Oke," said Lilong. "I trust her." Only after he'd left did she realise how flawed that statement was. She was, after all, planning to betray the woman.

· ◦ ····——————···· ◦ ·

Turay's dhow was a thing of beauty. A lightly sailed vessel built from felled iroko, the most gigantic and scarcest tree this side of the island. Two huge triangular sailcloths, still wrapped, cast a long shadow on the beach. Lilong had seen fine vessels in her time, but she had never seen this before. There was no way Turay's daa would ever forgive him taking this to Ofen under a storm warning. It made her heart even warmer, the risk he was taking on her behalf.

Together, he and Oke lowered the dhow from its carrier into the waterline. Turay helped them onto the dhow, then drove the carrier and its team of ten mixed animals—kwaga, ox, ass—back to the settlement, to tuck it into safety. On deck, the dhow bobbed, even though it had not yet hit full water.

Lilong took off her footwear to feel the wood underneath her feet. She had never sailed much—never liked sailing, in fact. Too windy for her liking, the way the White Iborworkers pushed into the sails while controlling the gusts around the vessel. She preferred those who used oars. Slower, much more manageable.

There did not seem to be oars here, though. A crossbar in the middle held the sails, extending to the aft and secured to the deck. Sandsacks, scattered around, were for balancing. Danso and Oke went around, observing everything, while Lilong kept watch for Turay's return. When he arrived, she asked him about oars.

"Full iborworking on this one," he said. "If we must make it to and fro before storm hits, we need something much faster than oars."

Under Turay's guidance, Oke's eyes flashed grey, and water pulled onto the beach, gently shepherding the dhow into the sea. Once the bottom of the boat had left the sand, a white glaze settled over Turay's eyes. Lilong felt a cocoon of light surround her and the whole boat, an ethereal mix of fog and light and wind. Then Turay turned his attention to the sails, unknotting the ropes that held them down. The sails rose free, majestic, billowing, trapping the wind. The dhow rocked to its movements.

"Brace," said Turay, and Commanded a blast into the sails.

The dhow shot forward like an arrow.

Lilong

The Neverending Sea
First Mooncycle, 2–3

CIRCLING THE LONG SIDE of Namge was a surreal experience. Most of Lilong's dhow trips had happened in smaller dhows on the channel crossing to Hoor. The open Neverending Sea had always been a distant thing she could see from the beach or from the edge of her daa's compound. Now, the Great Waters opened before them, spreading in every direction, wrapped over the horizon, truly never-ending.

Storm warning signs persisted, clearer now that they were on the waters. With night approaching, the two moons peeked just over the horizon, but were obscured by the towering clouds spread out like cotton. Lilong was no cloud reader, but the angry, menacing clouds that now filled the sky worried her. The others seemed unperturbed and occupied by other things: Turay and Oke keeping the dhow steady and moving; Danso on the bow, his hands out to catch the spray, cheeks in the wind, eyes shut, taking everything into sensory memory.

The temperature had also dropped considerably, which made sense since they were headed southeast, into the northwest winds that brought storms to the seven islands. Even the wind had picked up, though Turay was doing the good work of redirecting it toward the sails, where it was useful.

Watching him work was exciting, causing Lilong's throat to dry up.

Perhaps because her lips had parted and let air rush in, as she was most occupied by the way his muscles moved as he wielded power, pushing air and light around. Moonlight fell on his features and gave them each outlines, spelled them out for whoever was looking: broad shoulders, sharp jawline, soft eyes. Lilong gulped, licked her lips.

The soft eyes turned and saw her watching. Turay winked, smiled. Lilong swivelled, facing the sea. A cat-and-mouse game with Turay sounded exciting, but she couldn't quite enjoy it now, could she? Not when she was so busy thinking about her daa and Issouf. Now that she was beyond the harry of running and hiding, and the overwhelming emotions of returning home under dubious circumstances, doubt had begun to flood her mind. Was it wise, this trip? Were her daa and Issouf still there? Were they even still alive?

Calm yourself, Lilong. Seated cross-legged near the stern, she took deep breaths, unsure what she needed more calming from—Turay or her daa and Issouf.

Not long after they hit the open waters, they come upon the twin islands—Edana and Ufua. Though Turay explained that there was no need to hide—he had sufficient ibor on him to obscure the whole dhow to and fro—there was so much movement on the shore that Lilong only felt safe when she ducked behind the hull board. She even suggested they all go below deck, but that would mean Turay and Oke being unable to pilot the dhow, so they stayed.

They shot past the twin islands quickly, as both were much smaller than Namge. Lilong regretted not being able to show Danso the green fields and rice plantations she had so eloquently described for him to write in his codex. Perhaps another time.

Not long after, in quick succession, they came upon the next set of near-twin islands: Ololo and Sibu-Sibu.

Turay slowed the dhow down to an easy float, and all stood on the board side to watch the towering mountains. It was noticeably colder here, though Lilong could not tell if it was due to the forth-coming storm or the coming of the cold season. From here, they could see the white tips of the mountains, where water had begun to freeze and solidify. No wonder the inhabitants left the mountains and moved into the valleys in the cold season—it had to be furiously cold up there.

"We learned about those at the university," Danso said, pointing to the frozen mountaintops. "The jalis say we used to have those on the tips of the Soke mountains too, but it stopped hundreds of seasons ago. They think that's when the weather began to turn."

Though each didn't say it, they were looking for signs of life and movement like they'd seen at Edana and Ufua, but luckily, there was none to be seen here. Not from this distance.

"Is that why they're all yellow, its inhabitants?" Danso asked. "Because they never, like, come out into the sunlight?"

"Ha, no, no," said Turay, chuckling. "Us being yellow has nothing to do with anything, and does not need a reason—just like you don't need a reason to be . . ." He mulled over the word, then opted for "You."

Danso nodded, pensive. "The caverns—can we see them from here?"

"Sadly not," said Turay. "This whole side is blocked by mountains—you need to be on the southwest side for that. But you know the caverns are not natural, right? They carve homes into the mountains to keep cool in the hot season, and likewise heat up in the colder season."

Danso's expression was one of captivation. Turay chuckled. "I know it must be surprising, but everything we do, no matter how strange it seems to you, is simply to survive. Just like everyone else."

Night fell completely, but thanks to Turay's work, they could see their path just as well, even while being shrouded in darkness. Other than the few times Turay and Oke stopped to rest—and more importantly, replenish via food (packed by Ma Guosa) and water—the dhow continued to shoot forward at great speed. Lilong calculated they would be at the tiny island by dawn.

Signs of the storm continued to persist throughout the night. Lightning flashed in the distance. The winds escalated, whistling through the sail-cloth, creaking the wood. Lilong could only manage fitful sleep, so she took most of the night watch, to give Oke and Turay some time to rest after their work. With Turay's light gone, the night was pitch dark, both moons nowhere to be seen. Eventually, Lilong herself drifted off.

The sharp smell of petrichor woke her up just as the sun prepared to peek over the horizon. As she rose and looked over the bow, the shape of land came into view.

"We're here," she announced.

Everyone else rose, and they began preparations to moor the vessel. The lightning from the night before was gone, but thunder had replaced it, rumbling overhead as Turay and Oke worked to sidle the dhow onto the nonexistent beach. Instead, all they met was a bay with a thick clump of forest close to the water. Finding a place to moor the dhow seemed impossible. Oke pushed the vessel around the bay with short twists of water, while Turay searched for a safe spot.

That was how they came upon the wreck.

Lilong did not recognise the dhow at first. Perhaps because it was fool-hardy to attempt to moor a vessel like that—it had been planted head first into the bay. But there was little sand to cushion it, so instead it had rushed into rocks and roots. Now it lay there, damaged bow stuck, stern bashed violently by the water. This dhow was not going anywhere anytime soon.

"It's daa's," she said to no one in particular, over the increasing roar of thunder.

Danso, Turay, and Oke crowded around her. It was his dhow, all right: the shape of the keel, the pattern of the beam assembly, the cut of the timber sections—she would recognise those anywhere, even though the sailcloths looked new.

"They're here," she announced.

Turay and Oke set about mooring the dhow in the same spot as the wreck, though doing it better—this was a good mooring spot, still. Lilong was unsure if she should be proud for being right, or worried if her daa and brother were still alive. *Surely daa knows how to moor a dhow?* If not him, then Issouf at least. But Jaoudou was old—*going on a hundred and how many seasons now?*—and his body had recently taken damage. Perhaps he had run out of ibor. Perhaps ibor had run him out.

The dhow was moored. They gathered everything they needed—weapons, food, water—and disembarked from the vessel.

As soon as their feet touched the sand, the first patter of raindrops began.

◦——————◦

Ofen was an island of green. Trees tall and short, shrubs large and small, grass welcoming and cruel—the island had it all. Together, they did not quite constitute a forest, but neither did they constitute brushes or grassland—just clump after clump of overgrowth that obscured vision wherever Lilong and her group turned. Rain, drumming on the broad leaves, drenched them quickly and did not help their cause. Cover was impossible, and so was open land of any sort. These conditions combined to delay Lilong finding any opening in the overgrowth that allowed for long-range sight, but soon she found one, and could finally spot the risisi they were looking for.

Even from this distance, the risisi shone in the rain, tall and proud. The statue was mostly head—elongated crown, small eyes, stretched nose, wide lips. Large enough to hold up to ten people at once, if there truly was a way to enter the statue. A good refuge from this storm, too, and any other kind of danger.

Once they set their new direction, they cut through the vegetation quicker than before. Not long after, they came upon the first sighting of open wetland. They waded through it, Lilong watching out for snakes and other creeping predators. Luckily for them, only frogs croaked back, aggrieved at their abodes being disturbed.

They did not have to upset the fauna much longer, as soon, they stood before the risisi. It towered above them—almost as tall as the dhow was when beached. They walked around it, seeking an entryway. Nothing.

Thunder grumbled overhead.

"Great," said Turay, frustrated, wiping rain from his eyes. "We sail all the way over here, and the thing that defeats us is a fucking door."

Lilong saw Danso with his head tilted, pondering, as rain dripped into his hair and face. She went up to him.

"Find anything?"

"No," he said, but squatted, hand on the black stone on the ground. "Do you feel that?"

Lilong squatted and did the same. A low thrum, the stone underneath trembling.

"Remember when we climbed into the Dead Mines?" he said. "It felt like this—like open space."

"There's something down there," Lilong said, then rose and announced to the group over the wind and rain: "Look for an opening—any opening! Not a door, but anything like a crawl space."

They circled the statue again. Soon, there was a shout from Oke. They ran to her.

The space she had found was not easily visible, but thanks to her powers of grey, she had managed to use the water to wash away a heap of mud, and suddenly there it was: a door. Or, not really a door—an opening, like a sinkhole shut off with stone, which Lilong quickly set aside with the help of her blade. A dark, long tunnel stared back at them. Warm air rushed out.

Turay went in first, pulling light from outside alongside him. Lilong went next, and Danso after. Oke came in last.

The tunnel went forward, then dove sharply, inclined at an angle sufficient for walking, but only if one held on to the walls. Turay lit the way. It was stone all the way through: top, bottom, and walls. Not a trace of sand or any kind of growth.

As they went forward, Lilong thought she smelled smoke. Then light. Without thinking, she jumped forward, past Turay.

"Daa?" she called, running. "Issouf? Daa?"

"Lilong, wait." Turay ran after her.

"Issouf! Daa!"

The darkness stretched forward, never-ending, but Lilong did not need light. She knew what she *felt. Almost there.*

"Issouf! Daa!"

Silence. Nothing but Turay's feet behind her.

Then, suddenly, as if from nothing, a figure appeared, weapon forward: a blade, catching the light.

"Who's there?" the figure said in a fear-stricken voice. "Show yourself."

Lilong stopped, her ibor responding, asking her to Draw, to pull the blade, defend herself. But Lilong held back, pushed down the desire, and instead, said: "Issouf?"

Turay came up behind her, the yellow of the figure's face lighting up with his approach. But Lilong did not need it to know who stood before her.

"Sister?" said Issouf, and lowered his weapon.

56

Lilong

PLEASANTRIES WERE SHORT-LIVED, RELEGATED to an embrace and rapid-fire questions from Issouf about how they got here, how they had known where to find them, did they know a storm was coming? Lilong's only answer was the same one each time: *Where is he?*

Issouf led the group down the tunnel, toward the light Lilong now knew she had truly seen. Her brother looked spent, eyes bloodshot, on edge. He kept glancing over his shoulder at the others—Danso, Oke, Turay—as if they were going to jump and attack him the next moment. Turay, who it turned out had formed a good relationship with Issouf after Lilong had left, managed to calm him down.

They came to the end of the tunnel and into a round, open space with light.

Elder Warrior Jaoudou lay in a swaddle of wrappers, sweating like an infant, shivering despite the incredible warmth of the space. Frail, dehydrated, hair dry and frizzy, yellow skin stretched over his collarbones like a tent in the desert. He breathed in long drags, each inhale a creak, each exhale a whistle, like a drained cow in the field.

Lilong fell to her knees beside Jaoudou, the warrior once renowned in Namge, hailing from a long line of equally fierce Abenai warriors—there he was, now reduced to nothing. Between old age, the attack at the

Weary Sojourner, and the ibor he must have expended to make his way here, Lilong could not tell which had eaten at him the most. Whatever the combination, it had all colluded to ensure he would not be breathing much longer.

"Daa," she found herself saying. The tears that had not left her eyes all this time began to roll down her cheeks. She forgot everything—the lies, the questions, the blame. All she wanted, in this moment, was for him to be *alive*.

His eyes, glazed, did not recognise her at first. Then he squinted, opened his mouth, and let out a raspy breath.

"Li-long?"

"Daa," she said. "I came back. I promised, and I came back."

"Lilong."

"I'm here, daa," she said. "I'm here."

The sounds of thunder outside and overhead continued to boom, even this far underground. Lilong sat next to her daa, dripping over him, holding on to his bony fingers. The others, unsure of what next to do, sat around and waited.

"You should never have left," said Issouf, out of nowhere.

"Issouf," Turay chided. They spoke Island Common, so the others did not understand.

"No!" Issouf rose, his face twisting in anguish. "You should never have left and put us in this situation. Now look at him—*look at him*!"

"You should not have brought him here," said Lilong quietly. "You of all people know this—you should have stayed and protected him from the league."

"Like you did?"

"You don't have to make the same mistakes I did, Issouf." Lilong rubbed the ashy yellow skin on the back of her daa's hand. "They need you. *He* needs you."

"And I did what he asked me to." Her brother's cheeks were wet. "I helped him see his dream through—repaired the dhow, helped him sail here. It's not my fault the dhow wrecked—I'm not an Iborworker, I've never sailed before!"

"No one is blaming you," said Turay.

"But it's *my* fault we're here," Issouf pressed. "I brought him here—I brought *you* here. And now we're all going to die."

"We're not going to die," said Lilong. "We'll ride out the storm here, then we'll go home on our own dhow."

Issouf was shaking his head. "He's too far gone. Our food's been finished for days. We can't go out to hunt or anything, and the storm is never going to end unless we leave here."

Lilong's ears pricked. "Are you talking about…the plagues?"

"Li-long."

Jaoudou's arm reached out for her now, to her face, touching her cheek. She leaned closer to catch the words escaping his lips.

"Come," he was saying. "Come." His other arm pointed toward Issouf.

"He wants us," Lilong said to her brother. Issouf drew forward and knelt on the opposite side of their daa.

Jaoudou, weak as he was, reached forward and took her hand in his, then Issouf's with his other hand. He put them together.

"Forgive me," he said.

"We do, daa," said Issouf, glancing at Lilong, as if to say *Don't we?*

Jaoudou was reaching over and tapping something—a sack by his side. Issouf gave it to him. He pulled out something rolled up and unwound it. A message, scribbled on cloth.

Forgive me, it read. *For bringing you into this dangerous journey, one that will cost you more than you deserve. Forgive me for sacrificing your childhood, your dreams, your desires. Forgive me for keeping secrets, for not trusting you enough. All I ever wanted was a better world for everyone. But along the way, I forgot that everyone includes you.*

No more secrets. No more sacrifices you do not ask for. So, take this, but do with it what you will. I will not impress on you anything, except one thing: Protect home, if you can. It is all we have.

Lilong flipped the cloth. On the other side was a hastily hand-drawn map.

"Risisi," Lilong whispered.

It was what the city might have looked like in its heyday. There were built areas, roads, rivers, forests, the coast. Nothing was named. Instead, there were simply three markings: a circle, a route, and certain spots cross-marked. Nothing about an entrance, though, or where to find the city itself.

"Protect," Jaoudou was saying, tightening his grip on his children's hands.

Lilong put away the cloth and turned to him. "We will never leave your side," she said, offering Issouf a softer glance. "We will get you home."

"Protect *home*," said Jaoudou, adamant.

The siblings glanced at one another.

"We are doing everything we can, daa," said Issouf. "I will do everything in my power to enter Risisi. I will complete your quest. I promise."

Jaoudou was still shaking his head. *"Pro-tect—home."*

His words grew slower, weaker, repetitive. The two leaned closer. But Jaoudou said no more. Lilong felt a long rush of warm air on her cheek, a finality to its egress. Then everything went cold.

. ·⋄·⋯————⋯·⋄· .

Lilong and Issouf cried—first apart, then together. Issouf shook in her arms, head in her shoulder, unable to look at their daa lying there. Lilong watched Jaoudou's face, wishing he would somehow open his eyes and everything would be different. But the more she looked, the more she saw that he was finally at peace, that he had finally found rest.

They wrapped the body in his own wrappers and covered him in the darkest part of the cavern, where they would not need to look upon him anymore. Once the storm died—if it did—they would take him back to Namge and send him off with an honourable funeral.

Turay, Danso, and Oke took time to offer their condolences with silent pats, arms encircling them in embrace. Afterward, all sat in silence, nothing between them but the continuous rumble of thunder in the distance, the howling of the wind through the trees, and the muffled drumming of rain on the rock above.

Lilong finally opened up the map again, staring at the hasty drawing, the incomprehensibility of it all. *This is it?* she kept thinking. After everything—it all boiled down to *this*?

"Tell me what happened," Lilong said softly, to Issouf. "Tell me everything."

He told her of how, upon his recovery, Jaoudou had asked for Lilong. Once it became clear she was gone in pursuit of the Diwi, he became despondent. But not for long. Soon, his mind was taken up by something else—a voyage south, to Ofen. He turned his attention to Issouf, convinced him that he had found the source of ibor, conscripted him into his plans to escape here and harvest as much ibor as they could before it was all lost.

"*Source?*" asked Turay, looking to Lilong. "Your story did not say this is the *source*."

"What story?" asked Issouf.

Lilong told him Oke's tale. Issouf shrank, feeling the same betrayal Lilong did of this secret being kept from him. But when she got to the plagues, his eyes widened.

"Oh no," he said, face going pallid.

"What is it?"

He gazed at them all. "We did it. We started the plagues."

· ◦ ⋯ꞏꞏꞏ ⋯ ◦ ·

Jaoudou did not tell Issouf about the plagues. But Issouf had begun to sense something was wrong when, the moment they set foot on the dhow, the storm clouds began to gather.

Despite his failing health, Jaoudou had done most of the sailing, helping keep their course by curtailing the violent sea. This sapped his energy so much that, upon arrival at Ofen, he couldn't even bring the dhow to a rest, crashing it into the rocks instead. Issouf had dragged him onto the island, following his directions until they arrived at this risisi, this statue.

That was when he saw the first beast: a massive sea monster—one-eyed, wet-furred, a large hole for a mouth—heading straight for the rocks. As he stood there, at the entrance, he heard more of them—large, small, chittering, roaring, swimming, bounding, leaping—all headed here, as if seeking something. He knew he had to get Jaoudou safe, so he crawled into the tunnel, found the cavern at its end, and tended to his daa there.

But Jaoudou wasn't in good shape, and the storm had begun to intensify. Issouf had been too scared to go out, for fear of the beasts. He was unable to leave too—he had no ibor, no powers, no dhow. So he put his best efforts into nursing Jaoudou, hoping that once he recovered, and the storm cleared, his daa could use his powers to steer their patched dhow back home.

But Jaoudou never got better. He knew he was dying. So, he told Issouf the truth: He knew why the beasts would be here. The moment the storm winds began, the air currents carried with them the stirrings of ibor. And the beasts, no matter where they were located in Oon—they rose and followed the scent, leading them here.

Which was why he then gave Issouf one last thing: directions to the buried city.

·◇·⋯——⋯·◇·

"You found it already?" Lilong asked.

Issouf nodded.

"Where?"

"Here."

"On the island?"

"No, *here*." Issouf gestured with his chin. "We're sitting on it."

Turay translated to High Bassai for Oke and Danso. The energy in the cavern changed, became galvanized.

"Are you *sure*?" Danso whispered.

"It is there," Issouf said, his High Bassai halting. "I show you, but we not enter."

"Why?"

"You will see," he said, then grabbed a torch and beckoned to them to follow.

They went back into the tunnel, but this time, took a detour that went even farther downward. So far down that they had to descend with their hands. After a series of such downward climbs, Issouf stopped, then knocked on what seemed like a wall.

"There," he announced.

Lilong felt the wall. It *thrummed*, like a cat enjoying itself. Perhaps it was just the vibrations of the storm raging out there. But this felt like something else—like something inside there was *alive*.

"Behind there is where the beasts go," said Issouf. "*That* is Risisi."

Lilong stared at the stone door, trepidation suddenly washing over her. She had thought it would simply be easy to come here, witness the city, then walk away and wait for it to destroy itself via the plagues, like the tale said it would. Now, she realised that if she wanted it destroyed, she might have to use her own hands to do so. And as she stood here, she realised she did not want to do that at all.

Protect home, her daa had said. No longer angry, her mind was clear, and she knew that destroying this place would not only be more impossible with so many beasts standing guard, but it would be doing the opposite of protecting home. It would be leaving home with nothing to protect itself with.

"Is it, truly?" Lilong asked Issouf. "The source of ibor?"

Issouf shrugged, then pointed to the marked circle on the map. "Here—he said this is a whirlpond. According to him, ibor enters here, goes into the Neverending Sea, appears on the coast."

Turay's eyes widened. "*That* is how we get ibor?"

He nodded. "And these—" He pointed to the cross-marks. "Enclaves, where the dangerous beasts are." His finger traced the marked route. "He said if I take this route, it leads to a deposit we can retrieve ibor from without alerting the beasts."

Oke had been right—the Plague of Beasts and Plague of Wind and Water had indeed been triggered by her daa and brother's journey here. They, too, had arrived, causing the storm to intensify, to draw nearer. Soon, the Plague of Fire and Dirt would follow.

All of Risisi could be buried and lost if they stayed.

It dawned on her, now: This was what her daa had meant by *before all is lost*. He knew that someday, somehow, someone would take this tale seriously and make their way here, trigger these plagues. So he wanted to come here before anyone did, retrieve as much ibor as he could. But he knew he could no longer take whatever he collected to the league, or trust them to make the right choices with it, just as Lilong could not trust them now, not after all their secrets and lies.

This was why he had told Oke the story, why he had brought Issouf along, why he was trusting her now. *This* was his mission. And maybe it wasn't a bad mission after all.

Lilong stared at the map, then at her comrades.

"Back to the cavern," she said. "I have a confession to make."

57

Lilong

Risisi
First Mooncycle, same day

"I NEVER WANTED TO save Risisi," she said. "I wanted to destroy it."

They were on their way back up, in the darkness of the tunnel, headed for the lit cavern ahead.

Turay's mouth was agape. "You *what?*"

"It wasn't—" She turned to Turay. "I swear to you, I did not deceive you to make you come along. I just . . . I just thought it would be better to rid Ihinyon of this burden. I just thought that—"

"No one should have this much power," Oke completed.

"Yes." Lilong eyed Danso. He refused to look at her. She turned to Oke instead.

"I'm sorry. I didn't want to lie to any of you."

Oke nodded slowly and sighed, waving a hand. "We have all sacrificed much to be here. Not a single one of us standing here does not want salvation—for ourselves, for our people, for all of Oon—from the hands of Bassa. It is human nature, I guess, that we all have different ways of thinking about that solution." She paused to hold Lilong's eyes. "The most important thing is not what intentions you came here with. It's what you intend to do now."

Lilong looked to her brother. "Issouf, daa trusted you enough to bring you here. He wanted you to find this city. What would you say he wanted you to do when you found it?"

Issouf bit his lip, shook his head. "I don't know. But I would not have destroyed it, even if I could. And I don't think he would have wanted me to."

Lilong nodded. "Then I will honour our daa's intentions."

She inhaled deeply with relief, glad to have finally made that proclamation. Perhaps they truly needed to protect themselves—the seven islands, for a start, then perhaps the rest of the continent beyond it. This, she understood now, was what their daa really wanted. To get here first and ensure that. She had done that first part. Now to complete it.

Lilong turned to Oke. "Our daa trusted you more than he trusted the league. And when he couldn't give you what he wanted, he settled for me, then for Issouf. But he wanted it all for us—to protect *us*." She nodded at Oke, at Turay, at Issouf. "So, you are right. We finish what he started."

"Well, too late, is it not?" said Turay. "The plagues are already happening."

"Maybe there is more than one way to finish it," said Lilong. She held out one hand. "Perhaps we do as you wanted, Oke. We go in, collect as much ibor as we wish, sail off to the desertlands or mainland, distribute it among worthy champions, ensure we never have one power too big to conquer anymore." She held up another hand. "Or we leave? Turn around and don't return?"

"And then what will happen?" asked Oke. "You think the plagues will...reverse?"

"Maybe, maybe not," said Lilong. "No way is guaranteed. But if you are willing to try, so am I."

"And if it doesn't work?" asked Issouf. "Then the plagues arrive anyway, and *then* we're left with nothing—not even a source of ibor anymore. Even *we* will be unable to protect ourselves from the mainland. If we go in now, at least we return home with something."

They had reached the light of the cavern. Lilong wanted to tell Issouf that the mainland was already here, and that the emperor of Bassa was the least of their problems, but she had not yet divulged that information to Danso and Oke.

This choice, however, was indeed a tough one to make. But she was done making decisions for others. She did not want to end up like her daa, regretting pulling others into her own sacrifices.

"We put it to a vote," she said, finally. "All in favour of leaving." She raised a hand. Turay, beside her, reluctantly raised his, casting her a glance that said, *We will talk about this later, but for now, I support you.* She smiled her thanks at him, grateful.

Oke, hand partially up, paused midway, looking around.

"Is that a vote or nay, Oke?"

The Bassai woman turned back to them, frowning. "Where's Danso?"

The door to Risisi was open.

It wasn't really a door, but something akin to a sinkhole, as if made by an earthworm burrowing underground—if said earthworm was a hundred times the size of a regular one. But the wall once there was gone, and in its place, darkness rushed out to meet them.

There was no point asking how Danso had managed to push the rock aside. The only thing that mattered was that he had slipped inside somehow. Worse, he must already have known his way around, having taken a look at the map and probably memorised it. And worst of all, if he so much as touched one single piece of ibor in there, or woke up any of those beasts meant to be gathered in there, disaster was sure to follow.

Turay led the way with his cloaked light. Issouf offered some more of Jaoudou's directions, making it clear that it was impossible to go in with a torch of any sort. Apparently, the beasts, most of whom lay there in slumber, reacted to such light. Therefore, it was a matter of Turay working his ibor so *they* could see, but the beasts could not. Which was useful, because even from this distance, there were telltale sounds of life down there—slithering, huffing, sniffing. None of it welcoming.

The way inside had something akin to crude steps carved on its face, and did not go down for very long. Soon, the suffocating dust-air of rock gave way to something cooler, sharper, much more expansive.

They stepped into a cavern, and there was a collective gasp.

The cave that opened up before them went on forever. Its black walls dripped with every kind of colour, caked with mould and moisture and seasons of abandonment.

Statues lined the walls.

At first glance, it was easy to mistake them for a burial grove of sorts. But a closer look revealed that it was indeed not, but instead the remnants of the people of a once-prosperous city, immortalized by stone-ash on the very day the city was destroyed. There they stood, captured mid-act—tilling fields, working iron, weaving cloth. Noble enterprises preserved in black stone.

Where the walls were not black and graced by ossified people, ibor stones arose, jutting out in a haphazard array like a collection of crooked teeth. All four colours—white, grey, amber, red—were represented, dispersed in a manner that would cast rainbows if light penetrated this place. And the sizes—large as boulders, small as pebbles. There was more ibor here than the seven islands had ever needed—than generations of islanders would ever need.

From here, they could see, a distance into the cave, a deep pond with a black hollow, water whirling without sound, its centre leading somewhere that was clearly not this cave. But even from this distance, Lilong spotted something else twirling in the pond that gave her worry. Large scales, iridescent, rippling underneath.

"I can't see him," Turay was saying, a hand out to hold the group back. "We should stop—we don't want to alert anything."

"Do—not—move," said Lilong. "Everyone—stand still."

Twirling scales aside, something else was flying above in the dark. Something black and near invisible, even with Turay's light. It sounded like it was hunting, preparing to pounce.

Then Lilong saw what had its attention. Danso, sidling along one of the black walls. He was making his way along the length of it, toward a nearby teeth-like deposit of ibor. His eyes were fixated on the mineral, almost entranced.

No, thought Lilong, breaking from the group.

Turay spotted Danso the same moment Lilong did, and stepped out as well, followed by Oke, Issouf bringing up the rear. They went over broken, slippery rock as silently as they could, but it wasn't long before something rolled down and splashed in the water.

The whirlpond gurgled, as if hungry. The fallen rock whirled with the motion, fast, faster, and was soon sucked into the gut of the pond.

The invisible flying beast above bellowed, a sound like a dry grinding stone. In response, a chorus of other voices followed, reverberating in the cave. It was impossible to know how many were there, camouflaged, hiding in crevices. Eyes—lights?—opened up in various corners, awoken, alert, angry.

Danso, who was now standing next to the teeth-like mound of ibor, heard the commotion and turned.

"Stop!" Lilong was saying. "What are you doing, Danso—stop!"

She felt a tickle of air on her arms, raising goose bumps. Turay, next to her, was extending the cloak to cover Danso. She could tell from the way his eyes shone white. Now it was not just invisibility, but he was using the air to cloak sound too, so they could hear each other but not be heard by anything else. Unfortunately, the ibor use was also being recognised by the beasts, agitating them even further.

"It's okay," Danso was saying, now that they could hear him. "I'm following the safe route the map said. *You* stop, you're waking them up!"

"Don't touch it!" Lilong spat. "You will destroy everything!"

"But that's what *you* wanted!" he shot back. "*You* wanted to destroy everything. And now you want us to just *leave*? Guess what, Lilong? *I* have people to protect too. *I* have dreams of making change, of bringing freedom to *my* people. So, no, you don't get to choose for me."

Lilong went cold. His rebuke shocked her so much that all the sounds around—the water, Turay and Oke and Issouf calling at her not to take another step forward—faded.

"People like me, people without power—we always die," he was saying. "Zaq, my daa, Kubra too. Even *your* daa. People like us need power like this to survive in this world, don't you understand? You don't know what it's like to be truly powerless, Lilong—you've always had power. So you make choices on our behalf and think you're doing better for us. But no. We deserve a say. We, too, want to *do something*. And this is me—*doing something*."

Lilong had never realised that Danso felt this way. A part of her felt proud, glad that he had finally found his voice. But the other part was scared for her friend, scared that his desire to change things was going to lead to his—and their—destruction.

She had to convince him.

"You are not powerless, Danso," she said. "And you are not going to die. I promise you, on my life."

"Let me guess," he said. "Because you'll always be there to protect me?"

"No. Because I have made sure your greatest enemy is dead."

Danso looked puzzled. "Who, Esheme?"

Lilong held his gaze and nodded.

His brow furrowed. "How?"

"She followed us here, Danso," said Lilong. "And they caught her, the sentries. She did not have the snake beast the blacksmith talked about. She was alone, and they captured her and we put her to rest."

Murmurs arose behind her, likely Oke registering her astonishment, but Lilong tuned that out for now.

"We won, Danso," she said. "You can stop fighting now. There's no one to fight against anymore." It was a lie, but she had to tell it. She stretched forth her hand. "Come back to us. Let us leave this city for now and find a way to save ourselves and our people without destroying everything."

Danso was shaking his head.

"We must look to the future now, Danso. But if you destroy this, there will be no future left. Or whatever future is left will be worse without ibor in it." She took a step forward, arm outstretched. "Just—step away from there, and we can plan this future together."

Danso stopped shaking his head, became silent. Then slowly, ever so slowly, he sighed and began to move forward.

Lilong breathed a sigh of relief, watching him follow the same path he had advanced by. The beasts, earlier agitated, began to quiet down.

When Danso was only a few feet away, he stopped again. His face was stricken with pain.

"You lied to me," he said in a low voice. "All of you. You knew she was here, and you lied. You deprived me of the satisfaction of seeing her fall. And now you want me to believe you." He took a step back.

"Danso," said Lilong, and behind her, Oke and Turay began to call to him too. Their calls fell on deafened ears.

"She is gone, moons be thanked," Danso continued. "But more will arise, will they not? Who will we depend on to fight for us then—you? You, in whom I can no longer place my trust?" He took another step back.

"Danso," Lilong was saying. "Please."

"It is as the Elders say: *Power concedes nothing without a demand.*" He took two steps back. "I'm sorry, Lilong, I really am—but I cannot go back to resisting with words alone. This Esheme may be gone, but for the next Esheme the world will bring forth, and the next, and the next, people like me—powerless, at the mercy of the world—must be equipped with more than just words. So I must take this chance, for all like me. Because if I do not, we perish anyway."

And with that, he turned and grabbed the nearest mound of stone-bone and pulled. A large chunk of ibor—red—came into his hands.

All the beastly cries went dead at once. Risisi dipped into sudden silence.

The cave rumbled, and the ground shook.

"What have you done, Danso?" Lilong whispered. "*What have you done?*"

A boom. The beasts screeched as one, splitting the former silence. Pieces of the cavern began to fall.

"To the opening!" Turay screamed, forgoing the cloaking Command.

They turned and ran as much as the black, slippery rock would allow. Lilong cast a glance at Danso, who was doing his best to keep up with them. He looked just as surprised by the suddenness of the cave's reaction, perhaps expecting it to have been delayed like in the stories. He'd tossed the stone-bone altogether—survival was all that mattered now.

"Come on!" Lilong slowed just enough for him to catch up. When he was within arm's reach, she grabbed him by the clothes and pulled him forward.

Then, out of nowhere, a tail, a tentacle, a limb, long and purposeful. It emerged from the whirlpond and whipped at them. Lilong, trying to avoid it, let go of Danso's clothes, and Danso, standing awkwardly, slipped.

Danso tumbled toward the pool, into the force of the bottomless pond's whirl. He screamed, scrambling to get back up, but the force was too great, pulling everything into that sucking hole.

Go, Lilong ordered her blade, and it flew, hilt-first, toward Danso.

"Grab it!" she screamed, but the tentacle was coming around again. She ducked, at the same time her comrades saw it. Turay turned around and whipped the tentacle away with a blast of air. Oke tried to Command water, but the water here moved of its own accord, as if against her Command.

Danso had caught the edge of the blade with one hand and was holding on to it for dear life, but the current pulled him away still, too strong.

Lilong strained her mind, expending the last of her ibor. She could feel it wither, get ready to dissipate. But she shoved everything she could into the blade, Commanded it further. *Pull, pull, pull!*

Another tentacle. She dodged. The second one, she didn't see, and it swept her away. She fell, hit her head, broke her concentration.

She turned to see the beast begin to crawl out of the hole. It was something between an octopus and a spider, with more eyes than either of those animals were allowed. Danso, she couldn't see anymore, now swallowed by the whirl.

Ahead, Turay and Oke and Issouf were pulling back, calling to her. *We need to go!*

But Lilong called for her blade again, finding it, finding Danso. She Commanded, and the blade stuck into a rock, pinning Danso in place, preventing him from drowning in the whirl.

"I'm coming!" she shouted.

There was another explosion, this one louder, bigger than any they had felt so far. It rocked the cavern's very foundations, so that the beasts screeched louder, and more of the cavern crashed around her.

Danso's hold began to slip, slowly.

No.

He was adamant, holding on with all he had. But he was not strong enough.

One of the tentacles grabbed Danso and pulled. The rock cracked, and the blade, nestled within, slipped. Both Danso and blade were swept into the whirlpond hollow—first in half, then in full—and then his screams were gone.

The cavern continued to rumble. Ibor fell from the walls, from the ceiling, and shattered on the ground. The beasts bellowed and growled, frantic. But all Lilong saw was Danso drowning, tentacles swinging to pull him in. She stared at the space for a long time, calling her blade, willing it to come forth with Danso attached to its other end.

But when the blade flew back to her, it was alone.

Turay was suddenly there with his light, pulling her out of the reach of the flailing tentacles, leading her toward the entrance. She let herself be guided, feet slipping over rock, until she was through the opening, back into the tunnel.

Another explosion erupted in the cavern.

She looked back. The pond was not a pond any longer, but a mouth, spitting salt water—water from the Neverending Sea—back into the cavern.

"Run!" Turay shouted.

Lilong jumped out and rolled the door back over, but it was only a temporary reprieve. Water began to gush out the sides. The rock trembled.

She looked left—toward the lit cavern, where her daa's body still lay. To the right—the opening to the outside of the rock, to safety. She froze there, undecided.

"Lilong!" It was Turay, running back into the tunnel to get her. "We have to go!"

Daa...she thought.

"Now!" Turay stretched his arm forward. "Take my hand!"

She took Turay's hand.

They crawled forward together for what seemed like eternity. Behind them, the sounds of something pushing against another intensified, and then a tumble. Water began to rush into the tunnel, flowing quickly downslope, luckily away from them but unluckily toward the opening where Jaoudou's body lay.

Rest well, daa, Lilong thought. *I'm sorry.*

The rock's opening lay ahead, Oke and Issouf already outside, urging them on. Lilong pushed her limbs to do the work. *Go on, Lilong. Go on.*

They were pulled out of the tunnel in time. As soon as her legs had cleared the entrance, water filled it to the brim, bubbling out like an underground spring.

"Hah!" said Turay, running a hand through his hair. "That was close." He chuckled nervously, then stopped. "Danso?"

Lilong bowed her head and said nothing. But something else struck her. She turned around, listening.

"There's no noise," she said. It was still raining, and there was still wind, but all was mild, like the storm had passed. *Too* mild, like the silence that had dropped in on them in Risisi right before everything caved in.

She looked up. In the skies above there was no sun, no cloud, just... nothing.

"There's no noise," she repeated, louder, getting their attention.

Then, as if in response, a great roar came, and darkness began to spread over the island.

They turned, as one, to look.

The wave was mighty—over a hundred persons tall. It was all the waves of the Neverending Sea put together, the Great Waters in final form, at her most vengeful. She rose and rose and rose, a shadow over the island. She snarled down at them, roaring in her greatest voice, tips shiny with foam, body grey and consuming. Before her came the Great Winds in warning, billowing through their hair, clothes, eyelids, announcing her intent: damage, decimation, death.

Lilong's heart sank. She turned around to face the people who stood with her and looked into their eyes, each stricken with fear, sorrow, and surrender.

"We tried everything," she said, her final words. "Let that count."

When the Great Waters descended and took them away, Lilong did not feel pain. She knew she was being swallowed, washed down the gullet of a monster more malicious than any beast she had ever met. Who could fight a vindictive god? Not even her. So she let the feeling guide her, transport her somewhere more important than here, holding on to nothing but the warm feeling that, in the end, she had at least done the right thing.

58

Kangala

Chugoko
First Mooncycle, 17–19

THE MAN BEYOND THE LAKE stood before an assembled crowd in the
Chugoko city centre and looked them over, row to row.

"Only a few fortnights ago, we were still a peaceful people," he began.
"Maybe not content, but peaceful. We crafted, sold, and traded in peace.
These borders were still open to us. We—you, and even I in my place of
privilege farther north—were living the best way our dear old imperfect
lives would allow." He paused. "And then came the Red Emperor."

Ngipa had spent her time back in Chugoko well. So well, that she dug
deep into the jali tales of the Red Emperor's triumph over Bassa, pored
over every record available of the event, and from it, pieced together the
speech the emperor had used to convince the Coalition for New Bassa to
rise against the Great Dome. A speech Ngipa had now taken, and from
it, spun a new one for Kangala in clean, clear Savanna Common, which
she helped him practice the night before.

"A usurper from Fourth Ward, hailing from a line that is anything but
noble, wielding a power that is foreign to us," Kangala continued. "But
what did she do with this power, my people? Did she employ it in service
of our—*your*—betterment?"

He didn't expect them to answer, and was not disappointed when they
did not, simply blinking at him, confused about where this was going.

But he waited. *Patience*, his eyes said to his children and their siblings behind him, all gathered with their companies.

"No, she did not," he answered the question himself. "Instead, she has opted to murder her own people and yours, set her peace officers, her Soldiers of Red, her swamp beast upon anyone she pleases." He jabbed a finger at them. "For seasons upon seasons, you have done nothing but obey Bassa, live according to her decrees even when there is no reward in it. You have remained steadfast, paid the taxes demanded of you because you are a loyal, loving people. But your loyalty has been met with nothing but disdain, disrespect, and violence." He paused for effect. "Today, I am here to dare you to say—no more."

He watched the mention of taxes slice the crowd like a blade through sand, sowing the seed of division he needed. Desertlander or otherwise, from oppressor advocate to the oppressed themselves to parties that pretended to be neutral—this was the one thing that united them all. There, in the far corner—the vigilante leader and the warrant chief he took orders from. There, in the shadows—a former mouthpiece of the Red Emperor's peacekeepers. There—civic guards from Bassa who were still waiting upon the emperor's return. There—merchants from Bassa, paused on their way to or from the northern trading route.

But Kangala was not foolish. He did not expect a sudden change of heart from anyone here. Not a single Chugoki or Bassai looked kindly upon him. Not when he'd arrived a day ago with news of the emperor's demise, and surely not now. He didn't blame them. After all, he was a Sahelian who had gone on a quest with their emperor and returned without her. Who would believe such a story—that the emperor had somehow succumbed to the wiles of the road and forest alongside the rest of her contingent?

They might not have attacked him yet, but they were definitely waiting for a moment to do so. Today, he would give them this opportunity. But first, he would open the ordinary Chugoki's eyes. He would move from *liar* to *saviour*, so the Four Winds help him.

"I dare you to dream of a life that does not centre Bassa and their ways," he said. "I dare you to think for yourself, to wonder if who you are is enough. I dare you to not require Bassa's approval, but yours and yours alone." He began to pace. "And I will go a step further and dare you to reclaim what has been taken from you. I dare you to follow me to Bassa and reclaim your land and your wealth."

It had been Ngipa's idea to have the full force of the company present. *Not just for protection*, she'd said, *but so that they can see you at the ready*. She was right. Because as soon as he said these words, all eyes swept to his children and their company of hundreds, as if asking *You and what army?* and immediately getting that answer.

But more importantly, Ngipa had gathered enough information to leave them confident of palpable dissent against the emperor, especially fueled by her visit. The Chugoki cup of obeisance was full, and they had thrown it out, ready to fill new buckets with a willingness for an end to tyranny. Which was why Kangala knew this next part would be particularly important.

"I am but a Sahelian of lowly beginnings," he said, "yet I stand before you, willing to take my own stand, and wishing you would join me." He clicked his fingers.

Oroe stepped forward, stopping next to a tall figure over which a large cloak was draped. He pulled it down.

A gasp cascaded through the crowd as the statue of the Red Emperor, in all its red glory, came into view behind him. Kangala seized this moment of stupefaction.

"Your emperor is no scion of moons!" he declared. "She is nothing but a usurper, a poser, a trickster." He jabbed his finger toward the statue to press home his words. "Every single deadly power she has wielded was not ordained by your gods, but mere evil sorcery. She is but an ordinary human, just like me, just like you. And if I, an ordinary man from Lake Vezha, blessed neither by the moon gods nor the Four Winds, can defeat her and her ferocious beast despite the power of this ibor sorcery"— he swung the finger around to point to the people—"then *you* can do anything."

Another click of his fingers. Oroe stepped forward with a heavy sledgehammer, leaned back, and swung it against the statue.

The Red Emperor came down in a shower of terracotta and bronze.

Shock and confusion rolled across the crowd like a bedsheet in wind.

Kangala's eyes scanned quickly, seeking those who had since been giving him dagger looks—civic guards, vigilantes, mouthpieces. Not a single one was in the position they'd last been, all already moving.

Kangala turned to his son Oroe and nodded. Oroe nodded back and, with a sharp command to his company, melded with the crowd. The remainder of his children pressed tightly around him, limiting the circle.

"Do not fear, Chugoko!" Kangala said, hands in the air. "You are the great city on the shoulder of the mountains, the gateway to the mainland. You have always been great. But you can be even greater, if you open your mind to it." He made a show of turning his head left to right. "If you fear the Red Emperor's wrath, look around. Do you see her here? Where is the Red Emperor you fear?"

From somewhere in the crowd, a cry of anguish, a scattering. A Bassai civic guard lay in the dust, fresh blood pooling around him.

Another cry, and another. And each time the crowd parted, someone was lifeless, painted in red.

"Where is your Red Emperor, defenders of Bassa?" Kangala announced, as cries of agony sprung up everywhere. "Where is your Red Emperor to defend you?"

Then, as soon as they had begun, the cries ceased. Bodies of civic guards, vigilantes, at least one warrant chief—all lay on the ground. A few members of the crowd who attempted to retaliate were quickly held at blade point. Kangala put up a hand in a show of control, as if stopping things from descending into chaos.

"People of Chugoko," he said, as every eye turned back to him in a mix of fear and reverence. "I dare you. I dare you to come with me to Bassa."

This part, he could say with the most confidence. Ngipa's research had also uncovered information about the Soke border. News of civic guards being withdrawn to be reassigned for some unrest in Bassa. Gossip about portions of the border left in half repair. Unfinished construction and fewer numbers meant only one thing: vulnerability.

Kangala spoke faster now, returning to his pacing.

"I dare you to come with me as I head out to the Soke Pass, to tear down the walls they have put up to keep us divided, to keep us from the good fruit of the land. We are as worthy children of this continent as any

Bassai, and we deserve just as much access to good water, good rivers. We deserve to dig wells that never go dry and reap of the humus. We deserve to mine the mountains and beautify our homes with the precious minerals that come forth. We deserve access to these stones of power, to the possibilities they bring. We deserve everything."

The crowd looked to one another, and somewhere within them, disagreement faded. Each look to a neighbour was to confirm that they were thinking the same thing. A gaze at the bodies in the dust, the crown and statue in pieces, the company behind Moy Kangala. It was hope. It was confirmation.

Kangala filled his chest with air and delivered the finale of his performance.

"Go home," he announced, a command rather than a plea. "Gather your households. Gather your friends. Gather your neighbours. Tell them that Moy Kangala, the Sahelian, the Man Beyond the Lake, says the day of reckoning has arrived. Today, we take back what is rightfully ours. Today, we march to the Soke border and tear it down. Today, you and your children walk into the mainland."

"Yes!" came a smattering of voices from the still stricken crowd. "Yes."

"I hear voices!" said Kangala, smiling. "I hear those who are not afraid to join me in this noble quest to throw open the gates of the Soke Pass for all desertlanders. And for you who have dared to speak, who have dared to march with me, I will open the gates of Bassa and beyond to you and your descendants forever. Never again will you ever lack."

"Yes!"

"Chugoko, I ask again—will you follow me? Will you take back what is yours?"

"Yes, yes, yes!"

Kangala opened his arms to the crowd, and an energetic cheer went around.

He looked at Ngipa, standing nearby. To Oroe, who had returned from the crowd, bloodied from the silent assassinations. To the rest of his children whose names he couldn't always remember. He nodded at them, and they nodded back, then began to chant.

Kan-ga-la. Kan-ga-la. Kan-ga-la.

The crowd followed, voices rising. Soon, they commandeered the chant and gave it new, full life.

Kan-ga-la! Kan-ga-la! Kan-ga-la!

Kangala lifted his arms to the sky, and the ruckus was the loudest the continent had ever heard since the taking of the Great Dome by the woman from Fourth Ward.

·—◇—···————···—◇—·

Capturing the Soke border was not an easy task, but Kangala set about it methodically. The first points of attack only required a handful of Oroe's best champions in the outposts where the wall was most vulnerable structurally and otherwise. Then, it was a matter of ambushing the civic guard reinforcements that arrived to recover them. That, of course, left other outposts open for taking, which did not even require well-trained champions to do so. When the reinforcements were pushed back, they did not have a place to return to, pinned in the narrow spaces of the border walls and caves by forces on both ends. A few fought to the death. Many opted to jump into the moats.

Kangala directed the desertlanders who had given up everything to follow him to the least taxing part of the attacks. Most of their work required taking down an outpost's pigeon coop, prevent them from lighting any signal fires, and in general ensuring word of these attacks did not get out until they were completed. Once each outpost was captured, Kangala gave the desertlanders who had survived the freedom to commandeer each outpost as they wished, including allowing whomever they pleased into the mainland. But many of the outposts were in the scraggier and less desirous parts of the mountains. Any immigrants who wanted to cross would have to brave treacherous climbs or go underneath the mountains and dare to face the moats.

So Kangala offered a third option, which the most sensible of them opted for: Convince more people to join the fight in liberating the Pass itself, and everyone could walk in unhindered.

Many opted for the latter. It earned significant returns, and Kangala's forces were boosted within hours.

Before the first day was over, Kangala had captured most of the eastern and western walls, where the moats inside the mountains were thinnest and most unguarded. The skirmishes were often not lengthy, though they were fierce. But the biggest battle was the final one—over the Soke Pass itself, where the moat was widest, the wall was tallest, and the gates most fortified.

Kangala arrived after a long day of capturing most lookout posts, set up his army of children behind the moats, and waited. There was no dialogue, no discussion, no demands. Whoever led the defence of the border ordered arrows to be fired whenever his people came too close, so they remained well out of reach.

All they needed was one drawbridge.

It took the rest of the night. Oroe, who had remained behind in the captured outposts, led the ambush from within. Kangala did not know how it went, but he knew when it began, because the arrows stopped, even when his children ventured forward and stood at the edge of the moat.

The first drawbridge dropped at dawn, and Kangala marched his army through.

The Bassai fought hard. The civic guards feared the Red Emperor's long hand more than they feared for their lives—perhaps even feared she could reach them in death if they did not do their utmost best to protect her empire. The thought of remaining soldiers even after death, yanked from eternal rest back into the empire's service, struck such fear into their hearts that they fought like crazed men. And like crazed men they also died, resisting the inevitability of Kangala's advancing forces and the losing battle of defending an empire that did not once consider them worthy enough to buttress their ranks and offer sufficient protection.

By dusk, the battle was over. When the iron gates of the Soke Pass were raised, blood dripped from them onto the sand that connected desertland to mainland. Kangala walked through, took off his sandals, and stepped onto mainland sand. It glued to his blood-slicked feet, nested between his toes, grainy when he rubbed them together.

The sand did not feel any different. He breathed in the air, and it did not feel any different. Save for these gates, these mountains, these moats, the land on that side and the land on this side were very much one and the same.

And he was just as entitled to it as anyone else.

59

Nem

Bassa: The Great Dome
First Mooncycle, 20

"Wake up. Wake up!"

Nem felt a tug—several, in fact—and woke into blinding light. It was morning, or afternoon—she couldn't be sure. Whatever the time, it was clear from the look of her Second staring into her face that something had happened yet again. Sounds of chaos filtered from outside the chamber, dampened by the shut doors. Satti's expression was taut, her movements jerky and anxious, a sculpture of consternation.

"You have to decide," said Satti, rummaging through a chest of wrappers. "Now."

Nem sat up. The small woman was never stern with her unless something was considerably wrong. And though there was always some ruckus in the Great Dome lately, Nem discerned that whatever was wrong was very immediate.

"Decide what? What's happening?"

Satti pulled a couple of wrappers from the bottom of a nearby chest, examining them. They were the oldest wrappers available.

"We are under attack." Satti said it calmly, as if relaying the available options for a meal. "The Soke Pass has been breached."

Nem felt all the moisture disappear from her throat. She couldn't swallow spit if she wanted to.

"Who?" was all she could ask. It came out in a squeak.

"Some desertlander," said Satti. "Not that it matters who." She began to undress, selected wrappers draped over her shoulders.

"What are you doing?" Nem asked. "Quick, help me get in my chair. I need—"

"You do not need to do anything," said Satti, continuing to take off and put on clothes as if the whole empire was not about to come crashing down on their heads, as if a Third Great War was not on their heels.

"MaaNem," said Satti, when she was finally done. "How long have you known me?"

"What is this, the local government office?" Nem began to pull herself over the edge of the bed. "If you won't get me my chair, then I will do it myself. But know that you will be sanctioned for this."

"You are going to lose," said Satti.

That stopped Nem in her tracks. "Excuse me?"

"No matter how you fight this, how you push back against it, Bassa is going to lose," she said. "And you, First Consul, having acted in the emperor's absence—you will be the scapegoat. You will never survive being the scapegoat."

Nem went quiet.

"Our attacker—they are calling him the Man Beyond the Lake. A Sahelian," said Satti. "Pigeon reports are scarce, but we hear of an army of hundreds, the full weight of the desertland behind him and his children-champions. Our civic guards have been outnumbered at every instance, taken by surprise. No squadron is complete because the Great Dome has plucked civic guards and spread them across the city—by the forest, near the blockade, in the emperor's caravan. The gates of the Soke Pass have been thrown open, and there is no one to defend it, to defend us, because we spent all this time pursuing other things."

Nem's palms sweated from this update. Satti wasn't pointing fingers, but Nem could see it already—the lack of preparation being blamed on her, on Esheme, even if they proceeded to battle now and won. The desertland army was already here. Even if she tried to summon every civic guard from across the mainland and mount a defence of the seat of the empire, it would be too little, too late. By Satti's estimation, the army was expected to be upon them within hours. The result of that battle was a foregone conclusion.

Satti was right. She had a decision to make.

"I told you, once, that I had a plan," Satti was saying. "The time has come. You can stay and stand commander over a war you will not win—not as First Consul, not from that chair you sit in—or you can come with me."

But, Esheme . . . was Nem's first thought, and Satti saw it flit across her face.

"She created this," said Satti. "You and I know it. I know you love and care for her because she is your flesh and blood. You feel guilty that you made her into who she has become. Or at least kindled the fire that now burns in her. But you have to agree—she made her choices, and her choices made way for this monster that now threatens to consume you."

The noise from outside dwindled into echoes, then into nonexistence. It felt like they were the only two people left in the Great Dome.

"Everyone has done the sensible thing and run away," said Satti, as if reading Nem's mind. "Even Yao—he never gave the last few orders you asked, and he is not here to give you this update either. He and the rest of the court have disappeared. The civic guard captains are out there, tired of waiting for orders. They're congregating on their own to decide on a next course of action." Satti leaned in. "They have chosen to forget you exist. This is a gift. Take it."

"Why are you doing this?" asked Nem, suddenly realising the question she should have asked all this time. "When I almost died, when my household almost crumbled—even now, when everything might just crumble again—why have you stayed?"

Satti shifted her weight from foot to foot, sombre, pensive.

"My family is safe," she said at last. "For now, at least. And you are the reason for that, so I will complete my duty to you. When you are safe, I will leave."

This was not the answer Nem expected, but she realised it was the answer to the question she did not ask. This was clearly not the first time the woman had thought about leaving. But this time, she had made up her mind. This would be her last act of service.

Nem took a long sigh, then nodded for Satti to help her to her chair. Once in, Satti began dressing her in the old clothes.

"I wonder what happens to the blockade now," said Nem.

"Perhaps it depends on what side of it one is on," said Satti. "If this Sahelian does end up taking over this Great Dome, then the Nameless Republic will become his problem too, and no longer yours."

Nem wanted to say Bassa would always be her problem, but was it, really? Here she was, being given an opportunity to leave the burden of all this behind, start afresh somewhere she was unrecognisable, a thought she had entertained many a time. But there was still the small matter of Esheme. Though Nem was against much of what her daughter did, she did not simply want to leave her behind.

"Where will we go?" Nem asked, as Satti pushed Nem through the empty hallways of the Great Dome. "Not too far, though? I want to be able to reach my daughter easily when she returns."

Satti wore a look that said she did not think Nem would be seeing her daughter for a while. But all she said was: "I hear there is a caravan of refugees headed to Whudasha."

Nem settled back in her chair. Whudasha was far, but it was close enough. When the dust of all this settled, she would find her way back to Esheme.

Satti swung her to the Great Dome's kitchen, which was also empty, as most of the domehands had fled. The Second quickly gathered some resources for their travel and stuffed them in a clothsack she slung over her shoulder. Then she shepherded Nem out through the domehand entryways and passages, stopping to pilfer a container of oil for protection from the sun.

Soon, they were outside, in a part of the Great Dome Nem had never seen. Satti wrapped a cloak over her nose and mouth, so that only her eyes were visible. She helped Nem do the same. They looked like different women, except for Nem's chair, which, thankfully, was a type commonly used in Bassa.

The two women turned and squinted west, shading their eyes from the sun.

The refugee caravan to Whudasha was well underway when Satti and Nem arrived. From every corner of the city came people of all caste and kind. Former Idu nobles now walked alongside immigrants. Despite the disguises of rags, hairstyle, and lack of jewellery, Nem was still able to distinguish between them simply by looking at their skin: polished, untouched by work or weather. And yet, pockmarked skin or not, all were headed for the safety of the Peace Fence, once a symbol of separation and subjugation, now a symbol of safety and—surprisingly—peace.

This fact did not pass Nem by, and she told Satti so. The woman scoffed.

"I've always thought peace was not the absence of war or violence, but the presence of one so silent it makes no sound," said Satti. "So, if you think about it, the Peace Fence has always been aptly named."

When they had melded with the caravan proper, the crowd swallowed them with alarming quickness. Stifling bodies aside, they soon realised that the Emperor's Road West, now well-travelled, was no longer the smooth and paved route it once was. Nem's chair was not built for such undulation. They had a long way to go, and continuing this way was sure to ruin it. Satti made it clear that under no circumstances was she carrying Nem.

They stopped by the roadside and waited for someone with a travel-wagon whom they could ask for help. But with so many being immigrants and Emuru—and Idu who did not want to be recognised as such—they stood there for a while without spotting a single travelwagon.

Until, that is, one pulled away from the crowd and parked by the roadside. The driver, an elderly woman, got down with the help of her daughter—granddaughter?—and went off on foot into one of the nearby bushes, likely to relieve herself.

Satti and Nem went up to the travelwagon.

"Dehje, maa," the girl greeted, surprisingly upbeat for someone escaping the possibility of war. "Are you going to Whudasha like us?"

"Indeed we are," said Nem, pulling down her veil to reveal more of her face. "I am Adodo, and this is my cousin, Olaye." She pointed. "This your maa's travelwagon?"

"Of a sort," said the girl, then pointed to Nem's chair. "You look like you could use some help."

"Indeed we do," said Nem, smiling. "Will you be opposed to helping a stranded elderly woman and her cousin reach the promised land?"

The girl laughed at *promised land* as if Nem had said something funny, then said: "Maa will make that choice. When she returns?"

The three waited together. Nem soon wondered if they had made the wrong choice, as the girl could not stop talking. She hoped the elderly woman was not as chatty. Could they last this journey with two such people?

"You know the Supreme Magnanimous of Whudasha is now back in Fifteenth Ward?" the girl was saying to Satti, who for some reason was giving all her attention. "Staying to join the Nameless Republic."

"You have been behind the blockade?" Nem asked. It struck her, now, that both the girl and the older woman bore distinctly Whudan features.

The girl nodded. "That is where the emperor put us."

Nem tried hard not to gulp. "You know what's happening back there?"

The girl shook her head. "We left very early, before they decided the outer wards are now independent of Bassa. Maa says there will be a war with the emperor soon, and we should not be there when it happens. That's why we're going back to Whudasha."

Nem almost chuckled at the idea. If only they knew all the fault lines underneath Bassa. Carnivorous forests, emergent beasts, an army from the north. The blockade was the least of their problems.

The girl was still speaking. "I think it's Whudasha we should be worried about, though."

"Why?" asked Nem, perking up. "What's there?"

The girl frowned. "You don't know?" Then she leaned in conspiratorially, whispering: "*Ibor.*"

Nem's chest locked up. Everywhere she went, it seemed this word just could not stop following her.

"There is nothing like ibor," said Satti, repeating the Great Dome's practiced answers. "Only people blessed by the moon sisters, like the Red Emperor is."

"Not what I hear," said the girl, smacking her lips. For some reason, chaos seemed to excite her.

"What do you hear?" asked Nem.

"Survivors," said the girl. "Ajabo. In Whudasha."

Cold washed over Nem. She glanced at Satti, who looked just as stricken. They were both thinking the same thing—that was *not* good news.

"Where did you hear this?" Nem asked.

"Everyone is talking about it," the girl said, waving her hand toward the road where more and more refugees poured toward the coast. "Gossip, but maybe true? The last Whudans who came to Bassa brought the news. They say people who can do strange things suddenly showed up there after it became empty. They think it's Ajabos—they say maybe not all of them drowned or returned to the islands and sank with them. They think a few survived and went to the southeast hinterland protectorates. Maybe their descendants kept their ibor. Now, people say they've returned to reclaim the place of their ancestors' first landing."

"It's not possible," said Satti. "Ajabos cannot be alive."

The girl shrugged. "I don't know—maybe we will see when we get there?"

Nem thought about how, only a few seasons ago, her biggest problem was wondering which First Elder's favour to curry. Now a revolutionary faction might be the last stand between the Empire of Bassa and its fall to the desertlands. And if this was true about Whudasha, then the lowly protectorate was about to be bestowed with great power, and therefore great influence. Worse yet, if Esheme's quest ended up being successful—if she wasn't dead and did indeed gain access to more red ibor—then that was what, four different groups holding power and all laying claim to the mainland?

Oon did not know it yet, but no matter what happened next, nothing would ever be the same on the continent again.

"Maa is back," the girl announced, as the elderly woman re-emerged from the trees. She was only a few seasons older than Nem, but seemed more weathered. She seemed too old to be this girl's maa, but also too young to be her grandmaa. Nem realised they might not even be related at all.

The woman's eyes caught Nem's, and her gait slowed in response, her expression stiffening. Nem realised she had left her face open. *Too late.*

"Dehje," Nem greeted warmly. "I am Adodo, and this is my cousin, Olaye."

The woman frowned and leaned on her walking stick, but said nothing.

"I am Rudo," the girl offered. To the woman, she said: "They want to ride with us because MaaAdodo's chair cannot go the whole road."

The older woman did not look convinced.

"We will offer all the food and resources we have," said Satti. "As payment."

After what seemed like an eternity of consideration, the woman angled her head, prodded the ground with her stick, then looked them squarely in their eyes and said:

"Those are not your true names, but I do not care. As long as you do not intend to harm us, you are welcome to travel with us and share in our goods, as we are to yours. But I swear to you, if you attempt to harm anyone, either here or when we get to Whudasha—" She lifted her stick and pointed it at Nem.

"We are simply concerned with seeking safety in Whudasha, like everyone else," said Nem, then gestured to herself. "Besides, who am I capable of harming in this state?"

The woman scoffed. "I have witnessed unspeakable harm come from less. Besides, I am not helping you because of your inability to walk—I simply am never one to abandon a fellow in need." The woman tapped her stick again. "My name is Biemwensé."

"Adodo is my real name," Nem lied, then pointed to Satti. "This is not really my cousin. She is my Second. But her name is truly Olaye."

The older woman nodded. "Fair enough. I must warn you, though: If it is safety you seek, perhaps you are on the wrong road. This one has a boiling pot at one end and a fire at the other. When we arrive at our destination, we hope to be alive long enough to discover which is which."

With that, she beckoned to her daughter—or whatever she was—to help her into the driving seat of the travelwagon. Satti opted to drive instead, and the woman surprisingly acquiesced, pulling herself inside the vehicle. Nem went in after her, and the girl shut the door after them.

The travelwagon pulled into the Emperor's Road and became one with the refugee caravan.

Epilogue

Tombolo Hamlets
First Mooncycle, 9

FATOI LIKED TO THINK himself an able fisherman. He was the first in his compound to rise every morning, first to pull his daa's old nets and head out before the sun rose fully. He wanted to be the first to catch something, anything, from the Neverending Sea before its tides went out too far and took all the fish with it. After, he would take his dugout canoe and row onto the Tombolo River and lay his newer nets there. Then he would wait for Memba, his rival from the next compound, the only fellow fisherman in their small hamlet of eight compounds, to arrive. By noon, when they would compare their catches, Fatoi would surely have room to gloat.

But as Fatoi marched with his nets on this morning, through the forest path and toward the beach, he studied the eerie orange sky, the settlement all but obscured in thick haze. Morning mistdew mixed with the remnants of yesternight's smoked fish fires.

What new evil could be coming this time? he mused.

Deep-coloured skies, thick haze—these were never good omens. The Tombolo hamlets had already seen more events within the last season than in their last ten: the new emperor's visit; new tax enforcement delegations from the Great Dome; lower and lower catch yields; lower and lower crop yields; wild, foreign beasts emerging from the Tombolo forests; the Neverending Sea eating farther into the coast, drawing closer and closer to their compounds. Only recently, the monsoon winds had blown heavy rainfall toward them for days, all but aborting their fishing plans. What more could the moon gods have in store?

He broke forest cover, the wind and waves still temperamental from the monsoon. That was when he saw the objects that littered the beach.

They did not glitter, but in the growing light of dawn, they seemed to in Fatoi's eyes. Gems—no, stones. Or bones, maybe? Different sizes, from chunks as thick as his head to some as tiny as his little toe. Different colours too—red, amber, grey, white. And they had coloured the water, the foam and wash of the beach imprinting rainbows in the sand.

But what Fatoi's eyes stopped and fixed on were the bodies.

This far away, he couldn't tell how many, but he was sure there was more than one. None of them were moving.

From deep within the Neverending Sea came a thunderous, monstrous roar that reverberated in his bones, shuddered every stem, trembled every branch.

The fishing nets dropped in the sand. Fatoi started running.

The story continues in . . .

Book THREE of The Nameless Republic

Keep reading for a sneak peek!

Author's Note

THE FICTIONAL CONTINENT OF Oon and its characters are inspired by cultures, events, myths, legends, and cosmologies from various West African ethnic groups (and other such proximate ethnic groups within the African continent). They are in no way intended to be accurate portrayals or representations of any nation, group, or community at any point in real-world history.

In the same vein, the mainland's hierarchy of darkness and lightness is not intended to be representative of real-world racism, especially not "reverse racism" or "inverted oppression." Rather, it is a demonstration of how a matter of genetic randomness such as skin shade (even when—especially when—it occurs within the same racial group) may generate illogical and groundless reasoning for the purposes of compartmentalizing power. Bassa's hierarchy of darkness and lightness is a product of the fictional city's own storytelling, born of tales rooted in its relationship to the land, the humus that forms the source of the nation's agricultural prosperity. While there may be analogues and analogies to draw from Bassa to the social, cultural, and political landscapes of today, Bassa's caste system is not a commentary on a particular system or place, but an examination of all caste systems—both visible and invisible—and a demonstration of how they take hold.

If a reader may draw any analogues from this series at all, they may do so in one instance. The people of the Ihinyon islands deemed "yellowskins" by the Bassai are a representation of the stigmatization and discrimination against persons with albinism across the African continent.

The rare genetic condition (affecting about 1 in 5,000 to 15,000 people in Sub-Saharan Africa, sometimes as high as 1 in 1,000)* results in a deficiency of the melanin pigment distinctive to Africans and their descendants, preventing it from colouring their skin, hair, and eyes in the same manner as their fellow darker-skinned compatriots. Early depictions of Lilong from the Bassai point of view mirror typical attitudes of many inadequately educated darker-skinned Africans and Afrodescendants toward fellow (otherwise Black) Africans and Afrodescendants with albinism. A discerning reader will realise that not only is said Bassai point of view false and damaging, it is also quickly overruled by various counter-portrayals of "yellow-skinned" islanders ("yellow," in this context, is the sometimes-neutral-sometimes-pejorative term Black Africans and Afrodescendants often employ in describing those with this melanin deficiency).

As a reader, I have long wanted to see more Africans and Afrodescendants with albinism be presented as their whole, ordinary selves on the page. As an author, it is a privilege to have Lilong, a character with albinism, be the full gamut of her human self on the page—the hero of her own tale, melanin or not. Long may it continue.

---

* United Nations, General Assembly, *Persons with albinism: Report of the Office of the United Nations High Commissioner for Human Rights*, A/HRC/24/57 (12 September 2023), available from https://undocs.org/en/A/HRC/24/57

Persons of Interest

(Stresses—upward intonations—are on uppercase letters. Flat intonations on lowercase.)

IN THIS TALE, in order of interest

Lilong (lee-LONG): Abenai warrior from Namge, one of seven islands in the Ihinyon archipelago. Fugitive of the empire.

Danso (DAN-soh): Formerly Bassa's brightest jali, now a fugitive of the empire.

Esheme (ay-SHEH-mee): The Red Emperor of Bassa, and daughter of Nem. Formerly Danso's intended.

Nem (nehm): Esheme's maa, and First Consul to the emperor. Formerly Bassa's foremost fixer.

Biemwensé (BEE-EH-mwen-SAY): Whudan potter and former Supreme Magnanimous of the Whudasha Youth. Also a fugitive.

Kakutan (kah-koo-TAN): Previously Supreme Magnanimous of the Whudasha Youth, now a fugitive of the empire.

Oke (oh-keh): Escaped daughter of the former Bassai Speaker. Now in league with the fugitives.

Igan (EE-gan): Second, advisor, lover, and confidant of Esheme. Once a general of the Coalition for New Bassa.

Pa Gaddo and Ma Gaddo (GAH-DOH): Leaders of the Gaddo Company.

Alaba (ah-LAH-bah): The Gaddos' son, partner to Oke and Ugo.

Kangala (kan-GAH-lah): A shrewd Sahelian businessman.

Oroe (oh-ROW) and Ngipa (nn-GEE-pah): Kangala's children and trusted hands.

Kubra (koo-brah): A general of the Gaddo Company.

Ifiot (EE-feeawt): Leader of the Nameless faction, a splinter group from the Coalition for New Bassa.

Hakuoo (hah-KOO-OH): A stealthy swamplander warrior and leader.

Turay (too-RAY): Abenai warrior, and Lilong's love interest.

Ugo (ooh-goh): Partner to Oke and Alaba.

Basuaye (BAH-soo-ah-YAY): Former leader of the Coalition for New Bassa, also known as the Cockroach.

Ikobi (ee-KOH-bee): Advisor to the Red Emperor. Previously Esheme's mentor at counsel guild.

Satti (sah-TEE): Nem's Second. Once caretaker of the MaaNem household.

Jaoudou (jah-OO-doo): Lilong's father and Elder Warrior of the Abenai League.

Issouf (ee-SOOF), Kyauta (kee-AW-tah), Lumusi (LOO-MOO-see): Lilong's [step] siblings.

Ma Guosa (GWO-sah): Lilong's [step]mother.

Afanfan (ah-FAN-fan), Owude (oh-WOO-day), Rudo (roo-DOH): Biemwensé's adopted children.

Thema (TEH-mah): Oke's infant daughter.

Pikoyo (pee-KOH-yoh): New owner, caretaker, and housekeep at the Weary Sojourner.

Gevah (GEH-vah) and Manemena (mah-nay-MEH-nah): Clan leaders from the hinterlands.

Mpewa (m-PEH-wah): A mainland immigrant in Fifteenth Ward.

Butue (boo-TOO-ay): A former Second Councilhand of Bassa.

Anuli (AH-noo-LEE): Chief physician at the Great Dome.

Jhobon (jaw-BAWN): False name for Danso used while in Chugoko.

Awa (AH-wah): Chief Warden of the Chugoko Central Prison (and his daughter, **Abunni, ah-boo-NEE**).

Sileya (see-LAY-YAH): One of Ifiot's advisors in the Nameless faction.

FROM PREVIOUS TALES, in no particular order

Abuso (ah-boo-SOH): Speaker of the Upper Council of the nation of Bassa, and Oke's father.

Abulele (ah-BOO-lay-LAY): A friend of Danso's, sometimes called Abu for short.

Aifu (aee-foo): A First Elder of Bassa.

Ariase (ah-REEAH-say): Ḍọta's Second.

Ḍọta (DAW-tah): First Elder and First Merchant of the Upper Council of Bassa.

Ebose (ay-BOH-seh): A priest of the moon temple in Bassa.

Habba (HAH-ba): Danso's father, formerly of the jali guild and later a private healer.

Idiado (ee-DEEAH-doh): Leopard Emperor, the Sixteenth Emperor of Great Bassa.

Ilobi (ee-LOH-bee): A priest of the moon temple in Bassa.

Indina (een-DEE-nah): A Whudasha Youth.

Isago (EE-sah-GOH): A First Elder of Bassa.

Mokhiri (moh-KHEE-ree): Zaq's lover.

Nogowu (noh-GOH-woo): Manic Emperor, the Twenty-Third Emperor of Great Bassa.

Nowssu (now-SOO): A friend of Danso's.

Oboda (oh-boh-DAH): Nem's Second, and later Esheme's Second.

Oduvie (oh-DOO-veeay): Danso's mentor at scholar guild.

Pochuwe (poh-CHOO-way), Uduuwe (ooh-DOO-way), Kachuwe (kah-CHOO-way): Danso's triplet uncles and Habba's brothers.

Sankofa (SAHN-koh-fah): A Whudasha Youth.

Tamino (tah-MEE-no): A general of the Coalition for New Bassa.

Tumwenke (toom-WEHN-kay): Emperor of Enlightenment, the Fifteenth Emperor of Great Bassa.

Ulobana (oo-LOH-bah-NAH): A general of the Coalition for New Bassa.

Uria (ooh-REE-ah): A friend of Danso's.

Usi (OOH-see): The DaaHabba household's kwaga.

Viasi (vee-AH-see): Oboda's leopard.

Zaq (zak): Danso's Second and only househand to the DaaHabba household.

Glossary

(Stresses—upward intonations—are on uppercase letters. Flat intonations on lowercase.)

TERMS

Abenai (ah-beh-NAI) League [of Warriors]: A league of sworn protectors of the secrets of ibor and the existence of the eastern archipelago of the Nameless Islands.

Ashu (ah-SHOO): The white moon, the smaller of the two moons of Oon's world. Represented as a hen in Bassai moon worship.

Bassai (bah-SAI): Of Bassa.

Bassai Ideal, the: An embodiment of the epitome of Bassai existence, which includes purity of lineage and devotion to the nation's protection, prosperity, religion, guilds, and social contracts. Sometimes colloquially referred to as *Prime Bassai*.

bushroad: Any minor road leading outside of the city of Bassa. Named for the bush paths that they often have to cut through.

cheto (cheh-TOH): A hair and skin dye used in beautifying the self.

Chugoki (choo-GOH-kee): Of Chugoko.

civic guard: A member of law enforcement in Bassa, mostly of Emuru caste.

Command: The third stage of iborworking: to mentally order an object, element, or inanimate being Possessed by ibor to carry out a task.

daa: Refers to (1) father; (2) mister, a formal form of address for any male household head (when used before name, e.g. DaaHabba); (3) a diminutive form of formal address for any man (when used after name, e.g. Danso-daa).

dehje (DEH-jeh): A formal greeting in Bassa.

Diwi (DEE-wee): A household heirloom of red ibor, belonging to Lilong's house.

Draw: The first stage of iborworking: to mentally absorb the power from an ibor piece by touch.

Elder: An honorific term used to refer to a leading member of Bassai society, especially in a guild or vocation. Sometimes preceded by qualifiers for members of the Upper Council; *Second Elder* for members of the Lower Council.

Emperor's Road: Any major road that leads out of the city of Bassa. Named for Bassa's first emperors, who built them to travel and establish trade with other parts of the mainland.

Emuru (eh-MOO-roo): The worker caste of Bassa and second in the hierarchy of all five mainland castes. Default caste for all mainland pureborns—mainlanders without any outlander blood—who are not Idu.

Gaddo (GAH-DOH) Company: A desertland group of semi-legal operatives.

High Bassai: The exclusive, highbrow dialect spoken mostly among the Idu caste of Bassa. It is the only language with a clear written form.

high-black: Bassai denotation of the darkest skin complexion of all mainlanders. The darkest and most desirable skin tone on the continent of Oon. Usually affiliated with humus, the Idu caste, affluence and well-being, and mainland pureborns.

high-brown: Bassai denotation of the darkest skin complexion of all desertlanders. Darker than low-brown but lighter than low-black. Usually affiliated with the Potokin caste and people of the Savanna Belt.

hunthand: A private bounty hunter.

ibor (EE-bor): A fossil-like magical mineral with the consistency of both stone and bone. Found washed up on the shores of island nations. Many believe it originates from the beds of the great seas, but it is unclear and unproven. Naturally occurs in four states: white, grey, amber, and red.

Iborworker: A manipulator of ibor who possesses the innate talent and training to wield each kind of ibor for their own use. White Iborworkers wield air and light, Grey Iborworkers wield fire and water, Amber Iborworkers wield objects with which they have established an existing connection, and Red Iborworkers wield dead entities that have once lived.

iborworking: The act of manipulating ibor.

Idu (ee-DOO): The noble caste of Bassa and highest in the hierarchy of all five mainland castes. Highly selective, only accessible through vocational inheritance (priests), economic accomplishment and guild leadership (First and Second Elders), politics (ward leaders), and scholarly merit (jalis, scholars).

islander: An indigene of any of the islands surrounding Oon.

Island Common: The crossover, easily understood dialect spoken all over the seven islands of the Ihinyon archipelago.

jali (JAH-lee): A trained oral historian, storyteller, musician, scholar, and information repository of the Idu caste. Exclusively trained at the University of Bassa (called novitiates while in training), the jali guild is highly selective.

landfowl (sometimes fowl): Any bird incapable of flight and restricted to land. *Fowl* may refer to birds in general.

low-black: Bassai denotation of the lighter skin complexion of all mainlanders. Lighter than high-black but darker than high-brown. Usually affiliated with the Emuru caste and poverty or less affluence.

low-brown: Bassai denotation of the lighter skin complexion of all desertlanders. The lightest and least desirable skin tone on the mainland, only darker than islanders and yellowskins. Usually affiliated with the Yelekuté caste and people of the Idjama desert.

Lower Council: Second-highest ruling council of the nation of Bassa with thirty members. Also doubles as government of the capital city, with two selected members each representing one of the city's fifteen wards. Usually of ward leaders, civic guard captains, high-ranking counsels, and local government officials, etc.

maa: Refers to (1) mother; (2) missus, a formal form of address for any female household head (when used before name, e.g. MaaEsheme); (3) a diminutive form of formal address for any woman (when used after name, e.g. Esheme-maa).

Mainland Common: The crossover, easily understood dialect spoken all over the mainland.

Mainland Pidgin: The dialect spoken northward of the mainland, closer to the Soke border. It contains limited vocabulary and is interspersed with other languages from the Savanna Belt. Sometimes referred to as *border pidgin*.

mainway: One of fifteen major roads that each divide and enclose Bassa's fifteen wards. May also refer to main roads or streets in other regions.

Menai (meh-NAI): The red moon, the bigger of the two moons of Oon's world. Represented in Bassai moon worship as a leopard.

mooncrossing: The celestial event when the orbital paths of both moons in the world of Oon, Menai and Ashu, cross over each other. Usually accompanied by festivities.

mooncycle: A "month," that is, the period of time between each mooncrossing.

Ochela (oh-CHEH-lah): An annual festival held in Chugoko, spanning many days and bringing together many communities in the desertlands.

outlander: Someone who hails from the opposite side of the Soke border or across the seas, especially relative to wherever the speaker is from (e.g. a mainlander would refer to indigenes of the deserts and islands as *outlanders*).

peace officers (and their mouthpieces): Empire-ordained bounty hunters sent into the desertlands to seek the escaped fugitives.

Possess: The second stage of iborworking: to mentally release power Drawn from an ibor piece into a target object, element, or inanimate being in order to Command it.

Potokin (poh-TOH-keen): The higher immigrant caste of Bassa and third in the hierarchy of all five mainland castes. Reserved only for immigrants who work directly for Idu caste members, including aides, pages, hunthands, and a select number of Seconds.

raffia (RAH-FEE-ah): The collective name for the leaves of the palm tree native to Bassa. Also refers to the fibre from the raffia leaves, used for making woven items.

risisi (ree-SEE-see): A colloquial term for "rock" or "statue" or "ancestor" in Island Common. Not to be confused with **Risisi**, the name of a (mythical) place.

runku (ROON-koo): A wooden club with a heavy bulbous end, usually carried by civic guards and Seconds.

Savanna Common: The commonly understood dialect spoken all over the Savanna Belt.

Shashi (shah-shee): The outcast caste of Bassa and lowest of all five in the hierarchy of mainland castes. Reserved for those of mixed blood between a mainlander and outlander, whether desertlander or islander. Also sometimes used to refer to the mixed-complexion appearance of Shashi caste members.

Soldiers of Red: Undead enemies of the Red Emperor, resurrected by Red Iborworking to become her personal protection unit.

stone-bone: A colloquial term for referring to ibor.

Upper Council: The highest ruling council representing the nation of Bassa, made up of ten First Elders and an appointed Elder Jali as a Speaker.

Yaya (yah-YAH): A Whudan title for an elderly maternal person.

Yelekuté (yay-lay-KOO-tay): The lower immigrant caste of Bassa and fourth in the hierarchy of all five mainland castes. Default caste for Seconds and all other desert-lander immigrants that constitute all the *-hands*: househands and all other workhands and servicehands.

yellowskin: Describes the albinoid people of the Ihinyon islands of the eastern archipelago (known to most on Oon as the Nameless Islands). Expression comes from the yellowish appearance of their skin, hair, and eyes.

ward: One of fifteen subdivisions of the city of Bassa, starting from the innermost and most affluent closest to the Great Dome (First Ward) to the outermost and least affluent farthest from the Great Dome (Fifteenth Ward).

weybo (WAY-boh): A highly intoxicating alcoholic spirit distilled from fermented raffia wine.

Whudan (woo-DAHN): Of Whudasha. Also refers to the language spoken by the people.

LOCALES

Ajabo (ah-JAH-boh): Refers to (1) the group of islands west of the continent of Oon, whose people were the first to migrate to the mainland; (2) the people of said islands.

Bassa (BAH-sah): Refers to (1) the nation of Bassa, formerly the Empire of Bassa, which spans all of the mainland except for Whudasha and a few hinterland protectorates; (2) the capital city of Bassa from which the nation got its name; (3) the region of the mainland over which the Bassai nation spans, one of the three major regions on the continent of Oon next to the Savanna Belt and the Idjama desert.

Breathing Forest, the: A forbidden forest on the western edge of Bassa whose floor undulates during heavy winds. Rumoured to possess supernatural creatures and is eschewed by the Bassai.

Chabo (CHAH-boh): A colony to the west of the Savanna Belt.

Chugoko (choo-GOH-koh): The biggest city in the Savanna Belt, standing between Bassa's Soke Pass and the Emperor's Road to the north.

Dead Mines, the: A cluster of abandoned mines of gold and other ore at the foot of the Soke mountains, west of the border.

delta settlements (*also known as* **deltalands, swamplands**): The southernmost part of the mainland, mostly uncharted, and harbouring various uncontacted groups.

desertland(s): Anywhere north of the Soke border. Indigenes referred to as *desertlanders.*

Enuka (EH-NOO-kah): A clan in the southwest hinterlands.

Gondola (gon-DOH-lah): A river on the mainland, intersecting with the Tombolo at the Tombolo-Gondola confluence.

Gwagwamsi (gwah-GWAHM-see): A settlement along the northern trade route.

Haruna (hah-ROO-nah): A small town in the Savanna Belt.

hinterlands: The internal regions of the mainland, often split into the southwest and southeast.

Idjama (ee-jah-mah) (*also* **Idjama desert**): The desert regions north of the Savanna Belt. Next to Bassa and the Savanna Belt, the third major region of the continent of Oon.

Ihinyon (ee-HIN-yawn): Collective name for the seven islands and the people of the archipelago east of Oon. A word that means "seven" in Island Common. Known as the Nameless Islands to mainlanders, for the seven islands it contains: Namge, Hoor, Ololo, Edana, Ufua, Sibu-Sibu, Ofen.

Lonely Roads East/West, the: Roadways of the Savanna Belt that lead east/west, respectively.

mainland: Anywhere south of the Soke border. Indigenes referred to as *mainlanders.* Sometimes synonymous with *Bassa.*

Oon: The universal name for the one continental body, consisting of three distinct landforms: the mainland to the south, the desertland to the north, and islands to the east and west.

outer lands: The regions on the opposite side of the Soke border or across the seas, especially relative to wherever the speaker is from (e.g. a mainlander would refer to the deserts and islands as *outer lands*).

Risisi (ree-SEE-see): Mythical buried city of ibor in the Ihinyon islands.

Savanna Belt: The savanna region between the mainland and the desert, north of the Soke mountains. Next to Bassa, the second most prosperous of the three main regions that make up the continent of Oon.

Sahel: The transition zone just north of the Savanna Belt. Its most conspicuous landmark is the Lake Vezha.

Soke (SOH-kay): Refers to (1) the Soke mountains separating the mainland from the desertlands; (2) the Soke border, the man-made border of moats and drawbridges built along the Narrow Pass (or Soke Pass) between the mountains to regulate southward immigration from the desertland into the mainland.

Tkithnuum (t-KEETH-noom): A port city on the northern trade route.

Tombolo (tom-BOH-loh): A river on the mainland, intersecting with the Gondola at the Tombolo-Gondola confluence.

Undati (oon-DAH-tee): A small mining location east of the Soke Pass. Refers to the location or the mines themselves.

Vezha (VEH-zzah), Lake: A lake in the Sahel belt, separating the Savanna Belt from the Idjama desert proper.

Wanneba (WAH-NEH-bah): A clan in the southwest hinterlands.

Whudasha (woo-DAH-shah): A western coastal protectorate on the mainland, separated from Bassa by a Peace Fence. Known as the land of the first landers—the Ajabo who first arrived on the mainland through the bight, now known as the Bight of Whudasha.

FLORA & FAUNA

genge (GEN-geh): An ancient desertland animal often found roaming in packs in the desertlands. Name translates to *monster* in a desertland dialect.

Ghost Ape: A gorilla-like animal with the camouflaging properties of a chameleon, rumoured to be found in Bassa's rainforests.

kwaga (KWAH-gah): A striped, hoofed equine with horns and a sharp bark. Primary transport animal on the continent of Oon.

naboom (nah-BOOM): A desertland cacti-like plant (or tree) with poisonous milky sap.

Ninki Nanka (NEEN-KEE nan-kah), or swamp dragon: A ferocious dragon-serpent with corrosive spittle. Native to the swamplands. Believed to be mythical.

Skopi (SKOH-pee), or lightning bat: A human-sized bat with the ability to call down lightning.

tepe (TAY-pay): A carnivorous tree that masquerades as other trees in the rainforest (often ubiquitous trees like plantains). Contains teeth and tentacle-like material within, ensnaring whatever living animal comes too close (humans included) and consuming their flesh but rejecting the bones, which can often be found at the foot of the tree. It is also capable of moving by "shuffling" its way through the forest.

The Written Codex of Danso DaaHabba, First Jali of Bassa to Journey over the Soke Borders

Hereafter lie his personal accounts of travels
and travails through the desertlands, from
the western vagabond colony of Chabo, to the
fabled eastern Forest of the Mist.

The Ninth Account: A recount of our journey across the Savanna Belt, through the Lonely Roads East and the Weary Sojourner Caravansary

The Tenth Account: *Why the Wind Howls: A Desertland Tale*, as told by Ugo, also known as Journeyman, once of Bassa, now of the desertlands

The Eleventh Account: *How the World Came to Be: An Ihinyon Tale*, as told by Lilong of Namge and the Abenai League (of the seven islands of the Ihinyon archipelago, known to some, inaccurately, as the Nameless Islands)

The Twelfth Account: *The Crab-God and the Gourd of Wisdom: An Ihinyon Tale*, as told by Lumusi of Namge, a tale which she has always known and in which she firmly believes

Acknowledgments

All my thanks to the village that made this book possible:

—My agents, Tamara Kawar and Alexander Cochran, for being stable beacons in the stormy waters of publishing.

—The good folks at Orbit: my superstar editor, Nivia Evans, who continues to champion this series and my work in general—I appreciate you; her able assistant, Angelica Chong, for ensuring this book got where it needed to on time; production editor Rachel Goldstein and copyeditor Vivian Kirklin, for ensuring series continuity—you are literally my series world bible; art team wrangler Lauren Panepinto for the awesome cover design (and Dan dos Santos for yet another badass cover art, and Tim Paul for the map); publicity wrangler Ellen B. Wright and able deputy Angela Man; Alex Lencicki and Paola Crespo in marketing (I'll always remember the *Son of the Storm* book trailer you made happen!); James Long and Nazia Khatun at Orbit UK—I salute your energy, always.

—My family: Dami and Dot, from whom I often snuck away to write this. Thank you for putting up with me.

—Writing colleagues and constant cheerleaders: Those who've blurbed this series so far: S. A. Chakraborty, Fonda Lee, P. Djèlí Clark, Shelley Parker-Chan, Andrea Stewart, Anthony Ryan, James Islington, Jenn Lyons, A. K. Larkwood; those who've been sounding boards: Rebecca Roanhorse, Tasha Suri, Evan Winter, Malka Older, S. L. Huang.

—Friends in Ottawa who helped me settle into a snowy new city: Amal El-Mohtar, Kate Heartfield; the good folks at CanCon: Marie Bilodeau, Brandon Crilly, and Derek Kunsken; colleagues Vicki Burke,

Kim Andrews and Alex Bowles, James Brooke-Smith and Sara Landreth, Tom Allen, the Jenns—Panek, Blair, and Baker.

—Bookstores and libraries who've supported this series so far: Long may your coffers fill.

—Newsletter readers at SuyiAfterFive.com: thank you, thank you, thank you.

—Anyone else who deserves a mention but whom I forgot to include: Forgive me. I wrote this at two AM.

extras

orbit

meet the author

Manuel Ruiz

SUYI DAVIES OKUNGBOWA is a Nigerian author of fantasy, science fiction, and general speculative work. He is the author of the epic fantasy trilogy The Nameless Republic (including *Son of the Storm* and *Warrior of the Wind*). His debut godpunk fantasy novel, *David Mogo, Godhunter* (Abaddon, 2019), won the 2020 Nommo Award for Best Novel. His shorter works have appeared in various periodicals and anthologies and have been nominated for various awards. He earned his MFA in creative writing from the University of Arizona and lives in Ontario, where he teaches at the University of Ottawa. Follow him on social media (as @suyidavies everywhere), or via his newsletter, SuyiAfterFive.com.

Find out more about Suyi Davies Okungbowa and other Orbit authors by registering for the free monthly newsletter at orbitbooks.net.

if you enjoyed

WARRIOR OF THE WIND

look out for

THE NAMELESS REPUBLIC: BOOK THREE

by

Suyi Davies Okungbowa

The sweeping saga of forgotten magic and violent conquests continues in the third novel of award-winning author Suyi Davies Okungbowa's epic fantasy trilogy....

Kakutan

The Nameless Republic
First Season of the Five States

First, tongue: seeking, tickling, finding. *Petals*, Kakutan thought, as small joys blossomed in her lower belly. Beads of perspiration gathered above her lip. She licked at them, an invitation.

Ifiot removed her head from between Kakutan's thighs, slipped fingers into her, and began to move. Her opposite fingers found Kakutan's lips, and motions above mimicked those below. Sharp fingernails, filled with slick, dug into her tongue, releasing flavours of salt and steel.

Kakutan turned over and let Ifiot enter deep inside her. Every movement a sensual brush, the tingling of a bell fingers could never reach. *Moons.* Satisfaction escaped Kakutan's throat, wisps of hair matted to her temples. Ifiot responded, stroking slower, deeper, all lean muscle and suffocating musk.

Sweat gathered in their armpits, charted rivulets down their backs. Kakutan bit her lip, fell to her elbows, arched herself. Thoughts melted away, replaced by an insatiable hunger for more, and more, and more.

Soon, she was atop a hill, then cresting. She opened her lips and let go, limbs quivering. Everything went white and empty and nothing existed. Then she was back to the wet, soaked present, after which it was time to return the favour.

· ◇ ··· ─────── ··· ◇ ·

Ifiot always dressed first, which Kakutan did not mind because she'd always preferred to lie in bed, smoke, and watch. There was something mesmerizing about that body, the way Ifiot's angular shoulders tapered into a back that was sturdy yet tender, and fed into buttock muscles that tensed on themselves whenever she moved. In the near-darkness of the room, Kakutan had trained her eyes to see and memorise every inch of her lover's body.

They were in one of the small abodes the Nameless faction once used as safe houses, before the blockade went up and they became an independent state. This one was tucked into an outskirt of Twelfth, with an entry level accessible only via a corridor. Which was why even though the light of late morning shone outside, their room remained shaded in shadow, like much of the Nameless faction had once been.

Kakutan took a drag of her pipe and watched Ifiot's tense buttocks disappear into a pair of pantaloons. She did not think it was fair that she was the warrior here, yet Ifiot was the one blessed with a warrior's angles. A body that was yet to feel the pressures of aging like hers. She did not hate her body, of course—curves and softness had their uses. It made people underestimate her, which was good. She was smaller, older, rounder—often invisible. They would not see her coming.

Especially at the meeting today.

"Nameless, eh?" Kakutan said as Ifiot put on her tunic.

"Nameless," Ifiot repeated, a wry smile tugging at her lips. The woman never dressed in Bassai wrappers, despite being Bassai herself, but preferred to wear desertlander clothing, often gifted to her by immigrant friends and comrades. It was part of her resistance—to *never put on the fashion of the oppressor*, as she would say—as well as a demonstration of her allyship with the now-free immigrants.

Kakutan blew a plume of smoke from her pipe. "They will want a name. And a leader."

"And I will tell them the same thing I have said many times over. It is not a nameless or leaderless revolution. It is—"

"—all our names, and we are all its leaders," Kakutan finished. "I'm aware."

"You can't cut the head off a snake if it has no head."

"Also aware."

"Then that settles it."

"For you, maybe. But this is war. Truth and reason don't apply here. War is politics, and sadly, politics is emotion."

Ifiot turned to regard Kakutan, who was still naked in bed. She gave her lover an endearing once-over and chuckled.

"Is that from the Supreme Magnanimous education you received?"

"Don't start."

Ifiot held up her hands. "I'm just saying..." She angled her head. "Our people say that *if you wrestle another into the mud, you must stay there to keep them down.* We got here by wrestling in the mud. We're not going to win now by trying to get out of it."

"This isn't about *winning*. These are our allies."

"*Everything* is about winning, Kaku."

"Maybe. But for this meeting, at least, we should be most focused on getting a good bargain."

Ifiot scoffed. "Bargaining is the tool of one who has already lost. You once tried to bargain for your people. Look how that ended."

Kakutan sucked deep on her pipe, biting down on the wood, trying not to show how much that stung. But the red of her pipe burned bright for too long, and Ifiot knew she had overstepped. She sighed and sat on the bed.

"I'm sorry. I should not have said that."

"Yes, you should not have," said Kakutan. "You young people have no respect for elders."

Ifiot burst into laughter. It was big and throatful, with a whinny buried within that made her sound like a little child and a mature adult all at once. Kakutan had no choice but to chuckle alongside her.

"You're not even twenty seasons older than me!"

"Fourteen seasons is enough."

"Let me guess, your friend Biemwensé used to say things like that."

Friend. Kakutan tossed the word in her mouth, savoured the taste. Once, she would not have thought that woman her friend. But after the places they'd been together, the things they'd seen and experienced, the truths about themselves and each other they'd come to recognise, *friend* was too inadequate a descriptor.

Sister, maybe. *Kin.*

"My *tribe sister*, Biemwensé," Kakutan corrected. "And yes, she's a big advocate of the elder argument."

Silence came after the laughter, as the weight of all that had been lost since the blockade settled on them. Aside from the loss of friends now trapped on the Bassai side of the blockade, times had become much harder for those living on the Nameless side too. Bassai or immigrant or Whudan—they all felt it equally. Even with support from the hinterlanders and swamplanders, who were now arriving in the outer wards no longer in trickles but in droves, there was still much to be desired.

For once, we should stop thinking about ourselves and start thinking about what they want. This was what Kakutan had promised Biemwensé she would do, that she would look out for her boys, that she would look out for their people here as Biemwensé would do back in the protectorate. The hinterlander and swamplander leaders were coming to the table to negotiate an allyship in what was surely a forthcoming war with the Sahelian who now led New Bassa. If their queries and demands did not serve the people's needs, it surely was an unwise time to play such politics.

Perhaps Ifiot was right: It was time to be rooted, firm and unyielding.

Ifiot, as if listening to her thoughts, rose then. Something shifted in her expression, and the jovial, laughing woman was no more. Instead, she went to the corner of the room where she often leaned her spear and grabbed it, then turned to Kakutan.

"The time for bargaining is over." Her tone was that of a soldier. "Now is the time for battle."

Then she angled her head and cracked a smile, and the tension dissipated.

"Get dressed," she said. "I'll check with my people to see if they've arrived."

After she left, Kakutan finished her pipe and went to the bathroom. As she scrubbed with a bath stone, she went over the plans she'd made with Ifiot to tackle the delegations. Somewhere within this, she remembered something Biemwensé once told her.

One former Supreme Magnanimous to another, your plans are often shit. Kakutan found herself laughing alone in the bathroom. That woman had a coconut head, but she was not wrong. Kakutan was really no good at planning. Thank moons she had Ifiot, who was more of a mastermind.

Together, they were going to be an unstoppable force. Starting today.

if you enjoyed
WARRIOR OF THE WIND

look out for

THE JASAD HEIR
The Scorched Throne:
Book One

by

Sara Hashem

Ten years ago, the kingdom of Jasad burned. Its magic was outlawed, its royal family murdered down to the last child. At least, that's what Sylvia wants people to believe.

The lost Heir of Jasad, Sylvia never wants to be found. She can't think about how Nizahl's armies laid waste to her kingdom and continue to hunt its people—not if she wants to stay alive. But when Arin, the Nizahl Heir, tracks a group of Jasadi rebels to her village, staying one step ahead of death gets trickier.

In a moment of anger, Sylvia's magic is exposed, capturing Arin's attention. Now, to save her life, Sylvia will have to make a deal with her greatest enemy: If she helps him lure the rebels, she'll escape persecution.

*A deadly game begins. Sylvia can't let Arin discover her identity,
even as hatred shifts into something more. Soon, Sylvia will
have to choose between the life she wants and the one she left behind.
The scorched kingdom is rising, and it needs a queen.*

Chapter One

Two things stood between me and a good night's sleep, and I was allowed to kill only one of them.

I tromped through Hirun River's mossy banks, squinting for movement. The grime, the late hours—I had expected those. Every apprentice in the village dealt with them. I just hadn't expected the frogs.

"Say your farewells, you pointless pests," I called. The frogs had developed a defensive strategy they put into action any time I came close. First, the watch guard belched an alarm. The others would fling themselves into the river. Finally, the brave watch guard hopped for his life. An effort as admirable as it was futile.

Dirt was caked deep beneath my fingernails. Moonlight filtered through a canopy of skeletal trees, and for a moment, my hand looked like a different one. A hand much more manicured, a little weaker. Niphran's hands. Hands that could wield an axe alongside the burliest woodcutter, weave a storm of curls into delicate braids, drive spears into the maws of monsters. For the first few years of my life, before grief over my father's assassination spread through Niphran like rot, before her sanity collapsed on itself, there wasn't anything my mother's hands could not do.

Oh, if she could see me now. Covered in filth and outwitted by croaking river roaches.

Hirun exhaled its opaque mist, breathing life into the winter bones of Essam Woods. I cleaned my hands in the river and firmly cast aside thoughts of the dead.

A frenzied croak sounded behind a tree root. I darted forward, scooping up the kicking watch guard. Ah, but it was never the brave who escaped. I brought him close to my face. "Your friends are chasing crickets, and you're here. Were they worth it?"

I dropped the limp frog into the bucket and sighed. Ten more to go, which meant another round of running in circles and hoping mud wouldn't spill through the hole in my right boot. The fact that Rory was a renowned chemist didn't impress me, nor did this coveted apprenticeship. What kept me from tossing the bucket and going to Raya's keep, where a warm meal and a comfortable bed awaited me, was a debt of convenience.

Rory didn't ask questions. When I appeared on his doorstep five years ago, drenched in blood and shaking, Rory had tended to my wounds and taken me to Raya's. He rescued a fifteen-year-old orphan with no history or background from a life of vagrancy.

The sudden snap of a branch drew my muscles tight. I reached into my pocket and wrapped my fingers around the hilt of my dagger. Given the Nizahl soldiers' predilection for randomly searching us, I usually carried my blade strapped in my boot, but I'd used it to cut my foot out of a family of tangled ferns and left it in my pocket.

A quick scan of the shivering branches revealed nothing. I tried not to let my eyes linger in the empty pockets of black between the trees. I had seen too much horror manifest out of the dark to ever trust its stillness.

My gaze moved to the place it dreaded most—the row of trees behind me, each scored with identical, chillingly precise black marks. The symbol of a raven spreading its wings had been carved into the trees circling Mahair's border. In the muck of the woods, these ravens remained pristine. Crossing the raven-marked trees without permission was an offense punishable by imprisonment or worse. In the lower villages, where the kingdom's leaders were already primed to turn a blind eye to the liberties taken by Nizahl soldiers, worse was usually just the beginning.

I tucked my dagger into my pocket and walked right to the edge of the perimeter. I traced one raven's outstretched wing with my thumbnail. I would have traded all the frogs in my bucket to be brave enough to scrape my nails over the symbol, to gouge it off. Maybe that same burst of bravery would see my dagger cutting a line in the bark, disfiguring the symbols of Nizahl's power. It wasn't walls or swords keeping us penned in like animals, but a simple carving. Another kingdom's power billowing over us like poisoned air, controlling everything it touched.

I glanced at the watch guard in my bucket and lowered my hand. Bravery wasn't worth the cost. Or the splinters.

A thick layer of frost coated the road leading back to Mahair. I pulled my hood nearly to my nose as soon as I crossed the wall separating Mahair from Essam Woods. I veered into an alley, winding my way to Rory's shop instead of risking the exposed—and regularly patrolled—main road. Darkness cloaked me as soon as I stepped into the alley. I placed a stabilizing hand on the wall and let the pungent odor of manure guide my feet forward. A cat hissed from beneath a stack of crates, hunching protectively over the half-eaten carcass of a rat.

"I already had supper, but thank you for the offer," I whispered, leaping out of reach of her claws.

Twenty minutes later, I clunked the full bucket at Rory's feet. "I demand a renegotiation of my wages."

Rory didn't look up from his list. "Demand away. I'll be over there."

He disappeared into the back room. I scowled, contemplating following him past the curtain and maiming him with frog corpses. The smell of mud and mildew had permanently seeped into my skin. The least he could do was pay extra for the soap I needed to mask it.

I arranged the poultices, sealing each jar carefully before placing it inside the basket. One of the rare times I'd found myself on the wrong side of Rory's temper was after I had forgotten to seal the ointments before sending them off with Yuli's boy. I learned as much about the spread of disease that day as I did about Rory's staunch ethics.

Rory returned. "Off with you already. Get some sleep. I do not want the sight of your face to scare off my patrons tomorrow." He prodded in the bucket, turning over a few of the frogs. Age weathered Rory's narrow brown face. His long fingers were constantly stained in the color of his latest tonic, and a permanent groove sat between his bushy brows. I called it his "rage stage," because I could always gauge his level of fury by the number of furrows forming above his nose. Despite an old injury to his hip, his slenderness was not a sign of fragility. On the rare occasions when Rory smiled, it was clear he had been handsome in his youth. "If I find that you've layered the bottom with dirt again, I'm poisoning your tea."

He pushed a haphazardly wrapped bundle into my arms. "Here."

Bewildered, I turned the package over. "For me?"

He waved his cane around the empty shop. "Are you touched in the head, child?"

I carefully peeled the fabric back, half expecting it to explode in my face, and exposed a pair of beautiful golden gloves. Softer than a dove's wing, they probably cost more than anything I could buy for myself. I lifted one reverently. "Rory, this is too much."

I only barely stopped myself from putting them on. I laid them gingerly on the counter and hurried to scrub off my stained hands. There were no clean cloths left, so I wiped my hands on Rory's tunic and earned a swat to the ear.

The fit of the gloves was perfect. Soft and supple, yielding with the flex of my fingers.

I lifted my hands to the lantern for closer inspection. These would certainly fetch a pretty price at market. Not that I'd sell them right away, of course. Rory liked pretending he had the emotional depth of a spoon, but he would be hurt if I bartered his gift a mere day later. Markets weren't hard to find in Omal. The lower villages were always in need of food and supplies. Trading among themselves was easier than begging for scraps from the palace.

The old man smiled briefly. "Happy birthday, Sylvia."

Sylvia. My first and favorite lie. I pressed my hands together. "A consolation gift for the spinster?" Not once in five years had Rory failed to remember my fabricated birth date.

"I should hardly think spinsterhood's threshold as low as twenty years."

In truth, I was halfway to twenty-one. Another lie.

"You are as old as time itself. The ages below one hundred must all look the same to you."

He jabbed me with his cane. "It is past the hour for spinsters to be about."

I left the shop in higher spirits. I pulled my cloak tight around my shoulders, knotting the hood beneath my chin. I had one more task to complete before I could finally reunite with my bed, and it meant delving deeper into the silent village. These were the hours when the mind ran free, when hollow masonry became the whispers of hungry shaiateen and the scratch of scuttling vermin the sounds of the restless dead.

I knew how sinuously fear cobbled shadows into gruesome shapes. I hadn't slept a full night's length in long years, and there were days when I trusted nothing beyond the breath in my chest and the earth beneath my feet. The difference between the villagers and me was that I knew the names of my monsters. I knew what they would look like if they found me, and I didn't have to imagine what kind of fate I would meet.

Mahair was a tiny village, but its history was long. Its children would know the tales shared from their mothers and fathers and grandparents. Superstition kept Mahair alive, long after time had turned a new page on its inhabitants.

It also kept me in business.

Instead of turning right toward Raya's keep, I ducked into the vagrant road. Bits of honey-soaked dough and grease marked the spot where the halawany's daughters snacked between errands, sitting on the concrete stoop of their parents' dessert shop. Dodging the dogs nosing at the grease, I checked for anyone who might report my movements back to Rory.

We had made a tradition of forgiving each other, Rory and me. Should he find out I was treating Omalians under his name, peddling pointless concoctions to those superstitious enough to buy them— well, I doubted Rory could forgive such a transgression. The "cures" I mucked together for my patrons were harmless. Crushed herbs and altered liquors. Most of the time, the ailments they were intended to ward off were more ridiculous than anything I could fit in a bottle.

The home I sought was ten minutes' walk past Raya's keep. Too close for comfort. Water dripped from the edge of the sagging roof, where a bare clothesline stretched from hook to hook. A pair of undergarments had fluttered to the ground. I kicked them out of sight. Raya taught me years ago how to hide undergarments on the clothesline by clipping them behind a larger piece of clothing. I hadn't understood the need for so much stealth. I still didn't. But time was a limited resource tonight, and I wouldn't waste it soothing an Omalian's embarrassment that I now had definitive proof they wore undergarments.

The door flew open. "Sylvia, thank goodness," Zeinab said. "She's worse today."

I tapped my mud-encrusted boots against the lip of the door and stepped inside.

"Where is she?"

I followed Zeinab to the last room in the short hall. A wave of incense wafted over us when she opened the door. I fanned the white haze hanging in the air. A wizened old woman rocked back and forth on the floor, and bloody tracks lined her arms where nails had gouged deep. Zeinab closed the door, maintaining a safe distance. Tears swam in her large hazel eyes. "I tried to give her a bath, and she did *this*." Zeinab pushed up the sleeve of her abaya, exposing a myriad of red scratch marks.

"Right." I laid my bag down on the table. "I will call you when I've finished."

Subduing the old woman with a tonic took little effort. I moved behind her and hooked an arm around her neck. She tore at my sleeve, mouth falling open to gasp. I dumped the tonic down her throat and loosened my stranglehold enough for her to swallow. Once certain she wouldn't spit it out, I let her go and adjusted my sleeve. She spat at my heels and bared teeth bloody from where she'd torn her lip.

It took minutes. My talents, dubious as they were, lay in efficient and fleeting deception. At the door, I let Zeinab slip a few coins into my cloak's pocket and pretended to be surprised. I would never understand Omalians and their feigned modesty. "Remember—"

Zeinab bobbed her head impatiently. "Yes, yes, I won't speak a word of this. It has been years, Sylvia. If the chemist ever finds out, it will not be from me."

She was quite self-assured for a woman who never bothered to ask what was in the tonic I regularly poured down her mother's throat. I returned Zeinab's wave distractedly and moved my dagger into the same pocket as the coins. Puddles of foul-smelling rain rippled in the pocked dirt road. Most of the homes on the street could more accurately be described as hovels, their thatched roofs shivering above walls joined together with mud and uneven patches of brick. I dodged a line of green mule manure, its waterlogged, grassy smell stinging my nose.

Did Omal's upper towns have excrement in their streets?

Zeinab's neighbor had scattered chicken feathers outside her door to showcase their good fortune to their neighbors. Their daughter had married a merchant from Dawar, and her dowry had earned them enough to eat chicken all month. From now on, the finest clothes would furnish her body. The choicest meats and hardest-grown vegetables for her plate. She'd never need to dodge mule droppings in Mahair again.

I turned the corner, absently counting the coins in my pocket, and rammed into a body.

I stumbled, catching myself against a pile of cracked clay bricks. The Nizahl soldier didn't budge beyond a tightening of his frown.

"Identify yourself."

Heavy wings of panic unfurled in my throat. Though our movements around town weren't constrained by an official curfew, not many risked a late-night stroll. The Nizahl soldiers usually patrolled in pairs, which meant this man's partner was probably harassing someone else on the other side of the village.

I smothered the panic, snapping its fluttering limbs. Panic was a plague. Its sole purpose was to spread until it tore through every thought, every instinct.

I immediately lowered my eyes. Holding a Nizahl soldier's gaze invited nothing but trouble. "My name is Sylvia. I live in Raya's keep and apprentice for the chemist Rory. I apologize for startling you. An elderly woman urgently needed care, and my employer is indisposed."

From the lines on his face, the soldier was somewhere in his late forties. If he had been an Omalian patrolman, his age would have signified little. But Nizahl soldiers tended to die young and bloody. For this man to survive long enough to see the lines of his forehead wrinkle, he was either a deadly adversary or a coward.

"What is your father's name?"

"I am a ward in Raya's keep," I repeated. He must be new to Mahair. Everyone knew Raya's house of orphans on the hill. "I have no mother or father."

He didn't belabor the issue. "Have you witnessed activity that might lead to the capture of a Jasadi?" Even though it was a standard question from the soldiers, intended to encourage vigilance toward any signs of magic, I inwardly flinched. The most recent arrest of a Jasadi had happened in our neighboring village a mere month ago. From the whispers, I'd surmised a girl reported seeing her friend fix a crack in her floorboard with a wave of her hand. I had overheard all manner of praise showered on the girl for her bravery in turning in the fifteen-year-old. Praise and jealousy— they couldn't wait for their own opportunities to be heroes.

"I have not." I hadn't seen another Jasadi in five years.

He pursed his lips. "The name of the elderly woman?"

"Aya, but her daughter Zeinab is her caretaker. I could direct you to them if you'd like." Zeinab was crafty. She would have a lie prepared for a moment like this.

"No need." He waved a hand over his shoulder. "On your way. Stay off the vagrant road."

One benefit of the older Nizahl soldiers—they had less inclination for the bluster and interrogation tactics of their younger counterparts. I tipped my head in gratitude and sped past him.

A few minutes later, I slid into Raya's keep. By the scent of cooling wax, it had not been long since the last girl went to bed. Relieved to find my birthday forgotten, I kicked my boots off at the door. Raya had met with the cloth merchants today. Bartering always left her in a foul mood. The only acknowledgment of my birthday would be a breakfast of flaky, buttery fiteer and molasses in the morning.

When I pushed open my door, a blast of warmth swept over me. Baira's blessed hair, not *again*. "Raya will have your hides. The waleema is in a week."

Marek appeared engrossed in the firepit, poking the coals with a thin rod. His golden hair shone under the glow. A mess of fabric and the beginnings of what might be a dress sat beneath Sefa's sewing tools. "Precisely," Sefa said, dipping a chunk of charred beef into her broth. "I am drowning my sorrows in stolen broth because of the damned waleema. Look at this dress! This is a dress all the other dresses laugh at."

"What is he doing with the fire?" I asked, electing to ignore her garment-related woes. Come morning, Sefa would hand Raya a perfect dress with a winning smile and bloodshot eyes. An apprenticeship under the best seamstress in Omal wasn't a role given to those who folded under pressure.

"He's trying to roast his damned seeds." Sefa sniffed. "We made your room smell like a tavern kitchen. Sorry. In our defense, we gathered to mourn a terrible passing."

"A passing?" I took a seat beside the stone pit, rubbing my hands over the crackling flames.

Marek handed me one of Raya's private chalices. The woman was going to skin us like deer. "Ignore her. We just wanted to abuse your hearth," he said. "I am convinced Yuli is teaching his herd how to kill me. They almost ran me right into a canal today."

"Did you do something to make Yuli or the oxen angry?"

"No," Marek said mournfully.

I rolled the chalice between my palms and narrowed my eyes. "Marek."

"I may have used the horse's stalls to ... entertain ..." He released a long-suffering sigh. "His daughter."

Sefa and I released twin groans. This was hardly the first time Marek had gotten himself in trouble chasing a coy smile or kind word. He was absurdly pretty, fair-haired and green-eyed, lean in a way that undersold his strength. To counter his looks, he'd chosen to apprentice with Yuli, Mahair's most demanding farmer. By spending his days loading wagons and herding oxen, Marek made himself indispensable to every tradesperson in the village. He worked to earn their respect, because there were few things Mahair valued more than calloused palms and sweat on a brow.

It was also why they tolerated the string of broken hearts he'd left in his wake.

Not one to be ignored for long, Sefa continued, "Your youth, Sylvia, we mourn your youth! At twenty, you're having fewer adventures than the village brats."

I drained the water, passing the chalice to Marek for more. "I have plenty of adventure."

"I'm not talking about how many times you can kill your fig plant before it stays dead," Sefa scoffed. "If you had simply accompanied me last week to release the roosters in Nadia's den—"

"Nadia has permanently barred you from her shop," Marek interjected. Brave one, cutting Sefa off in the middle of a tirade. He scooped up a blackened seed, throwing it from palm to palm to cool. "Leave Sylvia be. Adventure does not fit into a single mold."

Sefa's nostrils flared wide, but Marek didn't flinch. They communicated in that strange, silent way of people who were bound together by something thicker than blood and stronger than a shared upbringing. I knew because I had witnessed hundreds of their unspoken conversations over the last five years.

"I am not killing my fig plant." I pushed to my feet. "I'm cultivating its fighter's spirit."

"Stop glaring at me," Marek said to Sefa with a sigh. "I'm sorry for interrupting." He held out a cracked seed.

Sefa let his hand dangle in the air for forty seconds before taking the seed. "Help me hem this sleeve?"

With a sheepish grin, Marek offered his soot-covered palms. Sefa rolled her eyes.

I observed this latest exchange with bewilderment. It never failed to astound me how easily they existed around one another. Their unusual devotion had led to questions from the other wards at the keep. Marek laughed himself into stitches the first time a younger girl asked if he and Sefa planned to wed. "Sefa isn't going to marry anyone. We love each other in a different way."

The ward had batted her lashes, because Marek was the only boy in the keep, and he was in possession of a face consigning him to a life of wistful sighs following in his wake.

"What about you?" the ward had asked.

Sefa, who had been smiling as she knit in the corner, sobered. Only Raya and I saw the sorrowful look she shot Marek, the guilt in her brown eyes.

"I am tied to Sefa in spirit, if not in wedlock." Marek ruffled the ward's hair. The girl squealed, slapping at Marek. "I follow where she goes."

To underscore their insanity, the pair had taken an instant liking to me the moment Rory dropped me off at Raya's doorstep. I was almost feral, hardly fit for friendship, but it hadn't deterred them. I adjusted poorly to this Omalian village, perplexed by their simplest customs. Rub the spot between your shoulders and you'll die early. Eat with your left hand on the first day of the month; don't cross your legs in the presence of elders; be the last person to sit at the dinner table and the first one to leave it. It didn't help that my bronze skin was several shades darker than their typical olive. I blended in with Orbanians better, since the kingdom in the north spent most of its days under the sun. When Sefa noticed how I avoided wearing white, she'd held her darker hand next to mine and said, "They're jealous we soaked up all their color."

Matters weren't much easier at home. Everyone in the keep had an ugly history haunting their sleep. I didn't help myself any by almost slamming another ward's nose clean off her face when she tried to hug me. Despite the two-hour lecture I endured from Raya, the incident had firmly established my aversion to touch.

For some inconceivable reason, Sefa and Marek weren't scared off. Sefa was quite upset about her nose, though.

I hung my cloak neatly inside the wardrobe and thumbed the moth-eaten collar. It wouldn't survive another winter, but the thought of throwing it away brought a lump to my throat. Someone in my position could afford few emotional attachments. At any moment, a sword could be pointed at me, a cry of "*Jasadi*" ending this identity and the life I'd built around it. I recoiled from the cloak, curling my fingers into a fist. I promptly tore out the roots of sadness before it could spread. A regular orphan from Mahair could cling to this tired cloak, the first thing she'd ever purchased with her own hard-earned coin.

A fugitive of the scorched kingdom could not.

I turned my palms up, testing the silver cuffs around my wrists. Though the cuffs were invisible to any eye but mine, it had taken a long time for my paranoia to ease whenever someone's idle gaze lingered on my wrists. They flexed with my movement, a second skin over my own. Only my trapped magic could stir them, tightening the cuffs as it pleased.

Magic marked me as a Jasadi. As the reason Nizahl created perimeters in the woods and sent their soldiers prowling through the kingdoms. I had spent most of my life resenting my cuffs. How was it fair that Jasadis were condemned because of their magic but I couldn't even access the thing that doomed me? My magic had been trapped behind these cuffs since my childhood. I suppose my grandparents couldn't have anticipated dying and leaving the cuffs stuck on me forever.

I hid Rory's gift in the wardrobe, beneath the folds of my longest gown. The girls rarely risked Raya's wrath by stealing, but a desperate winter could make a thief of anyone. I stroked one of the gloves, fondness curling hot in my chest. How much had Rory spent, knowing I'd have limited opportunities to wear them?

"We wanted to show you something," Marek said. His voice hurtled me back to reality, and I slammed the wardrobe doors shut, scowling at myself. What did it matter how much Rory spent? Anything I didn't need to survive would be discarded or sold, and these gloves were no different.

Sefa stood, dusting loose fabric from her lap. She snorted at my expression. "Rovial's tainted tomb, look at her, Marek. You might think we were planning to bury her in the woods."

Marek frowned. "Aren't we?"

"Both of you are banned from my room. Forever."

I followed them outside, past the row of fluttering clotheslines and the pitiful herb garden. Built at the top of a grassy slope, Raya's keep overlooked the entire village, all the way to the main road. Most of the homes in Mahair sat stacked on top of each other, forming squat, three-story buildings with crumbling walls and cracks in the clay. The villagers raised poultry on the roofs, nurturing a steady supply of chickens and rabbits that would see them through the monthly food shortages. Livestock meandered in the fields shouldering Essam Woods, fenced in by the miles-long wall surrounding Mahair.

Past the wall, darkness marked the expanse of Essam Woods. Moonlight disappeared over the trees stretching into the black horizon.

Ahead of me, Marek and Sefa averted their gaze from the woods. They had arrived in Mahair when they were sixteen, two years before me. I couldn't tell if they'd simply adopted Mahair's peculiar customs or if those customs were more widespread than I thought.

The day after I emerged from Essam, I'd spent the night sitting on the hill and watching the spot where Mahair's lanterns disappeared into the empty void of the woods. Escaping Essam had nearly killed me. I'd wanted to confirm to myself that this village and the roof over my head weren't a cruel dream. That when I closed my eyes, I wouldn't open them to branches rustling below a starless sky.

Raya had stormed out of the keep in her nightgown and hauled me inside, where I'd listened to her harangue me about the risk of staring into Essam Woods and inviting mischievous spirits forward from the dark. As though my attention alone might summon them into being.

I spent five years in those woods. I wasn't afraid of their darkness. It was everything outside Essam I couldn't trust.

"Behold!" Sefa announced, flinging her arm toward a tangle of plants.

We stopped around the back of the keep, where I had illicitly shoveled the fig plant I bought off a Lukubi merchant at the last market. I wasn't sure why. Nurturing a plant that reminded me of Jasad, something rooted I couldn't take with me in an emergency— it was embarrassing. Another sign of the weakness I'd allowed to settle.

My fig plant's leaves drooped mournfully. I prodded the dirt. Were they mocking my planting technique?

"She doesn't like it. I told you we should have bought her a new cloak," Marek sighed.

"With whose wages? Are you a wealthy man now?" Sefa peered at me. "You don't like it?"

I squinted at the plant. Had they watered it while I was gone? What was I supposed to like? Sefa's face crumpled, so I hurriedly said, "I love it! It is, uh, wonderful, truly. Thank you."

"Oh. You can't see it, can you?" Marek started to laugh. "Sefa forgot she is the size of a thimble and hid it out of your sight."

"I am a perfectly standard height! I cannot be blamed for befriending a woman tall enough to tickle the moon," Sefa protested.

I crouched by the plant. Wedged behind its curtain of yellowing leaves, a woven straw basket held a dozen sesame-seed candies. I loved these brittle, tooth-chipping squares. I always made a point to search for them at market if I'd saved enough to spare the cost.

"They used the good honey, not the chalky one," Marek added.

"Happy birthday, Sylvia," Sefa said. "As a courtesy, I will refrain from hugging you."

First Rory, now this? I cleared my throat. In a village of empty stomachs and dying fields, every kindness came at a price. "You just wanted to see me smile with sesame in my teeth."

Marek smirked. "Ah, yes, our grand scheme is unveiled. We wanted to ruin your smile that emerges once every fifteen years."

I slapped the back of his head. It was the most physical contact I could bear, but it expressed my gratitude.

orbit

Follow us:
 /orbitbooksUS

 /orbitbooks

 /orbitbooks

Join our mailing list
to receive alerts on our
latest releases and deals.

orbitbooks.net

Enter our monthly
giveaway for the chance
to win some epic prizes.

orbitloot.com